I0840836

FRANKLIN HORTON

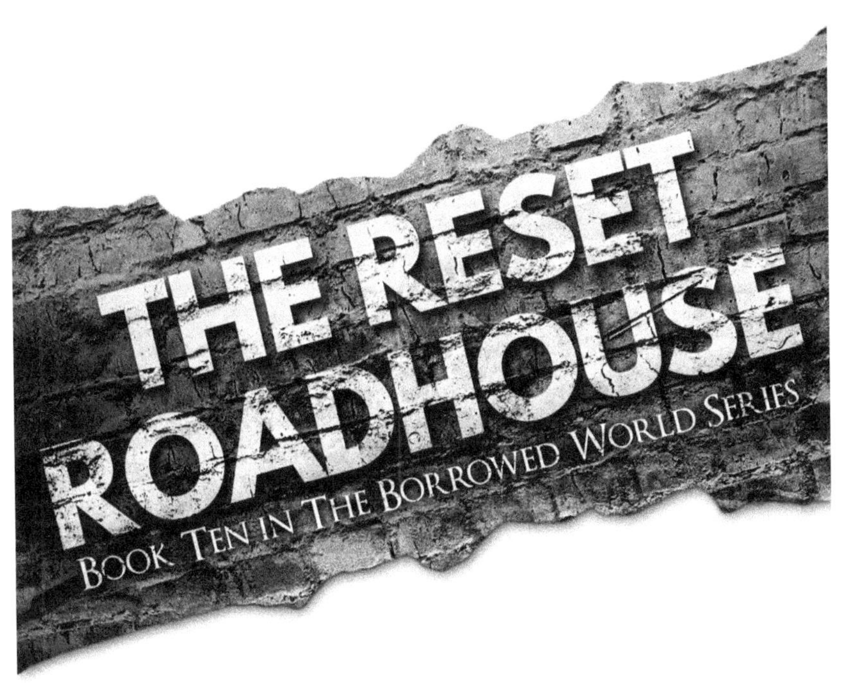

ALSO BY FRANKLIN HORTON

The Borrowed World Series

The Locker Nine Series

The Mad Mick Series

The Way of Dan Series

The Ty Stone Series

Random Acts

ABOUT THE AUTHOR

Franklin Horton lives and writes in the mountains of Southwestern Virginia. He received an English degree from Virginia Commonwealth University and has written over thirty novels. He lives a hermit's life on a remote mountaintop along the Clinch Mountain chain, splitting his day between writing and tinkering in his shop like one of his characters.

You can follow him on his website at franklinhorton.com.

While you're there please sign up for his mailing list for updates, event schedule, book recommendations, and discounts. He's also active on social media so follow him on Facebook or Instagram to keep up with the latest releases.

THE RESET
ROADHOUSE
MUSIC BOOZE GUNS

1

Jim

LLOYD SWAYED IN THE SADDLE, his hat pulled low over his eyes to block out the painful sunlight. Even at a walk, nearly every step of his horse provoked a curse as the movement aggravated the wicked hangover he was nursing. He'd arrived back at Jim's farm last night after spending a few months at the summer camp where the young musicians had been stranded with Sharon, the camp director. There had been a harvest party going on when Lloyd arrived at Jim's place and his unexpected return only added to the festivities.

"I think I'm going to die this time," Lloyd mumbled.

"You should have stopped drinking a little earlier," Jim said. "What time did you finally set the jar down?"

"What time is it now?"

"A little after 9 AM."

Lloyd made a disapproving groan. "No wonder I feel like shit. Who gets up at 9 AM?"

"Obviously not people who drink until the wee hours of the morning."

"I don't think it was the hour I quit that was the problem. It may have been the hour that I started."

"I didn't think you had moonshine at the music camp," Jim said.

"I didn't, but I may have made a few local friends during the time I was there. I don't know why but a banjo player seems to take up with all the men who love a drink."

Jim laughed. "It's because it takes liquor to numb the pain inflicted by a banjo. A sober man couldn't tolerate being in the presence of one."

Lloyd cocked an eye at Jim from beneath his hat. "Must be a burden toting all that wit around all day."

"So, did you drink every day of your ride back to the valley or just on the last one?"

"Eh, it was only a one-day ride."

Jim gave his old friend a suspicious look. "No way. It took us days to get out there to that camp. How the hell could you make it in one?"

"You're partial to camping in the middle of nowhere at night. I'm not so inclined. I'd like to think I'm cut of a finer cloth."

"You're what my grandfather used to call a 'house cat,'" Jim said. "A man more inclined to spending his day curled up on the couch. What you're really saying is that you were too scared to sleep in the dark by yourself, so you rode straight through?"

Lloyd managed a nod. "Little more than two days in the saddle. Might have slept some but only on the go. I drank to keep my nerve up. Hoped like hell I was remembering the route correctly."

"So, this hangover you're sporting isn't just from one night's overindulgence. It's the accumulated hangover from several days of hard living."

"That's about the size of it. Now don't you feel bad about being such an asshole and making me get out of bed so early?"

Jim laughed again. "What do you think?"

Lloyd shook his head sadly. "Nah, I guess not. There's not a single drop of human compassion in you. No sympathy for the weary traveler. No pity for the sick and afflicted."

"No tolerance for a lazy drunk is more like it. We got no time to waste. If you're serious about wanting to open a roadhouse, we need to make it happen before the weather starts getting colder. We might have two months. Three at the most."

Lloyd didn't reply to that. It was his typical response when someone slapped him with logic and he didn't want to accept it.

"You understand why we can't use your parents' house, right?"

"Too far out of town," Lloyd conceded. "I get it."

"Roadhouses out in the country were fine in the days when people had cars, or at least friends with cars. These days it needs to be closer to centers of population. Closer to town."

"I liked the idea of striking up a deal with those whores and perhaps sharing the house they were using."

Jim shook his head. "That house is too small and has too much baggage associated with it. It belonged to Hadley Wright and I don't want people thinking I killed him just to take over his criminal enterprise."

"Guess people in this town didn't know we were fully intent on starting *our* own criminal enterprise, did they?"

"Don't see a thing wrong with it," Jim said. "I see this as an expansion of our activities at the farmer's market. One more way of collecting intelligence and keeping an eye on what's going on around us."

"Well, if you don't want me turning my childhood home into a bar and you don't want to use Hadley Wright's brothel, what's your plan?"

"You'll see."

Lloyd didn't have the energy to try to pry the information from his old friend. If Jim wasn't going to be more forthcoming, Lloyd was going to do his best to try and catch a few winks before they got to town. He removed his hat and rested it over the saddle horn like it was a hat rack, then leaned forward with his arms draped to each side of the horse's neck. He looked like a cowboy who'd been shot and died in the saddle.

He only lasted in that position for a few minutes before he felt his stomach roiling and his gorge rising. Lloyd sat up abruptly, squinting against the harsh morning light. "Really bad idea."

Jim grinned. "You throw up on that horse and she'll throw you. No one likes to be under a puking drunk. Haven't you learned that by this point in your life?"

Lloyd crushed his hat back onto his head and said nothing for the rest of the ride into town.

Jim watched wildlife along the river, pleased to see deer, squirrels, and herons. He'd been afraid that these times of deprivation might have thinned the wildlife, as had happened during the depression. The difference was that America hadn't lost the majority of the population during the depression. Jim had no idea exactly how many people had died since the collapse, but anecdotal evidence led him to believe that they'd lost seventy to eighty percent of the local population. The good news for the wildlife was that fewer surviving people meant fewer hunters trying to eat them.

Thirty minutes later, Jim and Lloyd turned off Main Street onto a dead-end road. It led to some homes, the town park, and the sewage treatment plant.

Lloyd looked around, perkier than he had been earlier. "This is my old neighborhood. When my parents first moved here, we lived off this road."

"I remember. You and I met playing at the park."

"Hell, you think I forgot that?" Lloyd asked. "Worst damn day of my life. I've spent years trying to erase the trauma. Still can't get shed of you."

Jim ignored the jab. They rode a little further and Jim turned his horse into a cracked parking lot. "This is where I'm thinking we should open your roadhouse."

"The old sewing factory?"

The building looked like hundreds of thousands of other WWII-era small industrial buildings that were scattered around the country. It was a one-story brick factory with a flat roof, the parapet wall topped with terracotta caps mortared in place. The office section had modern windows but the shop area, where the actual work was done, held a row of high windows in thin iron frames. Some of the panes had been knocked out.

"The place has been vacant for years." Jim pointed to a For Sale sign. "It's owned by some commercial real estate company out of Richmond that bought it sight unseen. They haven't been able to get a tenant in there in twenty years, so I don't feel bad about borrowing it under the current circumstances."

Lloyd studied the building with an appraising eye. "I walked by this place hundreds of times as a kid. Rode my bike in this parking lot. Never imagined I'd open a post-apocalyptic roadhouse in the place."

"I've done lots of things in the past year I never imagined I'd be doing," said Jim. "That's the state of the world."

"What's the inside like?"

Jim shrugged. "I don't know. Let's see if we can get inside and take a look."

They rode their horses around back and tied them off in the brush that grew up against the building. The grounds had been severely neglected in the last twenty years, with only the more public aspects of the building receiving any attention.

Jim slung his pack onto his back and his rifle over his shoulder.

"You really going to need that?" Lloyd asked.

"You grew up here. It must be a bad neighborhood," Jim said. "I'm sure it's gotten even worse."

Lloyd didn't take the bait but grabbed his gear and set off through the brush with Jim. They soon found a side door that had been pried open with a crowbar. Jim tugged on the rusty steel door and the hinges protested with a squeal.

Before going inside, Jim raised his rifle and activated the weapon-mounted light. The door led them onto the factory floor.

"There used to be several sewing factories in our community," Jim said as he played his light around the room. "They provided a decent job, benefits, and retirement for a mostly female workforce. So many women in this area didn't finish high school, even when we were kids, but they could get a good job in a place like this, making clothing for major retailers. The factories began going out of business in the '80s and '90s when corporations started having their goods made in Third World sweat shops, often by child or prison labor."

"Mom had a lot of friends that worked here," Lloyd said.

The high windows allowed only a muted light to pass through their grimy panes, but it was enough to see that the factory floor was empty. At least it was empty of the rows of industrial cutting and sewing machines that had once filled the space. There was a scattering of broken bottles, grimy blankets, and empty cans. A charred place on the floor revealed that someone had once thought the interior of the vast space to be a good spot for a fire. Tiny bones that may once have belonged to a household pet revealed that it had been a cooking fire, however, none of it looked recent.

A double door led from the factory floor to the office section of the building. It was not quite as big as the factory area, but had over a dozen offices, a meeting room, and a reception area. The carpet and old network cables revealed that the offices had probably been vacant since around 1990. At least vacant from *legitimate* tenants. Graffiti, a deflated air mattress, and more garbage demonstrated that the offices had seen other forms of activity since the collapse.

Once they were certain that the place was empty, Jim let his rifle hang and switched to a handheld flashlight. "What do you think?"

"I think I'll take the biggest office."

"I don't think you'll need an office," Jim countered. "You'll be too busy. Someone has to make the liquor and brew the beer."

"Don't know nothing about brewing beer," Lloyd announced as if it were the final word on the subject.

"A small detail. We'll find someone who does. There's bound to be an amateur brewer around here somewhere."

For the first time since coming up with the idea of opening a roadhouse, Lloyd looked doubtful. Perhaps it was the exhaustion or his hangover, but his face was clouded with concern.

"What's the matter?" Jim asked.

"I'll be honest with you, Jim. Having a roadhouse was kind of a fantasy when I was stuck at that camp full of kids with no liquor. I thought it would be the best of both worlds. I'd have a venue for playing music, which is the thing I miss the most. Plus, I could drink while I was doing it. Looking at this place, though…it's a hell of a lot of work."

Jim nodded. "Yes, it is a lot of work, but this is the kind of project I used to manage at my job all the time, back when I had a job. I know how to break down and organize things like this. I don't see it as an insurmountable problem."

"I'm glad you're so cool about it. If I had to build a roadhouse, it might just end up as a circle of hobos drinking around a fire here in the middle of the floor."

Jim laughed. "I'll sit down tonight and organize the job on paper, then we'll put our heads together with a few folks and make it happen."

"What about all the physical work that needs done? Building stuff? Tracking down materials? Fixing windows?"

"That the part that scares you the most?" Jim asked. "Breaking a sweat?"

"I've sweated all morning," Lloyd protested.

"Sweating out a hangover isn't work, it's karma. But don't worry about that part. I can build us a workforce."

"How?"

"I used to work on a loading dock in Richmond," Jim said. "When we didn't have enough labor for the day, my boss would send me down to skid row and we'd hire day laborers. They'd get a bottle of wine for the day. No cash and no record keeping. They got their wine at lunch, so they weren't good for much after that."

"If I have to pay people in alcohol, that might not leave much to sell."

"I'm not thinking of alcohol," Jim said. "I'm thinking of food. We keep a cookpot going all day with a soup made out of the some of the things that no one wants to eat. Peas, canned lima beans, ramen noodles, the MREs and freeze-dried stuff that tastes like crap. We offer a big lunch each day and we'll get workers."

Lloyd waved a hand. "That's fine, man. Whatever. You figure that part out and just let me know what I need to do."

There was a whinny from outside, the cry of a startled horse. Lloyd and Jim looked at each other for a confused moment, then Jim sprinted across the factory floor. Along the brick wall, he braced his foot on a run of rusty conduit and boosted himself up to peer out a high window that looked out the back of the building. He caught sight of someone disappearing around the corner, leading their horses along behind him.

Jim dropped to the floor, looked at Lloyd, and mouthed, "The horses!"

Without waiting to see if Lloyd heard him, Jim ran for one of the front doors, hoping they weren't chained shut from the outside. He kicked the panic bar with a boot and the door flung open violently, bouncing off the brick wall. He spotted a scared man about thirty feet away, trying to hurriedly mount his horse. The horse was spinning away, not interested in letting the stranger mount him.

Understanding that in the world of rock-paper-scissors "shooting" beat "shouting," Jim fired off a warning shot. The round ricocheted off the bricks a few yards from the man's head. Message received, the terrified man flung his arms up in the air and stepped away from the horse.

"Don't shoot!"

"Where's the other horse!" Jim demanded, stepping forward with his rifle leveled on the horse thief's chest.

About that time, a second man emerged from around the same corner of the building with his hands raised in the air. Lloyd was behind him, his shotgun pointed at the man's back.

"Get over there with your buddy," Jim ordered.

When his prisoner did as he was told, Lloyd stepped off to join Jim. He'd learned to stay up-range when Jim's blood was running hot. It was easy to get caught in the crossfire.

With the two horse thieves standing side by side, Jim could tell that they were related. Both had bushy black beards streaked with gray and broad noses lined with broken blood vessels. Their pants sagged below their waists, but it was more a statement of their lack of food than of their sense of fashion.

"You best get that gun off me," the first prisoner said, emboldened. He wore a grubby t-shirt that may once have been white and advertised Newport cigarettes.

"Why?" Jim asked. "Stealing horses is a death sentence as far as I'm concerned."

"They was on our property!" Newport protested.

Jim furrowed his brow. "Your property? You're going to have to explain that to me. This was a public street last I heard. You own the town park too? What about the sewage treatment plant?"

Newport nodded confidently, indicating that he did. The man Jim assumed to be his brother was nodding along, though not looking quite so certain about it. Perhaps he was just playing along.

"My family lives down at the end of this road. All the other families moved out and moved on. We've seen the way other people around this town are claiming things for themselves. They're moving into houses that don't belong to them, taking stuff that don't belong to them, and generally doing whatever the hell they want. There some reason they can do it but we can't?"

Jim didn't have much of an argument for that. Newport was right. People were doing exactly as he said. Jim was too. "That may be the case, but you sure as hell aren't claiming my horse."

"Like my brother said, they was on our property," the other man said. He wore a grubby cap that said NAPA Auto Parts on it.

"I understand what you're saying," Jim said. "Property lines have been a little blurry lately. If something isn't being used, other people are coming along and putting it to use. I'm sure there's going to be a day where this all has to be sorted out and I'm not exactly sure how that's going to happen. It's going to be a mess for certain. That's part of the reason we're here."

Newport looked at Jim suspiciously. "Why? You hear something about us?"

Jim cocked an eyebrow. Apparently, the man was guilty of something, but perhaps no more guilty than Jim himself was. "I haven't heard anything about you people specifically. My friend and I were looking at this building. We wanted to put it to use for a project we had in mind."

"What kind of project?" NAPA asked.

Jim considered for a moment before replying. "I'm not ready to say yet. We're exploring our options."

"Can we put our hands down?" Newport asked. "If we're going to be talking business, we should be doing it as equals. I don't like staring down the barrel of a gun on my own property."

"Keep'em up!" Jim warned. "We're not talking business and you'll keep staring down the barrel of this gun until I'm comfortable that we're safe."

Newport cooperated but shrugged in disagreement. "Sounds like we're talking business to me. You're wanting to use a building that's on our property. That kind of makes us partners."

"Or it makes us your landlords," NAPA offered, flashing a grin that revealed a row of grimy teeth.

"Or my friend just kills you and we consider ourselves done with the whole matter," Lloyd suggested.

Jim frowned, not appreciating the way Lloyd so often told people that Jim was going to kill them. Why didn't Lloyd ever threaten to kill anyone himself? Jim supposed that this was the pattern of things. It was like Lloyd's drinking. Spend too much time doing a particular thing and you can't hardly get bent out of shape when people begin to associate you with it.

"We got family back in there," Newport said, gesturing further down the road. "You shoot us and start using this building, they'll figure out what happened."

"They must be smarter than you two," Lloyd said. "Didn't see you all as the analytical type."

"Lloyd, get those horses," Jim said. Then, to the two brothers, he added, "We'll be getting on out of here, but we'll get back to you on the building. You'll be seeing us again. Next time I suggest you don't try stealing our horses. You might not get off so easy the second time."

"You do that," Newport said. "We'll deal with you. We're not unreasonable men."

"Oh, I know exactly what kind of men you are," Jim offered. "The question is whether I can deal with men like you without having to kill you. The jury is still out on that one." No sooner had he said the words than he realized he was acting exactly like Lloyd always accused him of acting. He'd threatened to kill these men without a second thought.

Lloyd mounted his horse and led Jim's over to him, handing off the reins. Lloyd covered the two brothers with his shotgun while Jim mounted up. Casting a wary eye over their shoulders, Jim and Lloyd rode off as Newport and NAPA watched them go.

When they were back on Main Street, Lloyd had a lot to say about the encounter. His adrenaline must have been up because he was more animated than Jim had seen him all day.

"Surely you aren't thinking about dealing with those guys. We either need to find a different place or run those guys out of there."

Jim shrugged. "We've all done some questionable stuff, Lloyd. Especially where property is concerned, but those guys are right. How is them claiming that building any different than us claiming some of the empty houses in the valley for our people?"

"Those guys aren't using the building. They're thieves who didn't get away with our horses so they're looking for another way to shake us down. I'm not paying them rent. You can't let guys like that get a hook in you or you'll never be free of them."

"Let's look at a few other places," Jim suggested. "Then we'll get on home and figure something out."

Lloyd hung his shotgun over the saddle horn and got a biscuit out of his pack. The slightly crushed biscuit was wrapped in a dish towel and held a slice of cold roast beef left over from last night's feast. He bit off a chunk of the biscuit, then gestured at Jim. "Lead the way," he said, his words garbled by the mouthful of food.

Jim shook his head. "As my granny would say, you only got one manner, Lloyd, and it's *ill.*"

2

Jim

J‍IM AND L‍LOYD rode from one end of the town to the other, looking at various abandoned buildings on the way—empty retail spaces, law offices, convenience stores, automotive repair shops, tire shops, and beauty salons. Every place they checked out had something going against it. Some were too small or were impossible to secure against break-ins. Others were too close to residential neighborhoods and Jim didn't want to have to deal with complaints from neighbors. Other spaces were occupied, too damaged, or were owned by families still living in town.

Lloyd was more open-minded as to where the roadhouse could be placed. Like a lot of people, he had trouble looking at an empty, ravaged space and imagining it as something else. Jim understood all too well what it took to turn a vacant lot or the shell of a building into something else. He'd done it for years in his day job. Due to his experience, he had a list of requirements that he saw as critical to making this project become a reality. Some of those requirements were flexible, others were not.

"Hell, you shot down everything else we looked at," Lloyd grumbled. "Does that mean we're back to the sewing factory?"

"Maybe, if we can find some way to deal with those two assholes."

Lloyd laughed. "That may be the exact same thing they said about us after we left."

"Could be," Jim admitted.

On their way back through the town, they were riding along Main Street near the post office when they passed an ornate Victorian house with two women sitting on the wide porch. Their long legs were propped on the porch rail and both gave the men friendly waves.

Lloyd straightened his hat. "Obviously they recognize that I'm a banjo player. A man of distinction and talent."

Jim threw him a sideways glance. "Don't get too impressed with yourself. That's the brothel I was telling you about. There's a motive behind those friendly smiles and it's not because they want to hear your banjo."

"Oh," Lloyd muttered. "Well, maybe they'll take a tune in exchange for—"

"In exchange for Randi turning you into a eunuch with a rusty knife?" Jim asked. "You want to spend the rest of your life having to go to the mantel and open a jar to scratch your balls?"

Lloyd swallowed nervously. "I was just admiring the scenery. This is a pretty town, isn't it? Besides, a great philosopher once said that it doesn't matter where a man gets hungry as long as he goes home to eat."

"A great philosopher, huh?"

"One of them," Lloyd replied confidently. "Socrates. Shakespeare. Patton. Somebody like that."

Jim tugged on one of his reins and steered his horse toward the late Hadley Wright's house of ill repute.

"Uh, is this some kind of joke?" Lloyd asked. "You trying to get me killed?"

"Just business, Lloyd. Don't break a string."

Lloyd grimaced and nudged his horse in that direction. "If this gets back to Randi..."

The two women on the porch looked pleased that the riders were coming closer, hoping they'd lured in some early morning business. The blonde on the right lost her smile when Jim got closer. She must have recognized him. He'd seen that look on people's faces before when they figured out who he was.

He rode right up into the front yard and stopped alongside the porch. His horse lowered its head and began tugging at great clumps of grass. Jim opened his mouth to introduce himself but one of the women cut him off.

"I know who you are," the blonde said. "You were here with Charlie that night. When he came around asking where the Community Safety Council was going to be meeting."

Jim nodded. "That was me."

"You ended up killing all the folks who were at the meeting. You're the one killed Hadley too."

Jim opened his arms to concede the point. "You got me, but I never killed anyone who wasn't trying to kill me first. All those people deserved it. Especially that miserable bastard Hadley."

She crossed her arms and glared at Jim. "What do you want?"

"I'd like to talk business."

The blonde rolled her eyes and elbowed her friend. "That's how it always starts. They want to talk business, then they want a piece of the action in exchange for protection. Then, the next thing you know, you're doing all the work and they're taking all the money."

"Hear me out," Jim said. "I'm not here to be a pimp. Who's in charge now that Hadley is dead?"

The blonde stuck out her chin defiantly. "I am, though there's been no shortage of people coming by to talk 'business' just like you. Everyone wants a piece of the action."

"I'm Jim Powell. What's your name?"

"Blair."

Jim shifted on his horse. He was getting a little uncomfortable from so much time in the saddle. He slung a leg over the horse and got down. He started up the steps to the porch, but the ratcheting sound of a pump shotgun stopped him in his tracks. The shotgun wasn't pointed at him yet, but Blair wanted to make sure Jim knew she was armed. The weapon lay across her lap, barrel pointed in a safe direction for now.

Jim took that as a sign he'd gone far enough. He carefully took a seat on the steps where he could see both women.

"I think I'll just stay on my horse," Lloyd announced. "In case anyone cares."

Jim hooked a thumb in Lloyd's direction. "My buddy there, the one too scared to get off his horse, comes from a family of moonshiners. Lately he's focused more on the act of drinking liquor than making it, but we're hoping to change that. We're wanting to open a place on the outskirts of town and we're in town to scout out some locations."

"What kind of place?" Blair asked.

"A roadhouse," Lloyd replied. "Music, drinking, maybe some food. Thought some girls might round out the menu." He waggled his eyebrows at her.

Jim looked at the ground and shook his head. There was a reason he never let Lloyd do the talking. Blair exploded before Jim could try to rephrase the words that had just come out of Lloyd's mouth.

"Girls?" she snapped. "Mister, there's not a girl in this house that sold herself before the power went out. None of us ever imagined this is what we'd be doing to eat, but here we are. There's not much business most days and those that are coming don't have much to offer in trade. You bring in competition and we'll all starve to death. That what you want?"

Jim could hear a lot of emotions behind those words. Fear. Panic. Shame. Anger. Defiance. He held up a hand. "Hear me out. I'm not suggesting competition. I'm suggesting collaboration."

She raised her eyebrows. "So, we're back to you guys wanting to be pimps?"

Suddenly Jim felt like he was dealing with Randi. This was how their conversations usually went. It always seemed as if it was going to turn into a fight before they actually got to the heart of the situation. Now he was starting to get frustrated too.

"Will you listen to me for a second?" Jim asked. "We don't want your money or fees or whatever the hell you call it! We were just thinking that you all might help draw in customers. In exchange, you all get added security. We're going to make our money off liquor, so we don't need to take your money for this collaboration to be successful."

Blair appraised Jim before giving him a flat, "No."

He was surprised by her reaction. He'd finally managed to say his piece and she shot him down almost immediately. "Why?"

"Security isn't enough reason to change the way we're doing things."

"What are you thinking?" Jim asked.

"Well, for one thing, there isn't a one of us who can cook. We all hate the kitchen. It takes away from time that we could be working and earning. If you're going to be serving food, we want a guaranteed meal every day. One that we don't have to cook, pay for, or provide the food to make."

Jim considered this. It sounded reasonable. He'd already considered the idea that this may be the manner in which they paid for construction and continued to pay some of the staff after they opened. Food was perhaps the most important currency of the day. If they were already going to be preparing a meal, it might not be too painful to feed these girls too.

"How many of you are there?" he asked.

"Seven now," she replied, "although that number could change. There's been more of us at times and there's also been fewer."

"Is that all you want?" Lloyd asked. "Food and security? That's manageable."

Seeing that she was making progress, Blair felt emboldened. "No, it's not. I'm tired of having to run this operation too. I'm tired of having to manage customers and decide if what they're offering in trade is a fair deal or not. I'm tired of having to run off the troublemakers, worrying that they're going to come back when I'm asleep and hurt someone. It's a lot of responsibility."

"Now it sounds as if you're wanting a pimp," Lloyd pointed out. "The same thing you just said you *didn't* want. You're going to have to make up your damn mind, woman."

"Did you just call me 'woman'?" Blair snapped, sitting up straight in her chair.

Jim cringed. Lloyd and his big mouth again. He might be accurately stating the situation, but that technique never worked in an argument such as this.

Jim raised a hand before Blair could tear into Lloyd. "I hear what you're saying. It's not a pimp you're wanting. It's a madam, and I might have just the right person in mind for the job."

3

Jim

Two hours later Jim and Lloyd were sitting in the shade of Randi's porch laying out the story of what had taken place in town. No matter how Jim approached conversations with Randi, they always turned argumentative almost immediately. Jim always had difficulty telling whether Randi was genuinely offended or just being argumentative.

"Jim Powell, I'm not even going to ask why you'd think I was the right person for running a whorehouse." She slammed her fist into her open palm to emphasize each word as she spoke. "If it wasn't so hot, I'd get out of this chair and whoop your ass."

That wasn't the end of it. She soon tore into him with an almost ministerial rhythm, like she was a hellfire-and-brimstone preacher delivering a sermon and his everlasting soul was hanging in the balance.

"Being a single mom doesn't make me a whore. Getting pregnant when I was little more than a kid myself doesn't make me a whore. And when did it become a man's business what a woman does with her body anyway? We don't *need* your permission to do a damn thing.

Did Lloyd ask permission to be a sloppy drunk? Did you ask anyone's permission before becoming an asshole?"

Jim couldn't even get a word in edgewise. He sighed and rolled his eyes, which was exactly the wrong thing to do.

"You get my girls out here and ask them what happened the last time one of them rolled their eyes at me. You'll be picking them things up out of the yard and hoping you can fit them back in your head when I'm done with you."

"Will you calm down a second!" Jim demanded.

Randi fell silent and glared at Jim for a long moment. "Did you just tell me to calm down? Oh, you better hope the Lord can hold me back, Jim Powell."

"I ain't so sure it's the Lord got his hand on your chain, Randi. It's more likely to be Satan himself. Now hear me out."

Randi fumed like a pressure cooker about to blow, but she held her tongue. Jim knew she hadn't calmed down. She was simply waiting for the opportunity to attack again. He knew he better say what he needed to say quickly, or they'd be scrapping in the yard like kids.

"I want you to be part of the roadhouse because you're tough and you're good at managing difficult people. I thought your personality would be perfect for managing the *ladies,* dealing with tough customers, and negotiating the transactions. I saw you in action at the market and that's just the kind of attitude we need at the roadhouse."

Randi mulled this over. She continued to glare at Jim, wanting him to be fully aware that she wasn't giving up her anger easily. "I *am* good at managing people. I have a lot of experience in that department, but I'd be giving up things to come work at the roadhouse, Jim. It's a big commitment. What's in it for me?"

Jim shrugged. "We may have to work out those kinds of details on the fly. You mentioned you wanted to sell marijuana at the farmer's market. Maybe you can sell it at the roadhouse instead."

Her fury had not yet abated but Randi was at least listening. Jim could see the tumblers turning as she considered his words.

"I could supplement my income as long as I wasn't stepping on roadhouse business?" she asked.

"I don't see any reason you couldn't," Lloyd said. "The more services we offer, the more ways we have for drawing people in. That's how I see it."

"It's going to take a lot to draw people in," Jim added. "Especially since we're trying to overcome the repelling force of banjo music."

Lloyd smirked and mocked Jim. "Banjo music, banjo music... whine, whine, whine."

Randi let out a long sigh, releasing some of the tension she'd held in since getting riled at Jim. "My people have always had to fight and scratch for everything they got in this world. My dad farmed and raised cattle on some of the worst land God saw fit to create. Him and my brothers fixed cars, did carpentry work, plowed gardens, and shod horses. My brothers sold a little liquor, a little weed, raised tobacco, and sold scrap metal. Anything to make a dollar. You give me a seat at the table and I'll find a way to earn a dollar from it."

"Does that mean we're good, Randi, or do I have to watch my back?" Jim asked.

"Jim, we're practically family now. Being family means that you will always have to watch your back around me from now on. Ain't nobody that will jerk you around and whip your ass like family will. Remember that."

Jim didn't exactly find that comforting. Unlike his relationships with most people, the closer you got to Randi, the more dangerous things got. It was like standing next to a fire. There was a point where it went from being comforting to being painful.

Unable to arrive at an appropriate response to her statement, Jim cleared his throat and returned to discussing the roadhouse. "I'm going to try to get a handle on this project tonight. We'll have to divvy up some things. I'm hoping we can lure in labor by offering a free midday meal."

"There's the matter of the neighbors," Lloyd reminded him.

"What about them?" Randi asked.

"They're laying claim to the building," Jim said. "They want to be partners or charge us rent."

Randi looked confused. "Kill them. What's the problem?"

Lloyd nodded. "That's what I said."

"As much as I hate to admit it, they had a good point," Jim said. "Lots of people are assuming possession of properties they don't own for all kinds of reasons, including us. I can't kill people for doing something we're doing. It's the same situation as the house you're living in Randi. Same with Gary's family."

"Are there other suitable buildings?" Randi asked. "And are these people actually using this building or are they just being jerks?"

"Jerks," Lloyd summarized.

"And we couldn't find another building as good as this one," said Jim.

"Then what are you going to do?" Randi asked.

Jim swatted a bug off the back of his neck. "I'm going back with Hugh. He has a little more *presence* about him than Lloyd here does. Hugh's not a big guy but he's menacing enough that just having him along encourages people to want to work things out."

Lloyd looked offended at the suggestion that his presence wasn't suitable.

"I'm going to explain that we're determined to use that building since they aren't doing anything with it. It's not on their land and they don't own it," Jim went on. "They don't even have a use for it as far as I can tell. I'll offer them work during the construction phase and they'll get the meal that comes with that. If I have to, I'll offer them a credit they can use once we open the place. Maybe a certain number of free drinks a month. Something like that."

"They tried to steal our horses," Lloyd protested. "That should tell you all you need to know about what kind of people they are. They can't be trusted. If we try to deal with them, they're going to become a persistent pain in the ass."

"I didn't say I was going to trust them. Despite the impression you two have of me, this isn't a *killing* situation at the moment. It's a *talking* situation. When it becomes a killing situation, you'll be the first to know."

"I don't think we're the only two that have that impression of you," Randi said. "Seems to be common knowledge."

Jim stood and stretched. "Whatever. I'm tired of talking about it and I'm heading home. Lloyd, what's your plan?"

"I'm going to sit here with Randi for a spell."

"Better you than me," Jim quipped, heading for his horse.

Jim rode the well-worn trail between Randi's house and his own. When he reached his place, he let the horse drink at the trough while he removed the tack, then turned it out into the field. It rolled around on the ground a few times before it began to graze the late summer grass.

Jim stowed the tack in the barn, then carried his gear into the house, piling it on the floor just inside the door. Most of the garden had been harvested by this point but the family's main task each day continued to be the preservation of the late summer harvest. There were tomatoes, carrots, peppers, and onions in the garden, but fewer each day. Pops, Pete, and Charlie were now preparing the soil for the cold weather crops they'd plant soon. Jim had never done a late season garden before so he wasn't sure how it was going to turn out.

Without air conditioning, the house was muggy, and everyone preferred working in the shade of the back porch. Jim joined them outside and dropped into a chair, propping his feet on the porch rail. Nana and Ellen were slicing vegetables for dehydrating. Ariel was carefully arranging them on the old window screens they used as drying racks.

"How'd it go?" Ellen asked.

"Just another day in paradise," Jim said. "Only had to fire one shot all morning."

"At a person?" Nana asked. "Did you shoot someone again?"

"Someone tried to steal the horses, but we worked it out."

"That mean they're lying in a ditch somewhere?" Nana asked with a disapproving look.

Nana was more aware of how violent things were than she'd been a year ago, but she still continued to apply "old world" rules to their situation and they just didn't fit. The idea that her son had killed so many people didn't set well with her, even when those killings had been unavoidable–even when they saved her own life. Worse yet was the fact that her grandson had been forced to kill. To her, the loss of Pete's innocence had been the greatest injustice of this entire event.

Jim tugged his radio out of his shirt pocket and called for Hugh.

"Go for Hugh," came the reply.

"Hey, can you be down at my house in the morning? We need to make a little field trip into town."

"Sure. What time?"

"We can ride in when the rest of them are headed to the market. Will that work?"

"Not a problem," Hugh replied. *"I'll see you then."*

4

Jim

JIM'S PEOPLE had achieved a degree of infamy at the farmer's market now. While the booths operated by Gary's family and Randi had once flown under the radar, they'd been unable to keep their affiliation with Jim Powell under wraps for long. There were multiple reasons for that. It could have been the fight they got into at the market with Hadley and Isaac, the regional sheriff. More likely it was because of the now legendary speech where Jim stood on the roof of an RV in the parking lot and basically warned the entire town that he'd kill anyone who crossed him.

Initially it had appeared that people were appalled by Jim's speech. That was the reaction he'd expected, and he saw no reason to concern himself with how people felt about what he said. After all, he'd been public enemy number one among the residents of his community for so long that he'd gotten used to it. What he hadn't gotten used to was people threatening his family and friends. His speech that day had made it clear that those hostilities stopped immediately, or he'd kill everyone even tangentially involved in those actions.

However, he certainly *hadn't* expected that some of the things he'd said that day at the market would resonate with people. He called them out for their failure to work together to improve their situation. He chastised them for continuing to wait for rescue when it was apparent that rescue wasn't coming. He went on to give several concrete examples of things they could be doing immediately to prepare themselves for the coming winter.

Within days of his speech, Jim was approached at the market by a group of men. He was expecting trouble and readied himself for fight. Instead, the men wanted more information on those things they could be doing for themselves. He gladly rattled off a list, giving them plenty to keep them busy.

From that day forward, even more people began to view him as a resource rather than a rogue in their midst. When he was at the market, strangers would approach him with problems and questions. When he could, he'd give them advice.

He declined their requests to come look at their problems in person or help them make the repairs. He had too much to do already and wasn't looking at establishing himself as some kind of apocalyptic handyman. He was a firm believer in helping people to help themselves. If they weren't capable of performing the work that needed to be done, it was up to them to recruit the help required. The nanny state was dead and Jim wasn't about to revive it.

The valley people rode together as a group until they reached the street that led to the old sewing factory. Charlie, Pete, and Randi were going to be working their booth today. Gary, his wife, and one of his daughters had come to work their booth. They'd talked about combining their efforts into a single booth but had eventually decided against it. Having twice the number of booths doubled their opportunities to collect intelligence and that was one of the primary motivations behind their presence at the market. Should the road-house turn into a better intelligence-gathering resource, they might eventually be able to reduce their farmers market presence.

Once the rest of the riders peeled off for the market, Jim updated Hugh on the encounter he and Lloyd had at the sewing factory the previous day.

"You're sure this is the best location?" Hugh asked.

Jim nodded. "The more I thought about it last night, the more convinced I am that this is *the* place. There's even an old hot water boiler that we might be able to turn into some kind of heating system."

"Don't you need power for a boiler system? Don't they use circulating pumps?"

Jim grinned. "That's part of the beauty of this location. There's a creek not thirty feet behind the building. Besides providing water, it might allow us to put a hydroelectric system in place with a little experimenting."

"If we could use the water to crank a car alternator, we might be able to power a car stereo system," said Hugh. "Man can't live by banjo music alone. Occasionally he needs some Motorhead and AC/DC."

Jim was preparing to launch into his plan about preparing a daily soup for everyone willing to work, but the words died in his throat when they reached the sewing factory. A crude, hand-painted sign had been erected by the front door.

NO TRESPASSING. PRIVATE PROPERTY. KEEP OUT.

"Obviously you made your typical first impression," Hugh observed.

"Clearly." Jim frowned. "Some feelings were hurt but no blood was spilled."

"Feelings heal faster than gunshot wounds these days. People need to remember that. So, what you want to do?"

Jim sighed, then leaned forward to pat his horse. "They said they lived down this road. I reckon we're making a house call."

Hugh switched out the single magazine in his rifle for one that had another taped to it. It would allow him to reload his rifle simply by ejecting, then flipping, the magazine.

"I hope that's just a precaution," Jim said.

"Me too."

Jim had been down this road many times as a kid, usually going to the town park. There was also a sewer treatment plant, which sat idle and fermenting. Beyond that, a gravel road led to several houses and mobile homes.

When they neared the end of the road, the clatter of their horses' hooves on the gravel road caught the attention of the local dogs. One announced their arrival, then more joined in to spread the word further. The good thing was that this saved Jim from having to decide which of the dark and overgrown homes served as the operating base for the men he called Newport and NAPA. Within minutes of the dogs starting up, the two men he was looking for wandered onto the porch of one of the homes, hunting rifles in their hands.

"They're not alone," Hugh said in a low voice. "One at the corner of the house and another inside peeking out the window. There's two more in the door of that mobile home off to the left."

"I figured they had a whole clan back in here," Jim said.

"Well, you figured right."

Jim threw up a hand and waved. It was an awkward and pointless gesture. There was nothing congenial about the visit. He might as well have thrown up his middle finger in greeting. "Morning."

"Yeah, it is," Newport muttered. "You back for more trespassing?"

Jim grinned. "I guess you could say that. We talked about this yesterday. I acknowledge that the lines are a little blurry right now about who has a right to be where they are."

"Oh, you *acknowledge* it?" NAPA said. "That's nice. Makes me feel better."

Jim looked at Hugh and sighed. He was trying to keep this friendly, but it wasn't working. They'd bowed and curtseyed enough. He might as well cut to the heart of it.

"I don't see that you have any more legitimate claim on that building than anyone else. It's not on your property and it doesn't adjoin your property. You can't even claim that it used to be on your property. You're not using it for anything. Best I can tell, it's been nothing but a flophouse for homeless and druggies for the past year."

Newport squinted and cocked his head. "What gives you a right to come in here and claim it?"

"Only the fact that were going to provide a service to the community. It may end up being a service that you gentlemen will wish to partake of."

"What kind of service?" NAPA asked.

"I don't care to go into that at the moment."

Newport nodded as he considered this. "Well, then, I guess we're back to where we were yesterday with me wondering what's in it for us. I don't care for you coming in here being all pushy, telling us what you're going to do on our property."

Jim was losing some of his patience. "Not. Your. Property."

"It ain't yours neither," Newport repeated.

"Well, we're going to use it," Jim said flatly. "That part isn't up for debate. The only question is how much of a pain in the ass you're going to be. This going to require us shooting at each other or can we do it with talk instead of bullets?"

Hugh lowered his head and snickered. "Damn, Jim, so much for being diplomatic."

Jim's eyes continued to shift from Newport to NAPA, then to the other faces visible in the background while he waited for an answer.

"I guess taking you for an asshole wasn't just a first impression," Newport said. "You kind of follow through with it, don't you?"

"That's about the size of it," Jim said. "A man tends to stick with what he's good at."

Hugh bobbed his head in agreement.

"You said we might be able to do this with words," NAPA said. "Any point to that?"

"Definitely," Jim said. "This project we're about to start will require lots of work. It will create some temporary jobs. We don't have money to pay wages, but we'll feed everyone who can give us a couple of hours."

Newport laughed. "That don't sound like much of a deal to me. We're agreeing to cooperate with you and we don't get no more than anyone else. Same meal for the same labor."

"We have to start somewhere," Jim countered.

"How about we start with you allowing us to eat the meal you're offering in exchange for use of the building?" Newport said. "And we ain't providing any labor."

Jim considered. "Just the two of you?"

Both NAPA and Newport shook their heads.

"Not hardly," NAPA said. "We've got kin people in these houses that need fed too. The deal includes all of them."

Jim exchanged a glance with Hugh. Hugh shrugged, the gesture indicating he had nothing to offer. He wasn't any better at non-violent negotiation than Jim was.

"Okay," Jim conceded. "Here's my offer. We're a few days away from getting started so we won't be offering any meals until construction starts. You stay out of our hair, don't cause trouble, and I'll agree to let you and your family participate in the free meal. If it turns into a problem, we'll have to reconsider. Do we have a deal?"

Newport and NAPA leaned into a huddle and held a whispered conversation while Jim waited. When they finally broke apart, both men were nodding.

"I'll be damned," Hugh said. "You pulled it off."

"I doubt it," Jim said. He threw his leg over his horse and lowered himself to the ground. He faced the porch. "You willing to shake on it?"

NAPA and Newport came off the porch rather hesitantly and shook hands with Jim. Their dogs came in and sniffed at Jim, as if their blessing too was required to seal the deal. Jim wasn't impressed with the handshakes, deciding these weren't men accustomed to sealing bargains in such a manner. Their handshakes felt like those you got in a nursing home–a limp, clammy claw that contained none of the significance of a hearty shake.

Jim commented on it when he and Hugh were riding away from the neighborhood. "They shook hands like the dead."

Hugh gave a somber nod, well aware of the fate potentially foretold by Jim's choice of words.

5

Jim

Jim had never been big on cell phones. He didn't like most people well enough to want to talk to them on the phone. What he liked about a cell phone was having the internet at his fingertips and being able to keep extensive electronic lists. For a guy who worked as a project manager it was the ultimate portable organizational tool.

The previous night, Jim had sat down with a notebook and tried to organize the roadhouse project into a series of lists. He carried them around and sweated on them. He marked things out and added new things in the margins. All of it made him long for the ability to compile information electronically again. Though there was no cell service, Jim had multiple ways to charge his old phone, so that was exactly what he did. Overnight he charged the battered old iPhone he'd carried home from Richmond. After leaving NAPA and Newport, he stopped by the old sewing factory with Hugh. Somehow, having that mobile phone in his pocket made the job feel much more manageable.

"This place has ambiance," Hugh said. "Nice industrial feel. If you were going to open some microbrewery or hipster eatery, this would be the perfect spot."

"What about as a location for a post-apocalyptic bar and whorehouse?" Jim asked.

Hugh opened his arms and looked around. "I guess I could see that too."

"Good, because that's what we're shooting for."

"So, you don't plan to make this a family place?"

Jim chuckled. "For Lloyd, this is a place to play music in front of people and get back to the life he enjoys. For me–for *us*–this is an intelligence operation. Men don't spill their secrets in a family diner. They spill their secrets in the shady places where being overserved is completely acceptable. I'm sure it's been that way since the earliest days of brothels and bars."

"Now I see why you wanted it on the outskirts of town. It wouldn't do to have a place like this operating directly under the noses of the decent townspeople."

Jim grinned. "A lot of them already hate me, so maybe I have nothing to lose."

"I don't know. That speech of yours had a weird effect on people. I think you're building a following."

"Bullshit!" Jim drawled. "I'll believe it when I see it."

"I call them like I see them."

Jim began using his beat-up old phone to take pictures of the interior of the sewing factory. He then opened an app for taking notes and began listing the various top-level projects they'd be undertaking. Beneath those headings he'd list the mountains of smaller jobs that had to be done to complete each project.

"What are you shooting for?" Hugh asked.

"Medieval. Primal. A crude bar with lots of tables. Beer, wine, and liquor being made in the room. I'd like to get some chimneys in place so we can have homemade woodstoves for heating in the winter. I want outdoor restrooms for convenience and because no one wants to clean them. I'd like to have running water inside. Maybe a cistern on the roof or some system to pump it from the creek. We'll need plenty of water for cooking, drinking, cleaning, and making alcohol."

"Lloyd has a lot of big ideas about making liquor," Hugh said. "But you know what kind of follow-through he has. If I'm being honest, I'm not sure he's up to it. I know he's your friend, but he needs to produce his recipes and let us get some other people in here to run the daily operation of making alcohol."

"You're right," Jim agreed. "I was thinking the same thing. We have several positions that may need to be filled with people from outside our group."

"When you're done with those lists, we should head to the farmer's market. We can ask around and see what we may be able to scrape up in terms of supplies and equipment."

Jim held up a finger. "Which brings up the whole issue of getting those items hauled here to the roadhouse."

"We can ask around about that. Maybe there's someone around with more horses and something besides hundred-year-old hay trailers."

After taking dozens of notes on his phone, Jim tucked it in his pocket. He couldn't help but feel a little excited at starting at a new project. The last year had been chaos and Jim had struggled in numerous ways as he tried to manage it. Projects were something he understood. He knew how to break a big project into all the little steps that had to take place to complete it. That made sense to him in a way that dealing with the complexities of human emotion didn't.

They rode to the farmer's market and left their horses at the corral. The tender, an overall-wearing man named Hatfield, no longer charged Jim for leaving his horse because he'd needed some advice on a homesteading project at his house. They exchanged some small talk and Hatfield filled Jim in on his progress.

As Jim and Hugh started to walk off, Jim was struck with an idea and turned back to Hatfield. "You really a horse man, Hatfield, or is this just a business venture for you?"

Hatfield frowned. "Not sure what you're asking, friend."

"Are you just running this corral to earn a buck or are horses your thing? Did you go to horse shows? Do you have horses of your own?"

Hatfield grinned and shoved his hands in his pocket. He arched his body and rocked with pride. "Buddy, I was raised on horses. Spent as much time in horse barns as houses. Traveled to horse shows all over the south and went to every county fair in the area. My people probably had horses in every fair this county ever had."

"Well, I'm trying to get together a little project here in town. Between you and me, it's going to be a roadhouse. Music, drinking, food–whatever else we can come up with. I expect we're going to be needing some materials hauled. There are people in my valley who have horses and I've seen them cobble together a rig that allowed them to pull an old hay trailer around, but I'm looking for something better than that. Somebody with big horses and dependable equipment that can haul weight for a distance."

Hatfield shook his head like that was an inconsequential detail. "Son, you live in the wrong part of the county for that. I'm from the western side and it's different. Bigger farms and more cattle. That's where you find the real horse people. On the eastern side of the county, people wear ball caps advertising chewing tobacco and tractors. On the western side of the county, people wear cowboy hats. That right there tells you all you need to know."

Jim gave a satisfied nod. "Can you think of anyone who has horses and equipment like I'm talking about?"

"Abso-*damn*-lutely. You'll be wanting the Wolfords. They're cousins of mine, somehow. Grew up around them boys." Hatfield shook his head as he peered back through the mists of time to his childhood. "Whole family was rough as corn cobs. I didn't go to their house that I didn't come home scratched, bleeding, and beat all to hell. Had the time of my life."

Jim flashed a concerned look at Hugh. "No offense, Hatfield, but I'm hoping to get this moving quickly. I don't want to deal with a lot of...trouble. Are these Wolfords good workers or are they the kind of men that can't come to town without turning it upside down?"

Hatfield nodded somberly as he considered this. Coming to some conclusion, he regarded Jim. "They're hard workers. Part of why they're so rough is they grew up being worked like men from the minute they quit pissing their britches. They've raised generations of the biggest, strongest draft horses you've ever seen and they logged with them. They cut timber out of places a man couldn't take a piece of heavy equipment. That's dangerous work and every one of them boys, and some of the women, worked at it for generations. They also farm and sell some horses. Like I said, they're rough but they'll do you right. I tell you one thing–there won't be nobody messing with those boys. People take one look at them, shake their heads, and walk off. They decide it ain't worth it."

Realizing that there were times when physical intimidation could be useful, Jim immediately thought of his new friends Newport and NAPA. Perhaps having more big, scary people around would serve as a deterrent to those two, because Jim knew he wasn't done with them. He assumed they'd only agreed to his terms because they thought they'd find a way to squeeze even more out of the deal. He was determined to prevent that.

"How would I get up with these Wolfords?" Jim asked.

"I can talk to them," Hatfield said. "I usually head out and go home once the market starts to slow down so I can take care of my own chores at the house. I got a local boy comes in here and finishes out the day for me. What should I tell them?"

Jim thought about this. "I need a couple of days to line up some supplies and get workers started on the building. Two days from now I expect to be working at the roadhouse full-time until it's done. Tell them they can show up to negotiate or show up to work. Either way, I'm sure we can work something out."

"I'll take care of it, Jim. You can depend on me."

Jim waved. "Thank you, sir. Catch you later."

They wandered off to see Ian next. He was the vendor who made and sold improvised weapons at the market. He'd stuck his neck out for Jim's people a couple of times and Jim had come to see him almost as one of their own. He wasn't really interested in living in the valley, and that was fine with Jim. Having friends in town meant more opportunities to gather intelligence.

"We're going to open a roadhouse," Jim said.

Ian looked up from the welding rod he was working with. He'd been pounding the flux off the wire, grinding a point onto the end, and setting them into wood handles to make a stabbing weapon that looked like an icepick. He made the sheaths out of clear plastic oxygen tubing.

"A roadhouse," Ian mused. "That sounds rife with possibilities."

"It was Lloyd's idea," Jim admitted. "He wanted a place to play music and drink. He misses his old life. The more I considered the idea, the more I saw an opportunity there. Just between us, I see this as an intelligence hub. It's an information gathering opportunity that will help us stay better prepared for anything that might be coming down the pike."

Ian smiled. "Maybe give you a heads-up if the government is sending men to kill or arrest you? Again?"

Jim pointed a finger at Ian. "Exactly!"

"We're imagining music, alcohol and food," Hugh said. "Jim also has an idea of partnering up with some ladies of the night to help draw in more customers."

"But there's even more potential there," Jim admitted. "We've had good luck selling here at the market and this would give us a chance to bring some trade to us. We could sell more of the gear we've collected over the past year. We can take gear we need in trade."

"The old upsell," Ian chuckled. "You draw them in with the booze and hook them on the girls, the gear, and everything else."

"We were wondering if you might want in on it," Hugh said. "We need security. Bouncers. Employees get fed, so that's one less thing to worry about every day. You could also display your wares behind the bar, giving you another avenue for selling your products."

Ian didn't take long to think it over. "I'd like to be part of something like that. Winter will be here soon. I'm sure the market will continue but it's not going to be much fun sitting here in the cold. That sounds like a better gig."

"I'm glad to hear that," Jim said with genuine enthusiasm.

Ian brought a lot to the table. Physically, he was a big, brawny guy that might be able to defuse potentially violent situations by the sheer force of his presence. He also had the right mindset. He thought like Jim and Hugh did, innately understanding what information might be useful.

"When do you need me?" Ian asked.

"You're welcome to help with the renovation or you can join us after the work is complete. Whatever you want to do," Jim said. "I'm going to see about rounding up some materials now. We're going to need some distilling, brewing, and winemaking supplies too, so be wracking by your brain."

"I'm going to hang out with Ian for a bit," said Hugh. "Catch up with me when you're ready to head out."

6

Jim

JIM'S next stop was the booth beneath the covered pavilion where Randi, Pete, and Charlie were selling goods. As always, Randi welcomed Jim with the same expression one used when watching a heaving cat vomit on their carpet.

"Good to see you too, Sunshine," he said.

"There's a man looking for you," said Pete.

Most of the time that was bad news in Jim Powell's world. "What did he want?"

"It's that Cookie guy from the building supply," Pete said.

"Ah, that's good. He was on my list of people I needed to see today."

"You're on my list too," Randi said, giving Jim a side-eye. "And you know what list I'm talking about."

"Anything new or for the same old reasons?" Jim asked.

"Same old reasons."

Jim nodded. "It's good that some things in the world remain

consistent in these troubled times. The sun still rises and sets each day. Randi still finds reasons to be pissed at me."

"Yep," Randi agreed, watching the crowd for potential customers she could strongarm into buying something.

"Any idea where Cookie is? He around?" Jim asked.

Pete pointed. "He's talking to some guy at a booth over there."

Jim spotted the tall, red-haired man above the crowd. "I'll go talk to him then. How are you, Charlie?"

"I'm good. Staying busy."

Jim smiled at the boy. "Glad to hear that."

The relationship between the two had been strained after Charlie had left the valley a while back. By all appearances, he'd joined forces with Hadley Wright and Isaac, the regional sheriff. It turned out to be a ruse on Charlie's part, a misguided attempt to work as a double agent. While Charlie did manage to collect valuable intelligence, his mission took an emotional toll on everyone in their group.

The boy had been prone to overreaction ever since he'd lost his mother. His devotion to Jim and his people was almost unhealthy. He had no problem lashing out violently at anyone he saw as a threat to his new family. The only problem was that Charlie didn't have the maturity or experience to pick his battles. His first response was to try and kill anyone that threatened the stability of his new family because, in his simplified view, that was how Jim handled things.

"I'll see you guys later," Jim said and wandered off.

"Thanks for the warning," Randi muttered.

Jim ignored her, which he knew irritated her more than any response he could offer. He wove through the crowd, heading in Cookie's direction. Jim's presence at the farmer's market had always garnered some attention since he'd been labeled an insurgent by the government and had his picture posted on reward posters. He'd become even more infamous since delivering that speech atop an RV here at the market a few days ago.

The reaction to that speech continued to surprise him. He expected it to further alienate him from a community that already despised him as the violent troublemaker who'd prevented them from getting government aid. Instead, his speech had actually created some converts to his way of thinking. People began to seek him out for his advice. Others acknowledged him with waves or friendly nods. For once, Jim had done exactly the right thing, though it was purely accidental that it had worked out that way.

"Cookie!" Jim called out as he approached the big man.

Cookie spun around and his eyes flashed with recognition. "Jim Powell! Just the man I wanted to see."

"That's good, because I needed to talk with you too."

The two made their way outside to a quiet spot along a high retaining wall. There were people moving around them, but it was considerably more private than inside the pavilion.

"The market just gets bigger every day," Jim commented.

"People are not as scared now. They're wanting things to get back to something more normal and I guess they realized that might not happen without considerable work on their part. Some of that was your doing. That speech you gave was a kick in the pants."

"You guys making progress on some of those projects?"

Cookie nodded. "Hell yeah. Basically, every fenced enclosure in town has become a pen for stray livestock. Tennis courts, athletic fields, impound yards, car lots, you name it. It's taken some arguing to get a system worked out, but everyone agrees that it makes more sense to work at this together. There will be less waste if we organize the slaughter instead of people just killing an animal when they're hungry and wasting most of the meat."

"One hundred percent true," Jim agreed.

"We've got people guarding those pens day and night. We're working on establishing a list of houses with wood heat where people can go for winter. We've got people cutting firewood and winterizing houses. We even found a guy who worked at the water treatment plant and he's helping us set up clean drinking water stations at some of the old, abandoned springs around town. They were closed decades ago because of contamination from sewers, but we've been collecting the water in plastic tanks. This guy checks and treats those tanks every day."

"That's good to know. Now I've got a question for you. What's the situation with the building supplies at the place where you used to work?"

Cookie sighed. "We've been using some of the plumbing for the water projects and some of the fasteners to winterize houses. Not much got stolen over the last year because there were several of us employees living there. We all lived alone outside of town and decided we might have a better chance of survival if we teamed up."

"Good planning," Jim agreed. "What's the lumber situation like?"

Cookie looked a little uncomfortable with the question. "It was a long winter. A little cold too. One of the owners was staying with us. I hate to admit it, but we burned a lot of the lumber to keep warm over the winter. Some got stolen by people trying to do the same thing, but us being there onsite put a stop to most of that."

"What's left in the way of materials?" Jim asked. "I've got a project going on that might create some short-term jobs for people. The scale of the job depends on what kind of materials I can get."

Cookie considered this. "There's plenty of concrete and mortar mix. Metal roofing and shingles are in good supply. Fasteners, plumbing, electrical supplies. The fiber cement siding and panels are available. You can't burn that stuff, so nobody wanted it."

"I'm not entirely sure what I need yet," Jim admitted. "I wanted to see what was available before I got a list together. You think there's a way I could buy some of those materials off the owner?"

"We're not really open for business. No one is. She'd probably be willing to sell you what you needed as long as you could make a good trade."

"I don't have much in the way of food to trade," Jim said. "We're going to offer a meal every day as payment to the workers, so I expect that will cut into my food supply. I do have ammunition, some weapons, some extra gear, and a few other things."

"You get me a list together and we'll see what we can work out. Now, getting those supplies from the lumber yard to your jobsite is a different story. There's obviously no delivery available now and I doubt you'll find a man interested in carrying a bag of concrete mix across town. Everyone is too weak from hunger to have that kind of energy."

"I'm working on that," Jim said. "I'm trying to work out a hauling contract."

"As far as workers go, I can help you with that," Cookie offered. "I know every contractor, tradesman, and laborer in the area. I did business with them every day. Most of them are bored and hungry right now. I'm sure a few of them would be more than willing to sing for their supper, so to speak."

Jim stuck out his hand. "Thanks for the help, man. You going to be around tomorrow?"

Cookie shook the offered hand. "I'll be here somewhere. Once I talked to you, I somehow ended up being the coordinator of a lot of these projects around town. Guess that's what happens when you open your big mouth. Anyway, all that keeps me on the run. So, I'll be here, but you might have to hunt me down."

"I'll try to work up what materials I need and get together a list of what I can trade for them."

"Good deal."

The two of them parted ways and Jim headed back through the covered pavilion. He'd become so accustomed to the stares that he no longer reacted to the feeling he was being watched. It had become part of being in town. The downside of becoming comfortable with that sensation was that it made it easier to miss threats or those with malicious intent.

7

The Antique Dealers

THREE SETS of eyes followed Jim as he left Cookie and walked through the pavilion. The owners of those sets of eyes all had the same expression of thinly veiled contempt on their faces. None of the three had been injured either directly or indirectly by anything that Jim Powell had done since the collapse, they just didn't like him. They didn't like seeing people defer to him and seek out his opinion on matters. After all, Jim Powell was an outsider.

"I hear his mother was from West Virginia," said Pamela, the dark-haired lady on the left. Her nose was turned up in the air, reading glasses perched upon it. She gazed at Jim from beneath heavy, reptilian lids.

The couple to her side, a man and woman she'd been in the antique business with for decades, looked almost shocked at that revelation.

"Really?" the lady asked. Her name was Dixie and she was damn proud of it. She knew her name had inspired a great deal of jealousy among the other Daughters Of The Confederacy back when they'd been able to have those meetings. "His mother taught school here in this county for as long as I can remember."

Pamela sneered contemptuously. "Yes, she came here from West Virginia in the early 1960s, but *still*. It's not like being born here."

"His dad is native to the area," said Dixie's husband. His name was Mitchell and he typically didn't have a lot to say. He'd once been overweight but was now just sallow and fleshy, with ill-fitting clothes. He looked like a man resigned to his fate, sitting miserably between two overbearing and judgmental women from whom he could never escape.

Pamela shook her head. "His family may be native to the *region* but not to this *town*. It's not the same thing. His father's family might have had land, livestock, and education–I don't know or really care. They didn't contribute to this town. It was families like yours, mine, and a handful of others that carved this place from the wilderness before there was even a United States. If you look back at the oldest records, you know what names you'll find as well as I do. The Powell name is not among them. He's an outsider. He'll always be an outsider."

"An outsider who's up to something," Mitchell said. "He was public enemy number one a few weeks ago. Now he's like Mr. Wizard and MacGyver all rolled into one. I've heard people talking about him in a much more positive light since he delivered that atrocious, profane speech here at the market."

Dixie fanned herself. "Don't remind me. The mouth on that one. His mother must be so ashamed."

"I was embarrassed for her," Pamela said, "and I don't even care for the woman. He just made a public spectacle of himself, up there cursing and threatening decent people."

"Just pure trash," Dixie drawled. "That's all you can say about it."

The three at the booth had been in the antique business for over thirty years. Before the collapse, they had a store they opened a few days a week. They were fixtures at all the weekend estate auctions and had vendor's booths anytime there was an antique festival in the area. Antiques were their entire world.

Being both industrious and miserly, they had seen an opportunity in the collapse. Many of the goods they sold in their store and owned in their respective personal collections were designed to be used without electrical power. They were antiquated gadgets perfectly suited for the world in which everyone now found themselves.

They had butter churns, corn shellers, meal grinders, and even the handheld graters that everyone had disposed of for modern food processors. They had hand-cranked mixers, whisks, sausage grinders, and apple peelers. They had stove irons, crocks, and washboards, as well as several early hand-cranked tub washers. Expecting there might be a need for these things, they gathered a suitable sampling of their wares and brought them to the burgeoning farmer's market as soon it became a regular event. They'd experienced steady sales ever since.

All three were very astute bargainers, having more experience in haggling than nearly everyone they encountered. After all, no one argued over prices like antique dealers. Sometimes dealers could spend decades trying to negotiate a colleague out of a particularly sought-after item.

They drove hard bargains and got top price for their goods. Without too much compromise, they parlayed their antiques into food, silver, gold, and jewelry. As antique afficionados, they were students of history and knew the world would eventually right itself. They might as well take advantage of this opportunity to make money while they could. With most people seeing no value in cash, precious metals, and jewelry, it was a good time for the three to hoard as much of it as they could.

When they began to run low on inventory, Mitchell, Dixie, and Pamela were forced to take drastic measures to restock. The community of those who dealt in antiquities was rather small, so the three knew a lot about the customers who frequented their shop. They knew who the local collectors were. And from the way that antique enthusiasts talked and gossiped about their particular field of interest, the three knew who had highly prized items in their personal collections that they swore they'd never part with.

Such as the elderly farming couples living on land that their ancestors had peopled for more than a century. Their stately old homes were still decorated with the personal belongings of those who'd come before them. They were the people who could never be convinced to sell their antiques because they weren't part of a "collection." It was *mother's* glassware or *grandmother's* kitchenware. It was the tools they remembered grandfather using to build onto the house or repair his old Allis-Chalmers tractor. All the things the antique dealers saw as dollar signs, those old people saw as living memory. They were mementos. They were personal reminders of love, family, and the roots of where they'd come from.

Estates such as those were the holy grail of auctions. When one of the owners died, the last of a long, proud line, the antique dealers and their brethren didn't waste a moment lamenting the end of a lineage. They felt no remorse that the estate would no longer exist as a unified collection that represented the flesh, blood, and dreams of a family. Instead, they circled like buzzards and fought tooth and nail over each piece of furniture, each tool, each camel-back trunk, and each box lot.

The three antique dealers were practical people. While there were no more estate auctions taking place, they'd noticed over the last year that elderly people were dropping like flies. Just as all the doom and gloom prognosticators had predicted, there had been a massive die-off from starvation, disease, a cold winter, and violence. While it might not have been as high as the over ninety-percent figure that some reports had anticipated, it was probably close. The antique dealers did not shed a single tear at these deaths because all they saw was opportunity.

As everyone in the affected areas knew, there were more unoccupied houses in most neighborhoods now than there were occupied homes. On a street of ten homes, perhaps seven or eight sat empty. There were large neighborhoods where once hundreds of people had lived. Now, those same neighborhoods might now hold a couple of dozen people.

In the quest for food, gear, and anything that might help them survive, people plundered the houses of their friends and neighbors when it was clear that there was no one living there anymore. It was different than the thievery of those who didn't care whether anyone was home or not. Most of those who took from empty houses understood that there was a sense of indebtedness that came with the gray area of taking from the dead or missing. They tried to maintain a spirit of gratitude, making promises that they would try to make it right if there was ever a way to do so.

The antique dealers saw this as an opportunity to begin reclaiming and recirculating items from their former customers and fellow collectors who had died or moved on. They didn't see it as stealing, but as a way of stimulating the economy. They were taking idle assets and getting them in the hands of people who needed them. In their eyes, they were performing a *service*, and it was only fair that they be adequately compensated for it.

Each night after darkness fell on their community, the three loaded backpacks into the carts they used to carry their wares around. They'd use side streets, fields, and back alleys to visit the homes of people they knew had antiques. Even in the homes that had already been looted, many people ignored antiques. Often the antique dealers came upon situations where valuable antique furniture had been hacked into kindling and burned, with only a few scraps remaining to tell the tragic tale.

When they reached a target home, they all changed into mechanic's coveralls, pulled on dust masks, and grabbed flashlights. They entered through open doors if they found them or used pry bars to gain entry when no one had been there before them. They all knew the things they were looking for and were familiar with the places where people would keep those items.

It was somber work, more often than not conducted in the presence of the decomposing former owner of the items they were stealing. Sometimes the antique dealers found themselves apologizing to their former customer for what they were doing. However, most days they felt no guilt for their actions whatsoever, filling bags and pillowcases with the items they knew they could most easily sell at the market.

Initially, they'd tried to limit themselves to their original business plan of only stealing items that people in the community needed, but that idea quickly went by the wayside. They weren't just dealers, they were also collectors, and that was the problem. Within weeks of beginning to collect inventory from other homes, they widened the scope of what they found acceptable to take.

It was a weird dynamic. Mitchell and Dixie were married, but just as competitive with each other as they were with Pamela. They worked as an efficient team when they were purchasing items at auction to place in their store, trying to get the item as inexpensively as possible. That teamwork went out the window when one or more of them wanted a particular item for their personal collections. Then all bets were off and they brutally competed with each other, running up the bid to make the winner pay dearly.

Other times, if Dixie noticed Pamela making a note that she wanted to bid on a particular lot number because it held something she was interested in, Dixie might secretly remove that item and hide it in a lot that contained mostly junk. Pamela would bid high on the lot she thought contained the sought-after item, but she wouldn't get it because Dixie had stashed the item in a less expensive lot, which she then purchased herself.

Such tactics had led to many arguments, grudges, and hostilities, but the three of them were together all day, every day, just as they'd been before the collapse. They'd even moved in together shortly after the terror attacks because they felt it would be safer and a better use of their limited resources. They were like some weird family, a trio of overly enmeshed siblings that couldn't escape the matrix that bound them to each other.

That same competitiveness revealed itself when they lurked about the dark houses of their town, scrounging through the personal belongings of the dead and missing. It had become their unspoken routine that before they even looked for the trivial items such as eggbeaters and cast-iron skillets, they checked all the common hidey holes for items of much greater value.

In addition to the deep pockets of their grubby coveralls, each carried rucksacks into which they discreetly slipped items that caught their interest. There were coins and precious metals, as well as items of jewelry that would one day be marketable again. There were antique pistols, memorabilia from world wars, and early photographs of the town.

They tried to ignore each other during these questionable acquisitions, preferring to search in private, each in a room of their own. That didn't always work, and they sometimes raced to reach coveted hiding spots as soon as they made entry to the home, elbowing each other like customers at a Black Friday sale.

Despite the fact that they were all doing the same thing, there were times that one would catch the others gazing at them with judgmental eyes. However, their lust for antiquities was so great that each found their own way to rationalize and compartmentalize their deeds. Any guilt dissipated when they got back to the home they shared, gloating like misers as they unpacked their loot in the glow of a lantern.

$$8$$

Jim

After leaving the pavilion, Jim returned to Ian's booth to meet up with Hugh.

"I've learned a few things sitting here with Ian," Hugh remarked when Jim arrived. "Some of it might be useful."

"Like what?" Jim asked, dropping to the ground and sitting cross-legged on the warm asphalt.

Ian was focused on grinding a point on one of his welding rod icepicks. "I was telling Hugh I'd heard the vineyard on the edge of town was looking for people to pick grapes. You know the place?"

Jim nodded. "I know the people who own it. I've known them my entire life."

"Apparently they have vines full of grapes and not enough labor to pick them," Hugh said. "Usually, their families come in to help. It's a big annual celebration for them. For obvious reasons, their families can't get here for the second year in a row so they're looking at losing another harvest."

"You might be able to work out a deal with them," Ian said. "The guy wants to make wine, but he doesn't have the manpower for the harvest."

Jim grinned, pleased. "I'll try to get up with him today. We'll ride by there on our way out of town."

"I also told Hugh that there was a microbrewery about twenty miles from here in the town of St. Paul. You know the place?"

"I've been there several times," Jim said. "Good food."

"It burned down over the winter," Ian said. "Some guy from over that way was telling me about it. Apparently, the owner was living there and trying to heat the place with an improvised woodstove. Things got out of hand and the place caught fire."

"How bad?" Jim asked. "You think there's anything salvageable?"

Ian shrugged. "I don't know, but it's something you might check into."

"The booze is a big thing," Jim said.

"It better be a priority," Hugh said. "No booze, no roadhouse. Sober people aren't going to sit around listening to Lloyd banging on the banjo."

Jim laughed. "I try to tell him that." He stood and stretched his back. "Let's go to the vineyard, Hugh."

Hugh got to his feet and slipped his day pack onto his back. "I think I can fit that into my schedule."

The two men retrieved their horses from Hatfield and set off through town, riding back in the direction that would eventually lead them to the valley. Near the cemetery where Jim had recently had a gunbattle with Hadley Wright's bodyguards, he turned off the main road and followed a long driveway to a sprawling ranch house. Jim had visited the house several times when he was growing up but hadn't been there in years.

The family that owned the farm had been in the town for over two hundred years, finding their way into the forts and settlements long before the Revolutionary War. Over the years, much of the town had been built on land sold off by this family. After selling off land and splitting it between family members, they now occupied a much smaller footprint than they once had.

The vineyard was the dream project of one member of that family and his wife. Jim knew the guy but couldn't recall having seen him in the last twenty years or so. Still, he recognized him immediately when he spotted him picking late-season beans from an overgrown garden. The man straightened from his work and regarded Jim approaching in the distance. The guy was dressed in ragged bibbed overalls, wire frame glasses with round lenses, and a frayed straw hat, looking more like a hippie than a haggard survivor of the apocalypse.

Noting he didn't appear to have a weapon, Jim raised a hand and waved. "Teddy! It's Jim Powell."

Hugh chuckled. "You sure that shouting out your name puts people at ease these days? He's liable to throw those beans in the air and take off running if he knows you're coming."

Jim ignored Hugh, steering his horse off the road and toward the fenced garden off to the side of the house. With its rusty iron gate, cedar posts, and antique wire fencing, it was the type of well-established family garden that had likely occupied the same plot of land for four or five generations.

"Well, howdy, Jim," Teddy said with a smile. "Who's that you got with you?"

Jim threw a thumb up and pointed at Hugh. "That's my buddy Hugh. We used to work together years ago. He lives out there in the valley with us."

Teddy laughed. "Yeah, I've heard about you folks in the valley."

"What have you heard?" Jim asked, wondering what Teddy's laugh implied.

"Mostly that you've been butting heads with people. Everyone from the government to your neighbors. Gives people something to talk about."

Jim nodded somberly. "That's about the size of it. Can't catch a break. Things finally came to a head last week. I got a little riled up and went off at the farmer's market. Cussed out the whole town, depending on who's telling the story."

"That's what I heard." Teddy chuckled. "I got a good laugh out of it. What you all into today? Been to the market?"

"Yeah, I've got a little project going and I needed to do some legwork. I'm trying to track down supplies so I can get it going before winter."

"What kind of project?" Teddy asked.

"Can you keep a secret?"

Teddy shook his head. "Not a one. Drink too damn much wine."

Jim shrugged. "I'll tell you anyway because we might be able to help each other out. I'm looking at opening a roadhouse. The kind of place a man might come to get a drink, hear some music, and maybe get a bite to eat."

Teddy listened as Jim spoke but didn't appear convinced. "What the hell made you come up with something like that? You really think people will be interested in going out to a nightclub with the world being like it is? These aren't exactly festive times."

"It's not really a nightclub," Hugh said, "and people will definitely come. There's a lot who would trade for booze now if it was available to them. Just look at the vendors at the market selling weed. People are looking for an escape, something to smooth the edges off a harsh world."

Teddy gestured at a distant hill covered in orderly rows of grape vines. "I've thrown in the towel and closed the doors on the vineyard. My wife and I have been giving it a try, but we can't pick enough to make a difference. Can't hire anyone who will actually show up and all our family is too far away to come help."

"That's what I wanted to talk to you about," Jim said. "I heard about your problem. I was wondering if we might be able to work something out."

"What are you thinking?"

"If I can get those grapes picked, I wondered if you might be interested in giving us some of the wine."

Teddy mulled this over. "I might consider that, but it wouldn't help you in the short-term. It would take a couple of months to produce anything of decent quality."

Jim frowned. "I didn't know. I can talk about guns all day, but I don't know shit about wine."

Teddy raised a finger in the air. "But I've got bottled inventory in storage. I've also got wine in barrels that needs to be bottled. I've not had much of a stomach for the business this past year because of the state of things so I've just let it all sit and gather dust. I've got plenty of supplies though. Honestly, I miss the work. Making wine kept me busy and distracted."

"Well, maybe we can put you back in business," Jim said.

"What are people even using for money these days?" Teddy asked. "I have no idea."

"All kinds of things." Jim rattled off a list. "Medications, food, ammunition, guns."

Teddy pondered that. "I can always use food, but I don't reckon I need any more guns or ammo. I've had to fire a few warning shots in the air, but I've not had to kill anyone yet."

Hugh shifted in his saddle. "There's always tomorrow. You don't always get to choose when and where violence finds you."

Jim's face darkened. "Yeah, take my word for it, Teddy. I've had to make some tough calls. Lost track of how many times I've had to pull the trigger."

"I've heard," Teddy replied, raising an eyebrow. "How about you guys help me harvest the grapes and I'll take that as payment for getting you started with a supply of wine from what I've already got on hand? Once the new stuff is ready to bottle, we can work out a deal on that. Maybe by then we'll both have a better idea of what the wine is worth to you."

"Sounds good," Jim agreed. "If I could have you a half-dozen people here tomorrow, would that do it?"

Teddy considered. "Ten would be better, and we might still need a few days to make it happen."

"I'll try to have you ten then. They'll be here first thing in the morning."

"Sounds good, man," Teddy said. "You said you're going to have music at this roadhouse?"

"Hell yeah. My friend Lloyd came up with the idea in the first place. He's more interested in a place to play and drink than running a business, so I'm trying to get it off the ground."

"You'll have to introduce me to this Lloyd character. I don't think I know him, but I'd like to do some picking again. It's been a while since I've played with people."

"I'll hook you up," Jim said. "We've got to get on the road, but I'll have my people here first thing in the morning."

When they were heading down the driveway, Hugh pulled up alongside Jim. "You want me to go with you tomorrow or come over here and pick grapes?"

Jim looked a little sheepish. "I hate to ask that, but do you mind coming over here and keeping an eye on things?"

"I don't mind. Teddy may be a nice guy, but I'm not sure he's very focused on security. If we're going to have a lot of our people over here, I feel a need to keep them safe."

Jim nodded. "My thoughts exactly."

9

Jim

After a lot of discussion, it was determined that no one from the valley would be attending the market the next day. Everyone who was free was going to be engaged in picking grapes. The idea of the roadhouse sounded like a novelty to some in their group, perhaps even a waste of time. To others, it was as if they were creating a situation that would only lead to violence, conflict, and trouble. Jim faced an uphill battle in selling some of them on the importance of the project.

"This roadhouse serves us in multiple ways," he'd assured Gary's wife Debra, among the most reluctant to lend her support to the project. "We need the roadhouse as an intelligence hub. Knowing what's going on in town can help us avoid some of the trouble we've run into before. Just think about how much we've learned about the community since we started going to the market."

She wasn't convinced.

He kept going. "It also gives us a leg up on establishing a retail center for when the weather gets cold. You guys are doing well at the market but you're not going to want to sit out there all day when winter hits. If we have the roadhouse up and running, we can sell merchandise through there with a lot less effort. It'll be like some kind of pioneer trading post. I guarantee we'll have traffic even when the market is mostly empty."

Debra gave Jim a hard stare. "I'm going to be frank with you. I've heard there's a prostitution component to this project of yours and I don't support being part of that. I don't want my family associated with it."

Jim sighed. He didn't understand why people didn't get it. "I've tried to explain this. We are *not* going to be involved in prostituting anyone. There was already prostitution going on in town, but Hadley Wright was the one benefitting from it. He was basically a pimp. My plan is to give the girls an opportunity to work for themselves and run their own show. We're only offering the support that they asked for, like security and help in managing customers. Randi is going to take that on."

"You can rationalize it all you want, but it still sounds like we're taking over as pimps," Debra remarked, shaking her head in disapproval. "I don't even see why this part is necessary. If you kept the place a little calmer, set limits on how much people could drink, and didn't facilitate prostitution you might be able to create a nice family atmosphere. A place that more people in the community could enjoy."

"I agree. That's all true. It's not about helping families, though. It's about gathering information."

"So you keep saying."

"A family environment is not going to bring in the kind of people we need to monitor, Debra. We need to overhear the discussions between bottom feeders and riffraff. We need to know what the smugglers, the shooters, and the travelers are seeing and hearing. Those people don't hang out at Cracker Barrel, they hang out in strip clubs and bars."

Debra continued to give him a look that said she was not swaying from her opinion. "I know you're determined to do this, but I worry where this may end up, Jim. It feels like we're playing with fire."

"I hear what you're saying, and I acknowledge that possibility," Jim said. "You have to understand, though, that I feel a lot of pressure to right the wrongs I've committed. Not the people I've killed, but the risk I've exposed my friends and family to by burying my head in the sand for much of the past year. I've tried to keep us isolated and that's hurt us. That's on me. Now I'm trying to take proactive steps and this isn't some knee-jerk reaction. This is a very practical, calculated, intelligence-gathering effort that's critical to keeping us safe."

Debra looked Jim in the eye and stared at him for a long time. He felt she was assessing him on all levels. He hoped she saw his determination and utter conviction that this was the path forward for them.

She must have because she reluctantly conceded and was among the somewhat confused group that met at Jim's gate a little after sunrise. Gary was there with his arm still in a sling from his fight with the regional sheriff. His daughter Sara was there with her husband Will. Randi was there with Charlie and her daughter Carla. Ellen came along with Pete. Finally, Hugh rounded out the group, serving as both picker and protector. Everyone else remained in the valley to keep an eye on things, babysit, and perform the chores that couldn't be put off for the day.

On the ride into town, Jim discussed the deal he'd made with Teddy. While he was explaining, he noticed Randi pointing at people and counting.

"What?" he asked.

"You promised him ten people and there's eleven of us. Does that mean I can go home?" she asked.

Jim sighed, fully knowing how the next few minutes were about to go. "No, because I'm not picking grapes this morning, Randi. I've got somewhere else I have to be."

Randi waved her fingers in the air dramatically, almost like she was casting a spell. "Oh, big surprise there, Jim. You sold us all into indentured servitude but you're not going to help. How convenient."

"I've got a full day of riding ahead of me, Randi. I'm going to the brewery in St. Paul and that's no short ride."

Randi shook her head in disgust. Jim knew there was no way he could derail the performance she was putting on. Regardless of how sincere his motives were, she enjoyed raking him over the coals, especially in front of an audience. Perhaps there was nothing in her immediate life, with the exception of her grandchildren, that gave her such pleasure.

"For what it's worth, I can vouch for him," Hugh said. "Ian told us that the brewery in St. Paul had burned. If any of the equipment is salvageable, that could be a tremendous help with getting the roadhouse up and running."

Jim caught Randi glaring at him and took the opportunity to stick his tongue out at her. Yeah, it was juvenile, but it was all he had at the moment. Always ready to turn things up a notch, she replied with an upraised middle finger, sending Pete and Charlie into fits of giggling.

After crossing the creek and reaching Main Street, they said their good-byes.

"Be careful," Hugh warned. "Head on a swivel."

"And try not to be an asshole," Randi advised.

"That's the pot calling the kettle black," Jim mumbled as he hugged Ellen and Pete.

"You'll be home tonight, right?" Ellen asked.

Jim shrugged. "I can't be certain. It'll probably take me half the day to get there, then I have to track down the owner of the brewery. I'll be back tomorrow night for certain, whether I find him or not."

Ellen didn't look comfortable with the idea, but they didn't live in a comfortable world anymore. Nothing was routine. Nothing was safe.

10

Jim

FOR THE NEXT five hours Jim rode into the western end of the county. For the most part he stuck to the main road since there weren't any viable shortcuts. The road felt different than it had even a few short months ago. While it was a far cry from the old world with its cars, electricity, and general state of busy-ness, Jim didn't feel the pervasive, threatening undercurrent that he felt when traveling in the spring and winter.

He couldn't tell whether that sense came from the fact that so many of the desperate had died off or moved on. Maybe it was because those who remained were determined to begin digging out of this disaster and find a way to move forward with their lives. He'd seen that attitude among people at the market.

Life wasn't like it used to be, but people were accepting that it might *never* be that way again. It was a different time and a different world. They were a different people. That 1950s-era mentality–that normalcy bias–that tomorrow would be just like today, only a little better, had evaporated like a morning fog. People understood now that the expectation of a normal tomorrow had always been an illusion. It was fantasy. It was hopefulness.

They still had hope, only they held it differently. Those who survived had a grit and determination that came not from being Americans but from being human. There was a drive to survive that was irrepressible. There was a drive to improve and make things better. To seek stability. That was what would deliver them through this. That was how they would restore their world.

Jim didn't feel like he was being watched from the murky recesses of locked homes. The few people who paid any attention to him at all did so as they labored in fields, repaired fences, or herded livestock. Some waved in a generally friendly manner, while others paid him little mind.

His neck didn't tingle with the sense that people were watching him through scoped rifles. He didn't feel as if robbery was imminent or that he'd be killed for his horse. In this end of the county, the primary industry was farming rather than coal mining, and that produced a different kind of people. The coal miners had let their livestock go generations ago when they sold their souls to the mining companies. The farmers in this area had stuck with livestock, it was just a matter of rediscovering the old methods of taking care of them.

The strangest moment of the entire ride was when Jim passed the county fairgrounds. It was the site where the government and their United Nations' partners had started building one of those "comfort camps" that had caused so much trouble. Construction had already been underway when Jim flooded the power plant at Artrip, but the project was abandoned soon afterward. The government had decided that violent hillbillies and insurgents could do without comfort camps and electricity if they were going to act like lawless heathens.

To one degree or another, Jim had spent the last six months paying for that impulsive decision to destroy the power plant. People in the community had taken every opportunity to remind him that they too had paid a price for his actions. The comfort camp would have been a facility where thousands could have lived with the basics of electricity and hot meals, but at the cost of their freedom. The price had been too high for Jim, so, for better or worse, he'd made the decision for everyone in the immediate area.

Jim was getting saddle-sore by the time he reached the town of St. Paul. He'd eaten as he rode and had been drinking steadily from his water bottles, but it was a hot day. Before visiting the remains of the brewery, he took a short detour to the banks of the Clinch River and splashed cool water on his face. He soaked a bandana and ran it over his head, the clear water of the ancient river having a restorative effect.

Here, too, things felt a little more relaxed than they had. Some families fished the deep pools for smallmouth bass, red eyes, and catfish. At other places along the river, people swam and bathed on the rocky beaches as others had done for thousands of years before them. People paid him little mind. The presence of an armed man on horseback was not the strange and ominous sight it had once been.

Jim mounted his horse and rode into the town that had once been called the Western Front. There had been entire streets of bars and brothels where coal miners spent their wages. Men accidentally killed in bar fights would be laid out on the train tracks at night so the passing trains would destroy any evidence of what had taken place.

As coal mining declined, so went the town. It remained a community of nice older homes and brick storefronts, but there was none of the bustle and energy there'd once been. Riding through the streets, Jim spotted a farmer's market like the one in his own town. People carried purchases in their arms or strapped across their backs. He noted that there were more people on horses here than in his own town.

When he reached the side street where the upstart microbrewery had been located, it wasn't hard to tell which building had once housed the brewery. The front of the building, from the brick to the wood trim, was stained with soot. The plate glass windows had broken out into the street, the glass raked into a haphazard pile on the sidewalk. Even before he reached the building, Jim could hear banging coming from inside.

He stopped out front, tying his horse off to a parking meter and stepping up to the damaged storefront. "Hello?" he called.

The banging stopped.

"Hello?" Jim repeated.

Moments later, there came the scuff of footsteps across a gritty floor. Jim stepped closer and shaded his eyes, trying to see into the dark interior of the building.

A man in his early thirties emerged from the darkness. He'd been hard to see at first because everything from his face to his clothing was blackened by soot and ash. He looked like a coal miner wearily emerging from the driftmouth at the end of his shift.

Seeing that he didn't recognize Jim, the man wearily asked, "Can I help you?"

Jim understood the tone in the man's voice. He'd been there before too. It was the sound of a man near defeated but refusing to succumb. It was the voice of a man who'd had the rug yanked out from beneath him but clung tenaciously to a dream. To his life.

"Is this your place?"

He sighed. "What's left of it."

Jim stuck out his hand. "My name is Jim Powell. I rode six hours to talk to you. You got a few minutes for me?"

The man made the pointless gesture of dusting a black hand off on equally black pants before shaking Jim's hand. "I'm Ed Frye. Can't imagine why you'd ride that far to talk to me." His expression revealed more suspicion than interest, which was probably only natural under the circumstances.

"What are your prospects for reopening?" Jim asked, looking around the wrecked storefront.

Ed's face took on a look of disgust. "I'd hoped to brew up some beer this summer for the locals, but there's just too much work and not enough help. Everyone has their own problems to deal with. The local farmers can afford to hire help because they can pay in food. I've got nothing to offer."

"Is your equipment salvageable?"

Ed gave a half-hearted shrug. "I think so. Most of the damage was confined to the restaurant area. I was trying to heat the place and my fire got out of control. I lived upstairs so the fire affected my home as well as my business."

Jim gestured at the neighborhood around them. "Looks like there were plenty of other places to stay."

Ed shrugged. "Nothing close enough to allow me to keep an eye on the place."

Jim decided it was time to cut to the chase. "I have a proposal for you, if you're interested."

Ed didn't appear enthused, as if he couldn't imagine there was anything this stranger could say that might breathe life back into his deflated dreams. "Let's hear it."

"I'm opening a roadhouse over in Russell County. I have a friend who likes to make liquor nearly as much as he likes to drink it. We've found a location and just yesterday I secured a source of wine. If I could add beer, that would be perfect."

"I'm not sure what the point would be. Everyone around here tells me they have bigger concerns than having a drink. They give me the impression I'm wasting my time even trying to open this place back up. To be honest, there's been a couple of dark days where I wanted to jump off the river bridge and drown myself."

"You know as well as I do that taverns have a long tradition in this country. Those are the places where ideas are forged and alliances struck. That's what I'm envisioning. I passed your farmer's market coming into town. We have one just like it in my county but where are those people going to go when the weather turns cold? I want to get a jump on setting up a place where people come to us. Food, drink, weapons, and trade goods."

"I like the idea," Ed replied, "but I'm not sure this does me any good. I'm in no position to make any beer. I don't know when I could be operational. Even so, I couldn't get it to you in any useful quantities. You're too far away."

"I've got a different idea for you," Jim said. "We bring your brewery to us. We haul all your equipment to our building and let you set up inside our space. You make the beer in exchange for room and board at the brewery. We could reexamine the relationship in a few months and see if it still felt equitable. If not, we could make adjustments."

Ed laughed. "Do you know how much equipment is here? How the hell am I supposed to move it?"

Jim held up his hands. "I'm working on that. I'm in the process right now of trying to find men with wagons who can haul supplies for me. If it works out, they'd be able to take care of it. All you'd have to do is help take it apart so nothing gets damaged."

Ed sat down on the curb and stared off at the town.

Jim took a seat beside him. "Listen, I know this is a lot to throw at you, but it's not like I can drop back in next week or ring you up on the phone. I kind of need an answer today, or at least some indication if you're interested or not."

"Oh, I'm interested," Ed said. "I'd love to have all this working again. I enjoy brewing beer. I enjoy drinking beer. I don't enjoy whatever the hell I'm doing in there now. It's kind of like beating my head against the wall. I feel like I'm trapped in my worst nightmare."

"Is it just you?" Jim asked. "You have family?"

"Just me." Ed shrugged. "But the equipment in that brewery is only part of what I'd have to move."

Jim furrowed his brow. "What else is there?"

"Opening this brewery was part of a community revitalization project. There were government grants involved. I don't know if you understand how that works or not, but they throw a lot of money at you and you have to spend it all. I've got years' worth of brewing supplies in storage because I had to use the money before the deadline. And you were talking about making liquor? I've got a shipping container out back that's packed with new distillery equipment because there was grant money left and I decided to explore the possibility of making liquor. Hell, I didn't even have a place to put the stuff, but I couldn't pass up the opportunity."

Jim's head was spinning from this information. He's assumed that if he was able to convince this man to move his brewery to the sewing factory, he'd be hustling to scrounge up brewing supplies. Not only was Ed saying he saying he had years of brewing supplies on hand, he also had distilling equipment.

Jim cleared his throat. "You're saying you have a still?"

"I reckon it's more than a still. They sold us on a whole package. I don't even know enough about making liquor to know what it all is, but they said it was everything we'd need to run a distillery."

Jim couldn't help but wonder what Lloyd was going to think of this development. He came from a family of moonshiners who'd improvised everything. The equipment they used for making liquor had traditionally been cobbled together from items stolen, bought, or passed down through generations. He might not know how to make heads or tails of well-made, professional equipment.

"I hope it comes with an instruction manual," Jim quipped.

Ed nodded. "Several of them."

"Do we have a deal? Are you interested?"

Ed looked at Jim for a moment longer, appearing more confused than anything else. "I guess I am but what does that even mean? I can't imagine it's like we're going to sign some contract and money is going to change hands. How would this even happen?"

"How about I have someone here in a few days to haul the first load out? That gives me plenty of time to get the haulers lined up."

"I'm just supposed to take your word for that? I'm supposed to quit making repairs and start taking it all apart because some guy I don't know shows up and offers me a new home for my brewery?"

"My word is all I got." Jim stuck out his hand. "And this. It used to be enough for people. Maybe it can be again."

The two shook hands on it and Ed got to his feet. "A couple of days, you said?"

"That's right. Break down what you can, and I assume they'll be able to help move it."

"I hope they're strong," Ed said. "This stuff is heavy."

Jim recalled the things that Hatfield, the corral tender at the market, had told him about the Wolfords. "I hear they are."

Jim hoped it was true. A lot of his plan was going to require the movement of materials, some of it over long distances. He hoped these Wolfords lived up to their reputation.

11

The Antique Dealers

Dixie, Pamela, and Mitchell watched with matching looks of contempt as courthouse custodian Bobby "Backup" Bailey pawed through the items displayed on their table. He'd gotten his nickname from his habit of backing into stuff nearly every day as he'd left work. He'd hit dogs, pedestrians, parking meters, dumpsters, and other vehicles so often that it became a running joke. Every vehicle he'd owned since 1961 had a caved-in rear quarter panel and a crumpled bumper.

The reason for the displeased looks on the faces of the three vendors was that they'd never had to deal with people like Backup Bailey when they'd operated their antique store. Backup was more of the yard sale and flea market type. He was more likely to pay a quarter for a used NASCAR t-shirt or a buck for an old hammer than to spend three hundred and fifty dollars on an antique wormy chestnut table.

Backup would never have darkened the doorstep of their antique store, gazing down his nose at carbide mining lights with their grimy patina. He wouldn't have bought a turtle shell mining helmet, an antique fountain pen, or a hickory chair made by a local craftsman over a century ago. Now, people like Backup had a new appreciation for these three antique dealers and the items they sold. In particular, Backup needed the cast-iron skillet that he hefted so adoringly in his grubby hands.

"Lord, I can't tell you how many of these we throwed out over the years," Backup muttered.

Every antique dealer was used to hearing comments like these. People talking about the things they'd owned or how little they'd paid for an item now being sold as antique. Most dealers had comebacks already prepared since they heard them so often.

"You and a lot of other people," Pamela snapped. "Throwing out perfectly good cookware to buy some aluminum crap from a discount store."

Backup shrugged. "People wanted *new*. My mommy said she was throwing out all that old 'poor people' stuff back in the 1970s and getting the latest thing. She threw out the cast iron, the pottery, and all the glassware. She bought non-stick pans and those pretty Corelle plates, then she bought the awfullest bunch of Tupperware you ever did see. Everything from saltshakers to cups to bowls. We hauled all the old stuff to the dump."

The three antique dealers heard stories like that all the time, but it still made them cringe. There had once been a mansion there in the county that had changed hands in the early 1900s. The home had come with an entire library of books dating back to the mid-eighteenth century. The new owners weren't readers and had no appreciation for books. They had their farmhands haul all the books out into the pasture on a hay wagon and pitch them into a sinkhole, where they were eventually buried. Sometimes Pamela jerked awake at night, dreaming that she was trying to stop the atrocity but couldn't get anyone to listen to her.

Mitchell was good at blocking out people like Backup. He sat there and bobbed his head like he was listening without really paying attention.

Dixie was less patient. "You want that skillet or not?"

Backup cradled it against his chest as if it was more than a skillet. It wasn't just cookware anymore. It was representative of all that had been lost, both in his life and in the greater world. "What you getting for them?"

"If you grew up using one of those, you know how long it will last," Mitchell said. "That's not something you throw away every three years and replace. That's a lifetime skillet right there. You'll pass it on to your kids and grandkids, on and on."

Backup shook his head. "Ain't got no kids. My wife died before we had any. Car accident."

Dixie opened her mouth to ask if he'd backed over her, but somehow managed to hold her tongue. She decided that might be a little rude, even for her. Instead, she focused on the deal. "What do you have for trading?"

"Didn't really bring anything with me," he muttered. "Wasn't expecting to trade."

If he had nothing to trade, Dixie was done wasting time on him. "You can check back tomorrow. It might still be here. No guarantees. If you want it, come back with something of value."

Backup gently placed the heavy skillet back on the table, his sadness palpable. "Reckon I'm going to check on the courthouse. I might be back through later."

"What are you still doing up at the courthouse?" Mitchell asked. "Last I saw, that place was trashed."

"People in trouble with the law have been trying to get rid of all the court files. People that owe back taxes have been throwing those records out. It won't make any difference. All that's on computer and they'll just have to print it out once the power is back on. I just go up there and sweep the trash out every couple of days to keep someone from setting fire to it. They've tried a couple of times but so far it hasn't caught."

The idea of people trying to burn down their historic old courthouse wounded Pamela. She felt a little more sympathy for Backup Bailey and the work he did to take care of the place. She was almost feeling magnanimous enough that she was ready to give him the skillet for free. It would be an unprecedented act on her part, something she'd never done in decades of selling. When she opened her mouth and raised her finger in his direction, she was struck by a thought.

"Mr. Bailey, sir?" she asked.

Backup regarded her curiously, as did Dixie and Mitchell. Everyone detected the change in her tone. To Backup, it sounded kinder. Her business partners instantly knew that she was up to something. They'd heard that tone before.

Pamela gestured at the table and its displayed wares. "Mr. Bailey, you can see that my friends and I are interested in history, particularly the history of our little town here. I'm not sure if you're aware of this or not, but we all had ancestors who were here prior to the Revolutionary War. They were founders of this town."

Backup shrugged indifferently. "That was before my time. I don't know nothing about that."

"Of course," Pamela replied. "But as concerned citizens and history enthusiasts, can I ask how the town's historical archives have fared?"

Backup grinned and stepped closer to the table. He leaned in conspiratorially and whispered to the vendors, "I may be the only one still alive who knows where all that crap is."

"Why is that?" Mitchell asked.

"After the lights went out, the librarian asked if they could move some things out of their local history room. They didn't have a safe place to keep things at the library since there wasn't any power. They moved all their old records to the courthouse, and we stored all of it in the old vault downstairs. That's where all the history stuff is."

"It's all safe?" Dixie asked.

Backup chuckled. "Nobody has been in there. Ain't nobody wants that stuff. They want food and bullets. They want cast iron skillets. They ain't a damn thing in that vault that would help anybody. Besides, no one can break through that vault door and I'm the only one with an emergency key."

Mitchell and Dixie's eyes brightened with understanding. They knew where Pamela was going with this now. They understood her angle.

"You have a key to the vault?" Mitchell asked. "That's a lot of responsibility."

Backup leaned backward and hooked his thumbs in the waistband of his pants. "I've been there a lot of years. They trust me with pretty much everything."

Pamela rested her hands on the table and smiled at Backup. "I'd love to see what's in that vault. You think you might be able to let us in there sometime? I'd be *very* appreciative."

Backup shook his head. "I couldn't do that."

Pamela frowned. "Just when I thought we were starting to get along, Backup. Just when I thought we were becoming friends."

Backup gave an exaggerated wink at Pamela. "If someone was to give me that skillet, I might accidentally drop the courthouse keys on the table while I was picking it up. Of course, I'd have to come back around next week looking for my lost keys. I'm pretty sure I'd be able to find them again, right?" He winked again.

Invigorated by the prospect of looting the vault, Pamela felt like a teenager again. She was using her feminine wiles and looks to make a slow-witted boy do her bidding. "Why don't you take that skillet, Backup? A little token of friendship from me to you."

He grinned at her. "Why, thank you. I think I will." He used a grubby hand to remove a large keyring from his belt, then dropped it onto the table.

Pamela covered the key ring with her hand and slid it across the table, raking it into her other palm. "Enjoy your skillet, Mr. Bailey. I'll look forward to seeing you next week."

Backup hefted the skillet off the table. He gave Pamela a flirty little finger wave, then headed off into the crowd.

When he was gone, Pamela spun back to her partners with a triumphant look on her face, dangling the heavy key ring from a finger.

"That was like watching a train wreck," Mitchell said. "I couldn't turn away. I was mesmerized, impressed, appalled, and disgusted all at the same time."

Pamela frowned at the comment. While she knew it held praise, there was jab or two not so subtly concealed within his words. "Well, I guess you don't have to go with me if you don't want. Personally, I've always wanted to get into the town archives and see what I could find."

"No, we definitely want to go with you," Mitchell said. "This is a once in a lifetime opportunity."

12

Jim

JIM DIDN'T THINK he'd ever spent so much time in the saddle on a single day and he felt every single minute of it. He was sunburned and parched, his tongue tasted like the sole of a rotting boot washed up on a riverbank, and everything below his waist ached from sitting for so long. Even his back was sore, his spine feeling like someone had snapped him like a whip.

He'd taken a sleeping bag with him in his gear just in case he was forced to spend the night along the trail somewhere. He doubled it over the saddle about halfway home, desperately trying to cushion his seating arrangement. While it improved the situation, it brought guffaws of amusement from the other horsemen he passed along the way. It was good-natured ribbing and Jim laughed them off. He'd been told many times that he was a hard ass, but this trip was proving exactly the opposite.

Hugh was sitting on the steps of Jim's home when he finally reached his driveway. The sun was setting over the horizon, redness spreading in the sky like a blood-filled egg had been cracked to ominous portent. The rest of Jim's family was there too, lounging in the shade of the deep porch like hound dogs on a hot day.

Jim steered his horse toward the porch and reined it to a halt. "Pete, you think you could help me with this horse? I'm wore out."

Pete dutifully began to stand but Nana tugged him back down and glared at Jim. "You leave this baby alone and put up your own horse, Jim. Poor thing can barely even open his fingers after picking grapes all day. I can't believe you sent all these people out to work like that while *you* were off riding around the countryside doing Lord knows what."

Hugh covered his mouth with his hand, trying to stifle his grin. Even Ellen smiled at the vehemence with which Nana protected her grandchild.

Jim sighed and nudged his horse toward the barn. "Fine." He didn't have the strength to argue.

It wasn't like he'd been out on some recreational jaunt. He was making this effort for the good of his family, not for his personal entertainment. He continued to inwardly rant about the situation the entire time he was stiffly unsaddling his horse. When he was done, he turned it out into the pasture and hobbled back to the house with his rifle and pack.

As he was walking toward the house, he could feel the heat of his mother's gaze upon him. He looked up at her curiously. Wasn't she done with him yet? He'd put up his own horse and not troubled her precious grandson, hadn't he? Yet when he reached the porch steps, she was glaring at him.

"What?" he asked.

"I'm just sitting here about to burst with pride, my son," she spat. "It's hard to even describe the joy that I feel in knowing that all my hard work as a mother went to produce a *pimp!*"

This time Jim couldn't hold the eyeroll. He definitely didn't have the energy to go down this road. "Do we really have to do this? I'm exhausted."

"Yes, we do! I have something to say and you'll listen to your mother."

"Ariel, will you please go get me some cold water?" Jim asked.

"But I'll miss you *listening* to Nana," she whined.

Ellen got to her feet and took Ariel's hand in hers. Jim handed over his empty water bottles as they passed. Ellen cut him a look that both warned him this had been building and pled with him to remember that he was talking with his mother. Sometimes he got wound up and struggled to rein it back in. They'd all seen it.

Jim climbed the porch and sagged into the seat Ellen had vacated. His voice betrayed both his weariness at the day in general and with this topic in particular. He got so tired of being questioned all the time. It was one of the reasons he hated having any responsibility for other people. It was almost enough to make him want to ride off into the mountains, but he'd tried that already and there was no peace in that either.

"I'm not a pimp, Mother."

"Well, that's not what I heard! All anyone is talking about around here is my *son* opening a bar in town with a brothel. When I asked how the market went today, everyone told me that they didn't go to the market because they were busy picking grapes. You know why they were picking grapes? Because *somebody* needs to serve wine at their brothel."

Jim looked to Hugh again and saw him doing his best to hide his amusement. Jim was not amused at all, but neither was Nana.

"There's more to the story," Jim said. "Do you want to hear it?"

"Not if it involves you opening a brothel, Jim!" she spat.

"I'd prefer you address me as Pimp Daddy. Should I dress the part too? It's too hot for a fur coat, but I might be able to whip up a walking stick with a gold crown on top."

Pops frowned. "That's enough, Jim. Don't be talking to your mother that way."

Jim threw his hands up in the air. "What way? I'm just addressing the issue everyone acts like they're concerned about."

"I'm not concerned," Pete announced. "I want to work there."

Nana fanned herself. "I hope you're proud, Jim. Your son aspires to work at your brothel. Generations of hard work and education and this is where it's led."

Ellen returned with Jim's water bottles. She tossed him one and he promptly opened the lid to suck down a long pull.

"Pete, go play with your sister. She's at the barn."

Pete started to protest but a stern look from Ellen cut him off. He was mature enough to understand this wasn't the time to argue. He got to his feet and stomped off through the dust of the yard.

Jim took a long, cleansing breath and let it out. He forced himself to be calm and tried again. "Has anyone explained this to you, Mom?"

Ellen mouthed. "I tried."

"Hugh?" Jim asked.

"I'm staying out of this," he replied.

"What's this all about, Jim?" Pops asked. "I'm as confused as Nana is. I know people at the market told us there were brothels in town but what made you decide you needed to operate one? Don't you have a hard enough time staying out of trouble already?"

Jim drained the last of his water bottle and struggled to find patience. The desire to rant and overreact simmered within him like a kettle boiling on the stove. "Well, I'm starving and this is the wrong time to talk to me about this. Let me get a bite to eat and cool off, then I'll explain. Will that work?"

"I guess," Nana said.

Pops shrugged in agreement. "Fine with me."

"Good." Jim got up and slogged into the house, Ellen on his heels.

"I'll put a plate together for you," she said. "I can heat it up, but it will take a little longer."

Jim shook his head. "I'm hot enough already. Cold is fine. Maybe with a cold beer or twelve."

"Sorry, no beer, but I'm sure there's some liquor around somewhere."

"It's probably a bad idea. It'll only lead to the discussion with my parents getting very *animated*."

Ellen pieced together two BLTs on homemade bread and handed them over to Jim. He looped a finger though the strap on his water bottle and carried it to the back porch. Unlike the front porch, the back was empty. Jim took a seat at the metal patio table and attacked the first of his sandwiches. Ellen settled into a chair beside him and he could see that something was on her mind. He hoped it wasn't something that was going to make him lose his appetite because his sandwich was pretty damn good.

"I know you've had a long day and you have a lot going on, but I too have some thoughts about the...*sex workers.* "

Jim gave Ellen a weary look. He felt very isolated and misunderstood at the moment. He was working his ass off to make things better for everyone in the valley. He'd gone from ignoring the rest of their community to trying to get a handle on it. All he wanted was to better manage their security by putting a system in place for collecting intelligence. However, all everyone else wanted was to complain about the prostitutes.

"Go ahead," he sighed, chewing a little less enthusiastically when he returned to his sandwich.

Ellen sat up straight, put both her hands on the table, and began speaking. "I totally get what you're trying to do here. Honest I do. I understand that the presence of sex workers at your roadhouse will create this kind of subversive, outlaw atmosphere that you hope will bring in the kind of people you're looking to glean information from. But I also think it will hamper you in some very practical ways that you might not be aware of."

Now Jim was genuinely curious. He thought he'd thoroughly examined the situation from all angles, but maybe he hadn't. "Go on."

"You've said that you not only want this to be an intelligence operation, but to create a trading post that will benefit our entire clan. You want it to become a place where the people in our group can sell things for our collective benefit."

"That's true," Jim agreed.

"I don't know if you've considered the scale of what you're trying to do, but you're going to need all hands on deck, Jim. Depending on how long the country stays in this collapsed state, our kids could grow up in that business. Same for Randi's grandkids and Gary's grandkids. Nana's reaction won't be an isolated one. There's going to be a time when you need more people helping out around there and the whole 'brothel' aspect is going to hamper that. I wouldn't want Ariel working there and I'm sure most of the other parents in our clan feel the same. So even if this is supposed to benefit us all, I would guess that about half of the labor force in our group will not feel comfortable working there specifically because of the prostitution angle. You see the problem with that?"

Jim finished devouring his second sandwich, eating every scrap of bread and every last chunk of tomato. He didn't feel so defensive about listening to Ellen present her argument. He didn't know whether it was her less aggressive approach or their comfort in communicating with each other, but he didn't feel like he was being attacked in the way he had when he was on the front porch.

Most importantly, he began to see her point. She was right. He was creating a family business that much of the family wouldn't want any part of. How did he fix it? It would have been a much easier issue to disentangle himself from if he hadn't already talked to the women at the brothel about it. Despite their initial reluctance, they eventually warmed to the idea. Now he'd have to retract the offer to keep the peace within his own group.

He pushed his chair back from the table. "I guess I need to go talk to Nana and Pops."

"What are you going to tell them?"

"That Jim Powell's Pimp Palace is no longer on the table. We'll leave the brothel out of the business plan."

"Seriously?"

Jim nodded.

"Nana is going to be very happy. You may avoid a public spanking yet."

"I'm sure there's plenty of people in town who would like to see that or worse," Jim said. "Hopefully they won't get the opportunity."

13

Jim

THE NEXT MORNING started just like the day before, with everyone meeting at Jim's gate for the ride into town. Harvesting the small crop of grapes at Teddy's vineyard was taking less time and manpower than Jim had estimated. They'd made a lot of headway yesterday. With that in mind, people had taken it upon themselves to shuffle their plans accordingly.

Debra and Randi were going back to the market where they'd operate a booth together for the day. Randi's grandchildren would be staying with Gary while he babysat his own grandchildren. Ellen would also be staying home. The remaining grape harvest would be handled by Gary's daughters, his son-in-law, Randi's daughters, Pete, and Charlie. They hoped they would be able to complete the harvest by the end of the day.

Jim was going to spend the morning tracking down materials for the roadhouse project and he took a second round of abuse for sending his people off to be field labor while he attended to other tasks. Everyone who arrived at the gate that morning had something to say about it.

"What about Hugh?" Jim asked. "He's going with me, but I don't hear you guys giving him crap."

It was true. As congenial, loyal, and comforting as Hugh's presence in the valley was, people were a little leery of him sometimes. When someone cracked a joke at his expense, Hugh laughed along with everyone else but had that look in his eye that warned that the offender might pay for their words. Either way, it spared Hugh some of the grief that Jim took over his leadership indiscretions.

After everyone split up in town, Jim and Hugh's first stop was to track down Cookie, the man from the building supply store. They found him on the middle school campus, helping to catch a particularly rambunctious goat that was not interested in being penned up on the athletic field. It was entertaining for a while, but then the goat-wranglers prevailed, and the unhappy goat was led away.

When he noticed them watching from a distance, Cookie jogged over. His shirt and face were soaked with sweat. "Could have used some help."

"I noticed," Jim said. "I only chase goats with bullets, though."

"We're trying to carry out some of your suggestions," Cookie replied. "Most of those recommended keeping livestock alive as long as possible, not shooting it because you're pissed off."

Jim shrugged. "Do as I say, not as I do."

Cookie laughed. "I talked to the owner of the lumberyard about those materials you needed. Like I told you, most of the framing lumber got burned for heat, but there's plywood, fasteners, and most of the other stuff you had on your list."

"The owner is open to trades?" Jim asked.

"She's not willing to give it away because she doesn't know when she'll be able to restock her inventory, but she's willing to entertain fair trades."

"What kind of things would she be interested in?" asked Hugh.

"I'd offer guns and ammo," Cookie replied. "I've got good weapons. Some of the other people staying out there do too. She's running an old deer rifle. An AR, mags, and some ammo would probably go a long way with her. Delivery is another story."

"I'm working on that," Jim said. "Waiting to hear from a couple of guys right now."

"Well, when you can get a hauler set up, you come find me. Bring what you want to trade and we'll talk to the owner."

"Perfect," Jim replied. "Hopefully it will be within the next few days."

It would be much sooner than that. Jim and Hugh were headed back to the market when the clatter of hooves on pavement caught their attention. They were on Main Street, not far from the courthouse, and the sound reverberated off the face of buildings like the rumble of thunder. Jim spun his horse in the street and looked back the way they'd come.

In the distance, he saw a line of horse-drawn wagons headed his way. Jim noted that these were perhaps the largest horses he'd ever seen in his life. They were much bigger than the quarter horses he was accustomed to riding. He wasn't any expert but assumed these were Clydesdales or Percherons.

As the wagons closed in on him, Jim noted that the men driving the wagons weren't that unlike their hoses. They were big men, with thick muscles that didn't come from pumping weight in a gym. These were working men, raised on big meals and hard work. Each wagon driver had an armed passenger sitting beside them.

There were four wagons in the convoy. They were of newer construction with rubber tires and padded bench seats. However, those wagons were not the most impressive sight. It was what came at the rear of the procession, the vibration of its engine finally audible over the hooves. Someone was driving a big John Deere tractor and pulling a pair of four-wheeled trailers behind it.

Jim sat in the road until the first of the wagons neared him. The driver reined the pair of horses to a stop and regarded Jim blocking his path.

"You've been eyeballing me for a quarter-mile now," the man

growled. "Don't tell me I'm going to have to kill the first man I talk to in town."

Jim grinned. That was the kind of thing *he* said to people.

"You think that's funny?" the man asked. He was probably around fifty years old with dark, curly hair. He wore bibbed overalls with no shirt and his pants were tucked into high farming boots.

"Are you Mr. Wolford?" Jim asked.

The man tied his reins off to the brake lever on his wagon and hopped down. He stalked toward Jim and stared up at him with curiosity. "Who the hell is asking?"

Jim climbed down off his horse and stuck out his hand. "My name is Jim Powell. I talked to a man named Hatfield at the market about hiring some people to haul loads for me."

The man's glower turned to a grin and he shook Jim's hand. "I guess I'd be the son-of-a-bitch you was asking after. I'm Shade Wolford. Good to meet you."

Jim guessed that Shade must have been about six foot four and probably around two hundred and eighty pounds of pure muscle. He had a scar on his face and a couple of missing fingers. He looked like the kind of guy who might lose a finger, wrap some electrical tape across the remaining stub, and go back to work.

"Good to meet you, Shade. My buddy back there is Hugh."

Wolford nodded in Hugh's direction. Hugh tipped his boonie hat in greeting.

"Looks like you brought just the size army I'm needing. I hope we can work out a deal since you came ready for work," Jim said.

"It was a might far just to come and shoot the shit. I thought I'd come prepared. If you and I can't work out something, I figured we might be able to pick up some work before we headed back out of town. Maybe haul firewood for people or something."

"What about that tractor?" Jim asked. "We had diesel for a while, but it got water in it. Once we'd burned through all our fuel filters and water separators, we gave up using it."

Shade grinned and shrugged. "A man can't tell all his secrets, especially to someone he's just met. We've done okay this past year.

We've come across a few things here and there, like that diesel fuel, that helped us out. We've got an auxiliary tank on one of the wagons so hopefully that will keep us fueled long enough to do the work you're needing."

"Are you guys prepared to stay for a few days?" Jim asked.

Shade nodded. "Planned on it. The fuel wagon has tents, sleeping bags, and everything we need."

"I can let you stay in the building we're renovating," Jim said. "That may also keep people from stealing our supplies."

Wolford patted the pistol on his hip. "I've got a way with thieves, my friend. They don't stick around."

"I think we're going to get along just fine," Jim remarked. "How about you follow me and Hugh down to the jobsite. We'll go over a few things and see if we can strike a deal. If we can come to an arrangement, you guys can get to work today. I'm not one to waste daylight."

"Same here," Shade Wolford replied. "You lead the way."

14

Jim

JIM AND HUGH led the procession through town like they were parade marshals. Both the chorus of clattering hooves and the thrum of the diesel tractor drew the eyes of everyone they passed. By the time they reached the farmers market, perhaps half the remaining souls in town had either seen them or were currently watching them pass. Jim noticed that the attention didn't bother Shade. He wasn't as paranoid as Jim, being cool-headed enough to only deal with problems when they actually *became* problems. When that moment arrived, Jim had no doubt that Shade and his people were more than capable of dealing with the situation.

About twenty minutes after they'd first met in town, Jim led the convoy of wagons into the parking lot of the old sewing factory. The driver of the tractor turned it off, while the drivers of the horse-drawn wagons set their brakes. Drivers and passengers climbed down and stretched stiff muscles. A few rolled cigarettes from tins of tobacco or packed pipes, an easier way for most people to smoke when cigarette papers were in short supply.

Jim noted a similarity in the facial features of many in this group. It was evident they were related. It was also worth noting that among both the men and women of this group, there were several people comparable in size to Shade. These were big people. As with Jim's group, the women were just as heavily armed as the men. Nothing raised Jim's spirits like well-armed friends.

"This is it," Jim announced.

"Well, I see what it *is*," Shade said. "But what's it *going* to be? Shelter? Soup kitchen? Some kind of improvised medical facility?"

Jim sighed, meeting Hugh's eye. "No. All of those things might have been nice. I'm looking to build a roadhouse."

Shade looked surprised. "Like one of them old-time beer joints you used to see out in the country?"

Jim nodded. "Beer joint, liquor joint, wine joint, and maybe even a marijuana joint. A little food and some trade goods. Live music every night."

Shade nodded but appeared uncertain about the idea. "I ain't questioning your plans, friend, but I guess I'm wondering what the point is. Is this a money-making venture or what? It ain't exactly the Roaring Twenties out there. Folks are a tad on the gloomy side. You really think they're ready to go out drinking and swarping?"

Jim grinned at the use of the old expression. It was something you didn't hear very often these days. "Swarping" was a mostly Appalachian expression that equated to "going out and running around at night," mostly just for the purpose of being out with your companions.

Jim exchanged a look with Hugh. Hugh caught the meaning of the look but shrugged, leaving Jim to make the call himself.

Going with his gut, Jim asked, "Shade, can I trust you?"

"Well, if you tell me to keep my big mouth shut I probably will. You don't know me, so you'll just have to take my word for it."

Jim weighed those words and kept going. "Shade, I've screwed up a lot of things this past year. I'm more prepared than most folks and I'm not scared of tough times. I figured I could keep my family and friends safe. For the most part, I have. I made some major miscalcula-tions, though. A couple of times, I really dicked the dog."

"I reckon the same could be said of a lot of us," Shade admitted. "A situation like the one we're in is the kind of thing a man has to figure out as he goes. It sure as hell didn't come with any instructions."

"I've tried to stay on top of things, but I mess up about as often as I get it right. I ended up being the leader of a small group of my friends and their families. It wasn't something I figured on doing and I've tried to get out from under it more than once. I figured the best way to keep us safe was to isolate us out in the valley where we lived and cut off the rest of the world. That didn't work out so well. The short version is that I ignored what was going on in the community around us to the point that it almost got me and my family killed."

Shade nodded with understanding. "I hear what you're saying, but what's any of that got to do with a roadhouse? You trying to make amends to the community or just hoping to drown your sorrows with a sip of liquor?"

Jim shook his head. "Neither. I'm trying to avoid getting taken by surprise again. Instead of staying out of town and ignoring the world, I'm hoping to get a foothold here in town so I can keep an eye on things. I want to know what's going on and what people are talking about. I want to know every piece of gossip, every scrap of intelli-gence, and every rumor that passes through this place. I'm hard-headed and it took a while, but I finally figured out that my old approach didn't work. I'm trying to fix things now."

"Ain't a damn thing wrong with that," Shade agreed. "Besides, everyone knows a drink of liquor will loosen a man's tongue, don't they?"

"So, now you know what I'm up to. What's it going to cost me to hire you?"

Shade stared at the building, then at Jim. He looked back at his line of horses, wagons, and the diesel tractor with its hot engine ticking as cooled. "If you'd tried to get me earlier in the spring or summer, you couldn't have hired me at any price. We had too much to do around our own place. Things have slowed down now. I've got hay to cut in a few weeks but we're free until then. We'll need food and a place to stay. The preferred currency is ammunition. You have any to spare?"

Jim nodded. "Most of the common flavors."

"Then here's the deal," Shade said. "Fifty rounds a day will hire us. It has to be calibers we can use. None of that weird shit like 6.3 Bamboozle or 9.7mm Panamanian. And if we have to fire off any rounds to protect your cargo, I expect those rounds to be paid back in addition to the fifty we're getting for the day. I know it ain't cheap, but we're worth it. I'm sure you'll see that soon enough. Do we have a deal?"

Jim tried not to reveal his excitement. Had this ammunition been coming out of his own personal stash, he'd have been concerned about giving up so much. After all, he didn't know how long this project was going to take or how long this collapse might last. His ace in the hole was that they had a lot of ammunition they'd acquired through various sources. There'd been battlefield pickups, the stash they'd gotten when they killed Isaac at the cabin near Hidden Valley Lake, and the full ammo cans they'd gotten from the Power Restoration people back in the winter. He'd have no problem coming up with a thousand rounds for the Wolfords if it came to that.

They shook on the deal and Jim gestured toward the building. "I was going to let you guys stay here because that might discourage people from stealing building materials, but it's not the best place for keeping horses. Maybe you should come out to the valley where we live. It's a few miles out of town but there's water and grass for the horses. I got a barn you can stay in and you'll eat well."

"I like that idea," Shade said. "We're country folks and we'd sleep better outside of town. I'm glad to leave two folks behind if we need to. My brother Nooner is on the tractor over there. He could pull that thing inside and spend the night. I'll leave one of the other boys with him. Won't nobody steal nothing while they're here."

"Nooner?"

"Drunk by noon."

Jim nodded. "I got one of those. Sure you'll meet him soon enough."

"Doesn't hold him back none," Shade said. "Not sure how he does it. Hollow leg or extra liver or something. He's still dependable."

"Great. Then let's get to it." Jim turned to Hugh. "Why don't you get to the market and talk to Ian. He was supposed to be recruiting some carpenters and laborers. Tell everyone we'll take the first two dozen men to show up tomorrow and they'll get a free lunch out of the deal. Make sure they understand that lunch is payment."

Hugh nodded. "On it." He mounted his horse and trotted off toward town.

"What about us?" Shade asked.

"We're going to the lumberyard. I need to strike a deal."

15

Luther

LUTHER CARDONE HAD NEVER ENJOYED HIKING as a form of recreation. He figured he'd paid his dues in the military, walking enough miles to do him for the rest of his life. Since the collapse, his feet were now his primary mode of transportation again. With his sore back and aching feet, he was reliving some of the low points of his military career.

It had taken him two days to walk to Hidden Valley Road from Abingdon, Virginia, but he didn't feel like he had a choice. He had this oppressive feeling of anxiety hanging over him. The feeling that something bad had happened to his friend.

Luther was from Wallace County originally and returned there after being discharged from the Army. Like most folks, he struggled to keep things going after the terror attacks. Every day was a new mission—the search for food, clean water, and the basics of survival. Then a few months ago, an old friend showed up at his house. It was his Army buddy, Isaac, and he needed a place to stay.

"My house is your house," Luther said. "I wish I had more to offer you."

Isaac waved him off. "Don't worry about a thing. I got us covered."

While Luther had enough of the war, Isaac had continued to work as a military contractor after he was discharged. He liked the money and wasn't ready to give up the adventure. He'd taken a job with Catalyst Security and Luther was surprised to learn that Catalyst had kept Isaac busy even after the lights went out.

"I'm a regional sheriff now," Isaac had said.

Obviously, Luther had no idea what that was and said as much. Isaac had gone on to explain that the Department of Homeland Security had contracted with Catalyst to put a new law enforcement program in place. It was to be operated at the national level but would provide law enforcement at the regional level.

The government had decided this was a necessary step because of the local pushback that had come from the comfort camp program. The regional sheriff program would provide a way to yank insurgents into line if they became too resistant to new government initiatives. Regional sheriffs could crack down on locals in a way that their own sheriff's departments might not be willing to.

"How big is your territory?" Luther had asked.

"Far southwestern Virginia," Isaac had told him.

"Dude, there's no way. That's a lot of area."

Isaac shrugged. "It's not like I'm doing normal policing. I've got a horse and a radio. My boss radios me every couple of days with a list of people to keep an eye on. The goal is mostly to stamp out insurgency. I'm not arresting people or anything like that."

"What if these insurgents don't take to being stamped out?" Luther asked.

"Then I radio in and ask permission to escalate the response. They'll either tell me to back off, continue surveillance, or eliminate the insurgent."

"Eliminate?" Luther asked. "As in killing Americans?"

Isaac nodded. "It's a different world, my friend. This isn't the same government you and I worked for. I'm not sure who's pulling the strings now, but a man has to eat. If it wasn't for this gig, I don't know what I'd be doing."

"I get it. That's a tough position to be in though."

It hadn't been as tough to Isaac. He loved the work and the benefits it brought. Isaac's presence had been a windfall for Luther as well. Besides bringing news of the outside world, Isaac got regular deliveries of food, ammunition, and survival gear. It was a game changer for Luther. The emergency rations helped him put back on some of the weight and muscle he'd lost. Luther began to wonder if Isaac's appearance hadn't saved his life. Where would he have been if his old friend hadn't shown up?

Then, about a week ago, Isaac didn't return from his latest outing.

It wasn't anything unusual for Isaac to be gone for days at a time. That was the nature of the job. Unexpected things came up, leads had to be followed up on, and visits had to be made. Because everything was being done in-person, without phones, and with horses as transportation, the timeline for any investigative effort was more drawn out than it had been in a century. But still, Isaac usually got home within a day or two of when he expected to return.

Luther didn't know a whole lot about what Isaac was looking into. It wasn't like he made a great effort to keep his job secret from Luther, but Luther just couldn't grasp it, really. It was very alien to him to have a division of government spying on people at the local level for statements they made to their friends, family, and community.

It wasn't like they were even broadcasting their opinions on social media like people used to do. It was just talk. But even if he didn't fully understand the mechanism at work behind the regional sheriff program, Luther continued to share the benefits Isaac reaped from his position. In the end, that regular supply of food mattered more to him than any misgivings about what Isaac did for a living.

All Luther knew of Isaac's current investigation was that he had been working in Russell County because there was a high-level insurgent there who'd destroyed a power plant. Supposedly the man had died or disappeared, but then he showed back up. Isaac admitted he was probably going to have to kill the man eventually, but he'd not yet been cleared to do so by his superiors.

Luther knew Isaac sometimes stayed with a retired Virginia state trooper named Garvey who lived near Hidden Valley Lake. He also knew that his lead contact in Russell County was a local politician with the first name of Hadley. That was all he had but it was enough to motivate him to set off in search of his friend.

He knew where Garvey lived because Isaac had taken Luther with him once when he visited the man. They'd spent the evening fishing at the quiet mountain lake. So, when Luther turned off the four-lane highway he'd followed from Wallace County, he knew just what lay ahead of him: a steep ascent up the narrow mountain road to Garvey's place.

Luther had spent the previous night camping along the North Fork of the Holston River. He slept well and woke up early to get a jump on the hike ahead of him. The slog up the road toward Hidden Valley Lake was tough. It ascended gently at first, then quickly turned into a straight climb up the mountain. Even with his light pack, Luther found himself pausing every fifteen minutes or so as his legs became smoked from the exertion.

He saw a lot of empty houses and other homes which he couldn't tell were occupied or not. Occasionally, he caught a glimpse of someone working outside or ducking into a home. No one greeted him. Not so much as a wave.

He wasn't wearing a watch, but figured it took him around an hour to reach Garvey's driveway after leaving the main road. Despite the early hour, he'd sweated through his shirt already and his hair was soaked. He tried taking his shirt off to keep it dry but quickly fell victim to the merciless swarms of insects that lived in this deep forest. They fell upon him with a ravenous hunger and his body was soon covered in puffy red welts.

As soon as he turned down Garvey's drive, he could tell something was off. The last time he'd been there, Garvey had owned two large hounds that charged up the driveway like they'd been launched from a cannon. No dogs came after him this time.

"Hello?" he called.

When there was no response, Luther walked a little further. The driveway swung around a bend that offered a clear sightline to

Garvey's cabin. There, Luther was greeted with the sight of scorched rubble.

"Shit."

He took off running but slowed as he neared the cabin. He removed his pack and lowered it to the ground, propping his rifle against it. The place hadn't just caught fire, it had burned to the ground. Blackened copper pipes jutted from the ash like bones. The charred cinderblock foundation cupped the delicate ashes like an offering vessel.

Moving closer, Luther could see the deformed refrigerator and oven. He could see whisps of copper wiring looped like curls of hair through the fine ash. Occasionally, the blackened nub of a board lay charred on the perimeter, somehow having escaped the fate of everything else combustible.

Eventually rain would compact and flatten the ash, but it hadn't rained since the fire. The ash was fine and delicate, almost making Luther think that he could blow on it to reveal what lay beneath. Would he find his friend Isaac there? Would he find Garvey? The two dogs?

He didn't see any signs of bones or dead bodies, but he couldn't imagine that he would under these circumstances. With no fire department, the fire had been allowed to burn out of its own accord. That was why there was nothing but ashes. Any body in there would probably have been incinerated to dust and there was no way Luther was sifting through that ash for teeth or fragments.

Luther noticed that the barn behind the house was scorched but still standing. There should be horses in there. He'd take a look inside before he left, but he needed a moment to get his head together. He was tired and emotionally overwhelmed. He backed away from the house and took a seat on a boulder. He startled a snake and it slithered away, its retreat creating a faint whisper as it moved over dried leaves.

Something he'd experienced fighting in Iraq came back to him. It was an unavoidable sensation that he couldn't push away and he had to acknowledge it.

This place *felt* like a tomb.

He'd been in places like this during war. Places where you knew people had died, even if no evidence remained. This was such a place. Even if his friend Isaac wasn't dead, there had been someone in this house when it went. Luther felt it with the same certainty with which he felt the warm rock beneath him.

So what was he going to do after he checked out the barn? Was he going to go home and wait to see if Isaac returned? It was pointless to spend two days walking back home just to spend more time waiting. He'd come this far already. Another day of walking and he'd likely walk into the next town. He could ask about Isaac. If no one knew anything, he could try to connect with this Hadley guy and see if he knew anything.

Luther wasn't even sure what motivated him at this point. He had no official role. It wasn't his job to try and figure out what happened to Isaac. Maybe it was a sense of responsibility going back to the time they served together. Back to the brotherhood of those who watched each other's backs. Or maybe it was appreciation for the way Isaac's bounty of MREs and gear had improved his personal situation.

Either way, he wasn't done yet. Whether it was vengeance, brotherhood, or personal greed, something pushed at him, urging him forward. For the moment, Luther wasn't ready to fight it. He wasn't done.

16

Jim

With his convoy of teamsters, Jim tracked Cookie down in town and they headed to the lumberyard. While the wagons, horses, and Wolfords waited patiently in the parking lot, Jim and the owner negotiated a price for the items on his list.

"I don't know when I can replace that stuff," the owner argued. Her name was Kathy and her grandfather had opened the lumberyard over half a century ago. "What happens when things go back to normal and I can't restock? All these houses in town have fallen apart and I won't have anything to sell the people trying to repair them."

"You're looking too far out," Jim replied. "It could be years before you're doing business the way you used to. Even if the lights come on tomorrow, people aren't going to have money to spend. Insurance companies are probably going to declare bankruptcy. Banks will be defaulting. It's not going to be like the power coming back on after an ice storm. Nothing will be normal for a long, long time."

Kathy stared at the rusty steel buildings around the yard as she processed Jim's words. "Are you sure you're not just saying that so I'll cut a deal with you?"

"I wouldn't do that."

"He may be a killer, but I don't think he's a liar," Cookie offered.

Jim frowned at the big guy. "Not sure that paints me in a very good light, Cookie."

He shrugged. "Sorry, I was trying to help."

"Helping would be you making people think I'm a great guy. Helping is not scaring people into thinking I'll kill them if they don't make a deal with me."

"My bad," Cookie said sheepishly.

Kathy laughed. "It's not Cookie who's damaging your reputation. You do a pretty good job of that yourself, Jim Powell. The story of you throwing a fit at the farmer's market and cursing out the whole town from on top of that RV did get around. I heard it from at least fifty people if I heard it from one."

Jim wondered if he was ever going to live that one down. "Well, what do you think?"

"I want an AR-15 with a thousand rounds of ammo and some spare mags. I want a .38 revolver for my mama and some spare ammo for that too. And I want five hundred .22 shells." Kathy shoved her hand in Jim's direction. "Do we have a deal?"

Jim didn't immediately take her hand, doing some calculations in his head. Damn, she drove a hard bargain. Nothing wishy-washy about her. He decided the price was fair, but he was surprised she'd asked for so much. People who were inexperienced with bartering often shorted themselves on the deal. She'd clearly inherited some of her grandfather's business acumen.

He wasn't too concerned about the quantity of ammo this was going to cost him. They'd been accumulating more ammunition than they expended for some time now. Just recently, when he, Charlie, and Hugh, had gone to Hidden Valley Lake to kill Isaac and Garvey, he'd retrieved more than enough weapons and ammunition to cover this purchase. Plus, if the roadhouse worked out as he expected, they be accumulating even more ammunition soon because a lot of people would be using it to pay for drinks.

"It's a deal," Jim said, shaking her hand with a smile. "Can I deliver your payment to you tomorrow? I've got haulers with me today that I'd like to put to work, but I didn't know they were coming."

Kathy nodded. "Tomorrow by noon?"

"I'll be here," Jim assured her.

"Cookie, let his wagons in," Kathy said. She turned back to Jim. "This isn't a shopping frenzy. Make sure your people understand that. If you want anything outside of what we already negotiated for, it's going to require additional payment. Are we clear?"

"Crystal," Jim said.

Under Kathy's watchful eye, Jim and the Wolfords loaded wagons in the hot sun for nearly two hours. Jim picked up some cordless tools and spare batteries, planning to recharge them from his solar panels. It would be slow charging them on his low wattage system but better than using hand tools all the time. He picked up some cheap hammers and a couple of hand saws, as well as basic carpentry tools such as measuring tapes, chalk lines, squares, and levels.

They picked up fasteners and tips for the cordless drivers. They grabbed some PVC pipe, glue, and fittings. They bought an entire bundle of half-inch plywood, cutting the metal bands and loading it one sheet a time onto the wagons. They picked up some plexiglass for repairing windows and new locksets for securing the doors.

Jim picked up some metal roofing, which he planned to use for the construction of the outhouse facility, along with a few rolls of light-gauge wire, some wire nuts, and a sleeve of electrical tape. By the time he reached the end of the list, everyone was hot and drenched with sweat. Jim felt beat, but the Wolfords looked like they could have kept it up all day long.

"So, what did you people do for a living before everything fell apart?" Jim asked Shade as they were confirming that every load had been strapped down securely.

"We farmed, but sustainable logging was our business. We used the horses to pull timber out of places they didn't want chewed up by skidders and dozers."

"Interesting," Jim said.

Shade laughed. "A lot of our clients were hippies. I don't buy into their bullshit, but it kept biscuits on my table."

"I can relate," said Jim.

"And it keeps the horses happy. These are working animals. They're not built for looking at. They like to stay busy."

Jim nodded. "I can relate to that too."

Shade guffawed at that. "Then let's get on with it. By the time we're unloaded, we'll be able to call it a day."

17

Jim

IF THE HORSE-DRAWN wagons had garnered attention earlier, they got significantly more on this next trip through town. With their cargo of building materials, this was obviously more than a few strangers passing through town. They appeared to be people actively engaged in some endeavor.

The icing on the cake was the presence of Jim Powell at the head of the procession. For some in the community, he was the villain who epitomized all that had gone wrong with the world in the past year. He was the single point of incarnate evil that represented all they'd lost. For others, he was nothing more than a curiosity whose exploits gave them something entertaining to talk about in a world with no news channels or celebrity gossip.

A new and rapidly growing group was those who'd been motivated by his speech at the marketplace to try and improve their immediate situation. These were the people who'd designated Cookie as their de facto leader and were actively working on making a better life for themselves. They were establishing clean water systems and corralling livestock on the athletic fields. They were laying in firewood, preparing their homes for winter, and finally accepting the fact that help was most certainly *not* on the way.

Before the collapse, those curious about something unusual happening in their town might have called each other to ask questions. They might have waited until the weekly paper came out and checked for any articles that explained what they'd seen. Others might have posted their questions to social media to see whether anyone among their friends knew what was going on.

Options were limited in their current, pre-industrial world, so the curious resorted to a more primitive mode of information gathering. They decided to use the method of basic observation–to see for themselves. One person fell in line behind the convoy of wagons and began to follow them. Then, like ants marching toward an anthill, more and more people began to join the line, following at a safe distance.

Jim's radio had been silent nearly all day, but it chirped within a pouch on his web gear. He fished it out as Hugh's voice broke across the tiny speaker.

"*Hugh for Jim, Hugh for Jim.*"

"Go for Jim. Where you at, Hugh?"

"*I'm at the farmers market,*" Hugh replied, amusement in his voice. "*Have you checked your six lately?*"

Jim frowned and tugged a rein, wheeling his horse around in the road. At the tail end of his convoy, he found a line of people stretching down the road for perhaps five hundred feet. "What the hell, Hugh? Where did they all come from?"

"*Reckon they noticed the Wolfords coming into town earlier, then they noticed them going back again. This time they saw them with their wagons piled high with materials and I guess it was more than anyone could take. People are curious about what's going on.*"

Jim shook his head in disgust. "Well, what the hell am I going to do with them?"

Hugh laughed again. "*I've tracked down some labor for you today and tried to be lowkey about it, but I guess the time for 'lowkey' is about over.*"

You're going to have to go ahead and tell these people what you're up to. Consider it marketing hype. Build some buzz."

"What am I going to tell them?" Jim wasn't asking Hugh as much as he was thinking out loud, trying to come up with a plan.

"I guess you have about a half-mile left to figure it out."

Jim groaned. "I was hoping my last public speaking event was truly my last."

"Guess you were wrong about that."

"Yeah, no shit. Jim out." Jim guided his horse alongside Shade's wagon and tipped his head toward the crowd following them. "I guess the cat is about to be let out of the bag. We have an audience."

Shade looked back behind the wagons. "Lord, look at all them people. They friends of yours?"

"I doubt it. You could probably fit my friends in the back of your smallest wagon."

"Then what do all those sons-of-bitches want?"

"I guess they want to know what's going on," Jim said. "When we get to the roadhouse, I might get you guys to stop in the parking lot before we unload. I'll hop up on the back of one of these wagons and give a little press conference. Hopefully they'll go away then and let us get to work."

Shade took another look at the crowd. "They don't look like much. We could probably send them running with a little gunfire."

That cracked Jim up. "I'd probably have gone for that a couple of months back, but I have to look at them as potential customers now. That means I got to try to be nicer, no matter how much it pains me. I'm going to take the high road."

"Your call," Shade said. "I'm good with either as long as you're paying for the ammo."

When they wheeled into the crumbling and potholed parking lot of the old sewing factory, Jim directed Shade's wagon to where he wanted it parked. Shade hopped off after setting his brake and guided the rest of the wagons up alongside him.

Jim tied his horse off to the chain link fence, then scrambled onto the back of Shade's wagon. He climbed atop the pile of plywood strapped down there and watched the horde that had followed them from the market get closer.

"I swear the crowd has gotten even bigger."

Shade leaned against the side of the wagon, rolling a cigarette. "More people than I have need for. I tried to get you to let me run them off."

"The more you talk, the more I wonder if you might be my long-lost brother," Jim said. "You sound just like me."

Shade grinned and raised his eyebrows. "My daddy was a lady's man. He was known to dip his wick in a lot of wax." He stuck the completed cigarette in his mouth and lit it with a disposable lighter. "I reckon I got brothers and sisters scattered over five states."

As much as the idea amused him, there was no way Jim would even joke to Nana about the idea of being related to Shade Wolford. She'd flog him across the yard, then lay down and have a heart attack out of pure spite. Jim turned his attention back to the growing crowd as they began to gather around him.

Shade didn't like people crowding him and he especially didn't care for people touching his horses. His size and menacing glare guaranteed that most people kept their distance, but he issued a warning for those that might be slow on the uptake. "Those horses bite and they eat what they bite. Best keep away from them."

One look at those wide, slavering jaws was enough to give most people a very unpleasant image of what it might be like to have their flesh ground between those huge teeth. The crowed backed up and gave them a little more room.

When it looked like most of the crowd had caught up with them, Jim raised a hand to silence them. "Feels like it's just been a few days since I last addressed a crowd here in town. Didn't figure I'd be doing it again anytime soon."

The crowd didn't find his opening remarks to be as amusing as Jim did. Most of them weren't in the mood for small talk and they hadn't yet gained a taste for Jim Powell's sense of humor. They didn't think he was funny when he'd been cursing them from the top of the

RV at the farmers market and they didn't find him to be any funnier now.

"What the hell you up to now?" one man demanded. "We've all seen these wagons going through town today. Now they're loaded up with building materials and you're the very one appears to be behind it. This some kind of community project?"

Jim shook his head.

"You building winter housing for the elderly?" an older lady asked. "We need it. I about froze to death last winter."

"No, ma'am," Jim said.

The old lady frowned. "Selfish bastard. I should have known better."

"Then what is it?" another of the crowd demanded.

Jim looked around the assembly and noted their expressions. They were more curious than hostile. He saw some familiar faces, and even a few friendly ones, though the latter were in the minority. Maybe this wouldn't go so badly.

"I'm opening a business with some partners of mine. I can't say too much about it right now, but we hope to be open in a month or two. All I can say is that it's a business some of you might enjoy and appreciate. For others, you'll probably complain about it because some of you complain about every damn thing."

Jim caught Shade Wolford cracking up at that comment. Jim was seriously trying to be nice and keep things positive, but it wasn't easy. Public speaking brought out the worst in him.

"While I got you here, I'll just mention that we're going to be hiring both skilled and unskilled labor to help us get this building whipped into shape. We can't pay anything, but we'll feed you lunch. We'll hire on the first two dozen people to show up each day."

"Work all damn day for lunch?" someone in the crowd barked. He was mostly bald, with a fringe of hair that wrapped around his head like he was a friar. "What's that come to? Ten cents an hour?"

Jim bristled at the comment. "How much are you being paid now for sitting around with your thumb up your ass? If you're not interested, stay home and don't take the work. That's what it pays and it's non-negotiable. If you're hungry enough, that probably sounds like a damn good offer."

The friar shook his head and grumbled. Part of Jim wanted to tear into him, but he tried to let it go. If the guy opened his mouth again though, all bets were off.

"So you're just taking this building as your own?" another man asked. He was wearing a polo shirt and a lanyard, like he was on lunch break from his job. "Are you buying it? Renting it?"

Jim hated questions like that. Ownership and property rights were murky territory at the moment and he didn't have all the answers. Jim knew this building wasn't his and would very likely never be his, but they were at a moment in history when no resources could be wasted. He'd use the building until he couldn't use it any longer.

"No, I'm not buying the damn building and I'm not renting it either. It's owned by some company in Richmond, so it's not like I could get up with them and ask. I'm not taking the building as my own. I'm borrowing it. I reckon things will get back to normal one day and it'll go back to whoever owned it before. Meanwhile, I'm going to use it for this business we're starting."

"You can just claim something like that?" the man persisted. "What gives you the right?"

Jim's eyes bored into the man. "Let me ask you a question, Lanyard Man. In the last year, have you gone into an empty house and taken something?"

The man shrugged nervously. "I guess. I'm sure everyone has."

Jim nodded. "That's right. *Everyone* has. Stealing is wrong and I have no love for thieves. I've killed men for trying to take things that belonged to me or one of my group. But if the people who owned an item are dead or gone, is it more of a sin to take that item or to let it go to waste? Is it stealing to move into an empty house with a wood stove when your house doesn't have one? Is it stealing to eat walnuts from a tree growing on an abandoned farm? We've all done things that didn't feel right in this disaster, and we'll probably do more of them in the future because this isn't over. But no, I'm not stealing this building.

I'm going to use it until I have to give it back. That's all I've got to say about it. If you've got more questions, meet me around back in ten minutes."

Lanyard Man looked like he had more to say on the matter, but he let it pass. The suggestion that he meet Jim behind the building to continue the discussion obviously contained a threat. He tried to point that out to the people standing around him, but they ignored him. Everyone understood by this point that there was only so much you could argue with Jim Powell before things got ugly.

"Anyone else care to bitch, whine, or bellyache before I get back to work?" Jim yelled. "I'm getting tired of talking about this and I have things to do."

A lady with long white hair raised her hand. "I'm still confused. What are you going to do here?"

"A roadhouse!" Jim replied. "I'm opening a roadhouse. A bar. A beer joint. A saloon. I'll have beer, liquor, wine, and food. I'll be open in a month or two and you can come see for yourself. Meanwhile, get out of here and don't come back unless you're here to work. I'm done talking about it."

Jim hopped down from the wagon and stood beside Shade. Jim was agitated and wound up, shaking his head with disgust. "I try, man. I'm just not good with people. Everything they do pisses me off."

Shade cocked an eyebrow. "You sure you're cut out for working with the public? I'm not sure you have the personality that's going to draw crowds into a roadhouse."

"My people know that. I'm going to run the place behind the scenes. People better suited to dealing with the public will staff the place."

"Good plan," said Shade. "You kill a few customers every night and eventually business will dry up."

Jim had to laugh at that, while at the same time acknowledging the truth of the statement. "There's a loading dock on the end of the building. Let's pull around there and we can start unloading."

Jim mounted his horse and rode on toward that end of the building. He was going to head inside and open the dock door. That reminded him that he needed to change the locks on the building to keep their materials safe. He'd also like to start leaving someone inside every night as a guard, but he hadn't worked out the details yet.

As he reached the end of the long, narrow building he caught sight of two figures further on down the road. He had no doubt as to who it was. Whether drawn by his voice addressing the crowd or by the sight of the throngs of people gathered there, NAPA and Newport had come to see what was going on. Part of Jim was hesitant to unload the building materials in front of the two shady characters, but it couldn't be helped. There was work to be done and he was not going to schedule it around a couple of nosy neighbors.

18

Jim

THAT EVENING JIM killed one of the numerous goats that had taken to living in the woods around their farm. With Shade's help, they deftly butchered the animal and set the various cuts to roasting over an open grill. Chunks of hickory and oak stove wood provided hot coals that would cook and flavor the meat.

The rest of the meal came from remnants of the late season garden and from Jim's supply of pasta. They still had corn, tomatoes, peppers, onions, and some assorted beans. Nana and Ellen were so tired of canning by this point that they eagerly offered up fresh vegetables. Anything that was cooked and eaten was that much less that had to be canned.

The grape pickers had returned earlier, and some were lingering around Jim's place. Jim took the opportunity to introduce his people, and then Shade ran through the names of those who had come with him. It was a large gathering and the meal was the biggest prepared on the farm since the collapse. Jim couldn't feed that many people indefinitely, but he could do it long enough to get all the materials moved.

The more time Jim spent with them, the more he understood that the Wolfords might be good friends to have. They were strong and resourceful, possessing a lot of the same traditional Appalachian skills that Jim had been exposed to growing up. They were also tough people, not scared or intimidated by much. They didn't shy from hard work or the threat of violence.

"We finished the grapes today," Pete said, coming up to give his dad a hug. "I'm so sick of grapes I don't think I'll ever be able to eat another one again."

"I'm glad you guys finished," Jim said. "Maybe you and Charlie can catch up on some chores around here tomorrow, then join me at the sewing factory."

"Are you going to have tables in this place?" Pete asked.

"Yeah. I figured I'd either send people around to collect them from abandoned houses or we could make some."

"What about cable reels?" Pete asked. "Charlie and I were talking about that today. The old phone company office has dozens of those empty cable reels locked up behind their office. I saw it once when Charlie and I were riding around town."

"Did they not get burned for wood last winter?" Jim asked.

Pete shook his head. "Apparently not. They were there a few weeks ago. If we could borrow some bolt cutters, you could send Charlie and me with some of these guys tomorrow. We could get all the tables you need and no one would have to waste time building them."

"That's an excellent idea," Jim agreed.

Pete beamed. "I thought so. I'll go tell Charlie and we'll plan on doing that after lunch tomorrow."

As Pete ran off, Jim watched as Shade deftly rolled another cigarette. It was a smooth operation for a man missing part of several fingers.

"You raise that tobacco?" Jim asked.

"I grew up raising it. Put out a patch every year."

"Some of my people have been bagging old leaves off the floor of a curing shed. People who like to smoke were getting a little desperate. They've been selling some at the market."

Shade smiled. "It doesn't take nearly as many of these for a man to get his fix. It's one thing to smoke a pack of store-boughts in a day, but you're not going to find many people that can smoke twenty of these in a day. Straight tobacco has a little kick to it."

"How'd you lose the fingers?" Jim asked.

Shade splayed a hand and stared at the nubs. "My granny cut them off because I wouldn't quit picking my nose when I was a boy."

Jim had no idea how to respond to something like that. "That's…a hard woman," he finally managed to utter.

Shade slapped Jim on the back. "I'm shitting you. Now, my granny was a pistol. She might have done that, but she didn't. Lost them when I was a kid. Daddy had us logging from the time we could walk. I had them stuck under a steel cable while I was adjusting a choker. The horses shifted and pulled the cable tight. Pinched them right off."

Jim winced at the image, picturing that horrible moment of watching your fingers crushed and knowing there was nothing you could do to prevent it. "Your dad feel bad about it?"

"Not as bad as I did," Shade said.

"What did he say?"

Shade smiled and took a draw off his smoke. "He said, 'That'll learn you, won't it?'"

Jim winced but understood the truth of it. The old man had been right. A lesson like that did stick with you for life. Much like Jim's grandfather, Shade's father had been the product of a different generation. They were hard people who didn't see any benefit in softening the blows the world threw at you. The world was a tough place. The sooner you learned to take its punches, the better off you'd be.

"The old man gave me the rest of the day off, but just the one day," Shade said. "The fingers were too mangled to stick back on, so the doctor cleaned everything and stitched me up. The next day I worked a team of horses since I couldn't fasten chokers with one hand."

"You raise your own kids like that?" Jim asked. "Or did they get it a little easier?"

"I worked them but not like I was worked. I tell them that all the time. My daddy treated horses better than he treated people. I tried to raise my kids knowing they were at least equal to the horse."

Shade winked as he said it, but Jim wasn't so sure if he was joking or not.

"I hope the accommodations are okay, Shade." Jim gestured at the barn.

"They're fine but we'll probably sleep in the wagons. We pull a tarp over the beds, and it makes a nice place to sleep. I was more concerned about the safety of the horses and your place is a damn sight better than keeping them in town. Town people are...different."

Jim nodded. "They are."

Both men whipped their heads around as a loud hillbilly yell reached their ears.

Jim sighed. "That's my buddy Lloyd. He's the one who came up with this roadhouse idea. He's a banjo player so consider yourself warned."

"I was raised with musicians, so I've been tortured by the best of them," said Shade. "What I want to know is if he drinks like a musician. I haven't known of many banjo players who didn't have a taste for liquor."

"And I thought he was special," Jim mused.

"Naw, they're all like that. Loud drunks. Every one of them. Who else would play an instrument like that?"

19

The Antique Dealers

IT WAS around midnight when Mitchell, Pamela, and Dixie crept out of their home and set off through the dark town. It would take them at least thirty minutes to reach the county courthouse but the night was quiet. Unable to stay up late scrolling social media or binge-watching shows on streaming services, most people went to bed around dark and got up with the sun. No one was out at this hour unless they were up to something that required the cover of darkness.

They didn't bring their coveralls and dust masks on this night, figuring they wouldn't be skulking around the dusty interiors of abandoned homes or working alongside desiccated corpses. Instead, they'd be venturing inside the courthouse, which had been kept relatively clean and clear by the faithful custodian Backup Bailey.

The courthouse was in the center of town and was surrounded by a proliferation of litter. Every nitwit, degenerate, and petty criminal in the county had visited the courthouse at some point in the last year trying to destroy any record of the charges, fines, and settlements levied against them. They had thrown out files and burned them on the lawn. They had smashed computers and tossed phones out windows. They had vandalized pictures of esteemed judges and urinated on their polished wooden desks.

Each morning, Backup returned to the building and cleaned up the evidence of their pointless efforts. Backup knew that every vital record in the courthouse was archived on offsite backups. Even burning the courthouse to the ground would do nothing to erase criminal records, pending charges, and the like.

The trio pulled their carts around to the back door, the entrance where those attending court smoked cigarettes during recesses. Despite the number of broken windows in the building, Backup continued to chain the doors closed every night. It didn't stop everyone, but it deterred those too large or lazy to climb through a window.

Mitchell used one of the keys they'd obtained from Backup to unfasten the padlock from the chain. He cringed when the chain rattled and banged off the steel doors. When it was free, he stepped aside and held the door open for the ladies to enter the building, pulling the carts in with them. Mitchell followed them in, securing the door behind him and chaining the doors from the inside.

Now that they were concealed within the bowels of the building, they turned on their headlamps. They listened but heard nothing in the vast network of hallways. The three were not naïve to the risk involved in their nighttime excursions. Besides the tools they carried for plundering houses, each carried a handgun in a pocket. They hadn't been forced to use them on anyone yet, but they understood that it could happen anytime, and they wanted to be ready.

"Which way?" Dixie asked.

Mitchell cringed at the volume with which she spoke. Her voice carried in the empty building, ringing off the hard plaster walls and echoing down the hallway. He pointed to a nearby set of stairs. "Down."

Dixie rolled her eyes at him, miffed at the way he intentionally whispered the word. She understood he'd done so to admonish her without having to come out and say it. Her cart was a jogging stroller made to hold two babies. She tossed her head, grabbed it by the handle, and headed toward the stairs.

Mitchell sighed. If he had a dollar for every time he'd received a scowl, eye roll, or disapproving look from these two women over the years, he wouldn't need to be selling antiques. He'd be independently wealthy and sailing the Caribbean on his yacht.

Pamela grabbed her cart and followed Dixie down the stairs to the basement level. When Mitchell fell in behind them, he made note of the difficulty they'd have if they tried hauling anything substantial out of this basement. The carts were awkward enough going down the stairs. Coming up would certainly be worse.

At the bottom of the steps they came to another steel door, this one thick with a century of glossy brown paint. There were scars in the door where someone had tried to batter it open, but the stout old door had not yielded.

"Looks like someone was living down here for a while," Pamela said, pointing to a niche below the stairs.

There was a tangle of discarded blankets alongside a stained bra. A candle had completely melted onto the floor beside some discarded food packaging. An empty bottle of T.J. Swann Magic Moments wine lay on its side.

"Looks like the magic faded," Dixie said. "That's how it goes."

Mitchell didn't take the bait, using a different key to open the brown door. Once he had it open, they all hurried through the door as if they were pursued by some unseen and ominous force. It wasn't until Mitchell locked the door behind them that they all breathed easier, assuming they were now safe in this orderly and inviolate space.

Dixie sniffed the air. "Smells like mildew. That's concerning."

Pamela nodded. "You know that irritates my allergies. I'll be congested all night."

Dixie frowned. "I don't give a tinker's damn about your allergies, Pamela. I'm talking about how this dampness might have affected any historic documents stored down here."

"Without power, there's no HVAC and no dehumidifiers," said Mitchell. "It doesn't take long for that to do damage to fragile paper."

"That practically makes this a rescue mission," Dixie said with enthusiasm. "We're not stealing anything, we're *rescuing* it."

Dixie and Pamela shared a laugh over that. Mitchell wasn't convinced. No amount of sugar-coating changed what they were doing there. He'd accepted that. He was a thief in the night and he was fine with it.

"Down the hall," Mitchell said. "Backup said it was a room on the left side. An old door with an opaque window and no sign."

When neither of the two women appeared inclined to search for the door, Mitchell abandoned his cart and scooted around them. In the glow of his headlamp, the long black hallway almost looked like a mineshaft. Now that he was in the lead, Mitchell felt hesitant. He advanced carefully, like a man who knew that a precipice loomed ahead and was terrified of stepping off it.

Mitchell noticed that all the doors on this level appeared to have been passed over in the last century of renovations. These were paneled oak doors with locks and hinges made of solid brass. The top halves of the doors held opaque glass panels. Then, ahead and to the left, was the last door.

He stopped outside and noticed there was no placard stating what the room contained. Mitchell fumbled with his keys and located one so old and pocket-worn that the teeth were nearly smooth, rounded like the hills surrounding the town. Mitchell slid it into the lock and gently applied pressure. The key turned and the lock emitted a solid *thunk* as the bolt retracted.

Mitchell extracted the key, turned the knob, and shoved the door inward. It swung open with a slow creak, halting just before it struck an interior wall. Mitchell stepped inside and the air in the room was even worse. The humidity clung to them like an oily film. The smell of mildew filled their noses, seeping into their hair and clothing. It was one that would stay with them for days and linger on anything they took from the room.

Despite their disgust at the conditions, the three antique dealers looked about the room with a sense of awe and reverence. There was a long, oak library table in the center of the room. Institutional-looking chairs of green steel were pulled up to it, the seats covered in brown leather. There was a sign on the wall that designated the location as a Fallout Shelter and specified the occupancy. They all understood that there had once been a sign just like this one posted at the main entrances to the building, just as there had been on all the local schools.

The table contained file storage boxes and copy paper boxes, all marked as having come from the library.

"That must be the stuff they brought from the library," Pamela said, gesturing at the row of boxes.

There was a painting on the wall that Mitchell recognized as being General William Russell, the man for whom their county was named. Mitchell touched the canvas and felt the raised whorls of oil paint. It was an original and not a print. While not a masterpiece in any artistic sense, it was a priceless piece of local history.

"Look at that," Dixie said, directing the beam of her light onto a broad, framed map on the wall. It was an original map of the proposed county, drafted by the steady hand of an eighteenth-century cartographer. "I want it."

"It's too big to carry," said Mitchell. "That frame is the size of a door."

"I'll take it out and roll the map up," Dixie said. "There have to be storage tubes in here somewhere for blueprints and plats."

Mitchell focused on the rows of glass-faced barrister bookcases crammed with ragged books, sheaves of documents, and bound ledgers. There was a wall of fireproof filing cabinets, but none of the drawers were locked since the room itself was locked and assumed to be secured. Each drawer held reams of irreplaceable historical documents.

Dixie began to read the labels on the filing cabinet drawers, tugging them open, then slamming them shut. When she finally found the drawer she was looking for, her fingers riffled through the old typewritten labels. Then she paused and gently extracted a century-old paper folder from the drawer. When she opened it, there was a handwritten document preserved inside an archival plastic sheet protector. Dixie ran a nail down the document, reviewing the signatures.

"What is it?" Mitchell asked.

"The charter," she breathed with great reverence. "When the county established the town as the county seat. It's an original."

Pamela hurried to Dixie's side and began reviewing the document with equal enthusiasm. "There are the names. Our ancestors."

"The founders." Mitchell took off his auction company ballcap and held it over his heart.

As trite as the gesture seemed, he was genuinely moved to be in the presence of a document of such historical significance. He wasn't the only one. They were all in awe, regarding it with all the reverence of some ancient holy relic. Just as the three of them were now gathered in this room, there had been a time some two hundred and fifty years ago when each of them had an ancestor who stood around this document, dipped pen in ink, and lent their support to the creation of the very town they now lived in.

Dixie closed the folder and gently laid it atop her backpack. "Honey, you're coming home with me."

20

The Antique Dealers

NONE of the three showed any restraint at all as they looted the local historical archives. Despite knowing how heavy a load of paper could get, each of them crammed their carts full of irreplaceable pieces of local history. They took documents, ledgers, census rolls, and everything else that struck their eye. Dixie in particular latched onto anything related to the civil war, nabbing old muster rolls, pensioner documents, and notes related to troop movements or encampments in the area.

When they tried to get up the stairs, it was just as they feared. It took all three of them working in tandem to awkwardly haul each of the heavily laden carts up the steps. By the time they were done, they had to sit down and rest in the dark courthouse hallway before they ventured out into the night. Despite the effort they'd gone to, despite the work that lay ahead of them on this night, they were energized and enthusiastic.

"We're coming back tomorrow night," Pamela huffed. "We didn't get through everything."

"It's not tomorrow night," Mitchell said. "I suspect it's already the wee hours of the morning, so you mean tonight."

"You know what I mean, you contrary old fool! Why do you insist on being difficult?" she snapped.

Dixie sighed. "You can't talk to my husband that way, Pamela. Only I can talk to the contrary old fool that way."

The two of them cackled like amused witches.

Mitchell got to his feet. "If you've got wind enough to laugh, you've got wind enough to walk." He stuck out his hands and helped the two ladies to their feet.

They groaned but accepted his help, struggling to their feet. Each of them got behind their cart and headed for the exit door.

"I'm feeling my age tonight," Dixie said. "I wasn't out this late this often even when I was young."

"Oh, honey, I was," Pamela cooed. "I made the most of it."

Mitchell smirked. "Because you were a tramp."

"It was the 1960s, asshole. I wasn't a tramp, I was a free spirit."

"Free is right," Dixie quipped. "You gave away more samples than the Hickory Farms."

Mitchell cracked up, laughing all the way to the door. He fished around in his pocket, found the keys, and unfastened the chain securing the door. He was still snickering as he held the door open for his partners in crime.

Pamela elbowed him in the gut as she passed. "That's for calling me a tramp!"

Mitchell grabbed his belly and scowled at her, but kept his mouth shut. He could never win with Dixie and Pamela. The best he could hope for was to get in the occasional jab and he'd learned to relish those moments.

"Turn those headlamps off," Mitchell warned them. "Your eyes will adjust in a few minutes." He was going to leave his own on until he had the door secured.

While Mitchell was chaining the door back, the two ladies pushed their carts out into the back street behind the courthouse to wait on him. That was when an unfamiliar male voice addressed them.

"Little late to be taking those babies for a stroll, isn't it?"

Mitchell's bladder nearly let loose from the shock of it. He'd not heard anyone approach. He tried to shove the building keys in his pocket, fumbling as his fingers sought the opening in the garment and missed. He dropped the keys and had to bend over to pick them up. When he finally got them stowed away, he turned toward the speaker, his headlight illuminating an unfamiliar man in a backpack casually standing in the street.

The man raised a hand to cover his eyes. "Do you mind getting that light out of my face, please?" His words were polite, but his voice was authoritative. It might have been a request, but the implication was that he expected immediate compliance if this was to remain friendly.

Michell turned his head to move the beam of light off the man, then fumbled with the tiny switch that turned the headlamp off.

"You scared the pee out of me," Dixie said. Her voice was a little too loud, carrying both accusation and nervousness.

"I just came into town and saw the lights through the door there. I was looking for a place to crash for the night and thought there might be room for one more."

"So you're traveling?" Mitchell asked. His eyes hadn't adjusted to the darkness after turning off his headlamp. He had his left hand on his cart. The right was in the pocket of his hoodie, tightening around the grip of the .38 revolver he carried.

"You might say that," the man replied. "I have some business in town, but it took me longer to get here than I expected. Obviously, there's no hotels these days so I guess accommodations are wherever a man finds them."

"There are plenty of empty houses in town," Pamela blurted out. "Just pick one."

"That's a little too risky for me," the man replied. "I go walking into one that isn't empty and it might be game over for me."

"I guess that's true," she admitted.

"What are you folks doing wandering around town with these big baby strollers?" the man asked. "The grandparents out for a midnight jog with a half-dozen grandkids?" It was evident from the tone of his voice that he didn't believe that was the case. He was messing with them. Challenging them.

When the silence stretched on for an uncomfortable moment, Mitchell jumped in and answered him. "Most people don't go around talking about their business these days. It's safer that way. No offense, but we don't need to know your business and you probably don't need to know ours. Maybe we should leave it at that and go our own ways."

"If that's how you want to play it," the man replied. "And I was just about to ask if you guys might be able to put me up for the night. I'm assuming you folks must have a place around here somewhere unless you live out of these strollers."

This whole interaction had thrown Mitchell off. He hadn't recovered from the shock of the man's sudden appearance. He'd been anxious from the moment he heard the unexpected voice and that anxiety had steadily increased as the conversation grew more tense. His breathing was rapid and he could feel it quavering as he exhaled. He flexed his fingers, desperate for some way to regain his calm.

He wasn't sure whether his actions were motivated by a sense of self-preservation or whether he simply panicked from the surge of adrenaline, but Mitchell yanked the revolver from his pocket. Without a word of warning, he pointed it into the darkness, toward the general direction of the voice, and began yanking the trigger.

Dixie screamed as the first shot split the night. Pamela grabbed her cart and tore off down the back street.

Mitchell kept pulling the trigger. He couldn't see the sights on the pistol, but it was a weapon designed for pointing, not precision. Finally, the hammer fell on a spent round and fell silent. The flame flaring from the barrel had blinded Mitchell and he could no longer see anything in the darkness. With a trembling hand, he fumbled for the switch on his headlamp and snapped it on.

He braced himself for the sight of a man bleeding out in the harsh pool of his light, but there was no body. Mitchell whipped his head around, thinking the man might have made it a few steps before dying, but he found nothing.

He'd missed.

"I must have wounded him!" he gasped, his heart pounding.

"You missed him, you boob!" Dixie snapped.

"Go!" Mitchell ordered, pointing toward the direction in which Pamela had already fled.

Dixie didn't hesitate. She grabbed the handles of her jogging stroller and shuffled off after Pamela. It wasn't quite a running pace, but it was faster than a walk. Though Dixie enjoyed plundering for antiques she was not a fan of physical exertion, even when her life might depend on it.

When he failed to locate the body after a moment of searching, Mitchell didn't wait around for the man to reappear. He grabbed his cart and rushed off after Pamela and Dixie.

Mitchell's white New Balance "old man" shoes were much better for running than Dixie's Crocs. He was huffing and puffing, his heart rate maxed out, but he soon caught up with his wife. "Pick it up, woman! Faster!"

She mumbled a protracted curse, insulting everything from Mitchell's aim to his manhood.

When he detected no increase in the flapping of her Crocs, he said, "Don't waste your breath. I'm not waiting!"

When she didn't reply, he sped up and set his sights on catching up with Pamela.

"You leave me back here by myself and I'll cut your damn throat when you're sleeping," Dixie gasped.

"Keep dragging your ass and you won't make it home!"

Those words had some impact. As if some unseen hand reached down from the heavens and gradually increased the speed of her throttle, the flapping of Dixie's Crocs increased and she pulled alongside him.

"We keep...running...like this...none of us...will...make it...home," she gasped. "Not made...for this."

In the end it wasn't the logic of Dixie's words that forced them to slow but the inarguable truths of their own physiologies. Less than a hundred feet after Mitchell caught up with Dixie, they found Pamela flat on her back in the middle of the street. She was stretched out along the yellow dividing line like a dead possum.

"You think she's dead?" Dixie asked as they neared her.

Mitchell slowed down. "Are you kidding? She's wheezing like a seal."

"I heard that!" Pamela croaked. "I'm just resting. Help me up."

Dixie wiped the back of a sweaty arm across her equally sweaty forehead and swooned dramatically. "To hell with getting you up. I'm joining you." With that, she sat down perhaps a little harder than she planned, letting out a little sound of surprise when her butt hit the ground.

Mitchell sagged forward, resting on the handles of his cart. "This is pathetic. We're not even out of sight of the courthouse. If he's coming after us, he'll be here anytime."

"Let him come," Dixie moaned. "I'd rather die sitting than running. I have *some* dignity."

Mitchell didn't have the wind to argue with them. Perhaps it wasn't the nicest thing to do, but he did the only thing he could think of. He straightened up and cocked his head as if he heard something.

"What is it?" Pamela asked, detecting the shadow of his movement.

"I hear him. He's coming." Mitchell grabbed the handles of his cart and bolted off down the street. When he heard the sound of flapping Crocs behind him, he couldn't help but grin.

21

Jim

With Teddy's grape crop picked, the morning routine of the valley folks changed yet again. Pete and Charlie were going to stay home with Pops for the day so they could catch up on some of the chores around the farm. Randi's daughters, with Ariel's help, were going to babysit for all the families. Gary, his wife, and daughters would be running a booth at the market while his son-in-law Will worked at the old sewing factory with Jim, Hugh, and Lloyd. Randi, addicted to trading at the market, would be back to running her booth.

The entire Wolford clan was up before the sun. Ellen and Nana fixed a huge breakfast for everyone. They prepared a mountain of pancakes and served them with honey from the market since there was no syrup to be had. They fried ham and thick slices of bacon cut from a pork belly hanging in the basement. There were also fresh eggs from the chickens, served any way you wanted them, as long as it was scrambled.

Before he left for the sewing factory, Jim retrieved a couple of freeze-dried soup mixes, some canned peas, and some fresh corn.

There were some cuts of goat meat left from the dinner last night and he wrapped those up in a shopping bag. All of it was packed into two large institutional-sized serving pots that Jim had "borrowed" from a local school cafeteria early in the disaster.

Cookware suitable for large groups had been one of the gaps in his preparations. They figured out early on that less food was wasted if they cooked as a group. The only problem with that was no one had pots of the size required to feed an army. A few weeks of looking for the appropriate cookware had led him to the local elementary school.

Jim was hoping he didn't get stuck with preparing the lunchtime meal he'd promised everyone. There were times he didn't mind cooking, but he had other duties he wanted to concentrate on right now. He needed to be managing the project and making sure everything was done to his requirements, so finding someone who could do the cooking each day was high on his list.

When the market group split off from the roadhouse group, Jim got his first big surprise of the day. Approaching the old sewing factory, he found a line stretched a significant distance down the road. There must have been seventy or eighty people waiting there, presumably hoping to be selected for the job.

As Jim rode alongside the line, he studied the men with the same intensity with which they studied him. He stopped about halfway down the line, judging that to be the best point from which to address the group. "I guess you're all here wanting to work?"

There were nods up and down the line. Some looked back at him like it was a stupid question. He'd remember those faces. It was his project and he didn't have to hire smartasses if he didn't want to.

"Who here *can't* read a tape measure?" Jim asked. "And don't lie because there will be a test."

Over thirty hands went up.

"Thank you for coming out but I can't use anyone who can't measure," Jim said.

There was some mumbling as those illiterate in the ways of inches and fractions thereof tried to determine whether he was serious.

"I'm serious. Thanks for coming out but I can't use you if you can't measure. It's a basic life skill."

With a few curses and hard looks, those who were culled headed back home. The group was now about half the size it had been a few minutes ago.

"Any of you ever work as real carpenters or mechanical contractors before?" Jim asked. "Not nailing together an old shed in your backyard but *professionally* employed as a carpenter."

Seven hands went up.

Jim pointed off to the side. "You guys group up over there. Any of the rest of you ever work on a construction site? Day laborer? Concrete guy? Helper?"

Nearly a dozen more hands shot up as Jim applied this broader filter.

"Okay, you guys go hang out with the carpenters." He addressed the carpenters that he'd grouped off earlier. "You guys figure out if these helpers know their way around a jobsite. I need people who can carry and know the difference between a five-quarters deck board and a two by ten."

Jim spent a few minutes assessing the rest of the men and picked a few more, ending up with about two dozen men. Before he sent the last of the rejected men on their way, he asked one last question. "Anyone in here ever cook for large groups before?"

A single hand went up.

"Where at?" Jim asked.

The man hesitated before responding. "Prison."

Jim pointed at him. "You stick around."

He sent the rest away, telling them they were welcome to come back and try their luck the next day. He suspected some might come back, but others looked stung by his rejection and he wasn't sure whether he'd see them again or not.

When they were gone, he addressed his crew. "You guys hang out for a second while I get the haulers on the road. Where's the cook?"

The guy who'd said he cooked in prison raised his hand.

"Come with me," Jim said. "We need to get the lunch supplies off the wagons."

With the cook in tow, Jim headed for the wagons. Hugh was engaged in some amusing story with the Wolfords. Jim figured it was about him but didn't hear enough of it to know for certain.

"Grab that pot and the boxes beside it," Jim told the cook. "Haul them clear of the wagons but keep your eye on them. Don't let any of it walk off."

The cook began ferrying the lunch supplies from the wagon to a crumpled sidewalk that ran along the front of the building.

"So, what kind of fun you got lined up for us today, Captain Kangaroo?" Shade asked.

Hugh laughed. "I like it. That's a good nickname for him."

Jim didn't dignify the comment with a response. "You guys have a long couple of days ahead of you. Any of you know where the brewery is in St. Paul?"

Both Hugh and Shade nodded that they did.

"The guy who runs the place is named Ed Frye," Jim said. "I cut a deal with him to make beer for the roadhouse. His place burned down, but the equipment is salvageable. He's also got tons of brewing supplies and an entire distillery sitting in a shipping container. I need all of it moved over here."

"You're the boss," Shade said. "We'll go where you send us."

"It's a long haul," Jim said. "I made it the other day and didn't run into any trouble. The route along the road was pretty laid back. I ran into some folks, but no one was edgy. I took that as a good sign."

"Good to know," Hugh said.

"It'll take you all day to get there, load, and get back. You might even need to plan for an overnight there at the brewery if things move slowly."

"Got it," Shade said. "Today we'll do a quick trip to get what we can and get the lay of the land. Tomorrow we'll go prepared for an overnight stay if it comes to that. What do we do with the loads when we get back?"

"Hugh, when you get back, bring these guys into the valley along the back way, past Lloyd's parents' house," Jim instructed. "Since it's going to be a long day, we'll store the loaded trailers at my place overnight and unload them here in the morning when we have more hands. Sound good?"

Shade threw Jim a little salute. "Good enough, Captain. We'll see you tonight." He wandered off to get his people squared away.

"Hugh, these Wolfords seem like they can take care of themselves, but we don't know them very well. Keep a rein on things as best you can."

"I've worked with all kinds," Hugh said. "We'll be fine."

Jim scanned the group, locating Gary's son-in-law Will, and waved him over. "Will, I want you to go with Hugh and the Wolfords. I doubt you'll run into trouble but keep your head on a swivel and follow Hugh's lead. Got it?"

Will nodded. "No problem."

After the wagons, tractor, and Hugh headed off for the brewery, Jim joined his new construction crew standing around in the parking lot. "Today isn't going to be real organized," he announced. "Jobs sometimes start like that before they find their groove. Our main objective today is to secure this building so we can actually lock it up at night. I need all the doors and windows secured. For now, fill any missing panes in the old windows with plexiglass. I'll need someone to get measurements of all the windows too. I'm going to get bars made for all of them and we'll anchor those in the bricks."

"Do we have materials?" one of the men asked.

"We've got some," Jim said. "There might be some things we're missing or tools we'll need to gather, so make lists if you spot things like that. I'm also going to want a team building an outhouse out back. Dig a pit in the bank and shore it with plywood. Above that, we'll build a men's stall and a women's stall. Nothing fancy. I'll give you more guidance on that once we have the pit in place."

"Any demo to do?" another man asked.

"Some," Jim said. "I'll point out what's to be demolished when we get inside. How about you guys go in and get the loading dock door open. I'll join you in a minute."

When everyone wandered off, Jim turned to the one remaining person, the cook.

"What's your name?"

"P.J."

"Can you build a fire, P.J.?"

He nodded. "I got a lighter."

"You'll be cooking beside the loading dock. Go ahead and build yourself a fire ring out of some old cinderblocks or something. You'll need a place you can rest the pot and rake coals under it. I've got a filter on my horse and you can filter creek water into that giant kettle. Fill it about three-quarters of the way full with water."

"You been filtering your water?" P.J. asked. "What for?"

Jim didn't want to waste time going into the dozens of reasons one might want to avoid drinking unfiltered water. "Let's just say I like the taste better. But I definitely want it filtered. Got it?"

"If you want it filtered, I'll filter it. You're the boss."

"Good," Jim said. "While the water is heating, add everything to the pot. The powdered soup mixes, the canned food, and the fresh vegetables. Then I want you to cut up the meat in small pieces and add that. Got it?"

P.J. nodded. "Not a problem. And I appreciate you hiring me on. I been bored shitless."

"Well, if no one dies from your cooking you can come back and do it again tomorrow," Jim said. When P.J. didn't smile, he added, "That was a joke."

Then P.J. grinned. "Got it. No dead diners."

22

Jim

Hearing the sounds of construction, of progress, at the sewing factory that morning brought a smile to Jim's face. With the use of power tools, it sounded like jobsites from before the collapse. He'd charged all the battery-operated tools on the meager solar setup at his house, which had worked fine until they ran down on the job and he didn't have an effective way to recharge them. He'd have to figure something out for that because they didn't have nearly enough spare batteries.

Even with that minor setback, things moved along. A debris pile grew off to the side of the loading dock. Windows were fixed and doors repaired. Mildew-smelling carpets were stripped from offices and tossed onto the debris pile. A couple of determined men even got the pit for the outhouse going.

The occasional straggler wandered by on the road, drawn either by the sounds of industry, the rumor of Jim's project, or the smell of the cooking soup. Some asked questions and Jim did his best to answer politely. That politeness lasted for all of one visitor. By the time the second arrived, he was already running people off and telling them to come back in a month. He had no idea whether things would be done in a month or not, but he hoped it might buy him some time.

Lloyd, meanwhile, complained about nearly everything. He'd gotten into some moonshine with the Wolfords last night because he always enjoyed drinking with new people. He must have had a bit of a hangover because he was short-tempered and whiny.

Jim didn't cut him any slack. He talked about gross things that he knew would nauseate Lloyd in his hungover state. He spoke in a loud voice that made Lloyd clutch his head and grimace. As Jim tormented his friend, he remembered all the times Lloyd had given him grief about killing people. Payback was a bitch.

The only thing that succeeded in breaking Lloyd's unpleasant demeanor was the arrival of two ladies at the door to the roadhouse. Lloyd put on a smile that was intended to appear friendly, but came off as creepy. Randi had tried to point that out to him but gotten nowhere.

"You ladies here to see me?" Lloyd cooed.

They turned up their noses and shook their heads in tandem. The one in the front said, "Nah, just the guy you were with the other day."

That was when Jim recognized them. It was the ladies from the brothel in town. The same two he'd spoken to on the porch.

He realized that he'd completely forgotten about needing to go speak with them. At Ellen's suggestion, Jim had given up on trying to make the working girls part of the roadhouse. He'd just forgotten to tell those working girls. Now they were probably here to check out the accommodations and see where they'd be working. Jim was going to have to tell them. He couldn't put it off any longer.

"Morning, ladies," Jim said. "Can we talk outside?"

The ladies turned and headed out into the sunny day. Jim followed them, Lloyd on his heels.

"We need to talk about something," one of the girls said.

They did, Jim silently agreed, but he doubted they had the same conversation in mind. These ladies probably wanted to talk about colors and lighting. They probably had a list of things they were going to require in their rooms. Jim would hear them out. They'd come to him and it would only be polite to let them go first. Then he was going to have to give them *his* bad news.

"Okay," Jim said. "What's on your mind?"

The two ladies looked at each other and Jim recognized the look. The lady in charge was nervous and garnering her strength. She was steeling herself to ask something that made her uncomfortable. Jim wished she'd get on with it so he could get on with his own uncomfortable business. He doubted there'd be much to talk about after that. They'd probably stomp off angry with a few choice words tossed in his direction.

The madam laced her fingers together over her chest and looked at Jim. "Look, it was very thoughtful of you to try and incorporate us into your project. I appreciate that. I know you had your own financial motives, but I appreciated that you talked to us like people. Some people don't because of our profession."

Jim wasn't sure how to respond to that, so he just smiled and nodded.

"Like I said, I appreciate the way you spoke to us because we don't see a lot of kindness. People feel like the fact we're prostitutes means they can treat us like shit. I'm getting off topic, though. I do that when I nervous." She took a calming breath and pushed it out. "We've decided we can't go through with it. We don't want to be part of your roadhouse."

Jim was taken aback. He was obviously excited at this unexpected turn of events because it saved him from having to backtrack on his earlier offer. Still, his curiosity gnawed at him. "Why not?"

"No offense, but we don't feel like we should be associated with you. There's a lot of people in this town who have some hard feelings where you're concerned. They don't like you. Some even think you're dangerous. At the end of the day, I'm a businesswoman and I can't do things that are going to negatively impact our business down the road."

Jim was stunned. He was both relieved and insulted.

Lloyd, however, was eating it up. "This guy is my friend, ladies, but I have to admit that you're making the right call. Jim here is a little unstable. Hell, he's barely any better than a psychotic criminal. I couldn't tell you how many people he's killed. I doubt he even knows. You ladies would do well to distance yourself from him. I wish I had, but it's too late for me now."

The more Lloyd said, the more concerned the two ladies became. They'd gone from being uncomfortable because of what they had to say to Jim to looking uncomfortable at being in his presence. They started backing away.

"Listen, we have to go," the madam said. "No hard feelings."

They hurried away. Jim watched them go with a frown on his face, trying to make sense of what had just happened.

"Ain't that some shit, Lloyd? The town whores decided I'd ruin their reputation."

Lloyd patted his old friend on the back. "Sorry, buddy. Sometimes the truth hurts."

23

The Antique Dealers

Dixie, Mitchell, and Pamela were back at their booth at the farmer's market that morning, despite the unsettling night they'd had. They'd barely slept and all of them ached from the unusual level of physical exertion. They'd snapped at each other all morning, each of them blaming the other for the way things had transpired.

Mitchell had a notepad in his hand and they were working together to build a list of things they wanted to look for when they returned to the courthouse that night. Despite their encounter with the stranger, there was no question as to whether they were going back or not. They only had those keys for so many days and then they'd have to return them to Backup Bailey. During that short window of opportunity, they wanted to take everything from the county archives they could think of.

"Original plats of the town," Pamela suggested. "I want to see if we can find all the original real estate transactions and land grants."

"Court records!" Dixie blurted out, snapping her fingers. "One of my ancestors was once fined for failing to maintain the road that passed in front of his house. It's a shame that a founding father of this community should have such a blemish on his record two centuries later."

"All that stuff is online now," Mitchell said. "You can destroy the original, but it won't erase the record."

"It'll make me feel better," Dixie hissed, her lips taut. "I'm going to burn the damn thing personally."

"Expunge criminal records of all of Dixie's ancestors," Mitchell said aloud, adding that to the list.

She gave him a hard look and started to swat him, but they were interrupted by the arrival of a customer at their booth.

"Morning," Pamela said.

The man smiled at her. "Good morning." He studied their wares for a few moments, then looked up and studied each of their faces.

When his staring finally became uncomfortable, Pamela snapped, "Is there something we can help you with?"

The man got a sneaky look on his face. "Maybe. You guys have a late night last night?"

Pamela's eyebrow arched into a questioning expression. Dixie, who'd been occupied in giving a disapproving glare to a lady she didn't care for, whipped her head up to give their customer a second look.

Mitchell hadn't been paying much attention either but looked up from his notepad to see what was going on. When he got a look at the man standing in front of their booth, his heart nearly seized up in his chest.

"Have...have we met?" Pamela asked.

The man leaned forward and rested his hands on the table, intentionally ignoring the neatly lettered sign warning him not to do so. "I think we might have. I'm pretty sure I recognize you guys from a less-than-friendly encounter I had outside of the courthouse last night. One minute we're having a friendly conversation. The next, some idiot is blasting away at me as fast as he can pull the trigger."

It was on the tip of Mitchell's tongue to apologize to the guy, but he restrained himself. He kept his voice low and said, "Listen, I have a gun and I'm not afraid to use it."

"Clearly," the stranger replied. "But even at this range I'm not sure you could hit me."

"You need to leave," Dixie said. "You had no business scaring us last night and you have no business harassing us now. You just march your happy little ass out of here and keep moving."

"Or what?" the stranger asked, setting his jaw.

Dixie hesitated, then slapped Mitchell on the arm. "Well, tell him, Mitchell. Tell him what you're going to do. What are you waiting on?"

"What do you want?" Mitchell demanded.

"The same thing I wanted last night," the stranger snapped. "All I wanted was to ask you folks some questions and the next thing I know I'm getting shot at."

"Well, ask your damn questions and be gone," Pamela said. "How are we supposed to conduct business with you blocking our booth?"

The man straightened out. "Fine. My name is Luther and I'm from Wallace County. I'm looking for a friend of mine, a guy named Isaac. He was what you call a regional sheriff. Supposedly he was coming over here to meet up with some guy named Hadley, but he never made it back to Wallace County. I'm trying to figure out what happened to him."

"Oh him? I remember that one," Pamela said, fanning herself with an antique fan. "Big fellow, all dressed in black."

Luther smiled. "Now we're getting somewhere. So, he was here?"

"I just said I remembered him," Pamela replied, looking at Luther like he was slow on the uptake. "How am I going to remember someone who wasn't here?"

Luther sighed and glared at Pamela. If they'd given him this much attitude last night, he'd have been the one pulling out a pistol. "When is the last time you saw him?"

"I can't remember," Pamela said.

"Was it in the last few days?" Luther continued.

Pamela frowned. "I didn't know the man. It's not like I'd count how many days it had been since I last saw him." She looked at her companions. "Do you guys remember when you last saw him?"

Mitchell and Dixie shook their heads.

"What about this Hadley guy?" Luther asked.

Pamela shook her head. "Haven't seen him in a couple of days."

"Do you know where I can find him?"

Pamela resumed fanning herself, trying her best to look disinterested in Luther's interrogation. "Dixie, you remember where they buried Hadley? Luther here is trying to find him."

Luther let out a long breath. "He's dead?"

All three heads nodded.

"Then I don't suppose it will do me any good to find him then," Luther said. "How am I supposed to question a dead man?"

Pamela shrugged. "You didn't say you were going to question him. You asked me where to find him."

"Because I didn't know he was dead," said Luther.

"You act like that's a shocker," Pamela said. "Are people not dying over there in Wallace County? They're dropping like flies over here."

Luther raised his hands and rubbed his face. "Can I try this again? I'm concerned about my friend Isaac and I'm trying to find him. We served together."

"In prison?" Dixie asked.

Luther flushed. "No, smartass, in the military."

Dixie bobbed her head. "Well excuse me."

"You know what?" Pamela said. "I don't think I like your attitude, Luther. You need to move on. I'm bored with you and your questions. I find you offensive."

"That's fine. Then I'm going to make an announcement to all the people attending this market before I go," said Luther. "I'm going to tell them that I caught you three stealing from the courthouse last night and you shot at me."

Pamela's eyes flared with anger. "You wouldn't dare."

Luther turned his back to them and raised both hands in the air. "Excuse me, folks. Can I have your attention, please?"

"Do something!" Dixie hissed, swatting her husband again.

Mitchell stood and put a hand on Luther's shoulder. "That won't be necessary."

Luther turned back to the table. Many in the crowd were watching him, curious what was going on. "Oh, it won't be?"

"Lower your voice!" Dixie snapped.

Luther scowled at her. "I'm tired of you rude witches. Be nice and tell me what I want to know or I'm making my announcement." He raised his voice at this point, practically bellowing. "Do we have a deal?"

Pamela pursed her lips, breathing out her nose. "Yes! We have a deal."

Luther thrust out his hand. "Shake on it, sweetie."

She rolled her eyes at the comment, as would just about anyone else in town who might have heard someone refer to Pamela as sweet. There was nothing sweet about her at all. However, she shook on it, and that gesture dispelled the interest of the crowd. They simply assumed that Luther's outburst must have been part of a heated negotiation for some item he was interested in purchasing.

"So, who was Hadley?" Luther continued.

"He was a local politician with the county government," Mitchell said. "He was kind of a jerk. Always trying to make a buck for himself without having to do any work."

"He was an unpleasant little troll of a man," Dixie added. "He wanted to start taxing all us vendors here at the market, supposedly for the benefit of the county. We all knew where that money would have gone. It would have gone straight into his filthy little pocket."

"How did he die?" Luther asked.

"Hadley got pushy," Mitchell said. "He brought that guy you were talking about, Isaac, here to the market and they roughed some people up."

Luther looked confused by this. "That doesn't sound like my friend."

"All I know is what I saw. Those two came here to the market and they roughed up the wrong people," Dixie said.

"What do you mean by the *wrong* people?" Luther asked.

"They beat up some of that bunch from the valley outside of town. Those are rough people and they don't take to being pushed around," Mitchell summarized. "Don't get me wrong here. Jim Powell is a blight on this community, but Hadley crossed a line when they shoved Jim's dad here at the market. He's an old man and well-respected in this community. You can't do that."

Luther took this all in. "What happened after that? Did these valley people you're talking about take revenge?"

"Just one, as far as I know," Pamela said. "Jim Powell came into town in broad daylight and hunted Hadley down. Shot him in his own bed. He never even denied it. Hell, I think he was proud of it."

Dixie nodded in agreement.

"What about Isaac?" Luther asked. "If Isaac was involved in roughing his family up, did this Jim Powell kill him too?"

Mitchell shook his head. "I never heard anything about that."

"Me neither," said Dixie. "Not even a rumor."

Pamela agreed. "Same here. I never even knew that big guy's name until you told us."

Luther sucked in a deep breath and let it out. He shifted his pack on his sweaty back while he thought about what these people had told him. They might not have been much help, but they'd given him something.

"Where do I find Jim Powell?"

24

Luther

By the time Luther grabbed a bite to eat at the market and made his way through town to find the old sewing factory, two hours had passed. The three old relics he'd talked to at the market told him that Jim Powell was renovating this building as part of some secret project he wouldn't tell anyone about. They'd been critical of it, assuming that anything Jim Powell was up to was suspect at best.

Part of Luther wanted to stomp into the building, find Jim Powell, and pound some answers out of him. Another part of him understood that this wasn't always the best way to get to the truth. He was going to deal with this like the Army had taught him. He was going to treat it as an operation and start by gathering intelligence.

At first, he walked by the old sewing factory like he didn't have a care in the world. He wanted to look like a local just out for a walk on a sunny day. He noticed a pile of discarded material near the loading dock, likely from whatever they were so loudly demolishing inside the building.

Just beyond the sewing factory he ran into a sign warning him that the road was a dead end. Luther slipped into the bushes at that point and crept deep into the brush. He startled a blacksnake and it returned the favor, startling him. Eventually he found a spot that gave him a good view of both the main entrance to the old brick building and of the loading dock where so much of the activity was occurring.

He slid out of his pack and leaned it against a tree. Then he sat down on the ground, leaned against his pack, and rested his rifle across his lap. He wasn't going to do anything at this point except observe.

He'd bought a couple of extra skewers of goat kebabs at the market and the smell of them was taunting him. He'd planned on saving them for dinner that night but decided he couldn't wait. He'd eat them now, then heat up one of the dehydrated backpacking meals Isaac had given him for dinner later. He removed the grease-stained newspaper from his pack, unfolded it, and savored the smell of the grilled goat meat resting inside.

He'd never had goat before today, but these kebabs were the best thing he'd had in weeks. He grabbed the wire skewer and was raising it to his mouth when he heard a branch snap in the woods behind him.

Luther had grown up in the country. He knew the woods were never silent in the way they were portrayed in movies. There were always squirrels and chipmunks shuffling around. Birds hopped in the leaves. Deer sometimes moved like ghosts in the forest, silent and stealthy, but at other times they were noisy and easy to spot.

There was a certain sound that a branch made when it broke beneath a foot. It was loud, a sign that it had come from a branch thicker than most wildlife could break. At the same time, the sound had a muffled quality that came from the twig being compressed between a boot and the soil. Luther knew beyond any shadow of a doubt that someone was coming up behind him.

He spun hard to his right, rolling flat onto his belly and sending skewers of goat flying in all directions. He stopped rolling in a prone shooting position, rifle raised to his eye. The red dot of his optic rested on the chest of a sheepish-looking man standing perhaps thirty feet behind him. The man had his hands in the air, a grubby NAPA cap cocked on his head.

There was a second man immediately behind the first. His hands were also raised, his mouth gawped open in terror. Luther noticed that he wore a filthy t-shirt advertising Newport cigarettes.

"Don't move," Luther whispered, just loud enough for the two men to hear. He didn't want to compromise his observation post. Too much yelling or too much shooting might bring someone from the sewing factory to investigate.

The man in the NAPA hat was gesturing with his upraised hands for Luther to calm down. "Easy there, buddy. We saw you coming into the woods and didn't know what you were up to. Wondered if you might be lost...or something."

"What's it to you?" Luther demanded.

The man in the NAPA hat smiled nervously. "Well, friend, these are *our* woods. My family's place. We kind of like to know what goes on here. We have traps out for rabbits and squirrels and we keep an eye on them. Surely you can understand that. I know times are hard, but a man has to look out for what's his, you know what I mean?"

"I didn't know I was trespassing," Luther said. "You guys back on out of here and I'll be on my way." His tone didn't leave any room for discussion.

"What you watching there?" the Newport man asked, pointing toward the factory.

"None of your damn business," Luther snapped.

Luther's reaction apparently made NAPA think they'd hit a nerve. He pushed a little harder. "You watching that fellow working on that building yonder?"

Luther hesitated to respond. As far as he knew, these guys might be friends with Jim Powell. He had no way of knowing.

"We don't care if you are," NAPA insisted. "We got no love for the man neither. He's kind of an asshole."

"What do you know about him?"

"Can I put my hands down?" NAPA asked.

"Go ahead but any sudden moves and I'll drop you," Luther warned.

NAPA lowered his hands. "All I know is that we kind of claimed that building for ourselves and then he shows up and takes it from us. It wasn't like we were using it but it just rubbed us the wrong way. Don't know who died and left him boss."

"Which one is Powell?" Luther asked.

"Always wearing a pistol," Newport said. "Got a vest on sometimes, one of them military ones with all the whatnots and doohickeys on it. Ain't never far from a rifle, neither."

"What's he doing down there? Why'd he take the building from you in the first place?"

"I forget what he said he was doing," NAPA said, looking off and scratching his head. "He's got a bunch of people working for him. Hauling in all kinds of shit in wagons. Must be a big deal."

"They living in that building?"

Newport and NAPA looked at each other.

"I don't think so," Newport finally said. "We're up and down this road at night. We've poked around there a bit and ain't seen nobody."

Luther wasn't an idiot. He knew what that comment meant coming from men like these. The two of them must have been down there prowling around at night looking for things to steal. The fact they'd not been shot or run off must mean there was no one guarding the place at night.

"What about a big man in black military-style clothes?" Luther asked. "Seen anyone like that?"

Again, NAPA and Newport looked at each as if they shared a common brain and had to split it between two mouths.

"Ain't see no one like that," NAPA said.

Luther turned the situation over in his head and an idea came to him. Unfortunately, it involved these two cretins, but it might give him a way to get his foot in the door. "You guys be up for checking the place out with me tonight? I'm pretty good at getting in locked buildings but it's easier when you got someone to watch your back."

"They got all kinds of tools in there," Newport mused.

NAPA grinned. "And a fortune in lumber."

Luther fought to hold back a smile. He'd figured these two out. The idea of getting into that building and stealing whatever they could get their hands on was tempting enough to make these two let down their guard. They'd appeared willing to go along with whatever he wanted to do, assuming that no men were thicker than thieves.

"Meet me down there near the loading dock about two hours after dark," Luther said. "Can you do that?"

"Reckon we can," NAPA said. "Are we free to go now?"

"Yeah, go head. Better rest up. Might be a long night."

Newport rubbed his hands together with glee. "Hot damn!"

25

Jim

GOING BY THE SUN, Jim estimated it was about 4 PM when he told his crew to knock off for the day. Without a network to sync to, the phone he was carrying for pictures and lists didn't have an accurate time anymore. He had business he needed to attend to at home and there was no sense in pushing the crew too hard. There was no rush.

"You got work for us tomorrow?" one of the men asked as the crew gathered around.

"Are all of you coming back?" Jim asked.

There were nods and agreements around the room, but that didn't necessarily mean they'd be back. Some of these men might wake up in the morning, sore and blistered, and decide it wasn't worth a free meal to bust their ass all day.

The one dissenting voice was Lloyd. "I ain't coming back. You're a slave driver and a foul human being."

"Ignore him. Any of you that show up tomorrow will be hired for another day," Jim announced. "You put in a solid day. I might even bring on a few more men since we'll have some unloading to do."

"Will I still be cooking?" P.J. asked.

Jim looked around the room. "Anyone die today?" When a head count revealed that everyone had survived, Jim gave P.J. a nod. "You're hired."

P.J. gave a fist pump.

The men helped Jim load the tools in the steel tool chest and padlock it shut. Jim used a short length of very thick chain to secure the tool chest to one of the steel support columns and used another padlock to secure that.

As much as he wanted an overnight guard on this place, it wasn't right to ask one of the Wolfords to come back over here after the long day they'd spent on the road. He'd also considered asking one of the new hires to spend the night for some additional compensation, but he didn't know any of them well enough at this point to make that offer. He didn't want to come back tomorrow to find the guard gone and the place cleaned out.

Leaving Lloyd behind to watch the place was a bad idea for obvious reasons. Left to his own devices, he'd be drunk as Cooter Brown in an hour and passed out by the time darkness fell. On the checklist of things that made for a good sentry, Lloyd failed on all counts. Jim would have to think on it that night and see what he could come up with.

After everyone filed out, Jim secured the building and pocketed the new keys. He had a duffel bag containing all the batteries he needed to recharge overnight, and he tied that onto his horse. He didn't need to take the massive cookpot home because the new cook had washed the kettle, then boiled water in it to sanitize it. Tomorrow he'd return with more food to fill it.

"I don't know why you're bitching about the hard work, Lloyd. You remember this was your idea right?"

"I still think it's a good idea. Especially the drinking, socializing, and playing music part. The part with all the working and sweating is bullshit."

They gathered their horses, tied on their gear, and rode off through town. They were both quiet, though Jim wasn't sure it was from exhaustion or because neither of them was anxious to break the peace of the afternoon.

There had been so many times that this ride on the fringes of the small town had been outright terrifying. Jim and the people riding with him had been scared. The people watching them from inside homes had been just as scared. Everyone had been uncertain about what the future held for them and it made them rightfully distrustful of their fellow man.

It felt different now and Jim had to attribute some of that to the farmer's market. The event had served as an unlikely icebreaker. It had taken some time, but people were becoming accustomed to being around one another again. They were learning that it was okay to be friendly, to laugh, and to engage in conversation with people. They still had to be cautious, and carrying a weapon was always a good idea, but this was a step toward whatever the new normal was. The entire country had been clenched like a fist for the past year and now it was finally starting to relax its grip.

The ride home along the river was just as peaceful as the ride out of town and the old friends talked some as they rode.

"Care for some tonic?" Lloyd asked.

"Tonic?"

Lloyd removed a flask from his pack and held it up for Jim to see.

"Oh, you mean liquor."

Lloyd uncapped it and took a pull. When he was done, he wiped his mouth with a filthy forearm and handed the flask over to Jim. "We might call it liquor now, but there was a day when men sold it as a tonic or patent medicine. I'm a mere banjo player. Who am I to question those men of science who saw fit to label it as a medicine? Sure as hell feels medicinal to me. Good for what ails you."

Jim took a sip. It was the clear stuff, not the sweeter sugar shine, and it burned all the way down. "I don't know about medicine, but it's definitely a preservative. It *preserves* my sanity when I have to spend the whole day with you."

"You're the one that's hard to work around," Lloyd argued. "A little of the nerve tonic is all that keeps me steady. Never know from one minute to the next if you're going to go berserk and start killing people. Some poor son-of-a-bitch might cut a board too short and that's all she wrote for him. He'll go down in a hail of bullets."

Jim ignored the comment until he noticed Lloyd laughing hysterically and doing his best to muffle it. "What? You having some kind of fit over there?"

When he regained his senses, Lloyd shook his head, tears rolling from his eyes. "I'm just remembering the look on your face when the whores told you they weren't moving into the roadhouse because they were concerned about their reputation. That was priceless. I can't wait to tell Randi about it."

Jim knew he was in for it. Whatever Lloyd had given him, she'd be worse. Five times worse. Ten times worse. Lloyd was like a hammer as far as humor and insults went. Randi was more like a samurai sword. She could cut you to the bone with the slightest effort or, if she felt like it, she could lop you in a half with a single blow.

"I can't wait," Jim replied.

They passed Buddy's old house, the one where Pete and Charlie had been living. Lloyd stayed with them some days, but others he'd been staying with Randi. Lloyd didn't turn up that driveway though and Jim knew exactly what he was up to. He was going to follow Jim home so he could tell everyone about the girls from the brothel. He obviously understood that Jim might be reluctant to bring it up on his own. He needed prodding and Lloyd intended to be that prod.

At Jim's house, they found Pops, Charlie, and Pete cooling off on the porch. They'd had a long day of catching up on some projects that had fallen behind in all the recent activity. They'd done some routine maintenance on the spring, the spring box, and the gravity-fed water system. They'd also cut weeds and spent some time on the never-ending task of processing firewood for the coming winter.

Pete and Charlie volunteered to deal with Jim and Lloyds' horses, leading them off to the barn. The two took a seat in the shade and talked to Pops about their day. Pete and Charlie returned a few minutes later.

"I'm headed to Randi's house for a little while," Charlie announced. "You going, Lloyd?"

Lloyd looked disappointed. "Might as well. Nothing entertaining happening around here. Yet."

Jim cut him a look. "Good riddance."

"Besides, I've got a good story to tell Randi," Lloyd said with a grin. He followed Charlie around the corner of the house, heading for the path that connected to the two homes.

"What's Lloyd going on about?" Pete asked.

Jim shrugged. "Who knows? I think all that moonshine has affected his brain."

26

Jim

THE SUN WAS DOWN and the world was easing into the gloaming when the clatter of heavy hooves echoed through the valley. It reached Jim's ears a moment before the rattle of the diesel tractor engine.

"They're back," Jim announced.

This time of year, with the trees fully leafed-out, Jim could only glimpse one small section of road from his porch. A minute later, the first of the wagons entered that brief stretch of road. Jim couldn't help but grin at the sight of it. Even at this distance it was easy to see that the wagons were loaded down with cargo.

A short time later, the caravan turned down Jim's driveway and headed for the house. He got up from the porch and went to meet them. As they rolled up toward the barn, he could see pieces of brewing equipment that he recognized from the burned-out build-ing. Two of the wagons held loads covered with blue tarps and strapped down securely with ratchet straps. The tractor was pulling a hay wagon with two of the large beer vats strapped to it. Jim couldn't even speculate on how they got those loaded, other than some redneck engineering and a lot of brute force.

Will rode at the head of the line, steering his horse in Jim's direction.

"Where's Hugh?" Jim demanded, worried that he didn't see his old friend among the riders.

"He's at the brewery," Will replied. "That Ed guy was a little leery about us taking off with all his stuff. He wanted to come with us so he could see where we were taking it, but he was afraid of leaving his building empty for the night. Hugh volunteered to stay there with him as a guarantee that we'd be back tomorrow."

"Hugh as collateral. That's good, I guess."

"Yeah, Hugh said he'd try to get some more stuff taken apart and packed for tomorrow. Hopefully he'll have a load ready for us when we get there. Anyway, I'm going to get on home. I'm sure my wife is waiting."

Shade rolled up next, reining his team to a stop and setting the brake on his wagon. Like Will, Shade had soot stains on his clothes, arms, and face.

"Now that was a day," Shade said. "I think hauling logs might have been easier."

"Sorry about that," said Jim.

"Ain't nothing to apologize for. I thank the good Lord every day I'm able to work."

"We didn't know if you'd make it in tonight or not," Jim said. "We made a big pot of soup just in case. That way it'd be ready whenever you all got here. You want to eat now?"

Shade shook his head. "These horses had a long, hard day. We deal with them first."

Jim was ready to jump in and help, but there really wasn't much for him to do. The Wolfords were so accustomed to taking care of their own animals that they fell into the routine without exchanging a word. In less than thirty minutes, all the massive animals had been brushed and turned out into the field to eat, drink, and roll to their heart's content.

It was nearly dark when the horses were taken care of. Light and color drained from the day. Jim had retreated to the backyard where he built a fire in the firepit. Ellen hauled the pot of soup to an outdoor table, along with several loaves of homemade bread. There was a tub of butter to go with it, but it was made from freeze-dried powder and not churned with love by a little old lady.

By the time everything was ready, the Wolford clan began filing around the corner of the house. Jim directed them toward the table and watched while they filled their bowls. They were polite, but mostly talked among themselves. Shade was the only gregarious one in the bunch. Some of the men in the group were his brothers and uncles, but he was clearly the patriarch of the clan, the scarred and menacing leader of their tribe.

Shade took a seat beside Jim at the firepit. Jim knew the man had to be starving so he tried to not badger him with a lot of questions. Those unasked questions hung in the air and Shade apparently sensed them, responding without prompt once he had some food to sate his gnawing hunger.

"Long damn day," he mused. "That Ed fellow had a lot of it ready to go. Kind of surprised he did. You must have been really convincing. Takes a lot to trust some stranger who shows up out of nowhere with a bunch of promises."

Jim nodded. "Yeah, he agreed to my deal, but I wondered if he'd follow through with it once he had more time to think about it."

"He did," Shade said. "He had a lot of it taken apart and stacked. We loaded what we could. Those big old brewing tanks were the worst of it."

"How'd you get them out?"

"Tipped them over and put rollers under them. We used fenceposts."

"How many more trips do you think?" Jim asked.

"I'm betting all of four days. We'll leave the tractor at the sewing factory tomorrow after we unload tomorrow. Don't want to burn up all our fuel. We needed it today, though. Those tanks were heavy."

"Sounds good. Your people holding up okay?"

Shade grinned. "We all grew up working every single day. We worked on Sundays and on Christmas. Wolfords don't take holidays."

"Where did that work ethic come from?" Jim asked. "Any idea?"

"Goes back generations. Even my granddaddy said he was raised that way. I used to think it was about getting ahead, about bringing in enough money to own the dirt under your feet and live the way you wanted. As I've gotten older, I've begun to think there was a little more to it than that."

"Like what?"

Shade looked Jim in the eye. "I'll be the first to tell you that I come from some mean-ass people. Every one of us liked to fight. I'm not talking about just kicking a man's ass. I'm talking about fighting until the person you're fighting is either dead or will hurt every remaining day of their life. It's a dark thread that runs all the way back through our line. I've heard stories from the old people and I've seen it in myself. I think somewhere along the line, one of my ancestors figured out the only way to keep a Wolford out of trouble with the law was to work us so hard that we didn't have the time or energy to get in trouble."

"That's an interesting thought," Jim replied. "Does it work?"

"Most of the time. The school years are the worst time. None of us ever liked school, except that it was break from being worked like a two-dollar mule. We all stayed in trouble when we were in school."

"Even the girls?" Jim asked.

Shade laughed. "Especially the girls. Hell, they were the worst. If one of my sisters was to go walking down the hallway at school, the crowds would part like the Red Sea, everyone trying to stay out of their way. If two of my sisters was to walk down the hall together, people would flat out run to stay away from them. They'd fight anybody. I saw one of my sisters knock a boy out with one punch in the cafeteria one time."

"What for?"

"She got in front of him and he said something to her about it. That was all it took."

Jim laughed. He'd gone to school with a few girls like that.

"It's true," Shade said. "First day of school, every teacher in the building would scan her list of students for the Wolford name, praying they wouldn't find it."

"But coming from *hard* people doesn't make you *bad* people," Jim said. "I've spent a lot of time thinking about that. My grandfather was that way. Killed a lot of men in his day and never spent a day in jail for it. He lived in West Virginia when it was a rough, lawless place. That's why my mom ended up down here. She didn't want to raise kids around all that feuding, fighting, and killing."

"I'd have to agree with you there," Shade said. "Like all families, we've had a few bad apples, but we'd do anything in the world for people we like. We're good friends to have but the people who cross us spend a lot of sleepless nights worrying about the moment we catch up with them."

"I thought that being raised outside of that West Virginia part of the family made us soft," Jim said. "I thought my mom got what she wanted. She'd broken the cycle. I've had a lot of time to think about things over the past year, and I've realized that things like that are in your blood. You might think you've left them behind, but those instincts are in there."

"How'd you come to figure that out?" Shade asked. "If you don't mind me asking."

"I killed my first man on the very first day of the collapse. I was stuck in Richmond and we were trying to get home. A man wanted to steal our car since we had gas. He was swinging a lug wrench at my friend and I shot him without a moment of hesitation. Killing that first man kind of knocked me for a loop. It's a big step and it changes you in some ways. I've lost track of how many men I've killed since. Some I killed because they were trying to kill me, but others I killed because it was a bad idea to leave them alive. Every day I realize I'm more like my grandfather than I ever thought."

"What's your mom think of that?" Shade asked. "She ever mention it?"

"I don't know if she's made that connection or not. Every day is a struggle for her. She can't believe the world has come to this. I think she goes to sleep every night thinking she'll wake up to find out it was only some bad dream."

"It is a bad dream," Shade agreed. "But there ain't no waking up from it. Some of us are just better equipped for living in a nightmare than others, though I'm not sure what that says about us."

"Me neither," Jim agreed.

27

Luther

AFTER THE SEWING factory crew left for the day, Luther found a cool spot in the woods, stretched out, and took a nap. He woke as the sun was setting and prepared one of the MREs Isaac had given him for dinner. As he ate the mediocre meal, he thought longingly of the skewers of meat he'd lost when the two unexpected guests tried to sneak up on him in the woods.

When the sun had been down long enough for the sky to turn from blue to black, Luther used a red-lensed flashlight to navigate his way to the sewing factory. There, he turned off the flashlight, sat on the crumbling sidewalk, and waited to see whether the other men would show. He didn't have to wait long. A short time later he saw a light bobbing up the road. When they got a little closer, he saw the glowing cherries of cigarettes at head level.

Luther turned his red light on when the men got closer and flagged them down. They were startled at first but recognized him when he spoke, joining him in the parking lot.

The one in the NAPA hat dropped the stub of his smoke into the gravel and ground it beneath the toe of a cowboy boot. "Wasn't sure if you'd be here or not."

"I wondered the same about you two," Luther replied. "But here we are."

"Then let's get on with it," Newport said. "I'm anxious to see what they might have left for us."

They used Luther's red light to navigate their way to the back door. Luther held the small flashlight in his mouth while he retrieved a thin pouch of lock picks from his pack. He unsnapped the pouch, removing his favorite pick and a tension wrench.

"Where'd you learn to do that?" NAPA asked. "That would be a handy skill for a fellow to have."

"The Army," Luther lied.

He always told people he'd picked up the skill in the Army, but in truth it was something he'd taught himself. He'd bought the picks off the internet and watched YouTube videos to the point he could pick his way through most of the common locks. One thing that worked to his advantage was that most people were cheap and bought the least expensive locks they could find. Those were the easiest to pick. The new lock on the back of the sewing factory was commercial grade but not high security hardware. High security was too expensive and most places didn't even keep them in stock.

Luther inserted the tension wrench into the keyway and rested a finger against it to apply the lightest of pressure. He used the pick to rake the pins and get a feel for them, then tested each pin individually with the tip of the pick. Once he had an idea of how stiff the springs and pins were, he began lifting them and trying to find that elusive shear line that would allow the lock to open.

"They do it faster in the movies," Newport observed. "Maybe you need more practice."

Luther stopped his work, sighed loudly, then got back to it. He was going to glare at Newport but saw no point when the man couldn't see his face clearly. "Movies are fake. Haven't you figured that out yet?"

"Just saying," said Newport.

Luther tried to ignore the presence of the two men behind him and focus on his work. Once he got a feel for the lock, he got one pin, then quickly figured out the rest. It was a sweet feeling when the tension wrench yielded, twisting the keyway and unlocking the door. "There we go."

"Good job," NAPA said, his tone revealing he'd been just as impatient as Newport.

Luther tugged the door open and held it with his body while the other two men went inside. He stowed his lockpicks, then grabbed his pack and followed them inside. Both NAPA and Newport had flashlights, playing them over the stacks of materials and the heavy steel toolbox.

"Bet all the good shit is in there," Newport said. "Think we can bust it open?"

NAPA looked doubtful. "I haven't had much luck with them before. Those boxes are made to keep people like us out."

"There's a lot of building materials in here," Luther said. "Some of it might be handy. I see some wire too."

"Reckon I could use that big soup pot," NAPA said, pointing to the kettle in which the crew had prepared lunch.

Although Luther opened the loading dock door trying to be quiet, there was no way to quietly open a door like that. "Let's pile anything we want to take in the doorway. Then we can grab it on the way out."

NAPA hauled the big kettle to the door and set it down with a clang.

"Could you be a little louder?" Newport asked. "Not sure everyone in town heard you yet."

Luther stood by, playing his flashlight around the building.

NAPA noticed that Luther wasn't hauling anything over to the door. "Is there anything in here you want?"

"Just you two," Luther said. He drew his pistol and put a 9mm round center mass of NAPA's body.

NAPA grunted and sprawled over backward. Luther twisted and brought his handgun to bear on Newport. Newport was desperately trying to yank his own handgun from his pocket, but it was a revolver and the hammer was snagged inside the pocket. Luther put two rounds in him, then turned back to NAPA.

NAPA had rolled over onto his stomach and was dragging himself across the oily concrete floor. He groaned from pain and exertion. There was a wet whistling sound that Luther attributed to a lung shot. He raised his handgun and aimed for the back of NAPA's head. When he fired, the shot instantly dropped NAPA face-first onto the concrete floor.

Luther grimaced and tugged on an earlobe. The loud gunshots in the old factory had temporarily deafened him. If someone heard the shots and came to investigate, Luther might not even notice them if they didn't tap on his shoulder and introduce themselves.

He sucked in a deep breath and took a moment to get himself together. When his nerves had calmed, he set about preparing the scene. When he was done, he returned to the curb where he'd waited on the two men earlier. He checked his watch and confirmed he had several hours before morning. He laid down on the sidewalk and propped his head on his pack. If he'd learned anything in the military, it was how to sleep anywhere.

28

Jim

EVERYONE AT JIM'S place was up early the next day. Jim and his family prepared another large breakfast to feed the army staying at their home. When they were done, Jim loaded up more freeze-dried mixes for a midday soup. Pete and Charlie ate at Jim's house, but Lloyd had spent the night at Randi's and was slow to get moving. The whole gang was waiting at Jim's gate when he arrived there to open it for the wagons.

Jim could immediately tell from the look on Randi's face that she'd been waiting for this moment. She was squirming with anticipation. "Go ahead, Randi. Give it to me," he said. "I can tell you're chomping at the bit."

"I just think it's pretty damn funny that you came to my house and asked me to help run the business end of the brothel when you opened the roadhouse. Then it turns out the whores don't want anything to do with you. This just confirms what I've tried to tell you all along, Jim Powell. You're trouble! You're bad news! What does it say about a man that his reputation is bad enough to sully that of a whole whorehouse full of sex workers?"

Jim whistled and tried to block her out of his head as he held the gate, letting the massive horses ride through with their wagons.

Not to be outdone by the clatter of their hooves and their snorting exhalations, Randi raised her voice. "I know your mother didn't like this idea to begin with, but did you tell her that it was the whores who backed out?"

Pete and Charlie were not morning people. They'd been going through the motions of getting ready and getting on the road, but it was out of sheer habit. They were barely awake. At some point, the content of this conversation began to break through the fog of their sluggishness and the two looked at each other with surprise.

"There's not going to be a brothel at the roadhouse?" Pete asked.

Randi shook her head, her smile beaming. "No, Pete, there's not. Did you hear why? The prostitutes are worried about ruining their reputation by partnering up with Jim Powell. I'm not trying to be rude because I know you love your dad, but this is too good for me to pass up." She cackled hysterically.

Jim met his son's eye and caught the confused look there. "You know what the people in town think of me, Pete. It worked out for the best, though. Now Nana won't disown me."

"Have you told her yet?" Pete asked.

Jim shook his head. "I told her that I changed my mind about the brothel, but I didn't tell her this latest development. Not ready to get into it."

"You want me to tell her?" Randi asked.

Jim went wide-eyed with horror at the thought of it. "Absolutely not, Randi. That's the last thing I want."

She looked away. "I'll think on it."

Jim gave her a nasty look, mounted his horse, and headed off after the wagons. Lloyd couldn't wipe the grin off his face. He was enjoying it just as much as Randi was.

Randi continued to badger Jim throughout the ride to town and he let her have her fun. While she jabbered, his mind turned over the project ahead of him. As usual, the group split in town. Lloyd, Charlie, and Pete headed for the sewing factory with Jim and the wagons while everyone else returned to the farmers market.

When Jim came within sight of the sewing factory, he could immediately tell something was wrong. Instead of the orderly line of potential workers that he found the previous day, there were probably fifty people standing around the loading dock area.

"What the hell is the building doing open?" Jim said.

"We locked it," Lloyd said. "I was right there with you."

Jim kicked his horse into a trot and shot down the road. The men parted as he rode up to the loading dock. The dock door was raised about halfway and Jim could see two bodies in the shaded interior. After staring at them for a moment, he looked at the men gathered around him and spoke through gritted teeth. "Anyone know what happened here?"

He scanned the crowd. Most of the people were shaking their heads or mumbling that they had no idea. Then Jim spotted a man leaning against the loading dock. He had a large backpack at his feet with a rifle laying against it. Jim studied him for a moment, not recognizing him from yesterday. In the sea of shaking heads, he was nodding.

"You have anything to do with this?" Jim asked.

"Yeah," the man replied.

"You want to explain it to me?"

"I heard you were hiring people, but that you were only taking so many each day. I live outside of town, so I decided to spend the night here. I wanted to make sure I was here when you were doing the picking. I was sacked out in the grass around front and got woke up in the middle of the night by these guys banging around inside. I assumed they belonged here, that they worked for you or something. I was going to ask them about my chances of hiring on, but they flipped out when I went in and spoke to them. One of them pulled a gun and the rest was kind of a blur."

Jim climbed off his horse and handed the reins over to Pete. He hopped up on the loading dock and went inside to check out the bodies. They were face down in wide pools of coagulating blood but Jim didn't have to roll over the bodies to identify them. The displaced cap laying on the concrete floor told the story. It advertised NAPA Auto Parts. Jim was pretty sure that rolling over the second body would reveal a Newport cigarettes t-shirt. It was the two idiots from down the street.

Jim walked back to the dock door and regarded the man who shot the intruders. "What's your name?"

"Luther."

"Where'd you learn to fight with a gun, Luther?"

"The Army."

Jim looked at the items piled by the door. It was a pretty sorry pile of loot to lose your life over, but apparently the two thieves couldn't help themselves. If they'd waited a little longer, they might have been able to steal better stuff. Jim doubted, however, that anyone had ever accused NAPA and Newport of being smart.

Turning his attention back to Luther, Jim said, "Reckon hiring you is the least I can do after you killed two burglars for me."

Luther smiled and nodded in satisfaction. "I'd appreciate the work."

With that business dealt with, Jim addressed the group. "We've got a lot to do this morning and we need to get at it. I need everyone who worked for me yesterday to come on inside."

He did a quick count of how many he had versus how many he needed. He took on a few more men, then sent the rest home with the same speech he'd given yesterday. Once they were gone, he spoke to the crew. "Let's get these bodies out of the way, then get some buckets of water and rinse down the floor. We need to get these wagons unloaded so I can get my haulers on the road."

"You going to deliver these bodies back to their people?" Shade asked.

Jim shook his head. "It's the noble thing to do but it never works out right. It's a good way to get killed by someone wanting vengeance. Reckon we'll just stick them in a shallow hole and be done with it, unless anyone feels determined to reunite them with their kin."

Not a single hand went up.

"That's what I thought," said Jim. "Now let's get moving."

29

Hugh

HUGH DIDN'T SLEEP WELL in the burned-out brewery. For the last year or so he'd been living in the valley with Jim, sleeping in the quiet mountain valley with the customary sounds of rural Appalachia. There were roosters, dogs, and the cawing of crows. Occasionally there was a gunshot. At night, the calls of owls, nightingales, and whip-poor-wills lulled them into a sleep that only the occasional coyote would disturb.

The small town of St. Paul had been made even smaller by the die-off that had taken place over the last year, but it still felt like town to Hugh. Even though it was a quiet and non-threatening environment, he felt the pressure of civilization closing in around him. Just being among those buildings and paved streets felt artificial and unpleasant.

Despite his disdain for being in a town, Hugh hadn't minded staying behind to help Ed with the brewery. He was a nice-enough guy and Hugh firmly believed that Jim's idea of using a roadhouse for intelligence-gathering was a solid plan. He and Ed had plenty of work to do in breaking down the equipment and that had provided distraction until late in the night.

After they were done working, it had taken Hugh a while to settle in. Unlike Ed, he couldn't fall asleep in the partially burned-out building. It was structurally sound, but the smell of damp ash was unpleasant. Eventually Hugh wandered outside and stretched out on top of one of the steel shipping containers stored behind the brewery. While the sounds of the new locale were unfamiliar to him, he eventually found sleep there under the open stars.

When the changing light awakened him, he moved to the sidewalk outside the brewery. He was going to prepare instant coffee on his backpacking stove when he caught the aroma of what smelled like real coffee coming from inside the brewery. Following his nose, he found Ed boiling coffee on the propane range.

"I figured you for a coffee drinker," Ed said.

"You figured right," Hugh replied. "I didn't realize you still had propane."

"I've been rationing it, but it's about gone." When it was the right color, Ed strained the coffee through the basket of an old coffee maker. The filter lining the basket was perhaps the only item in the entire building that wasn't blackened with soot. When Ed had two full mugs, he handed one to Hugh and they stepped outside to drink them on the sidewalk.

Ed leaned back against the building and rested his cup on his thigh. "You know, this is all happening kind of fast. I had a moment of panic last night where it hit me that I'm putting my entire future in the hands of someone I don't even know. I spent years dreaming of opening this place, only to see it destroyed by a terror attack. Then Jim Powell comes out of nowhere, hangs out with me for a few minutes, and I totally uproot my life for the opportunity to bring this brewery back to life."

Hugh nodded as he listened, rolling the first cigarette of the day in his lap. He tried to read between the lines of Ed's words, assuming there was a question in there somewhere. When Ed finally paused,

Hugh put that question into words. "Are you wondering if he's full of shit or not?"

Ed laughed. "Basically, I guess. I'm wondering if I'm going to all this trouble for nothing."

"I've known Jim a long time. When we met, he was in high school and I'd just started college. Everything was different then. I've learned a lot more about him in the past year than I ever knew back in the day. In my opinion, he's a solid guy who's trying to do the right thing for his friends and family. He struggles but he's open about it. Part of him wants to tell everyone to go to hell and leave him alone, but he tried that and it didn't work. He seems finally to have come to the conclusion that the only way to keep everyone safe is to maintain a presence in the town and monitor what's going on there. This roadhouse is his way of doing that."

Ed took a sip of his coffee as he considered Hugh's words. "I guess all I really care about at this point is being able to make beer, having enough food to eat, and having a place I can lay my head at night."

"I'm pretty sure all those things are possible," Hugh said. "Besides, you can't bank on what things *used* to be like. We don't know what the new normal is going to look like for America. How are we going to move forward since the time for rescue has come and gone? It's never been clearer that it's up to the average American to take care of themselves. The government either isn't able or isn't willing to save them. Some people are more ready to accept that than others. You can see a shift now. They're starting to get it."

"I've spent most of the last year feeling sorry for myself." Ed stared down at the steam rising from his coffee. "Despite the uncertainty of moving my operation, I have to admit that this is the most excited I've been in some time. I'm feeling hope again."

"Jim has a way of motivating people. Sometimes it's by involving you in an exciting project. Other times it's by pointing out that you're a pathetic loser who's going to die in a puddle of your own fluids if you don't get off your ass and do something to save yourself. Both methods can work."

"Glad he used the first method on me," Ed mused.

After they finished their coffee, the two men finished breaking down the last of the equipment inside the brewery. Hugh and Ed stacked everything they could carry on the sidewalk in front of the brewery, then Ed began gathering items from the restaurant that he thought might be useful in Jim's roadhouse project. He still had silverware, glasses, pitchers, plates, and other supplies that hadn't been damaged from the fire.

"You think we can get all this in one load?" Hugh asked.

"Maybe what we have in the store, but not everything in the containers. I'm sure there's going to be at least one more load."

Hugh was a pretty stoic guy but even he was beginning to get excited about the roadhouse. It wasn't just the idea of a cold beer that appealed to him. It would be nice to have a distraction and maybe see people laughing again.

30

Jim

"How was your first day on the job?" Jim asked, checking in on Luther toward the end of the day.

Luther had been assigned to the crew building the outhouse and they'd made significant progress. A six-foot-deep trench had been dug and the walls shored with treated plywood to keep the sides from caving in. The bottom would remain bare soil to allow liquids to drain into the ground over time.

"Not bad," Luther said. "It's nice having something to keep me occupied all day. My biggest problem with the past year has been boredom."

"That puts you in a very special group," Jim replied. "For a lot of folks, the struggles have been around starvation, disease, staying warm, and not getting murdered."

"Fortunately, I survived all those things." Luther shrugged. "Somehow."

Luther had been the cut-man, sawing boards to length when measurements were shouted out to him. They'd been using a battery-powered circular saw to cut the plywood but a cross-cut hand saw on the dimensional lumber to save battery life.

"You interested in coming back tomorrow?" Jim asked.

"Definitely."

"You have a place to stay?"

Luther shook his head. "No, and it took me about six hours to walk here. Not exactly a manageable commute. I figured I'd camp out somewhere."

"Would you be interested in staying here at the jobsite overnight?"

"What would I have to do?"

"Well, I'm mostly trying to prevent more of what happened last night," Jim said. "You did a pretty good job of handling that. I can't pay you any more, but it will be a free roof over your head in exchange for keeping an eye on the place."

Luther agreed immediately. "I'll take it."

"Good. Tomorrow, I'm going to have you guys build the floor over the outhouse trench and then we'll position the stalls."

"Are we going to enclose the whole thing?" Luther asked. "Put a roof overhead and all that?"

"I was going to," Jim said. "But today I went wandering around the sewage plant looking for parts and I found they had some of those portable toilets sitting out back."

"Jobsite Johnnies?"

"Exactly. They're clean and unused. I figured we could cut holes in the bottom and drain them into the trench. It's faster than anything we can build. They'll be weathertight and easy to clean."

"That's a good plan."

Jim was preparing to go into more of his plans for the next day, but not particularly because Luther needed to keep abreast of them. It was more out of Jim's need to think and process out loud when he was chest-deep in a project. However, that train of thought was interrupted by the arrival of Shade's tractor.

While Shade had decided they didn't have enough fuel to take the tractor to the brewery today, Jim had convinced Shade to let the tractor and driver stick around the sewing factory to do some local hauls. The driver, Nooner, seemed like a decent guy and a hard worker. Before the collapse he worked for Shade or any of the neighboring farmers who needed help cutting hay, fencing, or herding cattle. About the time everyone else was digging into their coolers for lunch, Nooner would be pulling out his first tall-boy beer of the day.

Jim had put Pete, Charlie, and Lloyd with Nooner and they'd been running loads from the phone company offices the entire day. Using a pair of bolt cutters to gain entry, they'd liberated a few dozen empty cable reels from the fenced lot behind the phone company building. These were large reels and they'd make excellent tables for the roadhouse.

Using the cable reels would save them time. It was one less thing to build. Jim also had a line on some chairs, but he wasn't going to mention his source to anyone outside of the people he sent to retrieve them. He'd already faced some complaints about using the sewing factory and "borrowing" the cable reels.

Jim went to the loading dock and waited while Nooner backed the trailer up to the dock. This was their third and final load of cable reels. The rest were already lined up in a neat row in the sewing factory. Jim and some of the crew rolled the heavy reels off the trailer and stored them with the others.

"Any trouble?" Jim asked.

Pete shook his head. "Not a bit. Just people gawking at us as we passed through town, trying to figure out what was going on."

"Your daddy is used to that," Lloyd offered. "He worries people, so they like to keep an eye on him. I'm the same way around him."

Pete looked offended and Jim caught a flash of anger in his eyes. For a moment he thought Pete was going to pounce on Lloyd and take him to the ground. Pete had grown enough in the past year that he was nearly the same size as Lloyd.

Lloyd must have caught the look too because he held up his hands and smiled. "Easy there, Pete. I'm just teasing your dad. He does the same with me."

That flash of loyalty made Jim proud of his son. It was an

acknowledgement that even when he felt like he'd screwed up so many things in the world, he was raising good kids. They were better people than him.

"What have you got in mind for us tomorrow, Chief?" Nooner asked.

"Chairs," Jim said in a low voice.

"You're going to need a shitload of them, all these tables you got," said Nooner.

"I know where to get a shitload of them," Jim replied. "And I'm going to have you all pick them up first thing in the morning, before everyone in town is out moving around. I'll catch some grief if people figure out where I borrowed them from, so I'm going to keep it quiet. I'd appreciate if you could do the same thing."

"You're asking us to lie for you?" Lloyd demanded, acting as if that crossed a moral boundary for him.

Jim frowned. "Half the time, Lloyd, you lie for no reason at all. Don't act like it's straining your morality. Don't forget this roadhouse was *your* idea. Would you rather be running the construction?"

Lloyd sighed. "No, I'm not interested in switching roles with you. Being the boss requires too much sobriety. Me and my new buddy, Nooner, aren't fond of things that require sobriety, are we?"

Nooner shook his head. "Not a damn bit."

Jim studied Nooner and Lloyd. From their instant camaraderie and enthusiasm, Jim expected they'd bonded over sips from one of Lloyd's jars over the course of the day. Jim had known many men like Nooner over the years, men who'd never worked a sober day in their lives.

At the mental health facility where he'd once worked, he'd often met men like that in the detox facility. They were usually in their fifties, missing teeth, and reaching the stage of life where the non-stop party was being impinged upon by the appearance of alcohol-related health conditions. Brain damage, liver failure, pancreatic disorders, and a host of others showed up to rain on their parade.

Suddenly sober, many had no idea where the last forty years of their lives had gone. They'd missed entire marriages and children;

the deaths of their parents; the destruction of nearly every relationship they'd ever had; and the loss of jobs they couldn't even remember having taken.

"What do you need us to do next?" Charlie asked.

The question made Jim smile. Pete and Charlie were anxious to help. Judging by the look on Lloyd's face, however, he was hoping they were done for the day. He and Nooner were probably anxious to find a porch they could perch on with a banjo and a fresh jar of liquor.

"Charlie, you and Pete stay with me. Lloyd, you and Nooner are free for the rest of the day. I'm sure you'll find some way to occupy yourselves."

"Damn right," Lloyd said. "I have a banjo and a Mason jar with my name on them. If you all don't mind bringing my horse home with you, I'll just ride with my buddy Nooner."

"Go on then," Jim said.

Jim gathered the rest of his crew together and addressed them on the loading dock after Lloyd and Nooner had gone. "We're making good progress. You all have been doing a good job and I appreciate the help. I need to remind you of something for tomorrow. We're running low on the foam cups we've been using to serve soup at lunch. Tomorrow, you need to bring your own cup and spoon with you. We might have a few left but we're going to run out soon."

There were nods around the room. It was a small request and easy enough to accommodate.

"Tomorrow," he continued, "we're going to start wiring in some small lights and we might be able to finish the outhouses. As soon as we get the brewer here, we can start setting up some of his equipment. There's plenty of work to be done."

Jim was taking a breath to say something else when his radio chirped. He'd been using it for communicating on the jobsite since most of his people were too far away to reach him by radio.

Lloyd's voice came across the speaker. *"Hey, don't send everyone home yet. We just passed your wagons on the road. They'll be there in a few minutes."*

"Copy that," Jim said. "Thanks for the heads-up."

"Sorry we aren't there to help."

"Lying bastard," Jim replied. He replaced the radio in its pouch, then addressed his crew. "Guess you heard that. We'll unload these trailers and then everyone can head home for the day."

The trailer loads were heavy. Besides the brewing equipment there were sacks of the various ingredients required for making beer, the restaurant supplies Ed had brought, and some of the pieces of distilling gear from the shipping containers. Jim was in awe of just how much they'd managed to fit onto the trailers. Despite the size of the team they had unloading the trailers, it took nearly an hour to get everything situated inside the building.

Hugh had returned with the convoy. Ed Frye was with him, riding on one of the wagons. Jim introduced Ed to Pete and Charlie, then to the rest of the crew. Finally, he introduced him to Luther.

"I guess you two will be roommates for the next little bit," Jim said. "Luther will be sticking around until the construction is done."

Ed stared into the vast, dark factory with a backpack on his back and a suitcase in each hand. "Is it all like this?" It was obvious from the tone of his voice that these accommodations weren't much better than the burned out building he'd just left.

"No, there's offices at the other end," Jim said. "I suggest you pick one and start making it your own, since you'll be here a while. There are some spare locks in the building materials. If you want, go ahead and put one on your room so you can lock your gear up. Is this all you have?"

Ed shook his head. "No, there's more in the stuff we unloaded. I'll dig it out tonight."

"I can help you with that," Luther said. "There's not much else for me to do around here."

"I'd appreciate that," Ed said.

"Not to change the subject, but is that dried blood?" Hugh asked, pointing to a spot on the floor.

"Yeah," Jim replied. "I'll tell you about that on the way home."

"One day," Hugh lectured, shaking his head. "I was gone for *one* day."

Pete and Charlie cackled.

Jim dug into his pack and removed a few spare MREs he'd tucked in there. He handed them to Ed and Luther. "It's not much, but it's food."

Luther held the pack up and nodded in appreciation. "Thanks. Beats what I had last night."

"What was that?" Charlie asked.

"Nothing at all," Luther admitted.

31

Luther

AFTER JIM and his crew headed out for the evening, Ed and Luther were left alone on the loading dock. Luther rolled the door down and locked it for the night. Jim had suggested they keep the visible entrances closed so no one walking by would be tempted to venture inside. Ed and Luther were obviously welcome to go out as much as they wanted, but Jim just didn't want the building to look as if it invited theft.

"So how do you know Jim?" Ed asked.

Luther shrugged, wondering for a moment just how much detail he was going to go into. In the end, he decided to keep it simple. "Just met him this morning. I'd heard there was work in town. Even though it only pays in food, that's a good deal for me. My cupboard was getting pretty bare."

The two of them went out back, took seats on the concrete steps that led from the building, and tore into their MREs. Both were too hungry to wait.

"I had plenty to eat, but I was slipping into a dark place," Ed said.

"How did you have plenty to eat?"

"My brewery had a restaurant. I had these cases of spaghetti noodles and rice that I bought for specials. They store well and they're cheap, so I bought them in bulk whenever my supplier had them on sale. As a result, I've had a cup of rice or pasta for every meal for the last year. It kept my belly full but I'm sick of them both."

"You eat them plain?" Luther asked, tearing into a slice of MRE bread.

Ed tore into his own MRE, sniffing it with concern. He was new to MREs and still figuring out which were acceptable, and which bordered on toxic. Those Hugh had shared with him at the brewery were the first he'd ever had. "Usually not plain. I covered them in different kinds of sauce packets that we kept on hand for takeout meals–salsa, ketchup, mayonnaise, mustard, salad dressings, hot sauce, or lemon juice. I watered down ketchup and pretended it was pasta sauce once I ran out of the real thing. I mixed mustard and hot sauce. Anything to add variety."

"How did you and Jim meet?"

Ed shook his head like it was the weirdest thing that had ever happened to him. "He just showed up out of the blue a couple of days ago. Said he was opening a roadhouse and needed brewing equipment, hopefully with a full-time beer brewer to run it."

"He made you an offer you couldn't refuse?" Luther asked.

"Hell, I was living in a burned-out building that leaked when it rained and couldn't be sealed against the weather. I was afraid to move into something better because my whole life was tied up in that brewery. When he told me he'd put a roof over my head and all I had to do was make beer, it was hard to say no to that. I have to admit, until they showed up to move the equipment, I wondered if it was all a dream. Like maybe I'd imagined him because I was so desperate for things to get better."

"Wasn't a dream," Luther said, gesturing toward the building behind them. "It's not a roadhouse yet but it should be soon."

"I can visualize it," Ed said. Then, with a little less enthusiasm, he added, "Kind of."

The conversation wound down a little as they dug into their meals. While he ate, Luther thought about the mission that brought him to this community in the first place and wondered whether Ed might have come across Isaac in his town.

"You ever have any experience with the regional sheriff program, Ed?" he asked.

Ed considered the question. "It's a small town. I knew a lot of the town police and some of the county deputies from my area. Some of them ate at the brewery when they were off duty. They were afraid to be seen there in uniform."

Luther waved his hand. "No, not the normal county sheriff–the *regional* sheriff program. These were guys hired by the Department of Homeland Security to cover large regions of the state. Most of them were military contractors."

Ed looked shocked at this revelation. "No, I never heard of anything like that."

"I guess they must not have made it down your way."

"Yeah, I didn't get out much over the last year, but it seems like the kind of thing people might have talked about," said Ed. "I never heard anyone mention it."

They finished eating in silence. The MREs sated their gnawing hunger, but they weren't the kind of meal that inspired enthusiastic conversation.

When they were done, Ed stood and balled up his trash. He tossed it into a pile of scrap material waiting to be burned. "I'm going to pick out a room and get my gear situated while there's still some light."

"I'll come inside in a little bit and help you out," Luther said. "Maybe tomorrow you can ask around and see if anyone knows of a bed that's available. If you're going to live here long-term, you're going to want to get off that concrete floor."

"Thanks. I'll do that."

With Ed gone, Luther listened to the soothing water in the nearby creek. He wondered what he should do. He'd found no sign of Isaac, nor had he run into anyone who knew of his whereabouts. The

Hadley lead had fallen apart once he'd learned that Hadley had been killed.

Should he just confront Jim Powell and ask him if he knew anything about Isaac? Should he question the people close to Jim, like those two young men, Pete and Charlie? They'd probably be less suspicious of his questions than someone like Hugh would be. Then again, perhaps the smart thing to do was pack up his gear, slip out early in the morning, and go back home before he got himself into a situation he couldn't get out of.

Several times he'd asked himself what he was even doing there, but the answer was complicated. Sure, he'd served with Isaac, but he wasn't sure that his motivations were completely tied to the brotherhood they'd shared in the military. It was more what happened after the war that bound them together. Specifically, it was what had happened in the last year.

As much as Luther tried to convince himself that he was doing okay when Isaac showed up, hindsight told him that he'd been slowly starving to death. The daily hunt for calories was expending more than he'd been taking in. There was nowhere to hunt game in the town he'd lived in. Every animal even close to town had been cleaned out. Cats, dogs, squirrels, chipmunks, rats, rabbits, and migrating geese had been killed for food. Even as the population declined over the winter, there still wasn't enough food around to feed everyone.

Starvation had thrown off his brain chemistry and Luther had felt himself circling the drain. He'd been sitting there depressed one day, staring at the walls of his dark house, with nothing to focus on but the burning hunger in his gut. He'd wondered if he might be better off putting a bullet in his own head. He'd not eaten in two days and had no prospect of when he might eat again. He imagined himself lying there and dying in the same dirty clothes he'd been wearing for weeks.

He'd managed to keep his living room warm by isolating it with plastic sheets and burning everything that would burn. He'd gone through most of the furniture, the back deck, and the privacy fence that encircled the back yard. The 1960s-era fireplace was designed to be decorative and didn't throw a lot of heat out into the room. While he could improvise a method of heating, he couldn't create food from nothing. He couldn't survive on heat alone. There was no comfort in warmth when his body was slowly digesting itself.

It had been there in those darkest of times when Isaac had arrived with a packhorse in tow. Luther had barely been able to make it to the door when his old friend knocked. His head spun as he braced himself in the doorframe and welcomed his old friend into his home.

Isaac had seen starvation before and understood the condition his old friend was in. As soon as he'd unloaded his horse and tied them off in the backyard, he prepared some food for Luther. While Isaac regularly apologized for imposing on Luther, they both knew that Isaac showing up when he did was all that saved Luther's life. Isaac had nursed him back to health with vitamins and a steady diet of high calorie meals.

Once a month, Isaac would ride out of town with his packhorse in tow. He'd find an empty field with no houses around and use his radio to coordinate the regularly scheduled airdrop of fresh supplies. He always came back to Luther's house with more ammunition, medications, gear, and food.

As much as Luther was ashamed to admit it, it wasn't entirely his friendship with Isaac that brought him to Russell County in search of his missing friend–it was the fear of losing those monthly supply drops. He tried to convince himself that this mission was mostly about Isaac, but with each day he was away from home, it was harder to fool himself.

What was this mission to going solve anyway? If he found that Isaac was dead, it was over. The supply drops would be done and he'd be back to starving to death in his barren, depressing home. If Jim Powell was responsible, what was he going to do about it? Was he going to kill him? That wouldn't accomplish anything. Isaac would still be dead and the supply shipments would still be over.

A new thought entered his mind. It was something he'd not even considered before at all. He had to acknowledge that he felt a certain degree of contentment sitting there on those steps. It was something he'd not felt at any time since the terror attacks, even when he'd been hanging out with Isaac. He'd done an honest day's work and been fed well for his effort. He had a roof over his head for the night and he was looking forward to what lay ahead of him tomorrow.

Was it possible that fate had led him on this mission for some purpose beyond finding Isaac? If he could keep his mouth shut and do his job, maybe it would lead to something better than what he lost. He needed to keep his mind open to that possibility.

32

Becky

BECKY GILES WAS an enigma within the town. She was descended from the prosperous Giles men and women who'd settled in the town over two centuries ago. Since that time, they'd been doctors, lawyers, gentlemen farmers, and educators. They'd held political office, been active in their churches, and participated in every civic organization within the town.

In their prime, her family had accumulated land, fine old homes, money, and cattle, but the Giles dynasty was in decline. Many recent generations had failed to marry or failed to have children if they did. Their family reunions had become gatherings of the elderly, with few children or grandchildren playing off in the grass.

By the time the Giles family realized what was happening to their dynasty, it was too late. Many in the family were forced to leave their estates to distant cousins, nieces, or nephews. With each death, the history and legacy of the once proud Giles family dissipated like a bottle of ink poured into the ocean.

Amongst this high-profile and active family, Becky Giles was a ghost, perhaps the least known of any of the Giles family. Some of that was her own doing, though not all of it. Becky Giles was in her forties and a bit of a recluse. She'd been blind since birth and had attended a school for the blind in her youth. Because she'd been sent away from the town as a child, she'd failed to develop many local friendships. She'd missed out on that crucial bonding period when small town children often formed the peer groups that would follow them throughout their lives.

She hadn't resented being away from her family. It was probably the best thing that could have happened to her. She'd pursued her schooling all the way through the college level, obtaining a master's degree in English. Her plan had been to return to the same school for the blind that she'd once attended and take an instructor position, but it didn't happen. When her mother was diagnosed with cancer, Becky returned home to assist in her care.

After her mother passed away, Becky stayed on to help care for her father. He'd always been a force of nature to her. Loud, intelligent, and constantly involved in a whirlwind of activities. Every day revolved around business deals, civic organizations, and lunch meetings with his friends. After he lost his wife, the cyclone was reduced to a doldrum, and her father rarely left the house. He aged decades in the space of a year.

As much as Becky had wanted to return to school and to what she considered to be her life, her friends, and her passion, how could she walk out on him? She couldn't. The pace of her life slowly spun down to match his and she remained with him until he passed away some three years prior to the terror attacks.

By that time, Becky was firmly stuck in the glue trap that was small town life. With her parents both gone now, Becky was now free to move to an urban area where she'd have more opportunities to meet people. She could take that teaching job she'd been offered. With the money she'd inherited and the property she had available to sell, she could have done anything she wanted. Instead, she did nothing.

Living a quiet life with her parents in their large old home had turned her into a hermit. She had more house and money than she needed. She was small town rich. With no heirs, she made arrangements with the family attorney to have her entire estate willed to Leader Dogs for the Blind upon her death. Then she fell into a simple routine of reading, taking walks around town, and writing in her journal.

Before the attacks, she had a housekeeper who came by each day to take care of the shopping, clean the house, and drive Becky anywhere she needed to go. Having served the Giles family for over thirty years, the housekeeper was the closest thing to immediate family that Becky had. Even after the collapse, the housekeeper continued to visit Becky and help her as she could. Then one day, she failed to show up.

For several days, Becky anxiously waited for her to appear, but she never did. Becky considered going to look for her, but she wasn't familiar with the neighborhood where the housekeeper lived and it was a good distance from her home. Navigating the uniform structure of the city blocks where she'd attended school was easier than wandering around rural neighborhoods where there were no sidewalks and the streets often meandered. There was also the matter of the frequent gunfire and the occasional screams Becky heard through her windows.

Becky's home was at the end of one of the town's oldest streets. It was the only brick Tudor in town and was well-appointed with features that had been considered luxuries when the home was built. Becky knew the home like the back of her hand.

When she finally accepted that the housekeeper wasn't coming back, she understood that her survival was in her own hands. She'd once read Pat Frank's apocalyptic classic *Alas, Babylon* and, as far as she was concerned, this was exactly the same kind of scenario. The terror attacks she'd heard about on the news had obviously thrown the country into some kind of apocalyptic collapse.

Like many men who came of age during the Cold War, Becky's father had been concerned about nuclear war. He'd been a member of the local Civil Defense committee and had even gone as far as quietly having a fallout shelter built in one corner of their large basement. He was proud of it and had taken Becky down there ever since she was a child, telling her what to do if a nuclear attack came and she was the only one home. She remembered running her hands over the jugs of water, the cans of foods, and the boxes of medical supplies as he talked about each item stored there.

Even after the Civil Defense system was replaced by FEMA in the 1970s, Becky's father didn't abandon his fallout shelter or his interest in survival. Though he didn't speak of it to Becky unless he'd had a few glasses of Wild Turkey in the evening, the men's group at the church he attended continued to fuel his fears of an apocalyptic disaster. Even as they were supposed to be discussing the bible, the men discreetly shared flyers about the dangers of the Trilateral Commission, a group started by David Rockefeller, which was rumored to be working to usher in a New World Order. Up until the last years of his life, her father continued to purchase buckets of survival seeds and freeze-dried foods that were advertised on his favorite television networks.

It took Becky months to eat her way through the well-stocked pantry in their large kitchen. It was neatly organized into sections with Braille labels that told Becky what to expect when she opened a can from that section. The dozens of buckets and cans of survival food in the fallout shelter were an entirely different story. While she felt blessed to have them, there were no Braille labels she could read. They'd intended to do that but had never gotten around to it. Now, opening each can, package, or envelope was its own unique experience. It had become a game in which she sometimes won but other times lost.

She'd eventually come to figure out how to distinguish between some of the freeze-dried items. Green beans felt like normal green beans, only harder. Potato slices kind of felt like potato chips but thicker. Butter powder had a distinctive smell and taste, as did the soup mixes. If she felt noodles, she knew it was a pasta dish. Even when she basically knew what the item was, it was no guarantee she was going to like it, but she ate everything she opened, uncertain of how long this event might last.

Since she couldn't read the labels, she guessed at how much water to add and eventually figured out a system. She'd add a certain amount, then check the texture after ten or fifteen minutes had passed. If the texture was still "crunchy" she'd add more water and give it more time. This system had served her well, but it wasn't perfect. Not all of her meals had been properly prepared, but they'd been edible. Most importantly, they had kept her and her leader dog alive.

Her dog, Nancy Drew, was her best friend. Yet she was more than that. She was Becky's eyes, and in some ways she was also her guardian. In the big, empty house, Becky had fully expected that someone would try to break in and rob her, but it hadn't happened yet. It almost made her feel invisible there at the end of the street, as if time and the disaster itself had somehow passed her by. As if the world had simply forgotten she existed.

Becky and Nancy Drew stuck close to the house for an entire year. Each day she made a field trip across the backyard to collect water from the tiny stream that separated their house from the cattle farm that was part of the property. One bucket at a time, she'd haul water to the house while holding the rigid handle of Nancy Drew's harness in the other.

She'd eventually figured out that the survival food came with a water filter. With some experimentation, she came to understand that it functioned like a pump, suctioning the unfiltered water into one side and pumping potable water out the other. She used this filtered water for drinking and cooking.

The back patio of the house featured a built-in barbecue grill her father had added during a remodel of the house in the 1960s. The brick grill had been quite the conversation piece among his friends, an element of distinction at a time when most people preferred to cook inside. During warmer weather, Becky heated her cooking water on this grill, using twigs she picked up in the yard.

Building fires was one of those skills that never came easy to the visually impaired. Becky had burned herself multiple times. She'd also been terrified of using the old fireplaces in the house and had put it off until she couldn't stand the cold any longer. She was deathly afraid of an errant spark landing on the rug and starting a fire.

To minimize the chances of burning her house down, she removed everything combustible from that part of the room. She took up rugs, scooted furniture, and moved the stacks of magazines her father had read in his recliner each evening. She'd been fortunate that the firewood shed contained cords of wood her father purchased before his death. Even when he'd become so feeble that he was unable to build fires or carry wood, he insisted on buying more firewood "just in case." Becky was very thankful for his foresight.

The old family house had once held single pane windows throughout and used heavy drapes as an additional layer of insulation in the bedrooms. Even though the windows had been upgraded in the last ten years, those thick drapes still hung in the guest room. To the best of her recollection, no one had slept in that room since her mother's aunt had visited them in the early 1980s. Becky hauled those drapes downstairs and tacked them to the trim with tiny nails, sealing off the den in the hope that she could contain some of the heat from the fireplace.

Becky's final accommodation to the world she found herself in was to carry a weapon. Her father had been an avid outdoorsman throughout his life. Besides fishing, he enjoyed hunting deer, rabbit, and grouse. He also carried a .44 magnum revolver as protection against black bears when he was in the woods.

Not wanting his daughter to be defenseless, Becky's father had taught her to shoot the gun. Since aiming wasn't a factor due to her blindness, he focused on grip, function, the ability to accurately point the gun, and how to load it. Though she hadn't shot the weapon in years, Becky could still recall the loud report she associated with firing the weapon, as well as the recoil and the smell of the spent powder.

Her father had a well-worn leather holster in which he carried the weapon on his hunting trips. Becky threaded the holster on a belt and took to wearing it during the days. She wasn't scared of guns and she was practical enough to understand that there might be a time when someone decided to break into her house to look for food. She wanted to be ready for that eventuality.

She had several different loads for the pistol, but she ended up going with the plastic-tipped rounds. Her father had explained that they were like shotgun shells for the handgun and contained multiple projectiles that would spread in a pattern when she fired. He'd explained this might increase the odds of hitting her target in an emergency. As far as Becky was concerned, the situation she found herself in was about as much of an emergency as she could imagine experiencing.

33

Jim

THE NEXT MORNING, the Wolfords left the valley early to pick up Ed Frye at the sewing factory, then they headed toward St. Paul for what would hopefully be the last load from the brewery. Hugh would go with them as an extra gun.

Jim's plan was to send Nooner to pick up the chairs they were going to use at the sewing factory. He wanted them to get that task over with early so they wouldn't receive too much scrutiny from people heading toward the market.

"Where are we getting the chairs from?" Pete asked.

"I'm not going to be sending you this morning, Pete. Lloyd will be the only one going with Nooner because they won't need to be loaded on the wagon by hand."

"Why won't I need the wagon?" Nooner asked.

"There's a government agency in town that really doesn't do much more than hand out money for various local projects. They have a cargo trailer behind their building that's full of folding chairs. They only use them for groundbreaking ceremonies, so they're hardly ever used. You'll need bolt cutters to unchain the trailer, then you can hook your tractor up to it. Tow it to the sewing factory and we'll unload it there. Tomorrow morning we'll return the trailer to where we got it from. Hopefully no one will notice it was gone for a day."

Jim went on to describe their destination until Lloyd figured out where Jim was talking about. Since Lloyd had grown up in the town but had been gone for a number of years, Jim couldn't use modern landmarks. He had to provide directions based on forty-year-old reference points.

"I think I know the place," Lloyd finally said. "Let's get going."

Lloyd and Nooner unhooked the trailer from the tractor and headed off toward town. Everyone else prepared for a day at the sewing factory. Jim made sure he had enough food for P.J. to prepare the midday meal. As usual, they met up with the people heading to the market at the end of his driveway.

Unwilling to cut Jim any slack, Randi was on his case immediately. "You ever tell your mother that you cut ties with the brothel?"

Jim heaved a weary sigh. "No, Randi. I've been a little busy."

Randi started flapping her arms and clucking like a chicken.

Jim cracked up. "I don't know how you do it, Randi. You get one cup of instant coffee and a hand-rolled cigarette in you and you're loaded for bear. You come out of the chute and hit the ground running. I've had two cups of coffee and I still don't have the energy you do."

Charlie grinned. "Lloyd told me it wasn't coffee and cigarettes made Randi so spry in the morning. He said Randi was like an old banjo and needed tuning every day."

Jim wasn't even sure Charlie understood what Lloyd was referring to, but the comment cracked him up. A good part of his amusement was the shocked look on Randi's face. Jim wasn't sure if her expression was due to Lloyd's crass comment or the fact that Charlie had repeated it in front of the group.

When Randi had recovered her senses, she slapped Charlie on the arm.

"Ouch!" he said. "That stung."

Then she hit him again, right in the same spot. "That one's for Lloyd. Pass it on to that goofy bastard when you see him. Tell him there's more waiting on him when he gets home. We'll see who gets tuned like an old banjo."

Besides the pleasure he took in seeing Randi on the defensive, Jim was glad it also served to distract her from talking about the brothel. He knew she wasn't done with him yet, but at least he was getting a moment of respite.

When they reached the sewing factory Jim was pleased to note that people weren't clustered up at the loading dock as they'd been the day before. Hopefully that meant no one had been killed overnight, which was always a pleasant development. Ed Frye had been picked up by the Wolfords for the brewery run, but Luther was sitting on the loading dock eating the remains of an MRE.

Jim counted his returning workers, making sure the cook had returned. He picked a few new faces from the line to fill in some vacancies, then sent the rest of the people home with the advice that they could try again tomorrow.

"Pete, you and Charlie unload the supplies off my packhorse. Give the food to P.J. so he can get started on lunch. Pile the rest of it on the loading dock."

P.J. followed the two boys toward the horses. Pete had loaded the packs of freeze-dried soup mix and the cans of vegetables, so he knew exactly where to find them. He handed them off to P.J. along with a plastic bag of fresh garden vegetables.

While the cook wandered off to deal with the food, Charlie unhooked the heavy duffel bags from the packhorse and dumped them onto the dock. One held an assortment of old speaker wire, extension cords, and bulk wire in various sizes. Combined with the rolls of wiring, packs of wire nuts, and electrical tape Jim had purchased from the building supply, these supplies were to be the basis of his low voltage wiring system.

Jim addressed his crew while the boys unpacked the supplies. "I've got two guys on the tractor bringing in chairs this morning. I'm also wanting to knock out the toilet setup. Those portable toilets down at the sewage treatment plant don't have any liquid in the tank so they should be fairly light. Even though it's a bit of a walk, four guys could easily carry one that distance without it being too much of a struggle. I'm going to send eight of you down there first thing so pick up two of them. Once you're done, you can go back and get two more."

When no one had any comments, he continued. "I also want to start on the bar. It's not going to be anything fancy. I'm thinking a plywood top with corrugated metal along the front. Some of you can also be working on the wiring. I'm going to install lights over the bar, throughout the seating area, over the stage, and at the exits."

"Electrical lights?" Luther asked.

Jim nodded. "That's the plan."

"Do you mind me asking how you're going to power them?"

"My plan is to rob some batteries and alternators from vehicles. We'll harness the creek power out back to drive a shaft. We can use that shaft to drive the alternators using belts. The alternators charge the batteries and the batteries power a series of twelve-volt lights."

There was a murmur from the workers. Some of them were impressed by the ingenuity of the idea.

Jim could tell Luther was not as impressed. His brow was furrowed as he thought this out.

"What are you thinking, Luther? You have a better idea?"

"It sounds like you have a plan," Luther said. "I'm sorry I interrupted."

Jim shook his head. "No, I'm always interested in hearing ideas. If you have a better idea, I'd rather hear it now than after we're done."

Luther hesitated before replying. "I worked for the highway department office over in Wallace County before the attacks. We used to put out those big solar-powered highway message boards whenever we were doing construction. Even our small office had dozens of them. They were mounted on trailers, so we just had to pull them into place. There were solar panels on top and they had battery arrays in a locked compartment that could run the signs for days, even if there wasn't any sun."

It occurred to Jim at that moment that someone had mentioned the signs to him before, but he'd neglected to follow up on it. There was always so much to do that it was tough to pursue every idea that crossed his mind. "Maybe we should check into that before we go to the trouble of collecting alternators and batteries. It sounds like a simpler system."

"Do you have a highway department office nearby?" Luther asked.

"Not far," Jim said. "Out on Route 71."

"If someone could give me a ride, I'd be glad to check them out for you. I have some experience with them."

"I'll take you up on that," Jim said. "Once Nooner and Lloyd are back with the tractor, I'll send you guys on a field trip. Thanks for mentioning it."

"No problem," Luther replied.

Before he'd even finished taking the men through his list for the day, Jim heard the tractor returning. A few minutes later, Nooner was backing the cargo trailer up to the loading dock.

Jim counted out eight men. "I'm going to send you guys after those portable toilets." He explained where to find them, then sent the men on their way.

Nooner turned off the tractor and cut the lock off the enclosed trailer. Pete and Charlie opened the door, revealing a hundred or more neatly stacked chairs with padded seats. They began pulling them out two at a time and stacking them on the dock.

"I want the rest of you to finish up the deck overtop of the outhouse trench so we can get the toilets in place," said Jim. "The toilets will need holes cut in the bottom and they'll be positioned over holes in the outhouse deck. Don't forget to bolt them down, too. Without any liquid ballast in the bottom, they'll blow over in a good wind. When the toilets are done, we'll start on the bar and the lighting. Any questions?"

When no questions came, Jim sent them off to their various jobs. He jumped in to help with the folding chairs, leaning them up against a wall just inside the loading dock. He didn't count them but there were a lot of chairs. He couldn't imagine there would be that many people in the roadhouse at one time, but he could certainly dream.

Watching all the people at work around the roadhouse made Jim realize this project was near completion. It wasn't like construction in normal times when there were fire inspections and building official inspections. There was no paint, tile, and drywall finishing. This project only required a few basic things and it would be done before he knew it.

When they were done unloading the chairs, Jim flagged down Luther and took him to where Nooner and Lloyd were hanging out by the loading dock. Pete and Charlie were standing around drinking from water bottles.

"Pete, I want you and Charlie to take all those cable reels that we hauled here from the phone company and start setting them out like tables. When you're done, put chairs around each of them. Don't put them close to the bar or the area where we're putting the stage."

"Got it," Pete replied. He and Charlie hopped up onto the dock and disappeared into the building.

Jim faced the three men remaining on the dock. "Luther had an idea about powering the lights with some of those solar-powered highway signs. If they've not been stolen already, those would be simpler than what I had in mind. I want the three of you to go to the highway department offices and take a look. Luther used to work for highway department so he might be able to figure out which ones are best. If you can find some, let's haul them back and put them to work."

Nooner grinned and saluted, instantly making Jim question his sobriety, even though it couldn't have been much past 8 AM. Lloyd climbed up and perched on one fender while Luther sat on the other. Nooner settled in between them, started the tractor, and they were off.

Jim watched them go, then noticed two people watching him from the road. They'd had a steady stream of gawkers come by to check their progress so seeing people wasn't anything concerning in itself. However, these two people hadn't come from town, they'd come from the houses at the end of the road, making Jim instantly concerned that they might be relatives of NAPA and Newport.

When they started walking in his direction, Jim hopped off the loading dock and waited on them. He didn't go out to meet them, preferring to keep close to cover in case things got "shooty."

When they got closer, Jim saw that one of them was a woman who might have been around twenty years old. She had what he would describe as rat-like features. Her nose was too long and upturned at the end. She had large incisors that remained exposed all the time. Her eyes were dark and too close together. All she was missing were whiskers and a tail.

The man who was with her seemed angry even before he spoke with Jim, as if the Lord had punted him into this world against his will and he resented everything that had happened to him since that moment. Jim could see a resemblance to NAPA and Newport, but this man was older. Age was visible in the lines of his face, the way he moved, and in the gray that had overtaken his hair like kudzu swallowing a hillside.

"Can I help you?" Jim asked. He didn't particularly mean it. With the gruff tone he used, he could just as easily have been asking if he could shoot them.

The man hawked and spat. "We're looking for two of our kin that went missing the other night. They're nephews of mine. This here is their sister."

Jim's gaze didn't waver from the man. "Only men I've seen is the men I have working in there."

The man tipped his head toward the sewing factory. "You the one running this here job?"

"I am."

"You'd know these boys, then. You must be the one that told them you were using this building whether they liked it or not." The old man gave Jim a wary look.

"That's me," Jim admitted. "I did offer to let them to come over for lunch each day, but they never showed up."

"Them going missing worked out well for you, didn't it?" the sister said. "If they're missing, you don't have to feed them."

Jim laughed at that, looking at the ground and shaking his head. When he looked back up, he said, "I've killed people for a lot of things in the last year, but I've never killed someone just to avoid having lunch with them."

"You mind if we ask your people if they saw anything?"

Jim considered this. "They're busy right now. We knock off in late afternoon. Come back then and you can ask them anything you want."

"So, you ain't gonna let us talk to them?" the sister asked.

"Not while they're on the clock."

"What if we go in there and talk to them anyway?" the uncle snapped. "I ain't a man who takes to people telling me what I can and can't do."

Jim smiled. "I don't take to being pushed around either, so why don't you go on in and we'll see how this ends."

After a tense moment of giving Jim his hardest look, the uncle raised a finger and pointed at Jim. "This ain't over, by God!"

Jim stared at the finger, considering how much he'd enjoy snapping it to the side. He didn't get the opportunity. The uncle yanked it back, spat on the pavement again, and stalked off. The sister tried her luck at shooting Jim a mean look, but he'd received so many at this point in his life that they didn't have the impact they once did. Unless that mean look came while it was sighting down a weapon, Jim didn't get all that concerned.

Once he was certain they kept continuing down the road, Jim went back inside. He had work to do.

34

Becky

OVER THE HOT SUMMER, the inside of Becky Giles' house had become uncomfortably hot, humid, and smelly. Because her sense of smell helped compensate for her lack of vision, she was particularly sensitive to odors. After a long winter and a hot summer, it smelled stale and stuffy. There was a mildewy odor she couldn't get rid of, and as a result, she'd been spending more time outside. One day, one of the neighbors saw her outside and spoke to her for the first time since the collapse.

It was not lost on Becky that she'd known this woman her entire life. The lady was perhaps twenty years older than Becky and she'd lived right beside Becky's parents for as long as she could remember. Yet at no point in the last year had this woman stopped by to say hello, check on her, or offer any assistance. She had to have known Becky was there. For much of the winter, she assumed smoke had been coming out of the chimney since she'd been burning fires in the fireplace.

"You look good," Mrs. Eldridge said. "You must be getting enough to eat."

"Are you saying I'm fat?" Becky asked.

"Why no, I'm not!" the older lady replied.

Becky knew that Mrs. Eldridge wasn't calling her fat. Her actual motive was being nosy about how Becky had survived and what she'd been eating. Since Becky didn't want to talk about the fallout shelter or the survival food, she decided to act offended at Mrs. Eldridge's comment and see whether it would end that line of inquiry. It worked.

"How are you faring?" Becky asked, trying to divert the conversation away from her.

Mrs. Eldridge sighed. "It's been tough. Most of the neighborhood is gone. Some died and others moved. Some I don't know about. You and I are pretty much it at this point. Everyone else on this end of the street is gone."

Becky recalled that Mr. Eldridge had died of a heart attack several years ago. She could recall her father attending the funeral, but she hadn't gone. Was Mrs. Eldridge alone?

"Everyone else is gone?"

"Yes, dear, and not just on our street. The whole town is like that. Some people are saying the entire country is like that. I've gotten out some this summer and walked the neighborhoods above town. There are only one or two houses on each street that are occupied. Everything else is empty. It's been a tough year, Becky. More people died than survived."

While Becky understood in practical terms how this had happened, it was hard to fathom. They had lost *most* of their neighbors? "I wanted to grow a garden this summer, but it's a big job. It's tough when you can't see how the plants are doing. I'm sure my father's garden spot is pretty overgrown too."

"You should go to the farmers market," Mrs. Eldridge said. "That's what most people are doing."

"Where is it?"

"Same place it's always been. Down by the government offices. It's become the centerpiece of town life. You can get medicine, food, weapons, clothes, anything a person might need. There are vendors selling cooked food. Everything is about bartering and negotiation. What you're able to get depends on what you have to trade."

Becky found this intriguing. "What kind of things are people trading for?"

"Well, anything that people might need but have trouble getting. Old medications you don't need, ammunition, guns, knives, camping and survival gear, baby clothes, coats and shoes, and even old antiques that can be used without power. Things like those old crank mixers, potato mashers, apple peelers, oil lamps, that kind of thing."

"When is it open?"

"Every day," Mrs. Eldridge replied. "It's busiest in the morning. Things start to taper off in the early afternoon. A lot of the vendors go home around then. You should go sometime. You're welcome to attend with me, if you'd like."

"I'll think about it. Thanks for telling me." With that, Becky got to her feet and went inside. Once they were in the door, she removed Nancy Drew's harness and whispered to her. "There's no way I'm going to the market with that old bitch. I don't trust her any farther than I can throw her."

Unable to see facial expressions, Becky was left to sift through the nuances of peoples' voices and the general impressions she took from their interactions. It wasn't an exact science, lying somewhere between a psychic reading and a lie detector test, but it had served her well over the years. Whatever this sense was, it told her that Mrs. Eldridge was not to be trusted.

Even so, the information about the market had been interesting and Becky was determined to go. There wasn't anything in particular she needed to trade for, but she wouldn't mind interacting with someone besides Nancy Drew. Despite being a good snuggler, she was not particularly a stellar conversationalist. Becky grabbed her backpack from the closet and immediately began wandering through the house, searching for items that she might be able to trade off at the market.

Though Becky had never been to the farmer's market, she'd been to the government offices with her dad. She'd also taken walks through that part of town often enough that she was familiar with the route. Within her memory was a set of data points that corresponded to the route. She knew what to do at each intersection and at each turn in the road. Best of all, there would be no traffic to be concerned with. She shouldn't have to worry about her or Nancy Drew getting run over at an intersection.

It was several days later that Becky chose to attend the market for the first time and the appearance of the blind woman raised quite a stir. As much as people liked to think they were kind, mature, and sophisticated, they typically weren't. They openly gawped at anyone who was the least bit different from them. They whispered about the children with Down Syndrome. They shook their heads at the outbursts of children with autism. They blatantly stared at people with burns or artificial limbs or facial abnormalities. With her leader dog and red-tipped cane, many considered Becky Giles to be different from them too.

In the most important of ways, Becky was similar to everyone else at the farmers market in that she was a survivor. Perhaps that was why some were staring at her–they were shocked to see she was still alive. When so many had died, how had *she* made it? After all, she couldn't see and they assumed she required assistance with many basic tasks. All of their assumptions failed to take into account that Becky was an extremely intelligent, resourceful, and capable woman.

People at the market began to notice her as she walked down the sidewalk, Nancy Drew at her side. Becky could sense their eyes on her and she felt the murmur of the crowd change. More people were now watching her than talking to each other. She didn't care. She focused on the input from her dog and her cane, as well as what came in from her senses.

Besides the sounds of conversation, she heard someone pounding on steel. It sounded like blacksmithing, someone trying to shape something by repeatedly hammering it. She could hear the bleating of goats and the clucking of chickens. Someone played guitar and sang while a competing musician played drums on a plastic bucket. Occasionally, someone would bray with laughter or children would cry out as they played.

The smell reminded Becky of the county fairs she'd attended as a child. There was the smell of animal dung combined with roasting meat. There was the scent of strong tobacco in the air. A sweeter smoke hit her nostrils and she remembered being told when she was in school that it was the odor of marijuana, though she'd never tried it. She relied so strongly on her senses that the last thing she wanted to do was alter them in some utterly random manner.

Nancy Drew paused at the end of the sidewalk and Becky's cane told her there was a step. She felt gritty asphalt beneath her shoes and figured she was now in the parking lot of the government offices. She heard the scuff of shoes coming in her direction and she asked, "Excuse me, could you tell me which direction the vendor booths are in?"

A man cleared his throat, then spoke in a deep, friendly voice. "Well, honey, there's booths to your right, but there's also more booths up in the pavilion area. It's kind of behind you and to your left. You have to go up a set of stairs to get there. Can you find them on your own?"

She bobbed her head. "Yes, I'm good. Thank you."

"Then you have a good day."

She smiled at him, then turned to her right. She began to hear more people around her, which told her she was getting closer to the vendor area. Some voices quieted at her approach, but others continued with what they were doing. Some were negotiating purchases. Others were simply engaged in small talk about the state of the world.

Becky gripped the rigid handle of Nancy Drew's harness tightly. She trusted her dog to guide her safely through the crowd, but there was no way the dog would understand how to take her from booth to booth. Nor could her guide dog explain to her what wares were on display at each booth. Soon, Becky was totally surrounded by voices on all sides and figured she had to be in the thick of it. She paused and listened, processing everything.

"Can I help you with something?" a woman asked to her right.

"Is this a booth?" Becky asked.

"Ain't much, but I got a few things I'm hoping to trade," the woman replied in a friendly voice.

"What are you selling?"

"Eh, a little of this and a little of that. Items from my house that I don't need. Clothes the kids outgrew, a few tools, some camping stuff."

"Doesn't sound like anything I need, but thanks for telling me about it. Can you explain to me how this place is laid out?" Becky only took the chance of asking her because the woman had such a kind voice. She could tell a lot by a person's voice.

"Well, you're in the first row," the woman began. "It goes on for a bit with booths on both sides of you. There are three rows of booths here and there's a few people scattered around the edges. Some people are set up at tables and others just have items scattered out on blankets on the ground. There are more vendor tables up the hill at the pavilion."

"How far to the next booth?"

"You go about eight feet and there will be booths on both sides of you."

"Thanks," Becky said. "Good luck selling your stuff."

Becky started walking again, Nancy Drew staying in step with her. She had a good sense of how many steps it took for her to cover eight feet. When she'd made the distance, she stopped again and cocked her head to the right.

"Good morning. Can you tell me what you're selling?"

"I mostly do medications," an older male voice replied. "I used to be a pharmacist. Anything you're needing?"

"I don't really take anything except ibuprofen and Tylenol. I'm not on any prescriptions."

"That's good for you, but I've got both of those if you need them," the man offered.

Becky considered this. She *was* running low on ibuprofen, at least in bottles that had braille labels applied to them. She'd found some other large bottles in the house that sounded like they were full of over-the-counter medications, but she didn't dare take them when she couldn't read the label.

She'd thought several times how helpful it might be to have someone come in and help her label the items she was unsure about, but that came with a risk. Whoever she invited in would know what she had. They might try to steal from her or tell other people what she had. She was simply too terrified to take the chance. She knew a lot of people in town by name, but there were none that she considered friends and certainly none she trusted enough to bring them inside her sanctuary.

"I guess I could use a bottle of ibuprofen," Becky said. "What would it cost me?"

The man's voice got a little playful as he entered "trader mode." "The question is not what it costs, but what you have to trade."

Unable to see his eyes, Becky was uncertain if the man's tone of voice implied playfulness or something more malicious. It was just so hard to tell without the cues provided by facial expressions.

She'd brought medications to trade because Mrs. Eldridge had specifically mentioned that there were people buying and selling medications here. She had plenty of them at the house. Her father hadn't thrown out of any of her late mother's medications because it wasn't in his nature to throw out anything. Having inherited his same frugal nature, Becky had all her father's medications. Fortunately, all her parents' medications had Braille labels because she'd helped administer them and needed to be able to read the labels.

"I've got medications," she said. "Prescription stuff."

"Can I see what you got?"

Becky instructed Nancy Drew to sit and she released her grip on the handle. She rested her cane in the crook of her arm and removed her backpack. She reached inside and felt the labels. She didn't want to reveal just how much she had. She understood that showing all her cards too early in a negotiation was bad business.

"My dad took medication for high blood pressure," she said, removing a bottle and holding it out in his direction.

The man took the bottle and read the label. He shook it, then removed to the cap to get an approximate count. "I can trade you even for these, if that's acceptable to you. There's a lot of people with high blood pressure right now who need their pills. If you have more of his medicines, bring them by. Even if you don't take prescriptions, I have other things you might need. I got Tums, cold medicine, allergy pills, and cortisone cream. I have ChapStick for one end, hemorrhoid cream for the other, and a little something for everything in between."

His schtick made her smile. "I'll remember that. I'm mostly just looking around today."

He put the bottle of ibuprofen in her hand. "That bottle isn't even open. There's a hundred in there, just so you know."

She tucked it in her pack. "What else is around here? Can you tell me?"

"Across the aisle from me is a grumpy old buzzard selling canning jars. If you keep going straight ahead, the next booth is about ten feet away. You'll have a lady selling winter clothes on the right and a family selling meat rabbits on the left."

"Don't need any of those," Becky said. "What's past that?"

"There's someone selling backpacks, sleeping bags, and other outdoor gear. They're mostly wanting to trade for children's clothing because I've talked to them before. They're on the right. Across from them is a young couple selling marijuana."

That surprised Becky a little. Wasn't it illegal? Either way, she hadn't heard anything mentioned that she might need. "I appreciate it. I'll just keep looking."

She continued the approach that had been working for her, stopping at each booth and having them explain what they had. She'd then ask them what lay ahead of her. Though she didn't buy anything else in that first row, she learned a lot about what items in her home might be valuable trade items. She had the winter clothing that had belonged to her mother and father. She would also see whether she could find some .22 caliber shells because people were apparently using them like currency. She'd also need to poke about in the garage some and see if she could locate more of her father's old hunting gear.

In the next row there were several food vendors. She was able to trade a gallon baggy of fast-food salt, pepper, and ketchup packets for a couple of rabbit and goat kebabs. She split them with Nancy Drew, who preferred the rabbit over the goat. She traded a cheap flashlight for several pieces of homemade fudge. She knew the flashlight worked because she could feel the bulb end get hot when she turned it on, but she had no need for it.

After she'd passed down all the rows in the parking lot, she had someone point her toward the other vendor area. In the unfamiliar terrain it took her a few moments to get pointed in the right direction, but she finally made it to the pavilion with the assistance of a few strangers. There, she spent an hour doing the same thing that she'd done down below.

She didn't buy anything else, but she enjoyed being there. She wasn't really a social person, at least not there in her hometown, but being out in the world again felt good. It made her feel more hopeful about the future. For as unusual as the farmers market was, it was the most normal thing she'd seen since the power went out.

The only interesting thing that happened to her in the upper vending area was that someone recognized her. There might have been others in the crowd who knew who she was, but no one had said anything about it. Then, as she was passing by a booth, an older woman spoke to her.

"Excuse me, dear, are you Becky Giles?" the woman asked.

Becky had been walking along, preparing to ask what they sold at that very booth, when the woman spoke to her. She was stunned for a moment, but finally responded with, "I am."

"I thought I recognized you," the woman replied. "My name is Pamela. Pamela Johnson. I knew your parents."

Becky ran the name through her inner rolodex. She knew a

Johnson family that was prominent in the town. "The name sounds familiar."

"Why, darling, it should. My family and your family go way back. All the way back to when this town was nothing more than an outpost in the great wilderness. You probably know these other fine folks." Pamela gestured to her left.

Becky couldn't see the gesture but sensed that Pamela was expecting her to recognize someone. "You'll have to introduce us."

Pamela sucked in a breath. "Oh my. I'm sorry, Becky. I operate this booth with Mitchell and Dixie Meadows. Dixie was a Smith before they got married. As I'm sure your father could attest, both of those family names go all the way back to the beginning of this town. That practically makes us all related. The founding fathers and mothers of this fine community."

Becky could hear the smile in Pamela's voice but wasn't feeling the love. There was something in Pamela's tone that reminded Becky of all the things she hated about small town life. There was that ring of insincerity. That implication that two centuries of history somehow bound Becky to these people that she didn't really know. Even beyond that, something venomous oozed from Pamela. It was almost palpable.

Becky let out a long sigh. She was tired and getting a little overwhelmed by everything. It had been a good day, but after a year of seclusion this was a lot of "peopling" for her. She flashed a nervous smile and left abruptly. "It was good to see you all, but I need to be going. Good luck today."

35

The Antique Dealers

PAMELA STOOD with her hands on her hips and an unpleasant smirk on her face watching Becky leave the market. "Not exactly friendly, is she?"

Mitchell grinned. "If that ain't the pot calling the kettle black."

Pamela shot him a dirty look. "All I'm saying is that a girl like that, with *special needs*, should be a little nicer to folks. She might need help one day."

Dixie shrugged. "She made it this far, which is more than some folks can say."

"Why are you two defending her?" Pamela growled, retaking her seat behind the table.

"I'm not defending her," Mitchell said. "I'm not invested in her in any way."

"She does come from one of the founding families," Dixie said. "We've always argued that the founding families of this town deserve a little something extra. They should be memorialized with a big old plaque right there in the middle of town. People should know who we are."

"And bow when they see you in public," Mitchell teased.

Dixie swatted him on the arm. "I'm not joking. We should be treated special."

"Most of the founding families have streets named after them," said Pamela.

Dixie sighed. "Yeah, but so do some of the *lesser* families. I just think if you were here when the town was formed you should be entitled to certain things. Maybe we shouldn't have to pay local taxes. Maybe there should be a Founders Day celebration instead of the 4th of July festivities."

"Maybe you can bring that up at a town council meeting when things get back to normal," said Mitchell. "If such a thing ever happens."

"Don't think I won't," Dixie snapped. "I've gone in there and spoke my mind several times."

"Oh, I'm aware," Mitchell said, pained by the memory of some of Dixie's embarrassing and tone-deaf public diatribes. "I'm certain your name still comes up in closed sessions."

Dixie cut him a look. "What's that supposed to mean?"

"Oh...nothing," Mitchell said.

Pamela began painting her nails. She'd found it was a good way to hide the dirt that collected beneath them. Mitchell returned to trying to fix an antique mantel clock he'd taken in on trade.

"Where do you think she lives?" Dixie asked.

"Who? Becky?" Pamela asked.

Dixie nodded.

"Why, I think she still lives in that big old house their family owned on the edge of town, back behind the courthouse. Don't tell me you've never seen the house."

Dixie didn't respond, not wanting to give Pamela the satisfaction of thinking she'd seen something in the town that Dixie hadn't.

"By herself?" Mitchell asked. "With no one helping her?"

Pamela looked at Mitchell like he wasn't hitting on all cylinders. "If someone was helping her at home, don't you think they'd have come to the market with her today? Her mother has probably been dead for twenty years and her daddy passed away a few years back. I went to both funerals, obviously, and I remember seeing Becky there. I don't think she has any close family left."

Even in Pamela's innocuous statement there was a hint of accusation, the reminder that she had attended the funerals of two descendants of founding families that neither Mitchell nor Dixie had attended. In her mind, that was almost inexcusable.

"I forget about that house," Mitchell said. "It's kind of hidden back in there, off to itself."

"It's beautiful," Pamela said. "Either of you two ever been in there?"

Mitchell and Dixie shook their heads.

"I was there once to get her father's signature on some documents for the Rotary Club. It's a very nice house. I think it dates from the 1920s. Lots of ornate woodwork. Carved doors and high ceilings."

Mitchell exchanged a glance with Dixie, but it was her who put their shared thought into words.

"Antiques?" she asked.

Pamela raised an eyebrow and turned to face her partners. "Yes, there were a lot of antiques. That family had some nice things and they kept it within the family. They'd sell off land from time to time for a little extra cash, but you never heard of them selling possessions. Those stay in the family. But surely you're not suggesting...?"

"I hate to be crass but it's not like she'd see us," Dixie hissed. "Even if she did catch us, she couldn't identify us."

"This isn't an empty house," Pamela countered. "We've always limited our *visits* to houses where the owners are deceased or gone missing. That's part of how we justify what we do. In this case we'd be taking items from a living owner. That's a little different. A little more *common*."

"Yes," Dixie acknowledged. "It is a little different, but are you saying you're not up for it?"

Pamela considered her words carefully, letting out a sigh before she said, "No, I'm not saying that. I'm sure that poor girl doesn't even know what she has in that house. She can't identify all those old things that belonged to her family. If we don't take them, they'll just get thrown out eventually."

It was certainly easier for the three of them to justify their actions if they branded it a mission of mercy rather than a crime spree. None of the three were so naïve as to think that their liberation of those precious antiques was purely altruistic, but they simply chose not to think about that aspect of it. They all *wanted* to explore Becky's house and the only way they could excuse that behavior was by lying to themselves about their motives.

They certainly weren't strangers to that. They'd often had to lie to themselves over the last year, which didn't make them unique. It was likely that everyone who'd survived the last year had been forced to shift their values. The prospect of starvation was a powerful incentive.

"When do you want to do it?" Dixie asked.

Pamela watched the crowd as she thought, the same sour look on her face that it naturally relaxed into. For her, resting bitch face would practically be considered a smile compared to the expression she normally wore. "Tonight?"

Mitchell shrugged. "I don't see why not. No sense in waiting. If we're going to do it, let's do it."

"There is the matter of that dog of hers," Pamela said.

"We do *not* hurt puppy dogs," Dixie said firmly.

"Could we drug it?" Mitchell asked.

Dixie frowned at him. "Do you have a veterinary degree that I've missed? You give that dog some pill meant for a human and it might die. I'm not having that."

"What about a pot brownie?" Pamela asked. "There's a booth selling them."

Dixie snorted. "Duh, dogs can't have chocolate."

"Treats then, damn it!" said Mitchell. "We'll just take some treats and hope we can bribe the dog."

"I'm good with that," Dixie said. "Treats are fine."

Mitchell and Pamela shared an eyeroll.

"Don't think I didn't see that," Dixie snapped.

36

Ian

IAN GATHERED his wares and left the market early. He wanted to bike up to the sewing factory and see how Jim's renovation was going. He needed to head home first and store his tools and goods before making the trip. There was no need in hauling all that gear through town. With his stabby things stored in a bike trailer designed for carrying children, he stood on the pedals and climbed the hill from the market.

He turned right at Main Street, staying in the easy gears as he climbed another hill toward the center of town. Once he crested that hill, he pedaled a gentle downhill stretch, building up speed for the next hill. He worked the gears and cranked hard on the pedals, getting all the momentum he could before finally topping the hill at the courthouse.

At a dirty and broken traffic light, he turned right again, getting on one of the back streets above town. There were dozens of possible routes that would take him to his home, but he liked riding the neigh-borhoods. That allowed him to monitor which homes were occupied and which had been broken into lately. It also allowed him to look for any new faces. It was a way to keep a finger on the pulse of his neighborhood and see whether there was anything new he needed to be concerned about.

The treelined back streets were not as bucolic as they'd once been. They were lined with dusty cars, most with broken windows. Leaves and trash had gathered around them. Once-manicured lawns were grown high and matted with paths beaten through them by both animals and humans. Piles of trash were a common sight, as were the fire pits used now for both cooking and socializing. As they had for millennia, humans were once again crouched in the darkness, their imaginings stirred by the things they saw in the flickering flames of a campfire.

Ian had just turned onto a quiet street with the amusing name of Lively Avenue when a scream pierced the air. It was so close and so startling that Ian nearly wrecked his bike. He craned his neck, trying to find the source of the scream. The scream came again, this time followed by the boom of a large caliber weapon.

The gunshot served to provide Ian with a bearing and he dumped his bike, sprinting back toward the intersection where he'd just turned. Another scream came just as he reached the intersection. Up the street, to his left, he spotted a woman on the ground being attacked by three large dogs.

"Get out of there!" he bellowed, drawing his handgun and sprinting toward the fracas.

There was a woman with a backpack sprawled on the ground, a large revolver laying on the sidewalk near her. She was groping desperately for the handgun while trying to keep a grip on the leash. That was when Ian figured out that she must been walking one of the dogs when the other two attacked them.

"Get away from her!" he screamed.

He fired a shot as he closed in. It startled the dogs and they paused in their attack, but only briefly. A big Lab snarled and lunged at the German Shepherd. The Shepherd was restrained by its leash, impeding its ability to defend itself and its owner. The third dog, a lanky hound mix, snapped at the Shepherd's hindquarters while it was distracted by the Lab.

With each lunge of the Shepherd, the woman holding the leash was dragged a little further from her handgun. The Lab found an opening and sank its teeth into the Shepherd. The woman's screams turned to desperate sobs when her dog cried out in pain.

Finally upon them, Ian lashed out with a foot, connecting with the hound's side. The dog yelped then spun on him. Ian shouted at it but the dog only retreated a few feet, refusing to turn and run. Ian saw no other option. Presented with a clear shot, he aimed and fired. The hound flinched and toppled over. Ian fired again and it went still.

The Shepherd and Lab were now face to face, teeth bared and preparing to lunge at each other once again. Ian roared and charged at the Lab. Startled, it skittered backward, its attention now divided between Ian and the Shepherd.

Ian could see in the dog's eyes that it was trying to decide whether it should continue to go after the Shepherd or whether it was time to take on the big human. He didn't give it time to mount another attack. He fired, the round striking the dog in the head. It dropped instantly, one leg twitching before it died.

Ian gasped for breath, his adrenaline surging. He spun in a circle, checking for more dogs. His chest heaved and he could hear his pulse pounding in his ears like an approaching freight train. When he failed to spot any more threats, he lowered his gun to his side.

There was a wail from behind him. He turned to see the woman clutching the Shepherd to her. Bright blood coated her arms, face, and neck. It was only then that Ian took in the pieces of the puzzle he'd failed to spot earlier: the dog harness with the handle, the red-tipped cane, the woman unable to find her handgun when it lay so close at hand. This was the same woman he'd seen navigating the rows at the farmers market.

The *blind* woman.

Ian holstered his handgun. "My name is Ian. You're safe now. I'm going to help you."

"Is my dog okay?" she sobbed. "She's soaking wet. Is it blood?"

Ian laid a comforting hand on the woman's shoulder. She flinched at his touch and her dog snarled. "Easy there." His words were directed at both of them. "What's your name?"

"Becky," she snapped. "How is my dog?"

"She's bleeding. She's been bit, but I can't tell how badly through all that fur. Can I help you get up?"

She nodded and clutched her dog's face in both hands, planting a kiss on her forehead. "It's okay, Nancy. Good dog. Good dog, Nancy."

Ian could see now that the dog's leash was fastened to Becky's belt. That was why Becky had been dragged around the street. He could also see the empty holster sitting right at the center of her waist. "I'm going to reach beneath your arms and help you to your feet, okay? I'm going to make sure you're steady before I let go."

She nodded, wiping at her tears with a bloody hand. Her face was a gory mess with dog fur plastered to the blood.

Ian got behind Becky and slid a hand beneath her armpits. He lifted her to her feet and held on for just a second to make sure she had her balance. "You good?"

"Yeah," she said, her voice almost a whimper.

Ian leaned over to pick up her handgun. Just as his hand closed around the grip of the shiny .44 magnum, Becky startled him with an outburst.

"Dammit!" she shouted.

"What is it?"

She didn't answer him until she'd completed a long string of impressive curses. "Dogs! People let their dogs run all over the place. They always think their dogs wouldn't hurt anyone, until they do."

"Do you get out much, Becky?"

"No. Though I'm not sure what that has to do with anything."

"I only asked because there are a lot of wild dogs running around town now. Their owners died or abandoned them. It's a constant problem if you're out walking around."

"I didn't realize. I've been outside the house, but the property is fenced. I guess I've not really been off my property since the power went out. Today was my first trip out. I was excited about it, until it went all to hell." She leaned over and stroked her dog again. Her rage subsided and the tears came again.

"I have your pistol," Ian said. "Hold out your hand."

She straightened up and Ian placed it in her hand. She slipped it into the holster in a practiced manner that told him she was used to carrying the gun. As she should be.

"Listen, I dropped my bike when I heard you in trouble. I'm going to run back and get it, then I'll walk you home, if that's okay. Maybe we can clean your dog up and make sure she's not badly hurt."

She looked in his direction and cocked an eyebrow. Despite her inability to visually assess him, it was as scrutinizing a gaze as he'd ever experienced.

"Are you a murderer or a rapist?"

Ian almost laughed at the question but didn't when he saw that she was serious. "No, Becky, I'm not a rapist. I have killed when the situation called for it, but I don't consider myself to be a murderer either. I'm a neighbor from up the street. I sell at the market and was on my way home when I heard you cry out."

"I never let people into my home," she said.

"I understand. That's a good policy. I'll only go as far as you're comfortable with, but I do think you should let me help you clean your dog's wounds. She's got a few that are bleeding pretty well and they may need dealt with. Did you say her name was Nancy?"

"Nancy Drew," Becky replied. "After the detective. I enjoyed those books when I was a kid. Is there a vet around?"

"That's a good question. I've not heard of anyone providing veterinary services. I worked as an EMT, so I know my way around wounds. I also know a nurse who has a few more skills than I do if that's required."

"Okay, get your bike and let's go. I appreciate your help, but any funny business and I'll blow a big hole in you. I may be blind, but my hearing is sharp. And I only use shotshells in my pistol, so I just have to be close."

Ian chuckled. "Message received."

He picked up her cane and handed it over, then jogged back for his bike. He almost expected it to be gone but it wasn't. The gunfire must have discouraged anyone shady from venturing outdoors. He stood the bike up, then rode back to where Becky was waiting on him.

"Must be handy getting around town on a bike."

"It is," Ian agreed, climbing off to push the bike as he walked alongside her. "I can get around the whole town quickly. I've got a little trailer attached to the back that I use for carrying my goods to the market."

"What kind of goods do you sell?"

"Stabby things," Ian replied. "I make improvised weapons for people who might not want to carry a gun."

"That actually sounds kind of fun," Becky said.

They headed down a dead-end street that Ian had never traveled before. Since it didn't function as a shortcut, he didn't have any reason to use it. He was surprised when they headed for a massive brick Tudor at the end of the street.

"This is your place?" he asked.

"No, but I've always liked it. Thought I might be able to kill the owners and move in. Will you help?"

Ian stopped walking. "Are you serious, girl?"

She let out a tired laugh. "No, Mr. Gullible. I'm teasing. It's my house. The key is hanging around my neck."

Ian wouldn't have been surprised had her joke actually been a serious request. It wouldn't have been the first crime someone had asked him to commit in the past year. "It's a beautiful old house."

"That's what they tell me. It's big. I know that much."

"You live here alone?"

She hesitated before replying. Ian could feel her assessing him again, though he wasn't sure by what methods. He almost wondered if she was reading his mind or trying to.

"I do live alone," she finally answered. "My dad passed away a few years ago. I had a housekeeper who helped me out with things, but she disappeared when the power went out. I'm not sure what happened. She just quit showing up."

"How have you survived alone in this house?" Ian asked. He was both shocked and impressed.

Becky let out a sigh. "I'm not really comfortable talking about that."

"That's okay."

They went through an iron gate set into a low wall of cut stone, then followed a brick sidewalk to the front door. When they got to the porch, Becky removed her pack and leaned her cane against the door.

"Maybe we should look at her out here in the light," Becky said. "I'm assuming the light isn't as good inside since I keep the curtains drawn all the time."

Ian wasn't sure whether the light was the actual reason for examining the dog on the porch or whether she just didn't want him in her house. Either way, it was fine. He leaned the bike on the kickstand and took a seat on the steps.

"Can you sit down on the steps and help keep her calm?" he asked. "I don't want her eating my face off if I touch something that hurts."

Becky grinned at the comment and sat down, wrapping an arm around the big shepherd. "Nancy Drew wouldn't do that. She's a good girl, isn't she?"

"Where can I get some water?" Ian asked.

"I get it from a creek out back. There are full buckets on the back porch. If you walk around the house, you can't miss them."

"Back in a sec." Ian jogged around the house. He was back in a minute with a bucket in his hand. "You know, I'm surprised this creek water hasn't made you sick. You shouldn't be drinking it without some kind of treatment."

Becky frowned. "I filter it. I'm blind, not stupid."

Ian winced. "Sorry, no offense intended."

"It's okay. I get a little defensive when I feel like people are questioning my independence."

"Just trying to be helpful, but I understand your attitude. I'll try to think before I speak."

"Let me know how that works for you," Becky said. "Not sure that's something humans have mastered yet."

Ian removed a bandana from around his neck then dipped it in the bucket, grinning at Becky's defiant attitude. He squeezed the bandana over the dog's haunches, letting water run over the wounds, then dabbed gently at them to try and see the damage.

"Can you tell how bad it is?" Becky asked. Gone was the independent hard-ass. Now she was a woman concerned about losing not just her companion, but her eyes, her guide, and her freedom.

"There are a few small wounds that look like they'll heal on their own. There's one place on her hip where the flesh is torn and the muscle is exposed. I really think it needs stitched up. There's also a bite on the shoulder that's probably going to be painful. Antibiotics are in order too."

"Can you do stitches? I might have antibiotics, but I don't know. I'm not sure what you can give to dogs." Becky was thinking out loud, surrendering to the fear, and bordering on frantic.

"Easy now," Ian said. "I think she'll be fine. I'm going to get on my radio and see if I can reach a friend at the market. I could stitch her up if I had to, but my friend knows more about this kind of thing."

He fished around in his pack for the radio Hugh had given him. He confirmed it was set for the frequency Jim and his people used, then spoke into it. "Ian for Randi, Ian for Randi."

He repeated the request several times before Randi replied. *"Ian? What's up, man. You at the market?"*

"I was. I left a little bit ago and I've run into a bit of a situation. I don't want to go into any details on the radio, but I could use a bit of help. I'd owe you big time."

Randi laughed. *"I'm sure I owe you already. Didn't you save my ass down here at the market a few weeks ago?"*

Ian had. It was when Hadley Wright and the regional sheriff got into a scuffle with Gary's family, Pops, and Randi. Ian had intervened just when it looked like someone was about to die. "I might have."

"What do you need, Ian?"

"I've got someone that needs a couple of stitches and an antibiotic for a dog bite. That something you can handle?"

"I'll have to run home and put a kit together. It might be two hours before I can get back to town. Will that work?"

"Two hours would be fine. Can you come by my house?"

"Not a problem," Randi replied. *"Two hours and I'll be there. Randi out."*

Ian breathed a sigh of relief at having gotten her on the radio. If he'd had to bike back to the market to track her down, that would have added even more time. "I guess you heard that."

Becky tightened her lips and let out a sigh. "Obviously. I'm blind, not deaf."

Ian grinned at her defiance. "Will you be okay until we can get back here?"

If she had more smart responses, comments about how she'd been okay for the past year without any outside help, Becky held them back. "I'll be fine."

Ian got to his feet. "If I come knock on this door in two hours, will you let us in?"

"Knock and announce yourself," Becky warned. "I'd hate to shoot a nice guy like you by accident."

"I'd hate that too."

Ian offered to help Becky into the house but she waved him off. Once he heard the door latch behind her, he turned his bike, pushed through the gate, and pedaled off toward his house.

37

Ian

It was nearly three hours later when Ian finally heard a knock at the back door. When he answered it, he found Randi standing there, her horse tied off the porch railing. She had a shotgun in one hand, a medical kit in the other, and a backpack on her back.

"Is the patient inside?" she asked.

Ian shook his head. "Down the street a couple of blocks. Let me grab my stuff and we'll go."

He was outside a few minutes later with his weapons and a backpack. Randi had climbed back on her horse and was allowing it to graze Ian's yard. Ian headed around the house and Randi pulled her horse off the lush grass to follow him.

"What happened?" Randi asked as she fell in alongside Ian.

"Did you happen to notice that blind lady at the market today?"

"How could you miss her?" Randi replied. "People were staring at her like she had three heads."

"I noticed that too. I left the market early because I was going to head down to the sewing factory and see what kind of progress they were making. When I got off Main Street and was heading back into the neighborhood, I heard a scream. That lady's dog was being attacked by a couple of strays. She had its leash tied to her belt and she was being pulled along the sidewalk. I intervened and killed the strays."

Randi shook her head bitterly. "I hate seeing a dog killed. It makes me sick."

"I love dogs too, but I didn't know what else to do."

Randi held up a hand to stop him. "You had no choice. I get it. It's still tough. Did she get bit?"

"The woman didn't get bit, but the guide dog did. Her hip is torn open. She was a bloody mess. I walked the lady home and cleaned up the dog as best I could. It's going to need some help though."

Randi cocked an eyebrow at him. "My patient is the dog and not the woman?"

"You like dogs, right?"

"Yeah, but I'm not used to treating them. I thought I was coming here to treat a person. That's why I busted my ass getting here."

"I'm sorry, Randi. I didn't want to go into any details on the radio. Since the market opened, there's more and more people using them. If you could have seen her—"

"The dog or the woman?"

"Both of them," Ian replied. "But think about what this dog means to her. This woman survived alone for over a year. She told me that the trip to the market today was the first trip she's taken off her property since the collapse. That dog is everything to her. It would hurt any of us to lose a pet, but this is more than a dog to her."

Randi nodded as the she processed this. "How did she survive a year without leaving her house? And how did she survive a year without anyone breaking in on her? There's a lot of lowlifes around who would see someone like that as a soft target. It's horrible, but true."

"I don't have any idea. She didn't want to talk about how she survived, and I can understand that. I didn't ask her if she'd run into any trouble."

"I'll ask her," Randi said. "I'm *that* nosy bitch."

Ten minutes later they were through Becky's gate and Randi tied her horse off on a long lead so it could graze the high grass of the yard. Ian climbed the steps and banged on the door, while Randi lugged her gear onto the front porch. There was a bark from inside the house, but the heavy oak door prevented them from hearing any steps approaching.

Moments later, a nervous voice shouted at them from inside. "Who is it?"

"Becky, it's Ian. I brought my nurse friend with me to look at Nancy Drew."

"Nancy Drew?" Randi whispered.

"The dog's name," Ian explained. "After the books."

"Gotcha."

The door creaked open, revealing Becky standing there in the dark entryway. The large revolver hung from one hand. The other rested on the back of the large service dog standing at her side.

"Becky, this is my friend Randi. She's a nurse. Randi, this is Becky."

"Come in," Becky said. "I'm so glad you came. I was afraid you wouldn't."

Ian could tell from Becky's voice that she'd been upset and probably crying. He hated that she doubted him, but why wouldn't she? He was a stranger to her. He held the door wide for Randi, then closed it after she was inside. "I told you I'd be back."

"I know you did, but I don't know you. I just didn't know. That whole experience was terrifying. My worst nightmare."

"Is there a place I could examine the dog with a little more light?" Randi asked. "It's kind of dark in here."

Becky's brow furrowed as she considered. "I can show you toward the kitchen and den. You'll have to tell me which works better. I keep all the curtains shut for privacy and I don't need the light. Come this way."

Becky headed off through the house with Randi and Ian following. Nancy Drew stayed at Becky's side. The two guests couldn't help but look around with interest. This had once been a very nice house and perhaps would be again with a little care. It wasn't really neglected, just dated, with old wallpaper, old furnishings, and in need of a fresh coat of paint on some of the plaster walls.

The foyer area was paneled in dark maple and had a coffered ceiling of the same wood. There was a large brass and crystal chandelier and a staircase that led up to the second floor. All the downstairs rooms they passed through were formal, old-style parlors with antique furniture, expensive lamps, and décor that likely dated from the early 1950s. There were portraits on the wall, both painted and photographic. There were framed prints of pastoral hunting scenes.

The kitchen was also decorated with antiques. There was an iron rack hanging over a kitchen island that displayed copper pots and pans. A leather bellows for building fires dangled from a hook, alongside hand-wrought fireplace tools. There were high cabinets with glass fronts and a wooden pie safe with a punched tin front.

"This is the cleanest kitchen I've been in since the collapse," Ian remarked.

"What? You think blind people live in squalor?" Becky snapped. "I can clean up after myself."

"That's not what I meant," Ian replied. "It's just that without running water, people have tended to let things slide a bit."

Becky shook her head adamantly. "I can't let things slide. My sanity depends on orderliness and routine. I like everything to be where it's supposed to be or I might not find it again. If this place looks like it hasn't changed in forty years, that's because it hasn't. Before they died, both of my parents understood that change threw me off." Becky stopped in front of a set of French doors in a breakfast nook. "Is this better?"

"Yeah, it's good." Randi lowered her packs to the floor and propped her rifle against the door. "Will your dog lay down so I can examine it? More importantly, will it gnaw my arm off if I touch it?"

Becky sat down and patted the floor in front of her. "Come here, Nancy."

The shepherd circled once in front of Becky, then settled down.

"She's definitely being a little careful when she sits," Randi commented. "I'd say the bite is getting sore and swollen."

"Can you help her?" Becky asked.

The fear in Becky's voice made Randi's heart go out to her. Certainly, Randi could be a hard-ass, but she did have some soft spots.

Randi sat down in front of the dog and let it sniff her hand. "Nancy, I'm going to check out your sore places. I know it might hurt and I'm sorry. I'll try to be gentle, okay?"

"Are you waiting on verbal consent?" Ian quipped.

Both Becky and Randi frowned at Ian. As far as they were concerned, Nancy understood what was being said to her.

Randi removed some saline from her pack and began irrigating the wounds. They'd dried some already from the time that had passed, but the saline and gentle scrubbing with a clean cloth removed most of the crusted blood from the wounds.

When she had the wounds clean, Randi probed the area with the bite. When she went a little too far, Nancy Drew winced and Randi expected the dog to nip at her, but she didn't.

"Good girl, Nancy," Becky whispered. "I'm sorry it hurts."

"There's some swelling around the bite. Ian's right about the tear in her hip. That will heal better with some stitches."

"But you can fix her, right?" Becky asked hopefully.

"Fortunately, your dog is about the weight of a teenager so I can dose her with a human antibiotic. That's good because it's all I've got. I've got some pain meds, but I'll have to think about that. The hip is the big issue right now. I need to inject some lidocaine to numb up the wound before I stitch her up. Hopefully, she'll understand I'm trying to help her. How does she do with shots from the vet?"

"As long as I'm holding her, she should be fine," Becky said.

"I hope you're right," Randi replied, getting her supplies together.

The large shepherd flinched as the needle entered her flesh. She gave Randi a sharp, warning look, but Becky spoke to her in a soothing voice. She didn't growl or snap.

As the lidocaine began to do its job, Randi could tell that the pain in the dog's hip must have been bothering her. When the numbness kicked in, Nancy laid down and rested her head in Becky's lap.

"Is she okay?" Becky asked, a little worried.

Randi stroked the dog. "She's fine. She's just relaxing now because the shot made the wound hurt less."

Once she was certain the wound was numb, Randi used a razorblade to remove the hair from around the wound. It looked like one of the attacking dogs had gotten a tooth beneath the skin and ripped. The wound was jagged, but Randi was certain she could pull the skin together and close it.

When the hair was shaved back, Randi cleaned the wound again and began stitching it up. Nancy Drew looked up curiously, trying to figure out what Randi was doing to her. Since it didn't hurt, she laid back down and let Becky pet her.

After the last stitch was snipped, Randi applied a topical disinfectant to the wound. She had to figure some of this out as she went. It wasn't like this was a person that she could bandage up and threaten about keeping the dressing clean. Even if the dog stayed in the house until the stitches came out, they wouldn't be able to keep her from licking the wound and moving around. Dogs would be dogs.

When she finally had the wounds dealt with, Randi began counting out some pills into two separate plastic bags. "One of these is the antibiotic. One of these is pain pills. How can we label these for you so that you can tell them apart?"

"There's a braille label maker in one of the island drawers," Becky said. "We can label them. Can you get it, Ian?"

He opened a few drawers until he found what he was looking for, then handed it over to Randi.

"It's an older one," Becky said. "It doesn't need batteries."

As Randi began cranking out the labels, she decided to ask the question that had been on her mind since Ian explained the situation. "Forgive me for being a nosy bitch, Becky, but you appear to be doing fine here by yourself. Have you had help? How did you do it?"

"Ian asked that earlier," Becky said. "I didn't answer him because I was scared to say too much. I'm hesitant to talk about it, but I'm guessing you must be good people to go out of your way to help me and my dog. I do need you to understand one thing, though."

"What's that?" Ian asked.

"If you screw me over and I get killed, I'll haunt you all for every remaining day of your life."

Ian laughed, but Becky glared at him. "I'm serious, Ian. You'll never get an undisturbed night of sleep again. When you die, I'll do the same to your children, if you have any. I'll be the worst legacy ever passed down through your family."

Ian looked a little disturbed at Becky's threat, but Randi was smiling.

"We promise," Randi said. "Let's hear it."

Becky spent the next few minutes summarizing the story of her father's preoccupation with nuclear war and survival. She told them about the shelter he'd added in the basement, the survival food, and filtering water from the creek.

"That's impressive," Ian said.

Becky shrugged. "It's not like I did anything. My dad made all the preparations."

"Bullshit," Randi snapped. "He might have made the preparations, but it was your own grit that kept you alive. No one can take that from you. You alone kept yourself alive."

"Thank you," Becky said.

"We can help you out a little, Becky, if you're interested," Ian said. "We can use that label marker of yours to label your food, so you don't have to guess anymore. It might save you from a few unpleasant surprises."

Becky swooned at the suggestion. "God, you don't know how much I'd appreciate that. I was afraid to ask anyone for help because I didn't want them to know I had freeze-dried food. I was afraid they'd try to steal it."

"They probably would have," Randi said. "My people aren't like that. We wouldn't take your food."

Becky cocked her head. "What do you mean by 'your people'?"

"There's a group of us who live outside of town. Several different families in the same part of this valley. Ian here doesn't live with us, but he's become a friend. We've had a hard go of it, but we've managed to survive and do pretty well for ourselves. In fact, we're doing a little project in town right now, converting this old sewing factory onto a roadhouse. There will be booze, food, and we'll be selling some items."

"What kind of items?" Becky asked.

"Things people can use to survive. Kind of like the farmers market, but more like a store."

"I'd like to sell at the market," Becky asked. "I was thinking about that today. I have a lot of crap around this house that I could get rid of. It would also be nice just to see some new faces, so to speak."

"I sell there nearly every day," Randi said. "You're welcome to set up with me anytime. Then you wouldn't have to be concerned about shoplifting or anything like that. I could show you the ropes."

"I'd like that," Becky said.

"If you started with just a few things, I could help you get them there to the market," Ian said. "I pull a little trailer behind my bike. We could stick some of your gear in there and I could deliver it to Randi's booth for you. You could walk with me to the market if you wanted."

"That would be great," Becky said. "I hate to admit it, but my confidence is a little shaken by what happened today."

"If you've survived this long, I think you're truly over the hump," Randi said. "You're a genuine badass and no one can take that away from you."

"You want to try going to the market tomorrow?" asked Ian.

Becky considered for a moment before responding. "Yeah, I think I'd better. If I dwell on it too long, I'll talk myself out of it and I may never leave the house again."

38

Becky

After treating Nancy Drew, Randi and Ian stuck around for a couple of hours. They talked with Becky and got a start on labelling some of the foods she wasn't sure about. She enjoyed their company and that shone a harsh spotlight on how isolated she'd become since the collapse. She'd obviously become something of a hermit since moving back to her hometown, but at least there'd been some people in her life. Since the collapse there'd been none.

There had been her father up until he died, and the housekeeper until the power went out. She had friends from her old school that she communicated with online and exchanged texts with. Even though her universe had been small, it had not been empty until the lights went out.

If the day's experience had shown her anything, it was that she didn't want to go back to the isolation of the last year. Nancy Drew had been excellent company, but the conversation was one-sided. Becky hoped she might again have friends and people who could make her laugh. She couldn't even remember the last time something had spontaneously amused her.

Once Ian and Randi were gone, Becky began looking for a few things to sell at the market. For her debut as a vendor, she was only going to take some small items that would be easy to carry. She tried to recall the things that vendors told her they were selling when she'd stopped by their booths at the market.

She went to her father's closet and found a pair of his hunting boots. They didn't fit her, but they'd surely fit someone. While she was there, she found a couple of his sweaters and a lightweight windbreaker. She crammed those in her pack, then returned to the kitchen, locating the cabinet where her mom had kept her canning supplies.

Becky didn't think anyone had canned in this house in twenty-five years. There had been a time when her father raised a large garden and Becky helped her mother put up the harvest. She could identify the tools by feel. She placed a jar funnel in her pack, a set of tongs for lifting jars out of the canner, and several boxes of lids and rings.

There were other items in the cabinet she was uncertain about. One box sounded like a powder when she shook it and she assumed it was fruit pectin for making jellies. Some other little packets reminded her of the spices for making pickles or maybe salsa. There was another box that felt a little heavy. When she shook it, it sounded as if it contained sand. She opened the lid, stuck her finger in, and tasted it, confirming that it was pickling salt.

With all that crammed in the backpack, it was beginning to feel heavy. She decided this was enough for a first trip. There wasn't that much she really needed so she wasn't even sure what she'd ask for in trade. She supposed that people would have to make offers based on what they had, then she'd have to decide if they were offering something she needed or not. Randi would help her figure it out.

She cinched the pack shut and left it on the kitchen island. She'd be able to find it there when Ian came by in the morning. She'd warned him that he might need to knock loudly in case she was sleeping. Unable to see the cycles of day and darkness, she often got offtrack and kept weird hours. That had been a problem when her parents were alive. She'd often wake them up by accident when she was prowling around at night, listening to the television or making something to eat.

Becky had no clue what time it was, but she was getting tired. It had been a long, traumatic day and she'd not had anything to eat since the skewers of meat she bought at the market. At home, she ate soup a lot. She'd eaten most of the canned soup in the pantry because they'd already been labeled. Once those were gone, she'd started eating soups from the freeze-dried survival foods. She'd learned that there was a certain shape and feel to those packets which made it easy for her to locate them in the plastic buckets.

She built a fire in the masonry barbecue pit on the patio. Building fires was another of those things that had involved a learning curve for her. It was difficult for her to build them in a traditional manner because of her vision. In the early days of the disaster, she'd used the gas grill to heat food. When she ran out of gas, she'd found a spare tank in one of the outbuildings. Once that had been expended, she had no choice but to build fires, though she burned herself several times before she developed a system.

Her method now was to fill the firepit with two handfuls of kindling, then spray that kindling down with a solvent from the garage. She randomly picked spray cans from the shelves, assuming they were products her dad had used for maintaining the cars or the house. Some, like spray paint and WD-40, she could recognize by the smell. Others, like brake cleaner, degreaser, electrical parts cleaner, and waterproofing for boots, were unfamiliar to her.

Once she soaked the kindling with the solvent, she used a propane torch from the garage to light the fire. Her dad had used the torch to light charcoal in the fire pit, so she knew exactly where he kept it and how to start it with the pushbutton igniter. She could usually tell by how rapidly the fire was crackling as to whether she had a good blaze going or not.

She didn't need a huge fire. If she made it too hot, it was difficult to get the pot of boiling water off the grate. That had been yet another hard-learned lesson.

For heating fires, Becky used the firewood her dad had stored in the woodshed. For the smaller cooking fires, she mostly used scraps of wood from her dad's basement workshop. She kept thinking she'd run out of scrap wood eventually, but every time she explored the basement she found more. Her father had apparently been afraid to throw away even the smallest scrap of wood and kept it tucked into every nook and cranny.

When she heard the water beginning to boil, she removed it from the fire using an oven mitt and carried it inside to the stove top. There, she mixed in the packet of soup mix, put a lid on the pot, and waited about fifteen minutes before checking it. Since she couldn't read the instructions, she'd arrived at the fifteen-minute cook time through trial and error. Regardless of whether it was correct or not, it produced the best results. Any less time than that and she'd end up biting into powdery clumps of soup mix that were disgusting and made her gag.

She poured a glass of filtered water to drink with her meal, then sat down at the table to eat. She'd run out of crackers long ago, which had initially been irritating. She got over that tiny detail when she realized there were people out there who didn't even have soup, so she needed to be thankful for what she had.

When she'd eaten her fill, she fed the other half of the pot to Nancy Drew, dumping in the capsule of pain medication Randi had given her. Dog food was also one of the items she'd run out of quickly, so she and her guide dog now split most meals. She knew the soup probably didn't meet the nutritional requirements of a dog, but judging from the salt content, it probably didn't meet the require-ments of a human either.

Becky didn't even sit down to wait on Nancy Drew to finish her soup. It usually took less than a minute. The dog could lap up a bowl of soup in a fraction of the time it took Becky.

"All done?" Becky asked when the lapping stopped.

The dog obviously didn't answer, but when the lapping didn't resume, Becky took that to mean she was finished. Becky picked up the bowl and put it in the sink to wash tomorrow. Every couple of days she heated enough water to fill the kitchen sink, washing her clothes first, then doing dishes afterward.

"Ready to go upstairs?"

In the winter, Becky had slept on the living room couch, heating only that room. She'd moved upstairs for the summer. She didn't feel comfortable leaving a downstairs window open at night because she was afraid someone might climb through it. Upstairs, she could leave a couple of windows open and catch any breeze that might be blowing through.

The click of toenails on wood told Becky that Nancy Drew was at her side as they climbed the steps. They went into the bedroom and Becky shut the door behind her. She heard the bed settle as Nancy Drew leapt onto it, turned a few times, and lay down. Becky changed out of her clothes and put on cool summer pajamas, then lay down alongside her dog.

She stroked Nancy Drew's head. The dog sucked in a breath, then emitted a long, contented sigh that made Becky smile. She always took that sound as Nancy saying "goodnight" to her. Knowing she'd require a little more time to settle into sleep than her dog, Becky retrieved a book from her nightstand.

Her father had been an avid reader and insisted on building Becky a library of all the books he thought she should read. He was also good about buying books by authors he knew she liked, so she had an extensive library to work her way through. Most recently she'd been working her way through Sinclair Lewis and her current book was *Main Street*.

Despite the book having been written nearly a century earlier, Becky was amazed at how accurately the book reflected the life of her small town when she'd been growing up in the 1970s and 1980s. Apparently some things never changed. Sinclair Lewis had been the first American to receive the Nobel Prize for literature and she was beginning to understand why her father had so enjoyed his books. She felt a pang of regret at not having read the book when her father was alive, so that they might have discussed it and laughed at their little town.

Losing herself in the story, she was uncertain of just how long she'd been reading when she heard the distinct sound of steel scraping against brick. She laid the book down on her chest and listened. She was uncertain what she was hearing but knew these were sounds she was not accustomed to. More importantly, they were coming from outside her house.

Becky dropped a hand to Nancy Drew. Usually, the big shepherd was up and out of the bed at any strange sound in the night. She'd either be sniffing at the window or near the door, listening for any threat to her owner, but now she continued to sleep soundly. Then Becky understood it was the pain pill. The pain medication had knocked her dog out.

Becky had several thoughts at that moment and some of them were very troubling. She couldn't help but wonder if it was Ian and Randi who were out there trying to get into her house. They could have intentionally given her drugs to knock out the dog so they wouldn't have to worry about it when they broke into the house.

She thought about the things she'd told them. About her survival food, about the guns her father kept and the fallout shelter in the basement. She'd felt comfortable with them and had appreciated their kindness. Had it all been an act? Had they betrayed her?

Becky slowly sat up and swung her legs off the bed. She slid her feet into her slippers and retrieved the .44 magnum revolver from the nightstand. She carefully opened a drawer and retrieved more of the shotshell cartridges, dropping them into her pocket when she stood. She'd already felt like a victim once that day and she was not going to allow it to happen again.

39

"Do you think you could make any *more* noise?" Pamela snapped.

Mitchell turned around and glowered at Pamela. He was pretty sure she couldn't see the expression on his face but giving her a nasty look made him feel better. "Maybe if I had some help carrying things, I wouldn't have bumped into the wall."

"Whatever," she said.

Just as she couldn't see his expression, he couldn't see her eyeroll. Mitchell dropped to his knees and began working to fit the crowbar in between the cast iron door to the coal chute and the steel frame to which it was hinged. He was struggling to see by moonlight alone when Dixie turned on her flashlight.

"Turn that light off!" he hissed.

"Why?" Dixie replied. "Have we all forgotten that she's blind? She can't see it."

Mitchell *had* forgotten that Becky was blind. He was used to using stealth and not turning on a light until they actually entered the houses they visited on their missions. Dixie was right. In this case it didn't matter. "Most people forget about these old coal chutes. This one is either stuck or they've secured it from the inside."

"Keep trying. I don't want to break a window," Pamela said. "That dog of hers might hear it."

Now aided by Dixie's light, Mitchell was better able to work the tip of his crowbar into the lip of the coal chute and exert some pressure on it. With a thin creak, the cast iron door began to open. "Pass me that light."

Dixie handed her light over and Mitchell directed the beam into the gap between the chute door and the frame. Now he could see the problem.

"It's wired shut with a rusty old coat hanger. Hand me the bolt cutters."

Pamela turned her own light on and reached into the twin-sized jogging stroller that Mitchell used for carting goods back from their outings. She removed a small set of bolt cutters and handed them over. Mitchell slid the cutters into the gap he'd created with the crowbar and snipped the wires.

The heavy door was hinged on the bottom and fell open. Mitchell caught it with the toe of one boot, preventing it from banging off the brick wall. He handed the bolt cutters back to Pamela, then leaned down to peer through the opening.

"What do you see?" Dixie asked.

"It looks like they tore the coal bin out some time ago," Mitchell whispered. "I see lots of spider webs, some dusty shelves, and an old work bench with a few tools."

"Can you get through the opening?" Pamela asked.

Mitchell looked uncertain. "I can get through it, but I'm not sure about getting down once I get through." He stuck his head into the opening and directed the beam of the flashlight downward.

Apparently concluding that he'd come too far to back out now, Mitchell turned around until his back was toward the house. He leaned forward onto his hands, shoved one leg through the opening, then the other. His legs were now resting on the frame at thigh level.

In a push-up position, he began shoving himself backward. His arms tired quickly as he hadn't done anything resembling a pushup since around 1962. The rusty chute frame scraped his thighs painfully as he worked his way backward. He began to second-guess his awkward approach when the frame reached groin level. He grimaced and rocked his body, trying to avoid inflicting any permanent damage on his dangly bits.

"Don't worry about that. It's not like you're going to have children at this point," Pamela said. "Keep going." She topped it off with a giggle.

Mitchell paused and raised his head long enough to glare at her.

She shrugged her shoulders. "It's true."

Mitchell gritted his teeth and wiggled his legs. Moments later, he was through to his waist and his legs were dangling beneath him, trying to find purchase on the concrete foundation wall. Another couple of shoves backward and he was through to the ribs. Once he had his shoulders through, he lowered himself to the ground.

It took him a moment to get himself back together. His ribs and arms ached. The skin on the front of his body burned from being scraped over the frame. He was going to feel it tomorrow. He could tell.

"I'm next," Dixie said.

"Why are you next?" Pamela demanded.

"Because I beat you down here." Dixie was already trying to work herself through the opening.

Pamela shook her head. "You should let me go first."

Dixie tried to wriggle backward in the same way that Mitchell had done but was having trouble supporting her body weight on her arms. She was already breathing hard from the effort. "Why?"

"Because when your fat ass gets stuck in that opening, I'm going to be left outside," Pamela replied.

Dixie tried to support herself on one arm so she could use the other to punch Pamela in the thigh, the only part of Pamela's body that she could reach from her current position. The attempt to hit Pamela made Dixie lose her balance and she faceplanted in the dirt, crying out when her nose struck the ground.

"Serves you right for trying to hit me," Pamela growled.

Energized by pain, Dixie began moving again, wriggling backward on her elbows. "You see if we help you get inside, you old hag."

Inside the basement, Mitchell couldn't see or hear anything of what was going on outside. His wife's backside filled the entire opening. He grabbed her legs and tried to support her, attempting to spare her from scraping over the frame as he'd done. When she didn't seem to understand what he was trying to do, he gently tugged on her body.

He felt her advance toward him, but she began writhing in his arms and kicking her legs. "Quit kicking," he hissed. "I'm going to drop you." He suspected that she couldn't hear him, but he didn't dare repeat himself any louder.

Outside, Dixie grimaced as she was yanked backward, her breasts snagging in the frame. Pamela started giggling so hard that she had to sit down. Dixie began kicking wildly, afraid that Mitchell was going to do permanent damage if he didn't stop pulling.

Mitchell tried to grasp Dixie's legs tightly enough to keep her from kicking, but it was like wrestling a crocodile. Then one of her knees worked loose from his grip and caught him in the chin. Mitchell let go of her instantly and staggered backward. Lights flashed in front of his eyes as he fell against the old coal furnace.

He was leaning against it, trying to regain his faculties, when Dixie dropped to the floor in front of him. Her Live, Love, Laugh t-shirt was pulled up to her neck and her torso was scratched from the rusty frame of the coal chute. Black streaks smudged her stomach, elbows, and neck.

"You nearly knocked me out," Mitchell groaned, rubbing his chin.

Dixie shoved a finger in his face. "Not a damn word from you, Mister. We'll talk about this later."

Pamela shoved her face through the window, her devious grin illuminated by Mitchell's light. "I thought I was going to have to put my foot on your head and shove, Dixie. Your fat ass was stuck good."

Dixie yanked her t-shirt down and snarled at Pamela. "If I was built like you, like a twelve-year-old boy, I could have fit through there easily."

"You want us to let you in the front door after we get Becky's room secured?" Mitchell asked. He had a length of rope in his pocket. His plan was to tie it around Becky's doorknob, then tie it off to some other object in the hallway so she couldn't pull it open.

"No way! You guys can't be trusted. You won't let me in until you've found all the good stuff yourself." Pamela disappeared for a moment, then handed all their backpacks through to Mitchell. When she was done, she yanked her head out, shoved both legs through the opening, and dropped to the ground with the precision of a teenage gymnast. She threw both arms up with a flourish, then bowed. "That's how you do it."

Both Dixie and Mitchell regarded her with disgust.

"Let's get on with this," Dixie said. "We need to find her bedroom and secure the door."

They donned their headlamps and scanned the basement, spotting the stairs in the center of the space. As they walked toward them, they couldn't help but scan their surroundings with eager eyes. Noticing all the vintage tools and antique furniture gave them hope. This was the home of someone who didn't throw anything away and those were always the best homes.

At the stairs, they lined up with Mitchell at the front. Dixie and Pamela trailed him closely. As nervous as they were about entering the house, neither wanted to let the other get ahead of them.

When they reached the top of the steps, their headlights illuminated an old six-panel door of dark maple. The door hardware was brass and appeared original. The keyhole was for an old-fashioned skeleton key and Mitchell prayed it wasn't locked. He didn't have such a key on him and they didn't dare use the crowbar on this door for fear of waking Becky.

Mitchell reached out and carefully twisted the knob. There was a click and the bolt retracted. He shoved on the door and it swung silently open. He couldn't help but smile. "We're in."

Both of the women clutched at the tail of his shirt in excitement, all the cattiness from moments earlier forgotten. Mitchell took the final steps and found himself in the kitchen. He'd never been in the house before, but he'd been in others like it. He stood there listening for any sounds. There was no approaching dog, nor was there any snoring that might have told him which room Becky was sleeping in.

He held his fingers to his lips and hoped Dixie and Pamela could hold their tongues until they had Becky locked in her room. The two of them sometimes found it hard to restrain their snippiness. He led them out of the kitchen and began searching for the downstairs bedrooms. If they didn't find her there, they'd have to move their search to the second floor.

Even as they looked for the occupant of the house, Pamela and Dixie couldn't restrain themselves. They played their flashlights over curio cabinets and antique furniture. Mitchell knew they were both making mental shopping lists of the things they wanted to take. He felt like he'd be lucky to get out of there tonight without having to referee a fistfight between the two women.

40

Becky

WHEN YOU LACKED the ability to see, other senses moved forward to try and compensate. Hearing became more acute, the nose became more sensitive, and even the nerves of the skin rose to provide more information than a sighted person might be aware of. So, if the scrape of steel against her brick house hadn't convinced Becky that someone was out there, the sound of whispering did.

Sedated by her pain medication, Nancy Drew hadn't stirred. Becky would accept that as a blessing. She didn't want to endanger her precious dog by sending her out to potentially engage with burglars. Anyone willing to break into her house would probably be just as willing to shoot a dog and she couldn't risk that.

She eased out of her bedroom and gently closed the door behind her, making sure it latched. She listened but didn't hear anything within the house. She couldn't tell exactly what window they were trying to enter so she was afraid to go downstairs and confront them. If she incorrectly guessed their entry point, they could sneak up behind her.

The only stairs leading to the first floor descended to a landing before turning one hundred and eighty degrees and continuing down to the foyer. Becky paused at the top of the steps and listened but picked up nothing. She'd lived in this house long enough to know where to step to avoid making any noise. Without a sound, she descended to the landing and stopped there. This was as far as she dared go. From this position, she could hear if they were moving around downstairs. She'd also be able to deal with them if they tried to come upstairs.

She backed up to the wall of the landing and slid down to the floor. She cocked the revolver, the click producing the only sound she'd made up to this point. It sounded unnaturally loud in the silence of the house. She raised her knees and rested her elbows on them, aiming the gun toward the steps. Then she focused on her breathing and waited.

After several minutes of utter silence, she began to wonder whether she'd imagined the whole thing. Perhaps her exhaustion and the trauma of the day had conspired to make her think that someone was breaking into the house. Maybe she'd even fallen asleep and dreamed the entire episode.

Her self-doubt flew out the window when she heard a sound she knew very well. It was the metallic click of the basement door being opened. That explained why she'd not heard anything inside the house. Whoever these people were, they'd entered the basement somehow and she'd been unable to hear them through the thick oak flooring.

Becky heard them now. She picked up the almost inaudible sound of the basement door swinging open. Then she heard the scuff of multiple pairs of shoes transitioning from the basement steps to the ceramic tile floors of the kitchen. There was a single pop from the kitchen floor as they moved. Becky had heard that sound for her entire life. Her father had explained that one of the nails that held the floor to the joists had loosened and was allowing the floor to move.

There was a similar spot in the hallway floor outside of her mother and father's bedroom. Even as a child she'd kept odd hours and that creak had always told her that one of her parents was getting out of bed to check on her. This time it told her that strangers were moving through her house.

She heard another familiar sound. There was a spot in the floor of the formal dining room that shook the China cabinet a particular way when someone stepped there. The lips of two crystal wine glasses touched when the cabinet shook, producing a sound almost like someone making a toast. Becky heard the bell-like sound reverberate and fade as whoever was in her house moved out of the dining room.

Becky tried to keep her breathing steady, but she was terrified. It took everything she had to remain seated when she desperately wanted to bolt for her bedroom and hide in the closet with Nancy Drew. Then, she heard the most terrifying sound of all–the pop of the bottom step as someone transferred their weight onto it. The intruders were now coming up the main staircase.

They were coming for her.

The calm that Becky had so desperately sought up to now began to settle over her like an approaching fog. All her senses were focused ahead of her, toward whatever threat was coming up the steps toward her. All conscious thought ground to a halt and instinct took over.

She was no longer thinking about her guide dog. She was no longer thinking about the possibility that Ian and Randi had betrayed her. She was no longer thinking about how much safer she'd have felt with her father here. There was no thought of anything but the moment she was in and the moment that would come immediately after it.

The people coming toward her didn't speak, but she suspected now that there were three of them. One led the way and at least two others followed. Their shoes sounded different. Their feet landed differently. The whisper of their hands on the banister sounded different.

Then she heard the sound of their breathing and knew they were getting even closer. Soon they would be upon her. She had no idea if they'd be able to see her or not. Surely, she was hidden by the shadows. Then it occurred to her for the first time that they might be using flashlights and she felt totally exposed.

She had no time to dwell on it. She heard a man's breath catch in his throat and she knew they were upon her. She could sense him on the steps directly in front of her. He'd come close enough to the landing that he'd seen her sitting there on the floor waiting for him.

She could sense him trying to decide his next move. Then there was the whisper of fabric on fabric, a movement she couldn't interpret. Someone reaching inside a pocket? Someone going for a gun?

Becky pulled the trigger.

The explosion of the magnum revolver firing in the enclosed space of the house was deafening. Becky immediately realized that she'd compromised her senses with the shot, but it was too late now.

Mitchell's body pitched backward like a bowling ball taking out the remaining two pins. Dixie and Pamela instinctively threw their hands up to try and catch him but were thrown off balance by his weight and momentum. It happened so fast that the women couldn't even catch themselves. They fell with the sick feeling of someone knowing that they were going to be severely injured and there was nothing they could do to stop it.

Even through her impaired hearing, Becky heard the screams of two women as they fell backward on the steps. She heard a sharp crack as someone's head smacked against a wooden stair tread. She didn't hear the snapping of bone as Pamela's forearm shattered when she tried to arrest her fall, but Becky heard the cry of pain that followed.

Becky got to her knees, then used the stair rail to stand and align herself. Though the noises were muffled by the blast her ears had taken, she could hear something from the foot of the steps. Crying, groans, and perhaps even movement. She pointed the handgun toward the base of the steps and fired, knowing that the shotshell rounds would be very effective at this range.

At least two voices rose to shout at her, begging her to stop, but

Becky did not stop. She pulled the trigger and the double-action revolver fired again.

Pamela was silenced by the shot, but Dixie was not. She lay there at the base of the steps, both shielded and trapped by the bodies of her husband and friend. She was bleeding from where she'd struck her head on the steps. Her body was so wracked with pain that she was certain she'd broken her back. Still, she didn't want to die. She begged and implored. She threatened and made promises that Becky could barely hear.

Even if Becky had been able to decipher Dixie's words, they would not have swayed her resolve. She was calm and focused by all appearances, but inwardly she seethed with anger. She'd gone a year with no trouble and these people had violated her sanctuary. They'd broken her peace.

Becky held the rail with one hand, while the other kept the revolver raised ahead of her. She descended the stairs carefully, always terrified of falling in the empty house. When her counting told her that she was halfway down the steps, she paused and gripped the revolver with two hands.

"No! No! No!" Dixie whimpered.

Dixie's pleading only improved Becky's aim.

"You. Broke. Into. My. *House!*" Becky hissed.

The begging turned into a shriek as the gun fired again. This time Becky emptied the revolver, firing until the hammer dropped on an already spent round. As she'd practiced many times, she ejected the empties and they fell at her feet, rolling down the stairs with a musical ring.

One by one, she thumbed fresh rounds into the cylinder, then snapped it shut. As she worked, she listened, but understood she didn't have a chance in hell of hearing anything short of an explosion at this point. She wondered if she'd done permanent damage to her hearing. That would be a significant impairment on top of the challenges she already faced.

With the gun loaded, she considered her next move. Part of her wanted to go down and make sure these people were dead, but she didn't dare. What if one of them was still alive and grabbed her? There was no way she could fight someone off when she couldn't see them. Besides, they probably had weapons on them.

A scratching from up the stairs finally reached through her muffled hearing. The gunshots must have penetrated Nancy Drew's drugged haze and woke her up. The scratching was followed by a whine and then a bark. Becky understood that her girl was worried about her.

She decided she'd go back upstairs and wait until morning. That would hopefully allow enough time to pass that anyone she'd only injured would succumb to their wounds. Supposedly Ian was coming by to help her get to the market in the morning. If he didn't come, she'd have to assume he was the man now lying dead at the bottom of her steps.

Another bark spurred her into action. She took the stair rail and began climbing. Even before she reached her bedroom, she began speaking to her dog. "I'm back, Nancy. I'm sorry if I scared you. There were some bad people in the house and Mommy had to take care of them."

She used her knee to block the door as she opened it, afraid Nancy Drew would bolt for the stairs. The dog remembered her training and focused on Becky, licking her hand eagerly. Once she was inside her bedroom, Becky locked the door and took a seat on the bed.

Nancy Drew hopped up and began licking her face. Becky stroked her fur, apologizing again for scaring her, and taking the time to explain in detail what had happened. Becky assumed the dog didn't understand but Nancy always clearly enjoyed the sound of Becky's voice when she was explaining things.

Ian

LIKE MOST IN the powerless world, Ian's sleep cycle was mostly governed by natural light. He rose when the sky began to lighten with morning and began to wind down in the evenings when darkness fell. He decided to get an early start this morning, assuming he'd need extra time since he'd be walking with Becky instead of riding his bike.

While he packed for the day, he ate a few pieces of jerky and tucked away a few more pieces for his lunch that day. Most days he bought his lunch, but he wanted to have a backup plan in case there was nothing appetizing being grilled on a coat hanger today. When he had everything packed, he climbed onto his bike and pedaled off through his neighborhood.

A few minutes later he rolled up to Becky's house. He opened the gate and pushed his bike with the trailer all the way up to her front porch. He took the steps two at a time and rapped on her door with his knuckles. When there was no response, he knocked again, louder this time. Becky had warned him this might be necessary since she sometimes kept odd hours.

This round of knocking led to a window being opened on the second floor. Becky leaned her head out. "Who is it?"

"It's Ian. You still interested in going to the market for the day?"

She smiled broadly and nodded. "Definitely."

Ian was a little puzzled by her reaction. She knew he was coming, so he didn't understand why she was so exuberant to find him at her door. He supposed he'd find out soon.

Moments later Becky cracked the door open, shoving her face in the gap. "Is anyone else with you?"

"No," Ian said. "I'm alone. What's going on?"

Becky heaved a long sigh. "I know this is kind of getting to be a pattern, but I need your help."

There was something about the way she said it that roused a nervous curiosity in Ian. He was apprehensive, wanting to know what she needed, but almost afraid to ask. When she swung the door open, he smelled the situation before he saw it. It was that distinct slaughterhouse odor. The smell of blood and death. The smell of carnage and cooling meat contained within a confined space.

As his eyes adjusted from the bright daylight to the dim interior of the entryway, Ian spotted the tangle of bodies at the base of the steps. A wide pool of drying blood had spread out around the bodies, disturbed only by two sets of footprints. One was human, the other a dog.

"What the hell happened?" Ian said, reluctantly stepping inside. The odor made his head swim. If not for those years spent as an EMT, he'd be outside throwing up over the railing.

"They broke in on me last night. I heard them coming. I have to admit there was a part of me that was afraid you and Randi had come back to rob me. That your kindness had all been a ruse to get in my house and see what I had. I'm sorry for thinking that."

"It's okay," Ian said. "That would have been a natural reaction. Are you okay? Is Nancy Drew okay?" He looked at the dog calmly standing alongside Becky, delicately licking coagulating blood from between her front toes.

"We're fine. The pain meds Randi gave me knocked her out. She didn't even wake up until I started blasting my gun in the house."

"How did you even hit them?" Ian asked. "No offense, but I'm sure that's difficult when you can't see."

"Not as difficult as you might think. I waited for them on the landing at the top of this flight of steps. When they got close to me, I opened fire. When they hit the bottom, I emptied the gun on them. I figured they were all dead, but I locked myself in my room all night in case they weren't. I was hoping you might check them for me and make sure that's the case."

Ian didn't need to get any closer. "They're all dead. I can tell that from here."

"How can you be sure?" Becky looked doubtful.

Ian had no doubts. Both women lay there with their eyes open. A fly lazily landed on one and got no reaction. There was a fist-sized crater in the man's face. Blood coagulated on the oak floors, filling the gaps between the flooring. "Trust me. You don't want to know."

She bobbed her head. "Okay then, but what do I do with them? I've never killed anyone before. Does the town have a place that we dump them?"

Ian winced at the question. In some ways it was naïve, but it was also very practical. Considering the number of people killed in this town, they probably did need a municipal body dump. Body disposal was a very real and practical concern in their new world.

Ian had been fortunate that he'd never had to deal with it in his own home. The few times he'd had to resort to violence, he'd been able to leave any evidence of his handiwork behind for the scavengers. That wasn't an option when you had three corpses draining out in your formal entryway.

He let out a long breath. "They need to be buried but three bodies will require a big hole. Since you don't have any horses, hauling them out of town isn't an option. I'm not quite sure what to do. It would take me days to dig a hole deep enough and you don't want these things laying around here for days."

"Randi has a horse. Do those people of hers have more horses? Do you think they'd help me?"

"I can ask," Ian said. "How about for now, I get these guys wrapped up in something so they quit leaking all over your nice floors? I can drag them outside and stash them somewhere until we can figure this out."

"I have a garage. We can put them in there. That will keep any dogs and cats from chewing on them."

"Good idea. Now, do you have any idea where I might find some plastic around this place?"

Becky thought. "Maybe the garage or basement. If we can't find any, we can use some old blankets or shower curtains, right?"

"Where's the basement door?"

Becky told him and Ian headed in that direction. He removed a lipstick-sized flashlight from his pocket and played the beam around the basement. He didn't see any rolls of plastic, but he did spot the coal chute door laying open. When he peered out the opening, he saw the carts that the thieves had left outside in the bushes.

Ian slammed the chute door and used what was left of the old wire to secure it shut. When he was done, he jogged back up the steps and told Becky what he'd found.

"I knew they came through the basement, but I didn't know how," she replied. "Maybe I'll have to get someone to board that hole up a little better."

"I'm heading out to the garage. It may take me a second because I'm going to grab the carts that these people left in the bushes and hide them in your garage. I don't know if they had friends or not, but I don't want to leave any evidence that they met their demise at your home."

"Good thinking."

The garage was one of the oldest that Ian had ever been inside. It must have dated from the 1930s or 1940s. It was constructed of a type of concrete block that resembled solid stone. Instead of having a standard garage door that rolled upward, it had two hinged doors that swung closed and were chained together. Ian used the padlock key that Becky had pointed him toward to remove the old padlock.

Before going inside, he ran around the house and pulled all the carts around to the garage. One was a garden cart, but the other two were jogging strollers designed to hold two babies. They had a nice, large compartment and rolled easily. He'd have to remember that if he ever had to do any prolonged travel on foot.

Inside the garage, the concrete floor was stained a dark gray from leaking oil, dirt, and all the other things that men spilled over a century of use. The trusses and the underside of the pine boards that made up the roof sheathing had oxidized to a deep brown with age. The rafters were hung with fishing poles, a disintegrating trout net, a minnow bucket, and several pairs of rubber waders that were decomposing to a green dust.

A homemade rack held a pick, a mattock, and a couple of shovels. There was a coal scoop that served double duty as a snow shovel. An old floor jack was pulled out of the way and tucked neatly under a workbench. Rusting metal shelves held dozens of rusting cans of old paint. A red gas can with yellow lettering sat alongside a Sears riding lawnmower with four flat tires.

The place reminded Ian of his grandfather's garage in Akron, Ohio. It had looked nearly identical to this. The sight of it transported him back in time and he nearly forgot what he'd come for. He tried to picture how his grandparents would have coped with this event if they were still alive. Fortunately, they weren't. It was a mercy that they'd been spared the fate of so many elderly people.

Ian spotted a plywood cabinet with peeling blue paint. He opened one door and found it was packed with old camping gear. It was of a sufficient vintage that the tent and the tarps he found were made of canvas and not the nylon that dominated the modern market. Ian pulled out one of the olive drab tarps and unrolled it. There were a few holes that appeared to have been chewed by mice, as well as dozens of desiccated stinkbugs that hadn't survived the winter.

Canvas wasn't ideal for containing bodily fluids, but it was the best thing he'd found so far.

Poking around in the cabinet, he found a more recent blue plastic tarp. When he couldn't find anything else suitable, he unrolled the family-sized canvas wall tent and used his knife to cut the floor out of it. There was no way anyone was ever using that tent again anyway, between the mouse holes and the dry rot.

When he was done, Ian collected the two tarps and the tent floor in his arms. He topped it off with a hank of cotton rope he found in the camping gear and headed back into the house.

Becky was still standing where he'd left her. "I never knew dead people smelled so bad. I mean, I knew they'd stink once they rotted but they're not even rotting yet."

Ian laughed, despite the morbid nature of the comment. "The smell of death is something you'll remember forever. It's the same smell you'll find in a slaughterhouse."

Becky crinkled her nose. "Lovely."

Ian rolled out one of the tarps alongside the corpses. Using a pair of dishwashing gloves he found beneath the kitchen sink, Ian grabbed one of the women and tugged her onto the canvas. Seeing the face clearly for the first time, he realized he recognized her. After laying her out neatly, he checked the other woman and found that he recognized her too. He could assume who the man was by the company he kept, but there was too much of his face missing to positively confirm it.

"I'll be damned," he muttered.

"What is it?" Becky asked.

"I know these folks. They're vendors at the market. They sell antiques and crap."

"You know their names?"

"No idea," Ian replied. "I recognize the faces, but we've never really talked. They kind of seemed like...assholes, if you'll excuse my French."

"They're dead assholes now," Becky remarked.

Ian laughed. "I can't wait to introduce you to my friend Jim. He says shit like that. You guys might get along."

Before wrapping the first body, Ian removed the woman's backpack and tossed it aside. He did a hasty search of the body and removed everything that might be of use. When he was done, he wrapped it and cut off a few lengths of rope, trussing it up like a Christmas roast.

"I'll be right back," Ian said. "I'm going to haul this one to the garage and then we'll do the next one."

42

Jim

IT WAS near quitting time for Jim's crew when Nooner's tractor came putting down the road toward the sewing factory, Lloyd and Luther sitting on the fenders like gargoyles. Jim stuck his head out of the door to see if they'd been able to come up with anything and was pleased to find they had a whole string of the solar traffic signs stretched out behind them. He was still smiling when Nooner came rolling up to the loading dock and killed the engine.

"Forgive me for not backing up to the door, but...liquor." He held up a glass jar, certain it should provide explanation enough.

Luther hopped off the tractor, looking excited about the find. "I've got eight of these things behind here. I used a couple of ratchet straps to piggyback them together. Worked like a dream."

"So what should we do with them now?" Jim asked, the question intended more for himself than anyone else. "I'm guessing I better not leave them outside."

Luther threw a thumb back over his shoulder at the tractor. "The loader on his tractor will lift them if we do it one at a time. Eventually, you'll want them on the roof. They'll get maximum light that way and stay safe from thieves."

Jim, Luther, and some of the crew worked together to unfasten the solar signs from the tractor, then from each other. Lloyd and Nooner remained on the tractor.

"Operators don't do labor," Nooner said. "Union rules."

"And I've already lost fingers once in the last year. I can't lose anymore and still beat out a tune on the banjo," Lloyd piped in.

"*Beat* is right," Jim mumbled. "Hey, Luther, what do you call a thousand banjos at the bottom of the ocean?"

"What?" Luther asked.

Jim grinned. "A good start."

Lloyd snarled. "Oh Lord, he's starting on the banjo jokes."

"Hey, Nooner, what's the difference between a banjo player and God?"

Nooner shook his head.

"God doesn't think he's a banjo player," Jim replied.

Nooner burst out laughing and slugged Lloyd in the arm.

Jim wasn't done. Pete and Charlie were sitting on the loading dock laughing hysterically. Not particularly because of the jokes, but because they loved to see Jim and Lloyd banter.

"Hey Lloyd?" Jim said.

"I'm not going to be part of this," Lloyd slurred.

"What do you say to a banjo player in a three-piece suit?"

Lloyd didn't answer.

Jim lowered the pitch of his voice. "Will the defendant please rise."

"You're so funny," Lloyd said, rolling his eyes.

"Hey, Pete, what do you call a banjo player with half a brain?" Jim asked.

"Gifted!" Pete sang without missing a beat.

"Great," Lloyd muttered. "He's passed it on to the next generation."

Jim didn't run out of banjo jokes until they had the last of the solar signs unhooked. They chained the short trailers to the loader bucket and Nooner carefully placed each of them on the dock. Despite his intoxication, Nooner didn't miss a beat. He was steady, accurate, and even relatively safe. He reminded Jim of other men he'd known over the years who'd spent so long working drunk that it became second nature to them.

Once the trailers had been loaded on the dock, Jim called it a day and sent his crew home. Jim sent Nooner and Lloyd back to the valley, hoping they'd be off the road by the time the rest of them headed that way. Pete, Charlie, and Luther helped secure the building for the night.

"I'm not sure if the Wolfords will drop Ed off here tonight or bring him to the valley with them," Jim told Luther. "Guess it all depends on what time they get back into town. This was the last run so they might have had a long day."

"Doesn't matter to me," Luther said. "I'm going to eat some dinner, roll some cigarettes, and relax."

"I'm just telling you so you can be sure of your targets before you shoot," Jim explained. "If you hear someone creeping around, make sure it's not Ed before you drop them."

Luther laughed. "Roger that."

They left the building in Luther's care for the night, mounted their horses, and headed toward Main Street. They were only halfway there when Charlie pointed to an approaching horse in the distance.

"That's Randi! I wonder if she's wanting to see how the building is coming along."

Jim shook his head. "More likely she's here to give me a hard time about something."

Pete and Charlie looked at each other and smiled. There was no denying the truth of it.

43

Jim

JIM SHOT Randi a snarky look as they closed in on each other. "You in a hurry to harass me about something? Couldn't wait until we got back to the valley?"

"No, I need to borrow you for a while," Randi said. There was a degree of urgency in her voice that told him this was something serious. "I need you to take a look at something with me."

Jim's eyes flickered toward Pete and Charlie at his side.

Randi shook her head. "The boys need to go on home. We don't want them involved in this."

"If there's going to be a fight, I want to help," Charlie said. "I can shoot."

Randi smiled at Charlie. "There's not going to be a fight and we're not going to be in danger. It's just something you two don't need to be involved in. How about you ride on home and let Ellen know that Jim will be a little late, but not to worry."

Pete frowned at that. "She worries anytime someone tells her not to worry. She never knows if that means Dad is trying to kill someone or if they're trying to kill him."

Jim turned in the saddle and regarded his son. "She really thinks that every time I'm late?"

Pete shrugged. "Yeah, Dad. She does."

"Seriously, it's nothing like that," Randi assured them. "But we do need to get moving."

Pete looked at Charlie. "Okay, I guess we're leaving. It's clear we're not wanted here."

Charlie nudged his horse into a walk and pretended to break into sobs as he rode away. Pete broke into a fake wail and fell in alongside Charlie.

"Drama queens," Randi muttered, turning her horse. "Come on. Let's go."

"What's going on?" Jim asked.

"It's a long story," she replied. "I guess it starts yesterday with Ian. He was headed home from the market when he came across this lady who was out with her dog. She and her dog got attacked by two strays and Ian intervened. Her dog got chewed on a little so Ian radioed me at the market and asked me if I could come by later and check it out. He didn't really go into any detail, so I didn't know it was a dog until I got there. I assumed I'd be treating the person."

"So, you're a veterinarian now?" Jim asked. "Along with being a madam?"

Randi wagged her finger in the air. "Except I'm not a madam now because the local sex workers are ashamed to be seen with you, so there's that."

"Touché."

Randi grinned, satisfied with the quick way in which she'd dealt with Jim. "Anyway, I get there and help the dog. The lady is about my age and she's really cool. We hung out with her for a little while and talked. It turns out that yesterday was the first day she'd left her property since the collapse."

"And she's been able to survive?"

"She was scared about revealing too much since we were strangers, but she'd done well for herself. She's healthy."

"That's some bad luck then. First day out of the house and you have a run-in with some feral dogs."

"Her day got worse," Randi said. "The only reason she came out yesterday was that she'd heard about the market from a neighbor and wanted to check it out. She must have drawn the attention of some unsavory characters while she was there, because someone broke into her house. Ian went by this morning because he was going to escort her to the market. She was going to sell a few things at my booth and see how it went. When he got to her house this morning, she needed help."

"Was she injured?"

"No, but she had three dead bodies to dispose of and she wasn't sure where to start."

"Geez," Jim said. "Guess that explains how she survived. She's a badass."

"You don't know the half of it."

"What's that mean?"

Randi shook her head. "You'll see. Anyway, she hung out with me at the market all day, then Ian walked her home. He asked if we might be able to help her out. Like I said, she's really cool. In fact, you should consider bringing her on to work at the roadhouse."

Jim was surprised to see Randi so excited about someone she'd met. As far as he knew, she only liked one person in the world who wasn't related to her and that was Charlie. Jim wasn't even sure that she had much of a tolerance for Lloyd and they had some manner of relationship going. "We'll see. The place isn't even open yet."

Randi led him through town and onto the back street toward Ian's house. She refused to answer any more questions about what had taken place, just telling Jim he'd understand when he got there. He wasn't excited to take on any more people or any new problems, but he owed Ian a favor. Ian had defended his people at the market, possibly saving their lives, when Hadley and the regional sheriff had started a fight. If Ian wanted to help this lady, Jim would do whatever he could to make it happen.

They turned off onto a different street, heading toward some older, larger homes. Jim couldn't recall the last time he'd been down this street, but it may have been when he was a kid. When they reached the end, Randi dismounted at a stone wall and opened a narrow gate. She went inside and Jim followed her through.

"Why didn't you tell me about coming here to treat a dog?" Jim said. "I saw you this morning. You could have mentioned it."

"I had other priorities. Like giving you shit about your failed attempt at being a pimp."

"I wasn't trying to be a pimp," Jim said for what was probably the millionth time.

"That's not what your mother says," Randi replied in a childish, sing-song voice. "Honestly, it slipped my mind. I guess what happened yesterday didn't seem like all that big a deal. Killing three intruders is a bigger deal. I'd have remembered that."

The clatter of hooves on the brick sidewalk must have announced their arrival because the door swung open as they were tying their horses off. Ian stepped out of the house and nodded a greeting to Jim.

"I appreciate you coming, my friend. I know it was a lot to ask."

Jim waved him off. "I owe you, man. All you have to do is ask. If it's in my power, I'll do it."

Ian looked a little sheepish at that. "You better see the situation before you commit yourself."

Jim grabbed his pack and rifle off his horse. He was standing at the base of the steps, speaking with Ian, when Becky stepped out of the house and stood on the porch. She didn't have her cane, but she had a leash on Nancy Drew and held her tight to her side.

Then Jim noticed there was something about the way she looked at him. She had her head cocked slightly to the side, leading with her ear instead of her eyes. Jim had seen that look before. "Hell, you're blind!"

Becky frowned. "And you're ugly!"

Jim was taken aback. "If you're blind, how do you know I'm ugly?"

"Because you sound ugly," she snapped. "And I'm a good judge of people."

"Ignore him," Randi said to Becky. "He's like that. Not a bit of tact. Totally without class."

"He's the leader of your group? That's the best you could come up with?"

"No one else wants the responsibility," Jim said in his own defense. "Besides, I have some good qualities."

Becky folded her arms. "I'm waiting."

Ian and Randi exchanged an amused glance, enjoying the show.

Jim looked at the ground. "Well, I'm loyal to my friends. I've kept most of them safe and alive. We're kind of like a family, I guess."

Becky nodded. Combined with her stance, it was a gesture that oozed sarcasm. "Oh, that just means they like you because they have to. It's not a matter of choice or a statement that you're actually a good leader."

Jim sighed and looked at Ian. "Why am I here? Surely you didn't have me ride across town just to be berated by this foul-tempered woman."

"I *like* this foul-tempered woman," Randi said.

Ian nodded enthusiastically. "So do I."

Jim shrugged. "Then I'm just here to meet your new friend and playmate?"

"Don't be an asshole," Becky snapped. "You're here because they say you're very experienced in body disposal and I need some help in that department. I had a break-in last night and my poor dog here was too doped-up to even bark at them. She slept through the whole thing."

It was only then that Jim recalled Randi saying there were three dead bodies here. He'd forgotten that detail in the shock of finding that it was a blind woman they'd been talking about this whole time. How could Randi have failed to mention that? It seemed like such a relevant detail.

"Since you're not saying anything, I expect you're standing there slack-jawed and drooling on yourself," Becky continued. "Probably trying to figure out how this blind woman killed three attackers, but it's true. I wasn't sure they were all dead until Ian got here and checked them out this morning, but they were sure as shit dead. Now I just need to figure out what to do with them."

"Three takes a big hole," Ian confirmed. "That's a lot of digging for a bunch of thieving scumbags."

"How did you kill them?" asked Jim.

Becky dropped her right hand and reached beneath her shirttail. She yanked a large revolver from a leather holster. Ian, Jim, and Randi all ducked in response until Becky had the weapon safely pointed skyward.

"It's a .44 magnum. My daddy taught me how to shoot it using shotshells, so I'd have a better chance of hitting my target. It worked. I let them walk into a trap and I pulled the trigger until the gun was empty. I expect all three of them are in Hell right now learning what it feels like to be jabbed with a pitchfork and I hope it hurts."

Jim raised his eyebrows and looked at Randi, then at Ian. He could see what they meant about this one. She did have a certain charm about her. "Are they glued to the floor?" Jim had pried blood-encrusted bodies from the floor before and it could be an unpleasant experience.

"No," Ian replied. "I wrapped them and stuck them in the garage this morning. I was just helping Becky clean up the mess when you guys rode up."

"That's good," Jim said. "You're right, though. Three bodies take a big hole. Burying them would be a waste of time. I don't believe in breaking a sweat over the bad decisions of assholes."

Becky straightened defiantly. "Who are you calling an asshole, asshole?"

"Not you." Jim sighed. "The assholes who broke in on you. *Their* bad decisions."

Becky relaxed. "Oh, sorry. I thought you were talking about me."

Jim frowned. "Geez."

"I heard that," Becky snapped. "I hear everything. You remember that!"

"Do you want my help or not?" Jim asked.

"Yes," Ian and Randi said in unison.

"Yes," Becky agreed. "I'll be good."

"As I was saying before I was so rudely interrupted, we don't bury them," Jim began. "I've got the Wolfords on the road today, but they're supposed to be back tonight. Tomorrow morning they're going to unload the last of the supplies from the brewery in St. Paul, then I was going to pay them and let them go. They've hauled everything I need hauled."

"Who are the Wolfords?" Becky asked.

"They're people I hired to haul some loads for a project I'm working on," Jim replied. "They have large draft horses and wagons. Some of the biggest horses I've ever seen."

Becky looked concerned. "Can they be trusted?"

Jim nodded, then realized Becky couldn't see the gesture. "I think so. I've spent a lot of time with them in the past week or so. I trust them, and I don't trust many people at all."

"I guess that's good enough for me," Becky said, leaning over and scratching Nancy Drew's head.

"It's the best solution. If we haul the bodies out of here on horses, your neighbors will see them. People will talk. It will only serve to draw attention to you," Jim said. "If we bring in a wagon, we can cover the bodies up and no one will be the wiser."

"What will we do with them?" Randi asked.

"I say we throw them off the bridge into the river," Jim suggested. "The water will carry them out of town. Within a few weeks the snapping turtles, catfish, and other river critters will take care of them."

Both Ian and Randi were nodding in agreement at the suggestion, but Jim wanted to know what Becky thought. He hoped she wasn't one to have reservations about disposing of bodies in such a disrespectful manner. She didn't.

Becky cackled at the suggestion. "Good enough for them. Let the turtles eat their sorry asses."

"Any idea who they were?" Jim asked. "Starving? Druggies? Degenerates?"

"Actually, they were vendors at the market," said Randi. "When Ian told me he recognized them, it turned out they were up there in the pavilion with me. I'd looked at their booth before. Two old women and a man. They were snooty antique dealers."

Jim frowned. "Really?"

"It's an obsession for some people," Ian said. "They don't get over it just because the world has gone all to hell."

Jim looked as if he were having trouble reconciling that information. "I guess. You good with this, Becky? You fine with us picking them up tomorrow? It will probably be late morning because of having to unload the wagons at the sewing factory first."

"I was going to attend the market, but I'll stay here and wait on you," Becky replied. "Will you be coming with them?"

Jim raised an eyebrow. "Why? You prefer I stay home?"

Becky laughed at that. "No, but I won't open the door if I don't recognize someone."

"I'll come with them," Jim agreed. "You let us in the garage and we'll deal with it."

"Are you going to have to pay these people for hauling the bodies?" Becky continued.

"I expect so, but it's not a big deal."

Becky shook her head adamantly. "I'll make it up to you. I have things I can trade. I can also work it off. Randi said you were opening a roadhouse in the old sewing factory."

Jim gave Randi a dry look. Randi gave an apologetic shrug and Jim knew it meant absolutely nothing. Randi wasn't sorry at all. She always did what she wanted and if it irritated him, that was an added bonus.

"How about we talk about that later," Jim said. "Let's deal with the three dead stooges first."

44

Luther

LUTHER HAD PLANNED a relaxing evening on the roof of the sewing factory. There was a steel ladder permanently mounted to the brick out back for roof maintenance and Luther climbed it with an old lawn chair he'd found in the weeds along the road. He positioned it facing the sunset and settled in with a small jar of homemade liquor he'd gotten from Lloyd, trading him a Schrade Improved Muskrat pocketknife for it.

He took off his shirt and reclined in the lawn chair, slipping his sunglasses onto his face. He took a sip of the liquor and washed it down with a swallow of branch water from a canteen. He felt good. His muscles had that pleasing tiredness that came from a satisfying day of physical labor, and his belly was full, which was no small thing in this time of deprivation and hunger.

Hugh had lent him a paperback to keep him busy if he got bored. The book was the first in Jerry Ahern's series from the 1980s, *The Survivalist*. It was about a nuclear war, but the landscape of that novel sounded an awful lot like what people were going through now.

Hugh had told him that the book might help him understand a little more about the disaster they were facing. Luther could do with a little more understanding. He'd felt blindsided by the whole thing since day one. Despite his military background, he'd not expected the country to fall so fast or the collapse to last this long. Somehow, he always imagined America would spring back to its feet like Chuck Norris in one of his movies. So far, things hadn't shaken out that way.

Luther lost himself in the book and perhaps also in the jar of liquor at his side. He read until the sun dropped below the horizon, then had to remove his sunglasses to keep going. When it finally became too dark to read, Luther tossed the book down on his discarded shirt and stared at the sunset. He lit another cigarette and watched the light fade. He was as content as he'd been in some time.

He had another carton of smokes hidden at home, but this was one of the last packs he had with him. He'd been pleased to learn that Hugh and Randi had tobacco for sale. He'd not hand-rolled a cigarette since smoking Bugle in high school, but it beat quitting.

As he relaxed, Luther's thoughts returned to his original reason for coming to this town. It was as if that situation was the low spot in the floor and his mind constantly rolled back there the minute it wasn't occupied. He'd stayed here because of the rumors linking Jim Powell to the death of Hadley Wright. Luther assumed that if Jim had killed Hadley, he'd probably also killed Isaac.

Luther again found himself asking the same questions he'd been asking himself for several days now. What was his strongest motivation in making this trip to Russell County? Was it his loyalty to the friend who was quite likely dead at this point or was he driven by the fear of not having Isaac's supplies?

He'd originally manipulated his way into this job at the sewing factory to investigate Jim Powell and learn the truth about Isaac. He'd always assumed that the end result of this mission would be killing Jim Powell, then slipping off to return to Wallace County. Oddly enough, he often found himself so immersed in his day-to-day life on this construction job that he forgot his purpose in being there. His experience of working on Jim Powell's project at the sewing factory had not only been comfortable, it had become fulfilling.

Sure, he and Isaac had been friends, but Isaac was gone much of the time attending to his regional sheriff responsibilities. Looking back on his life of a few months ago, Luther realized he was often lonely and depressed. He might have had access to supplies, but he had no friends and nothing to occupy his time. Now he had both, even though he was hesitant to include Jim Powell among those people he considered to be friends.

What the hell was he going to do?

As he was considering this question, he caught the echo of gravel crunching beneath feet, the sound bouncing off the long brick wall to the front of the factory building. Assuming that Ed Frye might have been dropped off on Main Street by the Wolfords, Luther stood and walked toward the edge of the roof. The building was surrounded by a brick parapet wall that stood perhaps two feet above the surface of the roof. The wall was capped with terra cotta tiles that overlapped at the edges.

Luther already had his hand up in the air, prepared to wave, when he saw the dark shapes of two people walking toward the loading dock. One was a man and he was ranting. The other shape was either a woman or a smaller man. The voice didn't sound like it belonged to Ed Frye.

Luther crouched down out of sight and listened. The strangers rattled the loading dock door, cursing when they found it locked. Luther crept along the roof, staying close to the pair as they tried the other doors along the front of the building. He knew if they persisted in their search, they'd get to the back door eventually and their luck would change. Luther had left that door open to allow himself a way back in.

His mind wasn't working at its normal speed. Luther's thoughts were blurry from the alcohol and maybe a little frayed at the edges. He realized too late that he probably needed to get off the roof and beat them to the back door. By the time he reached the steel ladder, the figures were already moving along the back of the building, headed for the door. He was too late.

Luther crept back to his lawn chair and stood there a moment. He took a few deep breaths, trying to clear his head, then grabbed his rifle and went back to the ladder.

"They left this one open!" the man's voice said. "Dumb bastards."

"Get in there, then," a woman said. "Make sure there's no one inside."

"I hope there is someone inside," the man replied, venom in his voice. "I'll shoot them in the knees and leave them in here to burn alive."

Luther frowned. These two hadn't thought things out if they were planning on burning this building down. The walls were solid brick. The office area was framed with metal studs and finished with wall-papered drywall. There wasn't much that would burn, except for the wooden beams that spanned the ceiling and held up the roof. However, he doubted they could build a fire high enough to ignite them.

Then he remembered the wooden cable reels they'd collected for tables and all the lumber stacked inside. If they could start a blaze with those materials, it could eventually reach the ceiling. It might not burn the building to the ground, but it would certainly render it unusable.

"Well, shit," Luther muttered.

He stepped lightly, hoping they wouldn't be able to hear him walking on the roof. He slung his rifle around his back to prevent it from banging against anything, then transitioned to the ladder. As carefully as he could, he climbed off the roof, making sure he maintained three points of contact at all times. That was never so important as when a man was climbing drunk.

When he reached the concrete landing at the back door, he could see nothing but shadows. Only the depth of the blackness distinguished between what was outside, what was inside, and the open doorframe that separated the two.

Luther sucked in a deep breath to try and clear his head. He moved his rifle around to the front of his body. He tugged the charging handle back slightly and used the tip of a finger to confirm the presence of a round in the chamber. When he verified that he felt brass, he used his thumb to move the selector to the Fire position. Just as he was trying to figure out his next move, a flicker of light appeared inside the building.

Luther listened carefully, hearing a lighter being struck, the small sound echoing in the space of the building. Luther moved closer to the door and peered inside. When the lighter struck again, he spotted the two figures crouched at the debris pile, trying to spark a fire in the trash heaped up there.

He wondered what he should do. If he yelled at them to stop, they'd take off running and he'd lose them in the massive dark space. It would be like some horror movie with a killer loose in the funhouse. They could pop up anywhere. If he turned on his flashlight to look for them, it would be the same as sticking a beacon to his head that said "shoot me."

Though it was risky, he needed to let them get a small blaze going. That should provide just enough light that he could track their movements, then he could engage them without using his headlamp. Then Luther began to doubt himself. Did he really need to engage them at all? Couldn't he just fire a couple of warning shots and drive them off?

The idea of warning shots was pointless. What would that accomplish? If he didn't deal with them today, he'd be dealing with them another day. Perhaps when he was climbing the ladder to the roof, he'd take a shot to the back. Maybe he'd be crouched in the bushes relieving himself and get blasted with a shotgun.

No, these had to be the people that Jim had warned him about, the man and woman who'd shown up looking for the two men he'd killed here the other night. This was personal for them and they wouldn't let it go. If they weren't killed, they'd keep coming back until they found satisfaction.

Luther didn't want to live like that. Not with the persistent feeling that he needed to be looking over his shoulder at all times. When he'd fought in the war, every engagement had been scrutinized, reviewed, and second-guessed. They had to justify every life they'd taken, even when it was the life of an enemy intent on killing them.

As crazy as it sounded, there were no rules of engagement on American soil these days. Most of the time, no one questioned a killing. Well, that wasn't exactly true. The two people he was watching in the dark were there because they were questioning why two of their family members were missing. That was the extent of it, though. It was like the Wild West, but with even fewer rules.

Luther braced his rifle against the doorframe. With the alcohol impairing his balance, he needed every advantage he could get. He sighted on the back of the man and hesitated for a moment. Something from his childhood, some memory of someone telling him that fights should be fair, popped into his head. He pushed it away. That was a stupid rule for a simpler time.

He let out a breath and let the glowing red dot of his optic rest on the man's spine, directly between his shoulder blades. He knew he needed to get on with this. Hesitate any longer and they'd notice him. He pulled the trigger.

The woman screamed and twisted toward her companion as the boom of Luther's rifle echoed off the brick walls. The crouched man tipped over onto his side and arched his back, crying out at the pain. Luther fired again. This round went low but ricocheted off the concrete and struck the man he was aiming at.

The powerful report of Luther's rifle distracted him. Like many people who enjoyed shooting as a recreational activity, he'd spent so much time shooting with ear protection that the unimpeded blast of his rifle took him by surprise. He tried to force himself to focus on the scene ahead of him, but his vision skewed sideways, the alcohol making his head swim. He shook his head as if that might reboot his vision.

When he regained his focus, the woman had disappeared from the scene of the trash fire. Her companion was on his side, blood running from his mouth, his gory face reflecting the firelight. He'd taken two rounds but was still in the fight. He fumbled to pull a handgun from his pants and tried to aim at Luther but couldn't fully extend his arm. He pulled the trigger and a wild round struck the brick wall near Luther.

Luther flinched and jumped back, realizing again how the alcohol was impeding his ability to fight, and even to think. He should have finished that old man off when he was drawing his handgun, but Luther was almost mesmerized by the sight of it. Now he was torn between sending a more carefully aimed shot at the old man, taking cover, or trying to find the woman running loose in the building.

The old man squeezing off a second round made Luther's decision for him.

"The squeaky wheel gets the grease," Luther mumbled.

He placed his red dot on the distant man's chest and squeezed off a double tap. Both rounds hit their mark. The man immediately went limp, his head sagging to the floor and the handgun dropping from his hand.

Luther smiled. "Bingo!" He was proud of himself, despite having bungled the operation thus far.

His gloating was cut short by a muzzle flash in the darkness. There was a loud boom and a round struck the steel door behind Luther. Apparently, the woman was armed and a better shot than the injured man had been. Luther realized she might even be a better shot than him in his impaired state and that was a chilling thought.

He scanned the darkness but didn't pick up any movement. Either the woman was laying low, or the glow of the fire didn't reach her position. Unable to immediately spot her, he turned his attention to the growing blaze. It had spread from the trash pile to one of the wooden cable reels they'd intended to use as tables. Luther knew he was going to have to deal with the fire soon or it would be too large for him to extinguish.

There was a metal clank in the darkness that Luther recognized as being the latch on the dock door. He twisted in that direction but didn't see anything. The bright blaze had destroyed his night vision. There was a screech and the dock door began rolling upward.

Luther's instinct was to fire blindly in that direction, but he couldn't see anything to shoot at.

That changed as the door got a little higher. Luther could now distinguish a strip of lighter darkness at the bottom of the door. He could see outside. The screeching stopped and the door quit moving. Then Luther caught a flurry of movement as the woman dropped to the ground and rolled beneath the door.

Luther unleashed a cry of rage at the escaping woman and sent a half-dozen rounds through that opening, several of them ricocheting off the concrete. He hoped that some of them connected with her fleeing body but understood that was a longshot. If nothing else, perhaps they gave her a little more incentive to keep running.

With the second intruder now gone, Luther made his rifle safe, slung it over his back, and lurched toward the fire. He used a long piece of framing lumber to shove the burning cable reels away from the blaze, then used the same board to break up the fire. Wielding it like a push broom, he scattered everything that was in flames until it would burn out harmlessly on the concrete.

When he was done, Luther leaned against his piece of framing lumber like a proud farmer leaning against his pitchfork in an old painting. He decided to leave the doors open for a little while to allow the slight breeze to carry the smoke outside. He'd shut them when the smoke cleared.

He never got the chance.

His first indication that the woman had returned was when the long blade of the Old Hickory butcher knife slipped beneath his ribs and into his kidney. The woman yanked the blade out, intent on inflicting more damage. Luther reacted out of a mixture of pain and instinct, spinning to his right and catching her in the temple with his elbow.

The woman staggered back a step but didn't lose her grip on the knife. Nor did she lose her murderous rage. She screamed and prepared to lunge at Luther, but his range time and muscle memory paid off. He snatched his handgun from the holster on his belt and shot from the hip, the rounds from his 9mm Sig catching her center mass.

The first three rounds hit in such quick succession that she didn't even have time to drop before the next hit her. Then the knife fell from her hand and she toppled over, clutching her midsection. That Luther continued firing into her body even after she was mortally wounded was not a product of his training, but a purely instinctive response brought about by the pain of his injury. He was firing out of anger.

She was dead by the time Luther fell not far from her. He didn't have his blowout kit on him and wasn't sure he could reach his pack in the office section of the building. Getting to his feet and walking that distance seemed an insurmountable task.

He struggled to get a hand to the wound on his back and felt the blood pouring from him. He made a sound that was somewhere between a whimper and a cry of surrender. He felt nothing but defeat at the moment. He was seriously injured in a world with no 9-1-1 and no advanced medical care.

He let out a long breath and relaxed his body. When he did, his hand fell on the old paperback in his pocket. He'd shoved it there when he got up from his lawn chair on the roof, thinking he'd be climbing down to hang out with Ed. Part of him felt as if it was pointless to try and stop the bleeding, but another part of him refused to give up. He tore a page from Jerry Ahern's paperback and shoved it into the wound.

While people only grimaced from such actions in the movies, Luther understood in that moment that none of those people had actually performed that same task in real life. Had they done so, they'd have understood that it didn't produce a grimace–it produced a blood-curdling scream and blinding pain.

Beyond that, all Luther could think to do was to apply pressure to the wound. He struggled out of his t-shirt and wrapped that around the book. He positioned it under the wound, then rolled himself over on his back. With his body weight pressing down against the book, he could feel it trapped between him and the floor.

He stared upward but couldn't really see anything. It made him wonder if the blackness was the dark of the building or the darkness of his approaching death. Despite his grim situation, Luther found it ironic that he'd ventured far from home on a mission of vengeance and ended up stumbling into a life that he was beginning to enjoy. Had tonight not happened, it was likely that he'd have moved past his desire for revenge and continued to work for Jim Powell. Now all was lost.

Despite the warmth of this night, he felt the cold of the concrete floor seeping into his body. He thought of his parents. They were both dead now but had been wonderful people who'd given him the best life they could. He thought of his grandparents and the totally unconditional love they'd had for him. He wondered whether he was about to see them again.

He figured his parents would race to hug him if he got to go to the same place they'd gone to. The same for his grandmothers. The thought of that reunion made him cry in the darkness. His grandfathers, both practical men, would likely be inclined to smack him on the back of the head for getting himself killed.

45

Jim

THEY LEFT the valley shortly after sunrise, anticipating a long workday ahead of them. The Wolfords had arrived late in the evening last night, so dead-tired that they only took time to eat a quick meal in silence before stretching out for the night. Gary's family and Randi would be going to the market to open their booths, but everyone else in the group was headed to the sewing factory.

As usual, Jim expected to find a line of people looking for work when he arrived. The line had grown shorter over the weeks as people became discouraged that they weren't chosen, but there was usually still a line. Not this morning.

Everyone was gathered around the loading dock, just as they'd been when Luther had shot NAPA and Newport. At first, that was what Jim thought he'd find. The neighbors Jim had dealt with yesterday must have returned last night and Luther had taken them out. The situation was worse than that.

Jim rode his horse to the dock door. Inside, he could see two men crouched beside Luther's pale body. He lay in a large puddle of his own seeping fluids.

"Is he dead?" Jim asked.

"We just got here," one of the men standing at the dock said. "He's talking, though. He asked for you."

Jim dismounted, then hopped up onto the loading dock. He immediately smelled the odor of smoke and charred wood, then took in the sight of the other two bodies. Checking out their faces, he recognized them as the people he'd spoken to outside yesterday. He went to Luther's side, wanting to kneel close to him, but not wanting to stand in the man's blood. It seemed almost rude to do so.

Jim asked softly, "What happened, Luther?"

Luther's eyes were open and staring straight ahead of him, into the rafters and beams of the building. His breathing was labored and interfered with his speaking. "Those people came...back. I shot one but...thought the other ran off. She...got me with a knife while I was...putting the fire...out."

"We'll get Randi back here. I'll send someone for her. She's a nurse. She'll patch you up and you'll be good as new in a few weeks."

Luther's grimace briefly turned to a faint smile at the absurdity of it. "Hell, I'm...dead already...Jim. I'm just too...hardheaded to... accept it."

"Charlie!" Jim shouted, ready to send him to bring Randi back, but he fell silent when he heard the next words Luther spoke.

"I came here to...kill you."

Jim looked down with surprise. "What did you say?"

"I was a friend of...Isaac...the sheriff."

Jim knew exactly who Luther was talking about. Hugh, Charlie, and Jim had killed him at Garvey's cabin on the road to Hidden Valley Lake, then burned the cabin to destroy the evidence.

"We were...war buddies. He lived at my house. I came to find... what happened. Lot of...fingers pointed your...way."

"I killed him," Jim admitted. "But he earned it. One of us was going to die eventually and I didn't want it to be me."

Luther began to say something else, but Jim could barely hear him. Luther's voice was getting lower, as if there was less breath to push the words into the world. Jim grabbed a scrap of plywood and knelt on it, getting as close to Luther's face as he could.

"What was that?" Jim asked. "I didn't hear you."

Luther let out a long sigh and Jim was afraid that was the end of him. Afraid that long breath carried his soul and, with it, any unsaid words.

Instead, Luther swallowed and concentrated. "It's okay. I believe... you're a good man. Trying to...be. Wish I could have seen...how all this...turned...out."

When his words faded this time, there was no doubt that Luther was dead. He hadn't expired with a sigh, but gave the impression he was only hesitating to gather his thoughts.

"Son of a bitch," Jim muttered, pushing up from the scrap of plywood and turning away from the body. He hadn't noticed that Hugh had come inside and was standing behind him.

"You think he hung in there all night so he could tell you that?" Hugh asked.

"Either that or he didn't want to die alone."

"What should we do with these bodies?" one of the workers asked.

Jim knew what he was going to do with them. They were already going into town to haul off those bodies from Becky's place. What was a few more?

"Try to find something to wrap them in," Jim said. "Lay them out behind the building so people can't see them. We'll deal with them later."

"You need us to dig any graves?" another man asked.

Jim shook his head. "We don't have time for that. Just leave them outside for us and I'll take care of it."

They'd rigged up a system earlier in the week to pump water into a plastic tank on the roof. It was gravity-fed and didn't have a lot of pressure, but it beat the hell out of carrying buckets whenever they needed water. Once the bodies were outside, Pete used the hose to rinse the blood off the floor while Charlie scrubbed at it with a push broom.

"Never a dull moment around this place, is there?" Shade boomed, breaking the solemnity of the moment.

"That's the truth," Jim mumbled.

"It was a nice change of pace, but I can't wait to get back home," Shade said. "A man gets to missing his own bed after a while."

"I hope you'll come around sometime and have a drink with us," Hugh said.

Shade bobbed his head eagerly. "You can count on it."

Jim wasn't really unsettled by the death. He hadn't known Luther well enough to be upset at his loss. However, the admission that Luther had come to kill him was a little disturbing. Luther had been presented with plenty of opportunities in which he could have gotten the jump on Jim. There hadn't been any indications of bad blood or tension. Luther had played his part so well he'd likely have succeeded in killing Jim had he proceeded with his plan. Jim wasn't sure how anyone could be confronted with information like that and not be rattled by it. That could easily have been him lying there dead on the floor this morning.

To shake off those disturbing thoughts, he jumped into the task at hand and began handing out assignments. Once the floors were clean and the bodies stashed, they unloaded the last of the loads from the wagons. Ed supervised that part, having a good understanding of where everything needed to be for maximum efficiency.

While the equipment was set up, Ed discussed it with Lloyd, explaining what various pieces did. Lloyd's background was in home-made stills. Each piece was a unique sculpture in which the design was shaped around what materials were available to the builder. Some were well-crafted while others were cobbled together from salvage and repurposed parts. In Lloyd's family, the "pot" of the still was something that each man had to make for himself, while the coiled copper worm had been passed down through generations.

"Never used a fancy store-bought still before," Lloyd said. "This is going to be interesting."

"There's less chance of this one blowing up on you," said Ed. "And it makes distilling a lot simpler."

"We'll see what kind of liquor it makes," Lloyd said, casting a wary eye at the fancy equipment. "That's the real test."

With the sewing factory bustling with activity, Jim took a seat at the bar and worked on his punch list of all the items that remained to be completed. He was pleased at how much he was able to check off the list. With their crew, they'd been able to accomplish quite a bit. It was still a primitive building, more 19th century saloon than 21st century brew pub, but it was coming together.

With the construction phase winding down, Jim began to add other items to the list that would have to be addressed soon. First of all, they needed a name. Expanding on that idea, Jim thought it might be cool to have names for the various beers and liquors they'd be serving. Something appropriate to an apocalypse.

They'd also need a sign and maybe some other forms of advertising that they could stick up in town. The brothels handed out handwritten notes to advertise their girls. Perhaps they could have some of the people back in the valley write up flyers. Was it wrong to assign that job to the children? Jim didn't think so. This was a family effort.

He also needed to think about staffing. They'd need a manager each night. Security would be important, and it would probably require more than one person. There would need to be servers, dish washers, and in the cold weather they'd need people working the woodstoves and bringing in wood. The more he delved into it, the more his head spun.

He knew this was supposed to be Lloyd's baby, but Lloyd was a classic "Good Time Charlie." He'd never be able to run the place, but they'd let him think he was. He could perform on stage each night and address the audience.

Beneath it all, beneath the drinks and bustle of patrons, Jim's focus would be on building their network and gathering information for their area study. He didn't know what was going to happen in the coming months and years, but despite the bodies they'd dealt with recently, things were moving from a period of brute force and violence to a period that would require more intelligence and strategy. Jim wanted to be prepared for that and this roadhouse would be the culmination of that effort.

46

Jim

ONCE THEY HAD the wagons unloaded, Jim pulled Hugh to the side. When Hugh had reached the valley with Shade's people the previous night, Jim had filled him in on Ian and Randi's encounter with Becky and how he'd promised to help dispose of her bodies.

"I'm taking Shade Wolford and some of his people to haul off those bodies at Becky's house. We'll take Luther and the two dead assholes with us. Kind of keep an eye out while everyone is working. I don't know how many more people are going to show up looking for their dead family members."

"Got it," Hugh said. "Head on a swivel."

"We may need to figure out something for tonight, Hugh. I'm not comfortable with leaving Ed here alone. He's a brewer, not a fighter."

"The guy you've had cooking might be interested. If you trust him, I'll talk with him while you're gone. I don't mind staying tonight, but we need to work on a long-term arrangement. I can't handle too much *city* life."

Jim smiled at Hugh referring to this small-town side street as the city. It might not meet most people's definition, but Jim felt the same way about it. Town would always feel alien to country people. Too many souls and too much noise.

Jim headed for the loading dock and recruited some of the Wolfords to help him load the bodies into the wagons. They covered them with a tarp to avoid prying eyes. Shade recruited one of his nephews to ride shotgun with him, literally carrying a shotgun while wearing a bandoleer of twelve-gauge rounds. There was another man in the back of the wagon, riding with the bodies. He was a good worker but wasn't much for conversation. Nor did he seem to be too weirded out about riding with corpses. Maybe it wasn't the first time.

Since there was only one way through town from the sewing factory to the neighborhood where Becky and Ian lived, Jim set off down Main Street with Shade at a canter behind him. While cars and trucks may have been noisy, they had nothing on a team of massive horses pulling a wagon. The sound was so powerful that Jim felt it in his chest, like the thrum of a helicopter's rotors.

He tried to ignore the market when they passed but understood the market would not be ignoring them. All heads turned in their direction to investigate the clopping hooves. Jim wondered if the people at the market were still speculating on what he was up to or if they'd all heard about it by this point. Surely word of the roadhouse was making its way through the gossip chain.

They turned right at the confederate statue in the center of town and entered one of the oldest neighborhoods. Even with most of the residents dead or gone, those who were home came to their windows, yards, and doors to see what was passing by. Shade Wolford had none of Jim's concerns about stealth. He waved and shouted greetings to the people he passed.

"It's like riding in a parade with Santa Claus," Jim commented, pulling alongside the wagon.

"People need a parade sometimes," said Shade. "Look at those sour faces. Everyone is obsessed with gloom and doom. If I had candy, I'd be throwing it out along the way."

"A lot of them would rather mope around than do something

about it," Jim said with disgust. "That's what pisses me off. I've called them out on it before. It motivated some of them to get off their asses and do something about it, but there are still those who insist on waiting for help that's never going to come."

Shade shrugged. "Well, when the rest of the lazy ones die off, that's more bacon for the rest of us."

Jim cocked an eyebrow at him. "I've never heard that expression before."

"I just made it up, right this minute. Seemed to be a situation that called for an expression and that was the best I could do on short notice."

Jim laughed. "You know, Shade, I like you guys. I like the way you work and the way you think. I like that you don't let all the bullshit get you down."

"Life ain't never been easy for hill people," Shade said. "When they settled this country, we took the worst of the land because we thought it would give us some privacy. Then city people decided they wanted our coal and timber, so they put in railroads and it's never been the same since. It's always been boom or bust in these moun-tains, with the emphasis on the bust."

"I've said the same thing many times," Jim said. "Tough people settled this land, but the high-paying jobs brought in outsiders. Those people don't have roots here, but a lot of them stuck around even after the mining jobs were gone and now we can't get shed of them."

Now it was Shade's turn to laugh. "By damn, they're thinning out now. When this is over, only the hardy will be left. We'll be back to where hill people used to be. I hate to come off as excited about such an unpleasant turn of events, but I suppose I am. Might as well be honest about it."

"Yet another example of why I wonder if we might be long lost brothers," Jim mused.

After a few turns down maple-lined streets, Becky's house came into sight.

"That's it," Jim said. "I'm going to the front door to let her know we're here. Then I'll get you to pull around to the right. There's a driveway there that leads to the garage. That's where we're picking up the packages."

Shade threw a little salute and Jim headed for the gate set into the low wall out front. He climbed off his horse, opened the gate, and led it through. At the end of the brick sidewalk, he knocked on Becky's door.

"Becky! It's Jim Powell."

Never good at waiting, Jim gave it about fifteen seconds before pounding again.

"Keep your panties on!" Becky shouted. "I'm coming."

Half a minute later, she yanked open the door and glared at him. She couldn't see his exact position so her aim was a little off, but he got the message.

"I'm here for the trash," Jim said politely.

"I'll meet you at the garage."

She closed and locked the door. Jim stepped off the porch, grabbed his horse by the reins and began leading it across the yard. He waved at Shade, who snapped his reins and called to his horses. Jim reached the garage about the same time as Becky. She had her dog in the guide harness and Jim noticed she was also wearing a holster with a large revolver.

"That the same gun you used on these folks?" Jim asked. "The .44?"

"My dad's. He taught me to shoot it."

"Apparently quite well," Jim replied.

There was a wide gate for cars at the side of the property. When Shade reached it, the man in the back of the wagon hopped out to work the gate.

"Those sound like big horses," Becky said.

"The biggest I've ever seen."

"I rode horses sometimes when I was a kid. There was always someone leading them, so it wasn't like I got the whole experience."

"I was never a horse guy," Jim admitted. "Running out of gas gave me a healthy respect for them, though. I was in Richmond when the lights went out and I had to walk most of the way home. It sucked."

"In the land of the walking, the man on the horse is king," Becky said.

"Maybe not the king, but certainly blessed."

The horses reached the garage and Shade reined them to a stop, setting the parking brake on his wagon. Jim looked around to assess how much privacy they had and determined that no one could see what they were doing unless they came to the stone wall to gawp at them. That was good enough for him.

"And who is this fine young lady?" Shade asked, joining Jim in front of the garage door.

Becky blushed but smiled. "My name is Becky."

"May I shake your hand, Becky?" Shade asked.

"Certainly," she replied, sticking her hand out in front of her.

Shade took and shook politely. "Wonderful to meet you, Becky. My name is Shade Wolford and I'm at your service."

"Good to meet you too, Shade. I'm glad you're here. I understand you can help me haul off this garbage."

Shade cut Jim a look, apparently impressed that Becky was so casual about the cargo they'd be removing from her garage. "That's why I'm here, Becky."

She removed a lanyard with a keyring from around her neck and held it out. "It's the worn key with the round top. There are two notches cut into the side of it. My daddy did that with a file so I'd be able to tell it from the others."

Jim located the key and opened the padlock that held the wooden doors closed. With Shade's help, they swung them open just wide enough for someone to walk inside. The strong midday light illuminated the dark space, casting a stark beam across the three human-sized bundles.

"You did this?" Shade asked in Becky's direction, unable to hide how impressed he was.

Becky grinned and nodded. "I use shotshells so I only have to be close when I aim. I have good ears so I'm pretty good at picking out the direction where sounds come from. The one thing I hadn't counted on was how I'd lose my hearing after firing the first shot. If I hadn't trapped them on the steps, some of them might have gotten away."

"I'm still mightily impressed," Shade said. "Not to be nosy, but are you on your own?"

"No," Becky said. "I have Nancy Drew, my dog here. We did it together."

Again, Shade gave Jim a nod. Jim was fairly certain that Shade was completely taken by Becky. That was an interesting development. Shade hadn't mentioned having a wife and, as far as Jim knew, he planned on leaving this afternoon to head back home. Was this just a flight of fancy, a moment in time, or was this something more?

"Well, you seem like a capable young woman," Shade said. "It's been a pleasure to meet you. We'll go ahead and get this trash out of your way so you can get back to whatever you were doing."

Jim was almost ready to roll his eyes at the way Shade kept calling Becky a young woman. He was pretty sure Becky was older than he was. Then there was the way Becky blushed every time Shade said it.

Shade, his passengers, and Jim set about loading the bodies. They stacked them on the others and used one of Shade's tarps to cover them back up. While Shade's people were securing the load, Jim locked Becky's garage door.

In his most polite voice, Shade addressed Becky. "Was a pleasure to meet you, Miss Becky. I hope I'll have the good fortune to cross paths with you again one day."

"I was just telling Jim that it's been a lot of years since I rode on a horse," Becky blurted out.

Shade straightened up and winked at Jim. "Well, darling, it would be my pleasure to have you ride alongside me on this here wagon, if you're interested. She's got a comfortable ride. How far are we going, Jim?"

Jim let out a sigh. "Uh, maybe two miles past the sewing factory."

Shade looked in Becky's direction. "That gives us plenty of time for a ride. I'll have you back in a couple of hours."

Becky cackled. "How romantic! A sweaty ride across town to dispose of bodies. How could a girl say no?"

47

Jim

Since Shade wasn't local to the town, Jim couldn't just tell him where to toss the bodies and send him on his way. He had to escort the wagon to the old park outside of town. It was built along the same river that ran through his valley. The difference was that the river got deeper by the time it reached the park and deeper water was much better for carrying off bodies in the current. It was one of those little things you learned in a lawless apocalypse.

They didn't pass a soul as they followed the gravel road that ran back to the river. Shade parked his wagon as close to the water as he could get it. Becky stayed in her seat while the rest of them dragged the bodies off into the dirt. After some discussion, Shade and Jim decided that they'd rather leave the bodies wrapped like bloody burritos than unfurl their gory wrappings.

The wildlife would begin eating them more quickly if they were unwrapped, but what difference did it make at this point? There would never be an investigation. There would never be charges. Anyone downriver who noticed the bodies would regard them as little more than a curiosity and inconvenience. No one wanted a stinking body beached on their property. It didn't matter if it was a dog, a deer, a mud turtle, or a human. If one of the bodies snagged near someone's home, they'd do little more than dislodge it with a long stick and let it continue its journey downstream.

Once all the bodies had floated out of sight, Becky spoke from her seat on the wagon. "That was six splashes, not three."

"We had some items of our own garbage to dispose of," Jim said. "Obviously."

Jim rode alongside Shade's wagon until they passed the turnoff to the sewing factory. "Since you know the route, I'll head on back to the factory and get some work done. I'll catch up with you guys later."

Shade reined his horses to a stop and gestured to his two men now riding in the back of the wagon. "Y'all can go with him. I'm going to deliver Miss Becky home and I'll be back with you shortly."

Without a word, the two armed men climbed out of the wagon and stood alongside Jim's horse.

"Jim, are you still here?" Becky asked.

"I am."

"I appreciate the help, but I want you to consider letting me work at your roadhouse. I didn't realize how much I missed talking to people until these last few days. You wouldn't even have to pay me if you'd let me sell a few things from my house. Randi said you were going to use part of the roadhouse as some kind of store."

"We'll talk about it," Jim said noncommittally.

Becky frowned. "That's the kind of answer you give the little blind girl so she'll shut up and leave you alone. I'm serious. I want to work at your roadhouse. If you don't hire me, I'll show up every night and complain to the patrons. They'll think you're an asshole."

Jim laughed. "Too late. That ship has sailed."

"I'm sure Jim will do the right thing," Shade said, giving Jim a wink. With that, he slapped the reins and his horses lurched off down the road.

Jim sighed. The wink Shade had given him wasn't the kind of wink you gave a man when you were saying, "Go ahead. Humor the lady." It was the kind of wink you gave a man when you wanted him to act in a certain way and expected him to comply with your wishes.

Jim looked at the two men standing alongside him. "Reckon Shade's wanting me to hire that girl."

The boy who'd been riding shotgun gave a nod of agreement. "Yep."

Jim turned his horse and rode toward the sewing factory. "Well, shit."

Shade's men looked at each other, shrugged, and fell in behind him.

48

Jim

WHEN JIM REACHED the sewing factory, he found that Hugh had arranged for the overnight watch at the building. Ed was going to stay since he'd be living in the building anyway. Hugh had also talked to P.J. who was overjoyed at the prospect of being invited to stay.

"You did tell him that this wasn't permanent, right?" Jim asked.

"I told him it was on a trial basis," Hugh said.

"Are they armed? They won't be much use if they're not."

"Ed has a shotgun and a pistol. P.J. doesn't have anything. He was living in a halfway house in town when things went south. You can't have weapons there."

Jim looked off, watching P.J. working with some men at the bar. "What's your feeling about him?"

"As trustworthy as anyone else, I suppose," Hugh replied.

"Then give him Luther's stuff. Pack and weapons. All of it."

Hugh nodded. "That's a safe bet. Showing some trust in him will buy us a lot of loyalty."

"You're sticking around?"

"Me and Charlie both. Since we don't have Luther, I'm going to see if I can get some of those solar panels mounted on the roof. I think I have everything I need."

"I'm not sure we have enough wood left for building mounts. Do we need to get more?"

Hugh shook his head. "I sent Charlie and Pete out today to take down some traffic signs in the area. A lot of the newer signposts are made of square tubing with hundreds of holes in it. It's real flexible because you can bolt it into a lot of different configurations."

"Interesting," Jim said. "I hadn't noticed."

Hugh wandered off to find Charlie and get started on disassembling the solar traffic signs. Jim walked the building and compared the progress that had taken place to his lists, marking off things and adding new items. He was nearly done when Shade arrived at the loading dock.

By the time Jim got there, Shade's people were already ribbing him about his "date."

When Shade saw the grin on Jim's face, he opened his hands in surrender. "You got anything to add to it?"

"Not a thing."

Shade nodded with satisfaction. "Well, good. I will say that she's a nice lady and you'd do good to hire her."

"Yeah, I was expecting that. I got the impression that you were immediately invested in her success."

Shade arched his shoulders and smiled. "I will neither confirm nor deny."

Jim hopped off the loading dock and headed around back to his horse. He waved at Shade to follow. Jim removed a canvas backpack from his horse, struggling with the weight of it.

"My horse will be glad to be shed of this," Jim said. "This is what I figure I owe you, plus a little extra. You're welcome to count it out. I won't be offended."

Shade hefted the bag and made a face like he was concentrating. "Nah, feels about right."

Jim stuck out his hand. "It was good working with you. I enjoyed it. You're welcome back here anytime. And if there's ever anything I can do to help you, don't hesitate to ask."

Shade shook Jim's hand. "Likewise. Always good to know there's other people out in the world who think like you do."

They returned to the dock and Shade stashed their payment beneath the seat of his wagon. "Load up, folks! We're heading home."

There were more good-byes from people who'd made friends among the Wolford clan, and in five minutes they were turning their wagons and heading down the road. Nooner's tractor brought up the rear, two trailers hitched to the back of it.

"It's been a long day. Let's knock off a little early," Jim said to his crew once they were gone. "Tomorrow, we'll hit it again. I'm going to be hosting a meeting here in the afternoon so it might be another early day. Thanks for the hard work."

About that time, Lloyd came strolling in with a broad grin on his face. He was cradling a Tommy Gun in his arms like it was a newborn. "Look at this! It was a gift from Nooner."

"Is it full-auto?"

Lloyd shook his head. "It's a semi-auto replica, but I've wanted one my entire life. Your days of making fun of me for carrying a .32 pistol are over, Jim. From now on, this baby doesn't leave my side."

Jim rolled his eyes. "Great, I've got a drunken Elliott Ness on my hands."

Lloyd's eyes brightened at the mention of the old gangster television show. "*The Untouchables*! I loved that show!"

49

Jim

IT WAS early afternoon on the following day when Jim hosted a meeting at the sewing factory. The bar and restaurant area were set up approximately how they might be when the place opened for business. Today those seats were filled with members of Gary's family, Randi, Ellen, Hugh, Pete, and Charlie. Lloyd was there along with his new liquor-making buddy, Ed Frye. Seated alongside Hugh, P.J. the cook was looking a little nervous at being included among this group. Ian was also there and having conspired with Randi, had Becky seated between them.

After everyone had arrived and taken seats, Jim hopped up on the stage with a stack of papers.

Before he could even say anything, Lloyd began shouting. "Attention! Attention! Man with a clipboard! Everyone give him your attention please. Man with a clipboard!"

"Thank you, Lloyd. That was...special."

Lloyd saluted.

"Thanks for coming," said Jim. "This is an organizational meeting. We're just weeks away from being able to open the doors, but there are some things we need to iron out. First, I need to make some introductions." He went on to introduce P.J., Ed Frye, and Becky, whom many in the room hadn't met. For the benefit of the new people, he had his friends and family from the valley go around and introduce themselves too.

"Now that we all know each other, let's talk about how we're going to run this place. First off, Randi is going to be the manager. I have no doubt she can handle whatever this place throws at her. She's got a certain *way* with people, as I'm sure you all know."

Randi flashed him a fake smile. "That's kind of how you put it when you wanted me to run whores for you."

Jim grimaced and took a deep breath, letting it out slowly as he tried to find his patience. "Let's not mischaracterize what I asked you to do, Randi. I think everyone here understands that I initially had a plan to partner with those girls for their benefit and ours. I thought it would increase traffic at the roadhouse."

"Your mother was so proud," Ellen cracked.

There was snickering around the room. Randi cackled and high-fived Ellen.

"There are town whores?" Becky asked. "What all have I missed?"

Ian leaned over and whispered in her ear, presumably giving her a brief summary.

Becky covered her mouth, then giggled. "No one ever told me Jim was a pimp."

"I'm not a pimp," Jim clarified. "I'm lots of things but not a pimp."

"Only because the ladies didn't want you ruining their reputation," Randi pointed out. "Let's be clear about that. Apparently, the whores figured out the same thing we've all known for some time."

"Too late for you guys, you all are stuck with me," said Jim. "Let's move on, please. We have a lot to cover."

Randi shrugged. "If you insist, but I'm kind of having fun with the current topic."

Jim pointed to P.J. "Back to staffing. I introduced this young man to you a few minutes ago. He's going to be our cook. We'll start with one cook and see how it goes. The menu is going to be limited at this point. There will be a few dishes prepared in advance and people can choose to eat them or not. This isn't fast food and there's none of that 'have it your way' crap. It's our way or nothing."

"Looks like you're dealing with customer service the same way you deal with everything else," Lloyd said. "You going to kill anyone who complains about the service?"

"Maybe." Jim pointed at Ed Frye. "Our man Ed here is going to be brewing beer and liquor. He should have plenty of both available by the time we open. We're on a hunt for empty liquor bottles, wine bottles, and jars that we can wash and reuse, both for storing and serving. Ed will be brewing from Lloyd's recipes, as well as from a few of his own. Lloyd has generously volunteered to taste test every batch."

Lloyd threw his hands in the air. "Yay, Lloyd!"

There was a smattering of applause.

"I hope your blackberry shine is on-point," Jim told Ed. "We're nearly out and I'm having to ration myself."

"I got you covered," Ed said. "Or I will soon. Lloyd has shared his recipe and I've got people gathering the materials we need."

"Good man," said Jim. "You all know that the market has been really successful this summer as way to gain information, meet people, and convert some of our surplus gear into things we need. This roadhouse is to be an extension of that. I want to sell stuff here throughout the year. People can come here for food, drinks, guns, ammunition, knives, or whatever else we're selling. All of you are invited to display products here. We're working on collecting some display systems that will allow us to show items without them easily being stolen."

There were enthusiastic nods at this statement. This was one of the aspects that everyone was excited about. No one wanted to sit at the farmers market all winter, but they liked the idea of being able to trade items they didn't need for things they could use. This would be the next best thing to having an actual retail store.

"Ian and Hugh will be working security until we see what our needs are in that department. Randi's daughters, Gary's daughters, Pete, and Charlie have all expressed an interest in covering some shifts as servers, retail clerks, or whatever else is needed. Randi is going to be in charge of scheduling them. In the beginning, she'll also be in charge of bartering for drinks, food, and goods. As you know from the market, every transaction is unique these days."

Randi apparently took that as an indication that Jim was yielding the floor. She got to her feet. "Thank you, Jim. Yes, I did want to say a few words. I'd like to introduce my first bartender." She reached down and took Becky's hand, pulling her to her feet. "Becky is going to be the primary bartender. She and I have talked about this and have come up with a system that will work."

"I'm also going to help out with security," Becky announced. "I'm one hell of a shot. I'm also good at deterring fights. There's nothing that sends people running for cover like a blind woman waving around a big gun."

She started to draw her revolver in a demonstration of the principle, but Randi laid a hand over hers. "I think they get it, Becky. No need to demonstrate."

"Sorry, I'm just excited." Becky grinned, then she gestured at Jim on the stage. "I'd like to say a few things too. I'd like to thank Jim Powell for this opportunity. I told him when I met him that I suspected he was kind of ugly, based on his voice. I also called him an asshole and that wasn't based on guessing. As some of you may know, all the evidence supported it. Even if both of those things are true, however, I appreciate you giving me and Nancy Drew the opportunity to be part of your roadhouse and your group."

Everyone gave her an enthusiastic round of applause, especially since she took a few jabs at Jim. Seeing their welcoming attitude toward Becky, Jim stifled any smartass comments he was preparing. He'd save them for later.

"The ugly asshole thanks you," he said simply.

Becky smiled and sat down, leaning over and hugging her dog. Randi patted her on the back and whispered something into her ear. Jim was sure Randi was whispering something about him.

"I want all of you with specific assignments to start thinking about the things you'll need to do your job," he continued. "We need to outfit the bar, the kitchen, the retail displays–all of it. I have a creative challenge for you too. We need to name this place."

People started looking around, checking out the space with a critical eye, as if that might inspire them.

"Once we have a name, we'll need a sign," Jim said. "I also want you to be thinking about names for different liquors and drinks that we might serve. We're obviously limited by the items available to us. There won't be any rum and cokes, or margaritas, or hurricanes, or any of those kinds of drinks. Our liquor and beer won't be brand name either, but let's come up with creative and fun names for it."

"How will you pick a winner?" Ellen asked.

"We'll get together in a week. Right here, around the same time. People can throw out names and we'll see what sticks."

"Who's making the final decision?" Lloyd asked. His tone was suspicious, as if Jim might overrule any entertaining suggestions and go with his own.

"Group decision," Jim replied. "Then we can share the blame."

Ellen looked concerned, as if she was seeing the space in a new light and she didn't like what she saw. "I know you guys have worked hard on this place, so don't take this the wrong way, but it's kind of dreary in here. This reminds me of some place from the Middle Ages where barbarians might hang out. Are there any plans to spruce it up a little?"

"Yes, to an extent," Jim replied. "But this is an apocalyptic roadhouse and there's only so much we can do to improve that, using what limited resources we have. Most of our efforts so far have been on construction rather than those finishing touches. You'll find the place to be much different on opening night. Don't be surprised if you come in here on a cold night and there's open fires, the smell of roasting meat, and men slurping from mugs."

"As long as they're not wearing furs and necklaces of human ears," Ellen said, her nose turned up in disgust. "I prefer my apocalypse to be a little more civilized."

"What about rules?" Gary asked. "Is there a drinking age? Do people have to produce ID to prove their age? What are you going to do about that?"

"That's a judgment call," Jim said. "There may be times when young people are in here because they're in the company of an adult, so I don't think we should bar young people from entering. Most of us can tell by looking at someone if they're close to the drinking age or not. It'll be up to our bartender to look at the patrons she's serving and make that call."

Jim gestured toward Becky with a sweep of his arm, the problem with his statement hitting him in the face as he saw Becky's expression.

"Fine," she snapped. "Since I can't see them, I guess I'll be serving liquor to toddlers if they can hold a glass and speak in a deep voice."

Jim looked sheepish. "Well, I don't mean Becky *specifically* has to look at them. We can use common sense with how old someone appears to be. I don't think we can ask for ID. Becky, if you're not sure from talking to them, ask one of your coworkers what they think."

Becky nodded as she processed this. "So basically, I yell at Randi and ask if it looks like someone's nuts have dropped or not?"

There was laughter around the room.

"Yeah," Jim replied. "Exactly like that."

"I can do that," Becky replied smugly.

"Then, unless there are any questions, let's get on with it," Jim said. "Back in a week to compare notes and pick a name." He hopped off the stage.

Lloyd patted him on the back. "Good job, Jim, but we need to work on that stage presence of yours. You lost the crowd a couple of times. I can coach you through it."

"I really appreciate that, Lloyd," Jim replied, not meaning a word of it. "You get with Ed and keep working on this equipment. I'm going to get Pete and Charlie collecting firewood for you. Hopefully, you guys can do a test run soon."

"I hope so too," Lloyd said. "I'm getting a mite parched."

"That'll be the day," Jim quipped. "You sure you didn't mean that you were getting a mite *pickled*?"

Lloyd frowned. "I think I'll go somewhere I'm appreciated." He walked over and joined Ed at the distilling equipment.

"Are you going back home or sticking around here a while?" Ellen asked, joining Jim and slipping her arm through his.

"I really need to stick around here, but I don't want you riding back to the valley alone," Jim said. "Is anyone else going back?"

"Gary's family is going back," she replied. "They're done with the market for the day."

Jim saw they were headed outside, preparing to mount horses loaded down with packs, saddlebags, and assorted other kind of bags. "I'll walk you out to your horse."

"I'm leaving too," Randi said. "Ian is going to take Becky home, but we're having a smoke first."

"Sounds like a meeting I need to be a part of," Hugh said, digging in his pocket for his tobacco.

When they got outside, Jim spotted a group walking toward them from Main Street. Back in the valley, the appearance of people had always put him on edge. It was a much more common occurrence here in town and had taken some getting used to. His instinct was to let his hand fall to a weapon anytime he saw someone unfamiliar moving in his direction. Then he spotted Cookie's red hair.

"You know them?" Ellen asked.

Jim nodded. "It's the guy from the lumberyard and some of his friends. I've been giving them tips about preparing for winter, preserving food, and improving their water supply. He's probably got a question about something."

Cookie reached Jim before Gary and his family were mounted up. They exchanged greetings and Jim introduced everyone.

"So, what's up?" Jim asked.

An animated speaker, Cookie's arms were flying around as he

talked. He'd obviously been gearing up for this. "You know local government has been useless since the grid went down. Most of the elected folks quit showing up, except for the corrupt ones like Hadley Wright and that Community Security Council he tried to get going."

"I'm aware," Jim said.

"Well, we've seriously been trying to put all your recommendations in place," Cookie continued.

"I know you have," Jim said. "I'm glad to see it. You all have made amazing progress. It will save lives this winter."

"Organization is the problem," Cookie said. Other heads in his group nodded in agreement. "I kind of ended up coordinating this whole thing because I got inspired when you told us to get off our asses and do something to help ourselves. The problem is that I don't have any authority over people. There are people who could be helping but aren't, but they still want to share in the fruit of our labor."

Randi shrugged. "Kill 'em." She was leaning against the brick wall with one leg braced against it. She looked like some juvenile delinquent smoking behind the high school.

"I'd like to," Cookie agreed. "We're trying to come up with a *nonviolent* way to address this and we've decided we need some form of local government. We don't want anything complicated. Something small and simple."

"Then do it," Jim said, arms open, as if the answer was obvious.

Cookie grinned. "Oh, we are. That's why I'm here. On behalf of the people sweating their asses off to try and improve things, I'm here to ask if you'd be willing to be our mayor."

Jim's jaw dropped in surprise. Ellen guffawed, covering her mouth with her hand. Behind Jim, everyone else who'd heard the question began laughing hysterically.

Cookie looked around nervously. "Was it something I said?"

Randi couldn't let the moment pass. She pushed off the wall and approached Cookie, her cigarette dangling from her lip. She was shaking her head as if he was the most pitiful person she'd ever come across. She rested a hand on his shoulder, using the other to pluck her cigarette from her mouth. "Do you have any idea what you just asked?"

Cookie nodded. "I asked Jim to be mayor. He's the first man who had the guts to tell us what we needed to hear. All the things we've accomplished over the last few weeks only came about because of his advice and inspiration."

"Seeing a wolverine in the wild can inspire you to want to spend more time in nature, but that doesn't mean you should make the wolverine your mayor," Randi said. "Watching a documentary on a serial killer can teach you about the warning signs, but it doesn't mean you need to make the serial killer your mayor. You get what I'm saying here? Jim Powell is the *last* person you want as mayor. Hell, he stood on an RV at the market a few weeks ago and cussed at everyone in attendance. Is that mayor material?"

Cookie smiled at Randi. "I get what you're saying, but he's like a parent giving you tough love. He tells you what you need to hear, not what you want to hear. That's what this whole town needed. We deserved to be cursed at."

Randi shook her head as if Cookie were so simple that there was no getting through to him. She patted him on the shoulder. "Then good luck to you. You're going to need it."

Cookie looked eagerly at Jim, as if Randi had somehow given him permission to move forward with the idea. Cookie might have been safer had Randi talked him out of the idea. Jim was staring at him like he was a raving lunatic.

"No!" Jim said. "Absolutely not. I mean...I just can't...I don't even... what the hell?"

"You'd be perfect," Cookie assured him.

This provoked another round of laughter from everyone.

Jim sucked in a deep breath and let it out very slowly. He was a man attempting to thwart his own explosion, to defuse the bomb within him that threatened to blow up at any second and splatter everyone in the vicinity. "Listen, Cookie. You could literally pick anyone in this town who's still got a pulse and they'd be better at that job than me. I'm prone to violent outbursts."

"And murder," Randi added.

"And bad language," Gary piped in.

Jim glared at them before returning his attention to Cookie. "I admire what you're doing, but I'll be honest with you here. My motives are selfish. The things I do are designed to improve the chances of me and my people surviving. I don't really care how anyone else gets by."

"Not true," Cookie said. "If your motives were entirely selfish you wouldn't have been telling us how we could help ourselves."

"Even that was selfish!" Jim said, waving his hand in the air like a preacher delivering a sermon. "I was tired of looking at all those desperate people skulking around like starving dogs at the trash dump when there was something they could be doing about it."

"So, you're not interested?" Cookie said.

Jim groaned aloud and rolled his eyes. In the corner of his eye, he could see Randi snickering into her hand. She enjoyed seeing Jim squirm just as much as he enjoyed it when the roles were reversed.

"No, I'm not interested," Jim replied, struggling to maintain patience. "I appreciate the confidence but it's not happening. Part of the recovery effort is taking all the steps that you guys are currently taking. The next step may be establishing a formal leadership structure. Just do it without me."

"Well, okay," Cookie said, utterly demoralized. "If you don't want to help..."

"I am helping," Jim snapped. "But I hate government, I hate politicians, and I have no desire to be part of that."

Cookie looked uncertain, as if Jim might go for it if he just presented it a little differently.

Catching Randi giggling out of the corner of his eye, Jim spun and pointed to her. "Ask her!"

Cookie's eyes lit up and suddenly Randi didn't think the whole thing was so funny. Before he could even open his mouth to ask her formally, she unleased a string of profanity that left no doubt as to how she felt about the matter.

"I don't know," Hugh said. "That could have been kind of interesting."

"Keep it up, Hugh," Randi muttered. "This town ain't ready for that."

"This *planet* isn't ready for that," Jim added.

"Then I think I'll be going," Cookie said. "I've struck out enough for one day." He saluted and headed back for Main Street, his downcast entourage moping along behind him.

50

Jim

Three Weeks Later

It was a hot day in late September when they held the opening of the Reset Roadhouse, the name that had won out of all the suggestions. It had been Gary's idea. Charlie and Pete had been tasked with coming up with a sign, which they cut from scrap roofing tin that stood out well against the old brick structure. All the doors were open and the sound of traditional Appalachian music rolled out into the street.

While Lloyd considered himself to be the main attraction, he'd pieced together a band from surviving musicians he'd tracked down in the region. There would be no payment for their performance, but like Lloyd, they were desperate to be back on stage again. Then there was Lloyd's assurance that he'd get them drunk as boiled owls.

Besides the sound of the music, the Reset Roadhouse also had a certain aroma. There was the smell of woodsmoke in the air. Even on a hot late summer evening like this one, they needed fire for cooking, for washing dishes, and for the alcohol-making process.

There was the smell of roasting meat layered within the wood smoke. Ellen, Nana, and Ariel had spent the previous day making flatbreads on a griddle. If you had something to trade you could buy a flatbread pork sandwich with your choice of several sauces. There were also rabbit and chicken kebabs, roasted corn, and beans cooked with lard.

It may not have been a diverse menu, but it was the closest thing the town had to a place where you could sit down, order a beer, and eat a meal. It had been a year since such a thing was available. Nearly everyone in Jim's group was surprised that so many people were digging through their pockets to come up with something they could trade for a drink, but Jim wasn't.

Taverns, pubs, and little family-operated restaurants had survived in war zones for as long as there had been towns. No matter the hardship, people always searched for some respite from misery and suffering. They had to find some reason to keep going and maybe that inspiration came from finding a moment of normality within the bleak landscape of despair.

Jim's people had spent an extensive amount of time decorating the interior in the last few days. They'd salvaged interesting signs from burned buildings and hung hubcaps and emblems from antique cars on the walls. There were other unique elements like antique windows, doors with hundreds of layers of peeling paint, and antique photographs that came from various sources.

Though they weren't in use now, wood stoves had been placed throughout the building to give them a way to keep it warm in the winter. They'd be going through a lot of wood, but they had a plan to give out food and drink coupons in exchange for loads of wood.

The solar lighting that Luther had suggested to them had worked out well. Tiny twelve-volt string lights designed for RVs and campsites were strung across the room, powered by the array of solar panels and batteries sourced from the traffic signs. In places where they needed brighter lighting, they used car headlamps and bulbs run from the same power source.

The liquor and beer had turned out to be amazing. They held a sampling party for their family and friends and used that time to come up with creative names for the alcohol. Regardless of whether the name was accurate or not, they went with what sounded good. The Rifleman Rum they created was no more rum than the Teotwawki Tequila was tequila, but it was all still booze.

Some labels were more accurate. The Wasteland White wine produced by Teddy really was white wine, just as the Calamity Cabernet was actually cabernet. Lloyd had also assigned names to the various small batch moonshines that he created, though the names changed every day. So far, he'd produced Lloyd's Blackberry Busthead Liquor and Hellraiser Hooch, both of which produced results in the drinkers that were appropriate to the names.

There was no strategy behind their launch. When everything was ready, they passed out handwritten flyers at the farmer's market announcing that they were open. It was as simple as that. By afternoon, a steady crowd began to assemble. There was never a line stretched out the door at any point, but there was also never a time that the place was empty.

The big bottleneck of their business was settling on a price for the items they sold. It would be a while before all the servers knew enough to be able to handle negotiations on their own. Right now, all that was going through Randi. She'd come up with the idea of putting up a sign that listed suggested prices and that had proven to be helpful. Common currencies were ammunition, batteries, butane lighters, silver coins, and medications, but they'd accept damn near anything they could use or resell.

One surprising hit was how well Randi and Hugh's tobacco project had taken off. They'd grown a little tobacco patch over the summer, but also had buckets of cured tobacco they'd swept up out of an old curing shed they'd found back in the valley. In homage to the famous Prince Albert tobacco, commonly known as "Prince Albert in a Can," Randi had insisted their product be called "Princess Randi in a Can." She insisted customers call it by its proper name or she'd refuse to sell it to them.

Even customers not interested in food or drink would stroll into the bar and purchase tobacco like it was a convenience store from the days before the collapse. When many customers asked for marijuana, Randi decided that she wasn't going to be waiting until next year to grow her own plants. She chose to buy weed in quantity from growers already selling at the market. Those growers weren't concerned about the competition. They were excited at the opportunity to have a regular customer who bought in bulk.

Jim strolled through the roadhouse with a stupid grin on his face. He couldn't help but be pleased with how well things had turned out. People were eating and drinking, music was playing, and his people were occupied. He joined Becky behind the bar.

"How's it going?" he asked.

She gave him a harried nod. "A little hectic but I'm getting the hang of it."

"You're doing fine," he assured her. He leaned a little closer and spoke in a low voice. "Has anyone talked to you about my other motives for opening this place?"

"The whores?" she blurted in a loud voice.

Everyone in their proximity turned to look at them.

"Inside voice, Becky," Jim whispered. "And no, I don't mean the whores."

She flashed an apologetic smile. "Sorry, Jim."

"It's okay. What I mean is that my family had a tough time in the early days of the collapse and much of that was my fault. I kept us isolated because I thought that was safer. In fact, it put us at risk sometimes because we had no idea what was going on in the world around us. I'm hoping this roadhouse will become a place where we can gather intelligence that will help keep all of us safer. Let me know what kind of things you hear people talking about. Over time you'll figure out what's valuable and what's not."

Becky beamed. "Like a spy!"

"Low voice," Jim reminded her. "Yes, like a spy."

"Oh God, this reminds me of *Casablanca*. This is like Rick's Café."

Jim shrugged. "Maybe a little."

"I'll keep my ears open. I hear better than most people. I pick up things that no one else would hear."

Jim patted her on the back. "I'm glad you're part of our team, Becky, even if you called me ugly."

Becky laughed. "I was teasing. At least about that part. The other part, about you being an asshole—"

"Thanks, Becky. Let me know if you need anything."

Jim checked in on Ed next. Even with the roadhouse full of patrons, Ed continued to monitor the beer and liquor he was making along the back wall of the building. He examined gauges, tweaked knobs, and sampled his product with a discerning palate. He looked like some obsessed mad scientist, which was perhaps exactly what he was.

"It looks like your beer and liquor are a hit," Jim said.

Ed hadn't even noticed Jim's approach, but he flashed a broad smile. "I'm glad to hear it."

"You glad you came then? You glad you took a chance on the stranger who came out of nowhere and made you a crazy offer to move your brewery?"

"I think I am," Ed replied. "This feels right. I think this place is going to be big. This is how legends are made."

Jim considered that, imagining people a century or two down the road wondering what possessed a man to open a roadhouse in the rubble of a small town in a collapsed America. Would they see it as folly, as Nero fiddling while Rome burned, or would they see it as an act of inspired genius?

He doubted they'd ever understand the truth of it. That on one hand, it was a way for him to gather intelligence in his community. On the other hand, it was his way of giving something tangible back to his friends and family. A way for them to stay busy and engaged. A way for them to earn and be productive. Perhaps above all, it was a way of giving them a taste of normality amidst the backdrop of chaos.

Jim patted Ed on the back. "Let me know if you need anything."

He wove his way through tables toward his security people, the string lights he passed beneath reminding him again of Luther and how close he'd come to getting killed. Jim had gotten so comfortable with Luther that he'd let down his guard. Because Luther had killed those supposed burglars, NAPA and Newport, Jim had never doubted his intentions.

Jim couldn't even count the times he'd had his back to Luther throughout the days they'd worked on the roadhouse. How many times had they been on the roof together or alone behind the building? At any moment, Luther could have shot him and disappeared into the woods. Jim's family might never have learned who did it or why. Even Jim, as he lay there dying, would probably not have understood why Luther had shot him.

It was a reminder of why he'd been so interested in this project when Lloyd proposed it. He never knew who was working against him or what their motives were. If he had remained in isolated, ignorant bliss out in the valley, with his head in the sand, it would only embolden anyone working against him.

Now he was in their sandbox. His people were listening to their conversations, observing their movements, and learning their names. Over time, they'd develop contacts and cultivate sources. He'd learn the names of the players in this community, both the obvious ones and those operating beneath the radar. He'd build profiles on them, learning both their strengths and their vulnerabilities.

At any point, if he learned there were people preparing to strike against him, he'd strike first and he'd strike hard. The days of letting trouble come to him were long gone. He'd visit trouble on its doorstep and burn its house down around it.

Regardless of what people might think, this wasn't a case of Jim turning into what people had always accused him of being. It wasn't him becoming some badass wannabe. It was Jim becoming who he was always supposed to be.

The Scots-Irish people who settled this part of Appalachia did so because their experience in Europe soured them on being ruled. They didn't trust the government, and when they came to America they wanted to be as far removed from the government as they could be. In some ways, that manner of thinking persisted among those native to this region.

Certainly, that sense of independence had been watered down by government programs that allowed people to subsist without lifting a finger. It had been weakened by a reliance on coal, timber, and gas jobs. Yet among those who had been in these mountains since the beginning, that spirit of defiance was buried in their DNA in the same way certain sounds and smells could bring out the inner wolf within a domesticated dog.

"How are things looking?" Jim asked, approaching Ian and Hugh. The two men were leaning against one of the steel support posts that held up the roof.

"We were just talking about that," Ian said with a friendly nod. "It's kind of interesting."

Jim furrowed his brow. "How's that?"

"It's interesting how much you can tell about people without them even saying a word," Ian said. "I haven't had as much practice as Hugh has at assessing people as threats, but I'm learning."

"Anything in particular standing out?" Jim asked.

"Why don't we go stand outside," Hugh suggested. "Then we won't be so obvious when we're staring at people."

The loading dock door was open, as were all the other doors, to promote air circulation. It wasn't too stuffy inside the building now because the evening had cooled off nicely. The three men hopped down off the dock. A few others were standing around smoking cigarettes, marijuana, or sipping from drinks.

Hugh tipped his head toward the rear of the dining area. "Those guys right there could be trouble sometime, but I don't think it'll be tonight. It looks like they're deciding if the place can be robbed or not. They're much more interested in our employees and procedures than in hanging out and talking to each other. They're watching transactions, where bartered goods are stored, and they've clearly noted that Ian and I are the only so-called 'security staff.'"

Jim saw the table and agreed with Hugh's assessment. He hadn't seen the things Hugh had over his career, but his gut told him that Hugh was right. "What do you think they'll do?"

"I would expect that at some point in the next week, they'll come back at night to test our security measures. They might not even be planning to break in that night, but they want to know what they're up against."

"Any recommendations?" Jim asked.

"That's what we were just talking about," Ian said. "The people living here at night need to keep a dog or two as an alarm system, otherwise we're going to need to pull a nightshift to keep an eye on the place."

Jim nodded. "I was hoping people would be so glad to have *something* in the community that they'd cut us some slack. I guess that was naïve."

Hugh laughed. "Yeah, totally. The predators are already circling the herd."

"What else have you noticed?"

Ian spoke up. "You see that table of four? They're all sipping wine. The men are wearing polo shirts and one woman has her hair pulled back with a bandana."

"Ah, I see them," Jim said, spotting the table up front near the stage. They were watching Lloyd pound out clawhammer classics on his banjo but didn't exactly appear to be having a good time.

"They're putting off a weird vibe. Kind of disapproving and judgy. Every time one of them points out something to one of the others, they give this kind of a disapproving headshake," Hugh said.

Ian frowned. "Makes me feel like my home is being inspected by the homeowner's association."

"I don't know them," Jim said, "but someone will. I'm going to find out who they are so we'll have them on our radar if they pop up again down the road. Anyone else?"

"See the two girls by themselves at the bar? The ones with all the makeup? One of them wearing a tube top?" Ian asked.

"Couldn't miss them," Jim said. "They dressed to be noticed."

"You know why?" Hugh asked.

Jim indicated that he didn't.

"Advertising," replied Hugh.

"For what?" Jim asked. Then as he caught the looks that both Ian and Hugh were giving him, it clicked. "Oh, for that. You think they work for the brothel?"

"No idea," Ian said. "Either that or they're freelancers."

"Or maybe just looking for someone to buy them drinks," Hugh suggested.

"Sucks that they're here making money off our customers," Jim grumbled. "We should get a piece of the action if that's the case."

Hugh shook his head. "Haven't you been down this road before? Isn't that treading dangerously close to pimp territory?"

Jim sighed. "I guess you're right. We'll let them go on about their business and just keep an eye on them. If they start pestering people, toss them out."

"My thoughts exactly," Hugh said.

Suddenly, all the people standing around the loading dock area flinched as something moved in the darkness alongside them. They backed up and looked around, uncertain if something had been tossed in their direction or if it was a bat dropping from the sky to feast on insects drawn to the lights.

51

Jim

HUGH PULLED a tiny flashlight from his pocket and thumbed the switch on the end of the tube. In the circle of harsh LED light, they spotted something in the weeds off to the side of the dock. It was blaze orange, like the garbage bags that the highway department used when they picked up roadside trash.

Ian carefully scooped it up and held it out before him. "What the hell, dude! It's a tiny parachute with a bag attached."

At the same time, all three men turned their eyes toward the roof of the building. Hugh directed the beam of his light in that direction.

"Hey, is anyone up there?" he called out.

"Take a look," Jim said.

Hugh bolted for the back of the building. Jim pulled out his own flashlight and he and Ian examined the parachute.

"All clear up here," Hugh called out seconds later. "There's no one on the roof."

"Then where the hell did this come from?" Jim asked.

When he got back to the ground, Hugh pulled a more powerful

flashlight from his belt and played the beam through the trees behind the building. "I don't see anyone. Maybe they threw it from the ground?"

Ian shook his head. "Too light. If I try to throw this thing, it won't go more than a few feet."

"I know this sounds stupid, but do you think it could have dropped out of the sky?" someone off to their side suggested.

"There!" Hugh called out, pointing to a set of flashing lights on a distant plane.

Jim spotted it, but it was so high up that there was no sound coming from it. "Surely not. What would be the point?"

"Communication," Hugh replied. "Isn't that how they distributed those fliers telling people to be on the lookout for you?"

"Don't remind me," Jim muttered. "Maybe we should open this thing."

Ian passed around the sealed orange baggie attached to the plastic parachute.

Hugh hefted it in his hand. "There's definitely something in there, but it doesn't weigh much at all. Must be plastic."

Jim gestured at it impatiently. "Open it."

Hugh removed a Kershaw automatic from his belt and the blade locked into place with a solid *click*. He carefully pierced the plastic bag and made a slit in it. "Hope it's not a delivery system for a bioweapon."

Ian and Jim looked at him in alarm.

"Just joking," he quipped. "Sort of. Hold out your hand, Jim."

"Why me?"

"Because you told me to open it," Hugh replied.

Jim held out his open palm and Hugh tipped the bag into it. A tiny plastic device fell out that was maybe two inches by two inches square and around a half-inch thick. They examined it under the light, noting that there was a button and some holes perforating the plastic casing.

"Is that all?" Jim asked.

Hugh stretched out the slit in the bag and shone his light inside. "No, there's a piece of paper too." He fished it out.

"What is it?" Ian asked, staring at the device in Jim's hand.

"No idea," Hugh replied, unfolding the paper he'd removed from the bag.

"I've seen something like this," Jim said. "My kids used to get those greeting cards all the time that played music or allowed you to record a message. They couldn't resist tearing them open later and this looks like what they found inside. So, in theory, pushing that button should play a message."

"Or it releases a bioweapon," Ian said. "According to Humorous Hugh."

Hugh grinned at the nickname. Then, as he read the piece of paper he'd unfolded, his face became serious. "Oh shit."

"What is it?" Ian asked.

"Play it," Hugh replied.

Without further discussion, Jim pushed the button. Everyone in the immediate area stopped what they were doing to listen to the tinny voice emitted by the miniscule device.

"My fellow citizens, my name is Walter Lightspeed. Many of you may be familiar with that name because of the companies I own, the devices I make, or the technologies I've invented. I want to talk to you today about something entirely new and outside of my customary area of expertise. I want to talk to you about the future of your country."

Behind his voice, an acoustic guitar began playing an instrumental tune with an inspiring, patriot ring to it.

"For too long, our nation has been looted by special interests. You're still sitting at home in the dark with an empty stomach while politicians grow rich and fat on foreign dollars. That stops today.

"I, Walter Lightspeed, am taking over the United States of America as the sitting president. I know this is highly unusual, but you have nothing to fear. I am not a dictator. My solitary goal is to provide you with power, aid, and stability as quickly as possible. I know you've probably heard that before, but this is not just talk. I have the means to make it happen.

"Now, you're probably sitting there right now thinking that this Lightspeed guy is a billionaire. What can he and I possibly have in common? I'll tell you what we have in common. Common sense. You've all probably heard about the United Nations working here in America. Well, I threw them out. You've all probably heard about these comfort camps. Well, I also stopped those because I'm not scared of your guns and I have no intention of taking them away.

"If you're a liberal, about now you're probably thinking that I'm some cruel conservative who doesn't care about people. That's not true either. I believe we can have both freedom and social programs. We can have reasonable taxes and reasonable medical care. It's not about how much money we spend, it's about spending it smarter. For too long, Washington has been run on dumb ideas and I'm sure you're as tired of that as I am."

Jim knew who Lightspeed was. Everyone probably did. The guy sounded convincing and enthusiastic.

"In the coming weeks, we will begin electrifying the nation again. I have an innovative technology I've developed that has never been seen in the United States on this scale. Don't worry if you've lost lines, transformers, or electrical substations in your area. We don't need them anymore. We will be distributing all the parts you need in simple kits that every homeowner can install themselves. I know it sounds too crazy to believe, but it's true.

"I also have an assignment for you. I can't be dropping these little gizmos from the sky every time I have something to say to you. Over the next two weeks, I want you to find a friend, neighbor, family member, or someone in your town with a working radio. Every night at sundown, I want you to have someone in your community listening for the latest updates. They'll be broadcast at the 1380 frequency on the AM band. That's where you'll get the update on power restoration in the coming weeks. Consider this the Lightspeed version of Franklin Roosevelt's fireside chats.

"This is only the beginning of what you and I are capable of, America. There's a lot of work to be done but if you're an American who's feeling desperate tonight, know that help is on the way. If you're a politician who's hearing this message and thinking that there's no way you're going to let this happen, know that I'm coming for you. The politicians and bureaucrats

had their chance and they failed. Now it's time for science, logic, and common sense.

"We've had a year of loss and hardship, but that's behind us. Let this next year be about growth, recovery, and healing. I'm President Walter Lightspeed and I look forward to serving you."

When the message ended, Jim felt lightheaded. He couldn't believe the physical reaction he was having to the words he'd just listened to. He almost stumbled as he walked away from his friends, stepping out into the darkness as he tried to clear his head.

"Are you okay?" Hugh asked, reaching his side.

Jim leaned over and put his hands on his knees. "I guess I'm a little blown away, man. Does this mean it's going to be over soon? Have we survived the worst of it?"

Hugh put a hand on Jim's shoulder. "Don't get too carried away. That's a lot of hope to put in a cheap-ass piece of plastic that dropped out of the sky like bird shit. Ask me again after the lights come back on."

"When we get back to the valley, you need to get on your radio and start checking into this. See what you can find out. There has to be more to this story."

"I'm on it," Hugh replied. "Find someone to stay here in my place tonight and I'll start as soon as I get home."

"I can cover for you tonight," Ian offered. "I'll stay."

Jim straightened back up, feeling more like himself. He still couldn't believe that this information had hit him the way that it did.

"Do you think we should play it for the customers?" Hugh asked. "This is probably something people need to hear."

"I wish there was a way to amplify it," Ian said. "It's not going to carry the same weight if one of us reads it off that little piece of paper."

"I have a way," Jim said. "Lloyd has this little battery-operated PA system he brought with him. He was going to bring it out if we needed it, but they didn't because the acoustics are so good with the brick walls. They provide perfect reverb for a band."

"Where is the sound system?" Ian asked.

"Beside the stage," Jim replied.

"Let's go," Hugh said.

The three walked inside and made their way to the stage. As Jim climbed onstage to join Lloyd and his fellow musicians, they looked at him quizzically. When Hugh followed with the battery-operated PA speaker, Lloyd quit playing and the others soon followed suit.

"Are we not loud enough?" Lloyd asked. "Or are people having trouble hearing my angelic singing voice?"

Lloyd was joking but cut it off when he saw Jim's face. He hadn't seen him with such a serious expression in a while. "What's going on?"

Hugh placed the PA speaker at the front of the stage. He powered it on, then tapped the microphone with a finger to confirm it was working. He handed it to Jim.

"Sorry to interrupt the music," Jim said, "but I have something you need to hear. I know this sounds crazy, but this thing literally dropped out of the sky while we were standing outside." Jim held the device up to show them what he was talking about.

"Are you serious?" Lloyd asked.

Jim's expression made it clear that this was no joke.

"I want you all to listen to this carefully," Jim said. "This may be the most important news we've gotten since the attacks." With that, he held the microphone down to the device and pushed the single button.

"*My fellow citizens...*" the voice began.

When the recording concluded, Jim played it a second time at the shouted request of some patrons. He could already see that the message was impacting the people gathered in the Reset Roadhouse. Some looked stunned, just as he'd felt earlier. Others were sobbing quietly. A few were exuberant and cheered at the recording, only to be shushed by others trying to hear the words.

"Is this really the end?" Lloyd asked, eyes wide.

Jim shrugged. "I don't know, my friend. It could just be the beginning."

ABOUT THE AUTHOR

Franklin Horton lives and writes in the mountains of Southwestern Virginia. He received an English degree from Virginia Commonwealth University and has written over thirty novels. He lives a hermit's life on a remote mountaintop along the Clinch Mountain chain, splitting his day between writing and tinkering in his shop like one of his characters.

You can follow him on his website at franklinhorton.com.

While you're there please sign up for his mailing list for updates, event schedule, book recommendations, and discounts. He's also active on social media so follow him on Facebook or Instagram to keep up with the latest releases.